The Space Between Heaven And Hell.

A Novel by Jay Darkmoore

The Space Between Heaven And Hell.

TO THE READERS

Dear beloved reader,

I would first like to say a huge thank you for taking the time to read my work. I have always loved to write, and to have my own work in someone else's hands means more to me than I could ever express.

Secondly I would like to thank all the teachers, both in school and elsewhere, for helping me to hone my craft. Then there's the friends, family and those that have entered my life and then departed for one reason or another.

Finally, I would like to thank those who told me this wasn't possible, and those who told me I shouldn't pursue my dream. Without you, I wouldn't have the determination to prove you wrong.

The following work has been many years in the making, even before the first word was ever written.

- J

CONTENTS

"The meaning of life is to die before you die, and know there is no death."

- Eckhart Tolle.

AWAKE

Annabelle Jones saw the bright light as it revealed itself. She wasn't sure if she was dead, but she couldn't remember dying, or anything else for that matter. She couldn't recall falling into sleep so if this was a dream, she didn't know. She felt floaty, numb and befuddled. She tried to move her arms and legs but couldn't find them. Around the rims of her eyes was a solid black as the white light called to her, wanting her to go towards it. She felt calm and relaxed, like she was lying on a cloud being brought closer to it. The warmness of the light grew colder as the blackness around her vision disintegrated, slowly at first into a blur, but then faster. Annie saw shapes beginning to form around her as her vision became clearer. A pattern around the light, blue a simple. Chippings of paint and then under it, a long draping curtain on a rail. Her neck felt stiff as she turned her head. She heard the faint beeping next to her, and as she strained to turn, the beeping machine next to her came into view. Her body became warmer, as she felt the blood in her limbs. She tried to wiggle her toes and winced at the strip lighting above her. She moved her hand to offer relief from it. Her skin felt rough and cracked, as she saw the cannulas in her forearm, tugging gently as she moved. A strong smell of bleach married with citrus pushed its way up her nose, and her body slowly came into feeling. No longer relaxed on a cloud, but instead rubbing across itchy fabric of the gown she was in. As she tried to move her head more, her stiff neck hurt even more. She saw that the snaking tubes from her arm were fixed to several drips that hung next to her, one deep red, the other clear as crystal, feeding into her. Confused, she desperately tried to pull a thought from her haze, trying to pick up the fragments that were floating around her mind, unable to grasp them, like trying to grasp thick fog. Nothing came to her, and the buzzing on the heart monitor, next to her, grew faster. She let out a small whimper, like a dog left alone in the cold winter. She took the heart rate monitor from her finger and the beeping became a loud drone. She felt hot, nauseous, the serenity of the cloud long gone, like it had never been there at all. Instead it was replaced by fear. She sat up quickly, and her head exploded. Slamming her eyes shut, she ran her hands through her hair and found it to be matted together. Again she opened her eyes, and a new layer of confusion wrapped her. Her arm was bandaged heavily, and upon further inspection, so was her leg and her upper back.

She picked at the bandage on her arm and saw her skin was red and black from bruising. She saw tiny black beetles lining her skin, embedded in her tightly. She lunged to pull them out, her whimper now a low scream, but then something came to her from the fog. The beetles lost their legs, and instead she saw they were stitches, and she had seen them before. Not on her, but on someone else. A skin graft? A relief came through her dread, but was then again drowned by it. Hugo Black. "Hugo," she mouthed to herself, and it came flooding back like a train wreck in her head. She looked for the windmill she had been holding, but it wasn't there. Exploding tears ran down her face and she was shouting wildly now, looking around the ward, ignoring her brittle skin straining and tearing, the metal beetles coming undone as she thrashed looking for her. Where was she? She had just been with her on the hill? Her brown hair and little hands, soft like pearls, now gone. Mouthing something she couldn't remember, she heard footsteps rushing in the distance. The buzzing drone now a blaring siren. Her gown fell open as she stood onto the cold flooring, and splayed on the ground as her legs went from under her. She saw her body, bandaged, torn, bruised and bloodied. The smell of bleach was now gone, but instead replaced by the putrid smell of burning wood and smouldering ash. It all came back to her, a wicked slideshow presentation flashed in her brain on fast forward with the sound turned right up. The party, the fire, the gun shots, and the horned beasts and eels. She could see them again, large and monstrous. Then another, in the fire there was a woman, and screams of the dead infant made Annie scream louder into the floor, as she thrashed at the hands that held her and dragged back there into the fire. Their faces were malice personified as she laid her eyes on them. She grabbed and bit, scratched and spat at them, wailing for them to let her go, until she felt the sharp pain in her arm, and their hands as they held her on the bed, waiting for the sedative to kick in.

#

Annie awoke from a dreamless sleep. Her head hurt. That was the first thing she noticed. Like a beating drum played by a thousand energetic mice. She slowly opened her eyes. The room was still, her vision blurry. She felt heavy, her mind slow, body numbed. She heard scratching her ear. Turning her head, giving way to a pain that dulled in her, but wasn't quite there yet. A figure in blue sat beside her. She blinked a couple of times, each time harder than the other, until it came into focus. It was a woman writing on a clipboard. She was older, her hair silvered grey. She smiled warmly at Annie and stood up, leaving her alone as she passed through the curtain around her. A moment later, it opened again and the nurse came back, this time with another. An older man with a stethoscope hung around his neck and thick glasses. Annie tried to speak but her mouth fell loose and gaping, and all she can manage was a small babble. The pair didn't hear her, or if they did, they didn't take notice of her. They spoke amongst themselves, in voices that seemed a mile away. Then, the nurse drew into her and she smelt faintly of sweet flowers. Annie began sobbing from her soul. She bit her lip and tried to push away the ball in her throat. Again she tried to mouth to them, to ask them where she was. The girl with the windmill. The nurse was checking her bandages and Annie desperately tried to speak.

"What's that, pet?" the nurse whispered, looking intently at her. Annie locked eyes with her and tried to touch her face, but she couldn't. She looked and horror gripped her again, She was handcuffed on both sides to the bed. She rattled the cuffs, her voice again a low frightened moan. The nurse hushed her, and Annie drew back into her numbness. She mouthed again, and the nurse drew closer to her, and Annie could feel her breath on her neck as she whispered in her ear.

"Where is my daughter?" Annie waited for a reply, but one didn't come, and that was so much worse. Tears swelled on the lip of her eyelids and she couldn't even wipe them away. The nurse smiled warmly at her and held her hand, and then moved away. The doctor didn't speak to Annie. He looked the clipboard instead, scribbling away. He thumbed through the pages and then pulled out a pink piece of A4 paper with the words "ARREST HANDOVER" written in faded ink across the front. He sighed to himself, and Annie watched as he disappeared through the curtain again. "Where's my daughter?" Annie whispered as best she could again to the nurse. She drew in again, looking back at the curtain. Annie saw the wrinkles in her face, forming a mirror of sadness to her.

"I'm sorry, Miss," she said. "You don't have a daughter." There was the heart rate monitor again, picking up its dance in the background. Hot tears fell from her eyes as the nurse rubbed them with her gown. It didn't make sense. She was with her on the hill moments ago? She was right there with her. And then the rain, oh such heavy rain had fallen on them. Had she been in the fire?

"You're lying," she whispered. Her tongue felt like a wet sack in her mouth. Her eyes moved in and out of focus as the nurses face became blurred and contorted like a hellish devil, but then back again into a face of compassion, and again Annie heard the sound of the curtain rail. The nurse turned her head, then stood erect and stepped away from Annie. Annie relinquished her gaze, then peered at the tall bald man wearing a light pink shirt and suit pants and a woman wearing glasses with a black skirt and blazer that had walked into the room. The woman stood in front of the man, speaking clearly.

"Annabelle Jones," she said. Her tone was firm, and Annie instantly didn't like her. The way she stood, the way she spoke, the way she leant over the bottom of the bed. She didn't like her. Not one bit. "My name is Detective Sergeant Burnell and this is my colleague Detective Constable Ferris. I am arresting you on suspicion of arson with intent to endanger life and the murder of eight people. You do not have to say anything."

Her voice trailed off as Annie's hearing went mute. Murder? Her? Arson? So there had been a fire… but surely…. "If you do not mention when questioned…" Her mouth was moving but her face was like stone. The bald one continued to scribble something down in his brown book he had in front of him.

"Anything you may say can be used in court," She turned her head away from the sound of her voice. What was happening to her? Why was she here? Where was her child? She looked up at the ceiling, the strip lighting overhead appearing to get closer and brighter to her, and she wished it was the light you see before you die, either from heaven or from an oncoming train. "May be given in evidence." She stopped, and an uncomfortable silence was left after it, broken only by the slowing heart monitor and the scribbling of the officer's pen. "Do you have any reply to the caution I have just read to you, Miss. Jones?" Annie looked around the room.

"Where is Hugo Black?"

Chapter One

Ghosts

24 HOURS EARLIER

As dusk fell, the sun had begun to dip below the horizon of the meadow that surrounded the estate. High walls of thick hedges cast a speckling of dying embers of daylight that escaped through the tall metal gates at the foot of the driveway. A deep mix of red and purple creeped through the huge windows of the study where a large log fire burned and crackled, causing a dance of fire and shadow to merge with the fading day. Hugo sat quietly alone, staring at the fire. He sank back into his chair. A high piece, woven with blood red fabric and dark oak arms, encased around him like an open casket. His velvet dressing gown falling onto the cream carpet, now stained by the years of time and emotion, almost woven into fabric itself. Hugo held a large crystal whiskey glass, with distinctive edges but a rounded bottom, supporting a nipple in the centre that rocked a single ice cube inside his scotch. He rocked it, watching as the dance of flames cast a wicked morphing through the glass, and how the dark liquid inside blended with the arura of the burning wood. He took a sip then swirled it around his mouth and swallowed, leaving a citric yet sweet aftertaste that lingered there for a short time before disappearing. He arched his head up above the fire and admired his portrait that hung above, in a large golden frame. He stood the same way he had seen so many of the people in such paintings, tall, confident and proud. The background was that of a grey sky overlooking a tall mountain of slate and rock. He was wearing blue waist coat, covered by a light grey blazer coupled with high leather boots that protruded from under his grey trousers. He had a large bull mastiff to his right, who he, to this day, still doesn't know it belonged to. He just remembers the artist saying it would make him look powerful, so Hugo demanded the dog stay there for the duration of the painting. My figure back then he thought, was so mighty. There's a reason this carpet has such…history. He smiled and rested his hand on his stomach, which was now larger and softer than he would like to admit. He looked again at the fire, then at the design around it. Every time he did, he felt a boyish intrigue. He had the mantle of the fire place carved to resemble the nine circles of hell, depicted in Dante Alighieri's divine comedy 'Inferno.' He had been fond of that piece of literature and had always admired its imagination of how it captured the flaws of men. The mantle was carved from Canadian Redwood, and created by a Russian artist that was flown out first class by Hugo specifically for the piece. It depicted a man looking above into the clouds as an angry tyrant looks back down at him. From there the weavings of the wood become more erratic, casting the man down the circles of hell through greed, lust and anger, then down deeper into the chaos and more insidious ties and emotion of violence, betrayal and treachery, finally engulfed by Satan himself who holds the gurgling damned into the river of boiling blood. A true tail of judgement, and yet, Hugo found it somewhat fascinating to look at. He looked around his walls and appreciated his collection of expensive art work. A chalice from the Mayans, a stone from the pyramids of Egypt and a hand painted tapestry he bought from the London museum of Art, to name but a few. In between these paintings were swollen book cases filled with fine literature from Dickins to Poe, and music works from Brahms, Handel and Beethoven. He stood up, stretched his arms and back like an aging lion, then walked over to his record player that he hadn't noticed had stopped playing. He fingered through the selection of vinyl and picked one. He blew the dust from its cover and took out the disk from its sleeve. 'John hasn't been dusting correctly,' he said to himself. His voice sounding old and charred from the whisky. He opened up the record player and prepped the needle. A quiet crackling from the player came, as he put the disk inside and placed the needle down, the soft notes of Beethoven's

Moonlight Sonata's first movement began to play, and he was transported back to his night in Paris with his wife Claudia. He closed his eyes and lost himself, his whisky rocked in his hand as he remembered the large music hall. He remembered sitting in a private booth with a glass of scotch in his hand, overlooking the hundreds of meagre dressed members of the audience that sat below. "The acoustics are always much better in the booths," he said, turning to Claudia. She sat there, holding a glass of champagne which had just been topped up by a member of staff that looked almost as tired and as badly dressed as the poor souls he reigned over beneath him. Her bright smile complimented her olive skin. Her hair was naturally very dark, but it looked nearly invisible in the dim light, from the crown of her head and down her face blended into the dark walls of the booth, until revealing itself over her white dress that hung loosely from her shoulders, like a magician that hides a rabbit, only to realised it was there all along and you just weren't looking hard enough.

"Hugo, it's wonderful. Thank you so much," She said, casting an even larger smile at him.

"It's my pleasure. This is my favourite part," Hugo raised his arm and pointed to the pianist on stage below who played the epilogue of Beethoven's first movement of Moonlight. The keys and dynamics became firmer and more emotive, as the pianist closed his eyes and sweat could be seen forming on his brow. The slower things in life, the more patient and time staking practises are often the things that pay off the most. "Dedication," Hugo whispered, "Makes it all worth it in the end."

"Where did you hear that?" asked Claudia. Hugo tapped his nose and laughed. Claudia sat back and let the music drift her away. Hugo rocked the whisky in his hands remembering the night. The emotions from the carpet nestled in between his bare feet as it transported him again. The electrical atmosphere of the music hall, the laughter and clicking of glasses in the restaurant afterwards with the pallet of caviar and red wine. The way the presidential suite mattress at the most prestigious hotel in Paris supported his naked body while he made love to her. Then, something began to creep into his thoughts, like a ghost that crawled from under the beds of sleeping children. His heart picked up its pace. A silhouette was on top of him, enjoying his body quickly and firmly. She began to moan and arch her body back like a howling wolf. The eulogy of Beethoven's masterpiece swung around in his head, becoming louder and louder. He remembers his body beginning to panic but unable to move, a toxic secretion of sweat, ethanol and cocaine seemed out of his body and sank into the bed. The city lights of Paris cast a menacing glow onto the shadowed figure that was on him. He felt a sharp pain in his mouth and then a laughter that was not one he welcomed. Red hot pain dragged down him as deep scratch wounds carved themselves across his chest and abs. She was not his wife. This was not Claudia that was above him, defiling him. He saw Claudia next to him, stroking her body and gripping his lips to hers. He turned in terror and looked at the shadow. It stopped in a deadly pose, coiled and faceless like a viper in the dark.

"You're mine now, Hugo," she said. It leaned in closer and he made out her face, a face he had only seen in his nightmares. It was her. She whispered into his ear. "You are mine."

Hugo opened his eyes to see his glass empty. Its contents onto the rug that soaked it up thirstily, leaving a dark stain in front of the fire place, amusing the devils that infested its mantel. The vinyl had stuck in place, repeating the same bar over and over. He looked at the record player. Its dim bronze outline projected a burning twisted reflection of Hugo, like that of funhouse mirror. Hugo wiped his brow which was damp with sweat. Resetting the record player, he tuned to the window and a sheet of darkness. A knock came from behind. He turned to see John. He was dressed in a black tailored suit, with a white cravat and white gloves. Timeless, prestigious and classic. His black hair hung loosely around his eyes.

"Mister Hugo," he said in a Scottish accent. "I have prepared the welcoming drinks for the guests. The food is prepped and the downstairs has been cleaned". Hugo studied him, the images from his nightmare fading away, and walked over to the record player and picked up the sleeve of Beethoven. He walked over to John and without saying a word, pressed the dusty sleeve into his chest which was received with a thump and John gave a sharp exhalation. Hugo walked away. John's eyes following his step as he walked down the hallway and turned towards the bathroom. He looked down at the dusty sleeve and felt a grimace appear across his face. He ran his finger across the front collecting a thick covering of dust on his finger. He remembered being up here earlier cleaning and realized he must have missed it. He rubbed his arm and stroked the back of his head, face turned to worry. He waited a moment for Hugo to return like he had done many times before, but this time he didn't. His feet never crossed the threshold, and John allowed himself to believe he was safe. Then, he placed sleeve back into the stack, making a mental note to dust up here more thoroughly. He turned to exit and noticed the large stain on the white carpet. He pulled down the iron cask of the fire place with a fire poker and watched as the embers slowly faded away and died into the black charcoal. He looked at the stain again and made another mental note to order deep cleaner for the weekly shopping. He took out a linen cloth and gave the study a quick wipe down and picked off some lint from the fabric, before walking back to the entrance to the study. He placed his hand on the door knob and looked back into the darkened room, only illuminated by the bright light of the hallway. He shook his head and thought about Hugo, then about himself, and then about the night ahead. He closed the door quietly, then went about his preparation.

#

Hugo stood in the bathroom staring at himself in the mirror. He had grown weary recently and his body looked tired. His once chiselled six pack and hard pecks, now resembled that of Santa Claus, and his facial hair had started to turn silver and grey.

"At least if all goes to horse shit, I can tell elves what to do and lie to children for a living,", he said to himself.

He undressed and turned the shower to hot. He took off his jewellery and placed it on the windowsill, along with a large fluffy red towel on a heated steel rack that was mounted to the wall. "Play", he announced to the room, his voice reverbing back to him and mixing with the sound of the shower stream hitting the marble flooring, like a heavy storm in Rome. Music then began to play quietly, set to just how he liked it. 'Spring' from Vivaldi's 'Four Seasons' filed the air and Hugo let his shoulders relax and his knuckles un clench with a long sigh. He placed his gown on another hot rack before catching another glimpse of himself in his bathroom mirror. It reflected back poorly, a film of ghostly white over it, and he looked at himself through the fog, like observing a stranger in thick mist walking towards him. He wiped the mist away with and his shoulders tightened again, fists gripping the sink. He saw a figure behind him, a tall woman with wavy blond hair and jellied eyes staring back at him. He turned quickly, to see nobody standing there. He looked again into the mirror, once again clouded by fog. With trepidation, he wiped the glass clean once more, to find nothing but his worried face staring back at him. He closed his eyes tight and let the cold water run a second from the faucet. An icy slap of liquid forced a deep breath of air into his lungs. He turned off the faucet and opened the medicine cabinet. He studied the various white and brown bottles in front of him, like a child in a sweet shop. A thousand different varieties of 'feel good' from the local legal drug dealer, with medication from Adderall to Xanax. Hugo snapped open a bottle and crunched a couple before swallowing them down with a gulp of cold water. He stepped into the hot shower, Vivaldi's 'Spring' had now turned to Mozart's 'Ein Klein.' He rinsed his face and opened up a bottle of lotion. The citrus smell filled the air and floated him back to his times as a child, growing up in the centre of Manchester, England. An odd combination one may think. The smell of citrus fruit intertwined with the memory of a concrete metropolis with diesel fumes and taxi cabs. He remembered how he would find a quiet spot near a large apple tree where he lived, and hide away from the troubles at home. His father was a drinker, and his mother was not much of a person after the depression took hold of her. His father would drink and scream at whatever Hugo had done that day. Playing too loudly, not playing enough, speaking out of turn, being too quiet. It was all very toxic and overwhelming most of the time, and when he would seek refuge from his mother from his father's wrath, he was met by either a stone wall of a vacant woman, or the clink of a Gin glass half-filled with tears. Running from the house and hiding on a small patch of grass out of range of his father's belt, he had saved up enough money from recycling empty cider cans and vodka bottles, and bought himself a used Walkman. There, he would sit and bite into the half rotten apples, the sour and bitter liquid fill his mouth in a mushy texture, while lying on the damp grass looking into the clouds. It was where he met Vivaldi, Mozart, Bach and Beethoven, to name only a few. He knew he could time it perfectly, he would eat a handful of apples, fingering through the completely decayed ones to a half rotten one and if he was lucky, a fresh one the birds hadn't beat him to. He could have a handful, and listen to a couple of pieces, before returning back to his hollow home, where he could sneak into his tiny bedroom and don't feel compelled to leave, as his belly was full and his friends in his ears with him.

#

He washed his body and watched as the suds disappeared down the drain. As he watched, he saw something lying on the floor, a fist sized jumble of dark silk wire which bubbled as it rested on top of the drain. He crouched down and picked it up. He held a ball of damp black hair. "Claudia," he said to himself. He was firstly confused by the sight of this as he had not seen it before. Then remembered his dusty vinyl sleeve in the study and remembered why he hadn't seen it before, because John was paid to keep the house immaculate. And Hugo felt a wave of annoyance rise in his chest. He threw the ball of hair against the grey of the shower where it stuck. He let out a sigh and put it to the back of his mind. He brushed his teeth, pushing away the remnants of the scotch and replacing it with a refreshing minty taste. He spat into the drain and looked at the shower faucet like it was a hungry lion about to steal a baby. He repeated in his head over and over "Just do it. Just do it you pussy," his breathing became deeper. "Just do it. Just do it. Come on pussy just do" – In a quick explosion of courage and fear, Hugo flipped the temperature from hot to freezing, Braced himself, and the icy downpour rained down on him like a violent downpour, turning his muscles into stiff rocks and his body like iron. Hugo immersed himself under the water with a series of short high wails, breathing deeply and rubbing his hands over his body like he was on fire. Mozart's symphony had erupted into a climax of percussion and cellos, which mimicked Hugo's cries under the merciless cold. A minute or so passed and Hugo shut off the water, his skin tingling and adrenaline and endorphins raced through his blood. He felt his heart beat running through his head as he quickly grabbed a hot towel from the metal rack and wrapped it around him like a worried mother would hug her lost child. He held it tightly, laughing to himself and wondering why he does the hot and cold shower, but then he stops and relishes the feeling of his body. He felt alive. An immersion into the frightening. An aversion to discomfort is what will kill you. Comfort is not always your friend. You never feel truly alive if you're being rudimentary. Such were his thoughts. This, however, in his later years, is about as daring as Hugo would get, on a daily basis anyway. The past few months, since he met Claudia, he had slowed down a little. Cocaine and ecstasy would once do that for him, but since he was diagnosed with high blood pressure, this was about all he could handle these days. He began to laugh to himself at the absurdity of it all as he dried himself and tried to relax his goose bumps which had erected in ice. He again drew on his heavy gown and tied it at the waist, and announced "Stop," to the imaginary orchestra in the walls. The music died a little quieter before slowly slipping away in to silence. He could hear the faint noises of clattering and chinking down stairs. "John must be doing something useful," he thought. He walked to the windowsill and put back on his belongings, securing them to his wrist and fingers and checked his watch. '19:45'. The diamond incrusted hands ticking away at him, showing a dim reflection of himself looking back at the time that was ticking away. Clocks are a funny thing sometimes, we observe them to keep track of our lives, while they tick away and show us we were dying. He opened the bathroom door and walked down the hall to his bedroom. His home had a large array of halls which fed into large open rooms and studies. He had eleven guest bedrooms each en suite, two studies, a music room, a master bedroom, a gym, a cinema, a pool, a tennis court, a sauna, two large gathering halls, a pantry, two kitchens, an indoor pool and a meditation room. The latter was Claudia's. She was on some holistic herbal meditation detox since she left her aspiring career as a wine taster, a dog groomer and a personal trainer. His home had seen more Buddha statues than a palace in Tibet, more Kung Fu masters than China, and more exotic animal adoption reps that PETA. He swore one day he would awaken to Claudia meditating at the end of their bed, cuddling a chimpanzee while teaching it Tai Chi.

Hugo passed many rooms and doors that were closed, and ran his hands across the rosewood walls and mahogany paint as he walked. The white carpet below him lapping up the drips of moisture that fell from his wet body. He heard the sound of somebody whispering, and he stopped and looked around the empty hallways. He followed the sound and turned a corner. John was standing there, holding himself and pacing up and down on the spot, muttering lowly. Hugo observed him with a queer fascination. What was he doing? Who was he talking too? Hugo wondered why he was up here and not downstairs, his brow again forming into deep wrinkles. He watched him longer, and as he was about to announce himself, question what he was doing, he stopped. John had stayed in one spot, now muttering to someone, something. He couldn't see who, for John appeared to be speaking to something inside one of the guest rooms. No light bore from the void however, and the door was only slightly ajar.

The woman in the mirror. He jellied eyes and jaw hanging low.

He cast such thoughts from his mind, but John did indeed appear to be speaking to somebody. Claudia maybe? Maybe a guest had arrived? He listened intently, trying to get a hint of what he was saying, but all he could make out was faint incessant whispers, and this made him feel more uncomfortable. Finally, he made himself known. "John." John stopped and caught his eye, then immediately took out a rag from his pocket and began to wipe down the phantom door.

"Sorry Mister Hugo, I didn't see you there." John closed the door and continued to clean.

"Who were you talking too?" Hugo asked, eyeing at the closed door. John was on his knees now, picking up bits of lint from the carpet.

"Nobody sir. I was muttering a song, singing to myself."

"We've spoken about that, John." Hugo sneered. "You do not sing on my time. Correct?" John couldn't dare to look up.

"Yes sir." Then, almost immediately, "The guests will be arriving soon. You may wish to get dressed. I've nearly done up here too."

"Quiet," he said, still studying the door. He pressed his hand on it and found it unlocked. His skin began to crawl as he pushed it open a little, and then, seeing no devils upon him, he opened it fully and switched on the light. Nothing. Just a room. Neatly made and ready for guests.

"Mr. Hugo?" said John. He peered into the room once more, then killed the light and closed the door.

"Yes, John."

"Are you okay, sir?" his posture looking like that of a worried parent when their child starts to cry and won't tell them why.

"Yes, John, I'm fine. I'm just tired".

"Indeed, sir", John said, his Scottish accent masking his concern. He approached Hugo and felt his head with the back of his hand. "You do feel a little warm, sir. You have been under a lot of stress recently". Hugo pushed his hand away.

"If I wanted mothering, I would ask. If I wanted your opinion, I would ask. If I wanted you to give a shit, I would ask. Speak when spat at, and nothing more". Hugo bore a glare into John's brown eyes, again remembering the dirty sleeve and the hair in the shower. John, sadly was not shaken by these comments. He had been working for Hugo for around four years now. He knew when he would show concern and when he should keep his mouth shut. Sadly, this was the latter.

"Of course, Mr. Hugo." John said, head bowed, body small. "I shall continue making preparations". John stepped back. Hugo looked at him, he clenched his teeth, turned on his heal, a hit of friction catching them under the carpet, and continued towards his master chamber.

"Mr. Hugo," John called. Hugo stopped, let out a sigh and cocked his head to the side, his back still to John.

"Yes, John?" he spoke tiredly.

"I hope you feel better." Hugo, without missing a beat replied –

"I am not interested in your worries. You have a task to complete, now see to it." Hugo continued to walk away. As he turned the corner out of sight, he pushed the heavy door to his chamber open and shouted back "Now, clean this damn house!" and let the door slam shut, sending a crash of thunderous anger through the hallways. John walked to the end of the hallway to a small oak cabinet. He crouched down and opened it up and pulled out a grey plastic tub, filled with detergent, window cleaner and fresh bags for his handheld vacuum. He took out some anti-bacterial spray and began spraying and cleaning each door knob, each frame of art that hung on the wall, many of them of animals or vast oceans and mountain ranges and the odd vanity portrait of Hugo. Hugo did not have many pictures involving his people, and even less of him and his wife. But in the small few that did, they were often of him posing for an artist to capture his vanity. He continued through the hallway, cleaning the doors, the skirting boards, dusting the lampshades that sat on small tables. He felt a bead of sweat come down his brow and reminded himself to change his attire once he had finished. He could hear voices coming from the end of the corridor where Hugo's bedroom was. It sounded like he was pacing around, slamming his wardrobe doors and muttering to himself. A small hint of annoyance entered his mind. Such a vast estate and only him to maintain it. Him, and a gardener who came twice a month to trim the hedge animals and set traps for the wildlife that feasted on the ferns and rose bushes. Again, meticulous detail was required by Hugo. It was almost like he was obsessive about appearances as this covered his own insecurities. But alas, John continued on, anyway. Cleaning this, polishing that, dusting, mopping, cooking etc. He was a man of servitude in one aspect or another, despite how hard the whip was cracked and his ears numb from a berating over tiny sorts. He continued crouching down, picking off the stubborn lint with his finger tips that had dug into the insides of the carpet where it met the wall, the stragglers hiding away that had survived the powerful suction of the vacuum, only to be pulled away anyway. His back began to ache and he stood up and corrected his posture. His lower section torching and resisting the stretch, causing his hip to pop and his sternum to click. Considering his youthful age, his work at Hugo's manor had left his body sounding like crumpled bubble wrap. He had started getting up early in his quarters, before he would prepare Hugo his breakfast and morning black coffee with coconut oil. A new diet he was on, he didn't ask, he just provided. He would awaken just as the sun began to rise and peer over the outside meadow and light up his bedroom with deep oranges and reds, casting long shadows of oak and apple trees onto his body. He would stretch and complete a short workout routine that consisted of push ups, chin ups and body weight squats. He would then run around the outside perimeter of the meadow in his shorts and trail shoes which would usually make his body awaken further but not exhaust himself, before returning to his quarters and completing a quick yoga routine, a hot shower and then dressed for his duties all before Hugo had awoken. He would often prepare Hugo's breakfast, fresh Alaskan salmon which had been delivered in the weekly order which had been chilled on ice in the pantry, a handful of spinach and kale and two aspirins crunched inside Hugo's coffee to help with his hangover. He often thought of the irony of the whole routine. Feeding a hangover with medicine and good food, only to repeat the same routine again the following day. The definition of insanity is repeating the same thing over and over and expecting a different result. Claudia was always very welcoming in the morning, and he would often pass her on his run. Never much more than a "Good morning Ma'am," as they passed each other. Occasionally, they would stop and speak about the house and what their day entailed while Claudia sipped mineral water.

"Just getting my electrolytes up," she would say. Face red in the morning heat, her French accent pushing through the panting and sweat. She was always very calm and kind to those John had seen her meet. A true dichotomy of personalities between the couple. Hugo, a once marvellous spectacle of a man that reined his business empire with a solid white smile and tensed knuckles, who has since become a heavy drinker and bitter with fading health, and Claudia, a woman of affluence and education. Beautiful and well-travelled, she was clearly with Hugo for his money and he with her for a trophy wife, considering they had only been married a few months, and had only known each other for a little more than that and there were easily about twenty years between them. John had always enjoyed seeing her on his runs, which was partly the reason why he did them. He did enjoy seeing her in the mornings, but he was strictly professional with his boss' wife. John finished stretching and continued down the hallway to the small cabinet to put the cleaning products back. He could still hear Hugo moving around his suite, less energetically now and calmer. He opened up the cabinet and placed the items back and looked back at his work with satisfaction, wiping the beads of sweat from his forehead. Another irony he thought, most people could not dream of such expensive clothing, and Hugo has his house keeper wear it for dusting. A small scent of bleach filled the air and John proceeded towards the staircase to the lower floor of the house.

"John." He heard a faint whisper come from behind him. He turned and saw nobody with him, just the freshly dusted glow of lamps that lined the outside of the hall. He moved away but turned again at hearing the voice a second time, this time more immediate, more wanting.

"Jooohnnnnyyyy." A quiver of fear crept up his leg and he tensed, his chest and biceps became rigid.

"Hello?" He called into the silence. He heard the turning of a door knob, and the loud click of a latch releasing. To his left, the door to guest bedroom creaked open. "Mister Hugo?" he called, trying to stop his voice from shaking, a lump forming in his throat. He waited a moment for a reply, but again he could hear the faint clatter coming from down the hall. The door where he had been stood was now ajar, black night emanating from it, sucking in the light from the hall lamps into its abyss. A toneless voice crept from the opening.

"Come to me." The voice sounded familiar but he could not place it. Like the tune from an old nursery rhyme he couldn't remember. John walked towards the voice, inviting him into the dark. His mind became blank and he walked without fear, nearly robotic in his step. He was tense but become freer with his step. He got to the foot of the doorway and peered in to the night. Then, through the black he made out a figure, one he had seen before, like a nightmare you had revisited but forgot upon awakening.

"It's you," he whispered. He took a step into the dark, and the door closed shut behind him.

Chapter Two

Purgatory

Claudia was in the passenger seat, high on life and singing along to the radio. She looked out of the window and blurring trees and bushes that lined the sides of the country road. She hadn't seen another car for miles, and she loved it. She loved this part of England, away from the mess and the business of the city. It's something she had always hated about the modern world. How everyone was so obsessed with time and kissing each other's arse to climb up the corporal ladder, crawling over the weak and dead like rats. She compared people to a lot of things, maggots, cockroaches, but mostly rats. She had discovered that in this world, you need to do what makes you happy and to suffer through what it takes to get you there. She held up her wedding ring. A white gold band that had a rock on it the size of a babies fist, and she sighed again without realising it. She has made sacrifices for her happiness in ways that people could not truly understand. She has moved to another country and even though the jewellery she wore was nice and her home was amazingly beautiful, but the expensive make up she was given, wasn't enough to cover the fake smile each and every day. Her family had described her as spoilt, always wanting more. Others would say she was self-obsessed, beautiful and a dash or narcissism thrown in there for good measure. Her new lifestyle did give her one thing though, and that was fame, and she loved being the centre of attention. If it isn't shiny, she wasn't interested. Discounted? Forget about it. Where's the fun in buying a £2000 fur coat if you can't brag about its price tag. She had always had the best, but she always felt hollow inside, that a beautiful garden whose seeds were sewn in bog water, and her thirst for more was unquenchable. She wanted a real man, not a shell of one. A man in his prime, a man with influence and power. A man with whom if she were to walk into a room with, people would notice him and shut up. Then they'd notice her, and then they'd notice her clothes, jewellery and gossip about the cost of it all thus boosting her own ego. She lifted up her Hermes Birkin handbag from the footwell of the Bentley, the smell of the brown leather so strong she could taste it. She continued to sing loudly to the radio while the car cruised down the roads at sixty-five, turning smoothly around the tight corners and bends. She looked out the front window and saw a large set of black iron gates, illuminated by floor lights that cast a subtle welcoming white glow onto the entrance of the estate. She pulled open the golden zipper of her bag and took out a small mirror and a deep red lipstick. She puckered her mouth into the mirror and began to smoothly apply it to her bottom lip, her mask again applied. The Bentley hit a small bump in the road causing her to jolt to the side.

"Watch it," she snapped to the driver. He sat there in his dark blue tailored suite, both hands holding onto the steering wheel. He glanced back at her.

"Sorry, must have hit a pot hole." He smiled. A smile that never failed to warm her heart. A feeling she had forgotten since the accident. Since Emmanuel. Hugo had offered to take her to the Alps for their honeymoon, at a newly built hotel where the crest of the highest and most spectacular snowy mountains overlooked a giant green forest and where the sun sat just right over the horizon to project the natural beauty of the mountain range. But she had revolted at the thought and demanded they stay elsewhere. She wouldn't go back there, not ever. And as she felt her heart bleeding over that day, the way it often does, she allowed the locked box to be opened again, just for a moment, to be carried away into the night to that place, that day, when he held her again.

#

They had awoken that day the same as every other day before it.

Holding onto each other under the white sheets after making love. She would touch his olive skin with her finger tips, tracing down his face over his dark stubble. She would kiss his lips and tell her how much she loved him, and he would smile and tell her to stop being soppy. She ran her fingers through his shaggy light brown hair and he would trace the outline of her breast and torso. A once very talented tango dancer, Claudia made sure she kept her figure in tact as she never wanted to grow old and wrinkly, as she thought old women who let themselves go, never looked too great in fur coats. She would see them around the small mountain village where they had set up their home, many of the residents were old rich folk that had spent their lives chasing money and had now retired to the mountains. She thought of the irony of that. How people would spend their lives working tirelessly, sacrificing family, friends, love and time in the pursuit of more digits in their bank account, and when they had accumulated enough wealth, they would wear all their success in the form of high-end clothing and expensive meals, while their bodies were too racked and ruined to enjoy it. Emmanuel, however, had managed to secure his fortune early in life and worked for the pleasure of it, not the duty of it. "Rats," she would think, as she would stand looking outside her apartment window in her silk dressing gown half open smoking a cigarette out the cracked window. Emmanuel would lie in bed openly checking her out.

"You're beautiful," he said, his voice sounding like he was again seeing her for the first time.

"You told me to stop being soppy," she smiled, still looking out the window at the elderly people that drove through the village underneath, convincing themselves that their wasted years of pursuing money and fortune haven't been for nothing.

"I can't tell you you're beautiful now?" Emmanuel said, laughing. Claudia turned to him and walked to him in bed, her cigarette still lit and the morning sunlight mixing with the blue smoke that seeped out the top. Her long-tanned legs pursing through the bottom other gown which traced the top of her thighs as she walked.

"You can tell me all you like," she took another drag of the cigarette before blowing smoke into his face. He coughed a little and fanned the smoke away. Claudia smiled at him and turned back to the window, took one final drag and threw the cigarette butt outside.

"Leave it open," Claudia walked back to him and straddled him on the

bed. She leaned forward and rested her head on his chest, running her fingers over his smooth skin.
"Do you have to go today?" She asked, with a touch of sadness in her voice. Emmanuel placed his hand on her dark hair and twizzled a lock through his fingers. She lay on him and rested her chin on him, dark eyes looking into his blue.
"I do my love, but I will only be gone for a day. Not long at all."
"But I don't want you to go. You don't have too. Can't we go the beach instead?"
"No, I have to go, it's a quick meeting to look over some structural designs, and I'll be back tonight before the sun goes down." He sat up and placed his hands on her shoulders where the gown had slipped. "And tonight, we will go to Ruben's, eat some food, drink some wine and then relax in the hot tub to some music. Just me and you." He kissed her and ran his hands through her hair. They hadn't been married for a long time, but it was like they had known each other their whole lives. He fulfilled her needs, even the things she didn't even know she was missing. He was her knight, and she his maiden.
"I want a baby."

#

She returned to this moment, as they drew closer to the entrance of her home. She sighed and finished touching up her make up, and felt like an actor about to go on stage, the make up like the mask of a character desperately trying to play the part well, so the audience believes it all real when in reality, you can see the wires if you look close enough. They pulled up the driveway and began their accent towards the black gates, the estate still out of view. The engine of the Bentley gave out a low rumble as the wheels crunched lightly on the loose gravel. She turned to the driver once again, his suit bulging over his defined shoulders and biceps, and his white shirt slightly open, showing the top of his bare chest of steel.
"Are you ready for tonight?" she asked hesitantly. He gave her a glance before returning his view to the dimly lit driveway.
"I am." He said. "Just the way we talked about, yes?" he reached over to the passenger seat and took her hand. His hands were large like a shovels head, and they consumed her digits like the eclipse swallows the day light from the earth, rendering the sun mute.

"I can't do this any longer. I'm losing my damn mind here. Doing this shit over and over, pretending to care about him, about this house, listening to him whine about his back and his medication and how the house keeper is getting under his skin because the bins haven't been emptied on time". She reached inside her bag and pulled out a pack of cigarettes and took on out. She pressed the cigarette lighter in the control panel of the car, waited a couple of seconds then pulled it out and lit her smoke. She took a deep drag, the red embers from the tip projecting a deep glow on her face in the dark. She cracked the window and blew the smoke outside into the cool night air.

"You won't have to for much longer. We know what we have to do, and we know how we do it. Tonight, at his party is the right time, the right move."

"And what about Ima?" He thumbed his suit jacket and could feel her waiting for a reply, but he couldn't think of the right thing to say. More to convince himself, than to convince her. He was trying to justify this, all of this, to himself. He had all the right ingredients for a true underdog and knight in shining armour story. He hadn't always wore such expensive clothing, and that had given him the sympathy vote when he gained notoriety in charity work. Hearing her name again, spoken by Claudia, was like a knife to his vail of white, and it made a feeling of nausea creep into his stomach. They had met under the worst circumstances imaginable, but in hindsight it had helped propel his career. He remembers it vividly, way before his face was on the front of billboards and people before people wore his name as a bumper sticker "BRIAN CALLAHAN FOR MAYOR." He was working part time as a journalist for the local newspaper, a position he had competed tooth and nail for against vicious competition, like a pack of wild beasts tearing at each other apart for a nibble of a fat dead pig. He had been given the job of going to the local women's refuge to cover a story that was brewing. One of the press boys at the office had gotten some inside information about a woman that had been through some troubles from one of the local police officers he was sleeping with.

#

"It looks like its trafficking of some kind," he said. Brian looked at him in the office, smoking a cigarette with his feet up on a desk. "Jerry," Brian thought. "I think his name is Jerry." Brian hadn't worked there long and was eager to make an impact, to unravel the big stories, to be there through danger and injury with his notepad and camera to cover the most gripping and harrowing of tales that the world could conjure up. To capture the misery of mankind and to have his face all over it. He stood there holding his chipped cup of black coffee, wearing his £25 suit. He didn't have a jacket, only a beaten up light brown leather coat which he had borrowed from a friend. He had been working there three months and started to think that he had been sold a lie. The main office wasn't much bigger than the living room in his studio apartment. There were three tables each with large white computers and bundles of papers and binders scattered on the tops. There was a broken filing cabinet in the corner which had a further broken coffee machine on top. The boss of the firm, Jerry, sat back on his chair holding the only intact mug in the building, which had the words "Wake me when you're finished talking" on the front. The office was on the top floor above a local Chinese takeaway, and if the sounds of delivery trucks, frying pans and shouting chefs wasn't enough to make you lose your concentration, the blinking strip lighting that buzzed incessantly over the desks, then the ticking clock stuck between 4.58 and 4.59 definitely would. Jerry had resorted to throwing tight bundles paper at them, even screaming at them to shut up, as if it would listen. Still, the short explosion of anger broke the mundane tasks up of filing and typing, assuming you didn't spill your coffee over your shirt in the process.

"New guy," he said, pointing his cigarette at Brian. "I'll let you take this one. The firm needs a good story." He stood up and stubbed out his cigarette and hastily scribbled down something on a scrap piece of paper. He took out another cigarette and walked over to Brian who was half leaning, half standing on a wooden chair, praying it didn't give way. He wasn't sure if it was the opportunity of the story, or the five cups of double strength coffee he had drunk in the last ninety minutes, but he felt excited. Jerry took a drag of his smoke walking towards him, his greying moustache stained yellow. "Brett."

"It's Brian."

"Gazuntite," Jerry handed him a piece of paper, he looked fidgety and edgy, like a man who had been kept up for three days on cocaine. "Go to this address, take a camera with you, and speak to this gal and find out what the job is. If it's a pile of crap, then find something interesting. If you let those idiots from the Guardian get the scoop first, you're out of a job." Brian took the paper. "Sacred Sisters Refuge, 88 Argyle Street."

"What time do I have to be there? "Brian asked. Jerry walked away, lighting another cigarette.
"An hour ago, get lost." Jerry vanished into a side room which had a single sofa, a broken radio and no interior lighting or windows. He walked in, slammed the door and Brian heard a loud crash. From there, he took a breath, grabbed a small hand held video camera from one of the tables. He gave it a quick wipe, tucked in his shirt and set out of the door into the busy streets.

#

"Brian!" Claudia snapped. He jolted and looked at her. She was leaning to him, her face hard. "What about Ima?" The thought of her, what she had gone through and what she has helped him to achieve, and he swallowed what bit of pride he had left.
"It's in hand," he said.
"And Oliver?" 'Oliver', he was turning four soon. He saw his life as serving others in one way or another, every person he had helped to benefit through his charity work, his career into politics to make a difference, and his relationships and now, looking at Claudia sitting there like an eager child the night before Christmas, his affairs. He was always good at justifying his actions, despite how they may seem to others. If a lion murdered a wildebeest and ate it alive, it kicking up loose dirt in the savanna while the beast tore out its insides and muffled its screams with its jaws, one could look at that as a cruel twist of nature, the lion being the villain, and the wildebeest the victim. However, if the lion, after realising the wildebeest's limp lifeless corpse, dragged it back to feed its four starving cubs, nay a month old, then one's perception shifts. There are only actions in this world, no good or evil, just actions. The rest is up to interpretation. He loved his wife Ima, their son Oliver. But he also loved Claudia, and in their recent affair of fiery passionate lovemaking, great plans and limited baggage, looking at her, sitting there, her divine beauty emanating awe into his soul, made it a little easier to justify. He was trying to rescue her from a life she didn't want to be part of, from a shell of a husband who clung to his youth and power failingly, like a drowning man who tries to grab at mist to pull himself out of the depths. He wasn't a bad person; it was all perception. Or so he told himself. He squeezed her hand tightly.
"It's all in hand," he said again firmly.

"I'll explain it all to her once we are done here and we have a clear direction of where we are going."

Claudia continued to look at him, locking her gaze on the side of his face. They pulled up to the large black gate that was flanked by tall thick hedges, the lit cigarette filling the car with blue smoke. Brian's heart picked up its pace as she felt her stare boring into him. He pressed the brake of the car gently and it came to a gradual stop, its powerful LED headlight illuminating the bugs that flittered about outside, casting a twisted shadow through the bars and the emblem of lions warped into the metal. He turned to her, the idle engine releasing smoke into the air. Her face of stone cracked as she smiled and she leaned over and kissed him, hard, on the lips.

"I can't wait." Brian gave her another kiss.

"Me neither." He lowered the window with an electronic buzz and reached out and pushed the "Call" button on the small rectangular intercom that stood there like a pseudo gate keeper. A loud ringing noise pulsed. A second or two passed and a voice came from out the round dotted speaker, like a million bumble bees disturbed in their hive.

"Who is it?" the spectral voice said. Claudia reached over to the open window and threw her cigarette out onto the gravel below, resting her other hand on Brian's leg, out of view of the CCTV camera that was perched on top of the hedges, just out of sight.

"John, it's Claudia and Brian. Open the gate please," she called to the metal box. There was a pause and then –

"Yes, ma'am, opening it now. Come on in, there's champagne waiting for you both." The buzzing of the intercom went dead and the large gate began to creep open.

"I should really think about getting a key fob or something, so I don't have to do that every time I want to get into my house." She squeezed Brian's thigh again. "But after tonight I won't have to worry about that any more, will I?" Brian put the car in drive and moved through the opening gap. His eyes flitted to Claudia who was looking at him intently.

"Absolutely not, and I assure you Claudia, after tonight, you won't have to worry about me and you again." The warmness of her look grew larger and she turned away and let out a sigh. She continued to touch up the last bit of her make up as the car crept further up the snaking driveway, the large manor coming into view over the gradient of the hill. Brian looked into the distance and marvelled at the magnitude of the house. Its hundreds of windows glowing with inviting warmth, light casting away the darkness of the night. He thought about the night ahead and what he was going to do, and he was unsure whether he had spent this entire time reaffirming his intentions to convince Claudia, or if he was convincing himself.

#

Claudia and Brian cruised slowly up the drive way to the mouth of the house. Claudia sat there quietly, fingering the gold zipper of her £10,000 handbag, tracing the creases of the brown leather with her freshly done nails. Brian arched the rear-view mirror so he could see himself. His short cut black hair stood above the faded wrinkles of his forehead that rested below his solid hairline. He opened his mouth wide and then scrunched up his eyes, to see whether it was just the light or he was getting a set of crow's feet. "Botox," he thought. "Might need some more Botox," he adjusted his tie to a tight knot and pulled it up to his neck, his high collar perched over the lapel of his suit. After adjusting his cufflinks, he opened the car door. Before getting out, he turned to Claudia who was staring blankly through the windscreen, her gaze fixated on the giant set of double doors that led into the front of the house. "Are you coming?" he asked, like trying to ask a stone wall if it would move out of the way.

"One more night?" She asked, turning to him, clenching her bag tightly. He nodded.

"One more night." Claudia opened the car door and stepped out into the cool air and Brian followed suit. He locked his Bentley and adjusted his cuffs once more. He looked up at the magnitude of the house and honestly believed to be one of the marvels of the modern world. The house stood three stories high and stretched as far as he could see. The design was of dark stone with solid oak and mahogany, which blended together in an indecipherable fashion of architecture and art. The house had rounded pillars, similar to the world's most luxurious castles, that flanked the corners, which sat with a tall steeple on its roof, which housed stone gargoyles, that sat perched over the edge, looking down on those who stood below on the driveway beneath, as if they were ready to come to life and pounce down on their unsuspecting prey, with their exaggerated mouths filled with protruding teeth and sharp finger nails, ready to sink into flesh and tear bone from tendons. They reminded Brian of an Oni, a Japanese creature that comes into the bedrooms of children in the dead of night and would eat their souls. He saw his warm breath silently slipping away into the cold of the surrounding black and could hear the sound of an owl flitting in between the large amount of tress and hedges that surrounded the estate, unseen by all until it was upon its meal, beaks talons and all. He couldn't hear the sound of traffic, and he realised they were in the middle of nowhere. Claudia walked to the front door, her heels crunching on top of the gravel path. The front entrance was in a small alcove of stone, that arched over into a single point with the word "Caelum Et Infernum' calved into the stone. Hugo had told Brian that it was Latin for 'Heaven and Hell,' and had said that the architect who built and designed the fire place in the study, had convinced him to put it on the front of his home. Hugo had said to him in one of their golf games, that it symbolized that all homes and buildings have their secrets, their pain, their hatred and also their love. Four walls can look a million different ways, but their insides are all the same. A home is the amalgamation of both heaven and hell, and maintaining the balance is the key. Personally, Brian just thought it was a little morbid. He walked to meet Claudia at the foot of the door, she again pressed a small intercom on the side of the wall and awaited the buzzing bees to speak to her. He stood there anxiously, and Claudia was shifting in her step. In the silence he studied the doors, they were at least nine foot high and looked heavy. He thought that they looked new, as the red wood of the door looked freshly glossed, undeterred by time or nature. As if reading his mind, Claudia said "It's a new security system. Hugo has had all the doors, the windows and the front gate wired up. He's getting paranoid these days." Brian looked closer and saw the hinges dead bolted with thick steel. The windows that flanked him appeared the same. He wanted to ask Claudia why he had gone to such lengths for security, but then thinking of how crazy the world had been these days, a man like Hugo was a prime target, so he left it. The intercom came to life and a faint voice came from it.

"Claudia, is that you?" the robotic voice said. She rolled her eyes.

"Yeah, it's me John, like I said before. Open the door please. I'm freezing."

"Who's that with you? Brian?". She turned to him and her mouth was agape. "Yes, it's Brian and me. Are you going to let us in?" Brian smiled at the intercom, and Claudia tapped him on the shoulder and pointed to the large golden door knocker in the shape of a lion's head. Brian looked closer and saw that one of the lion's eyes were different, it was a small camera. The intercom went quiet for a couple of seconds and the couple looked at each other in confusion. Again, it muttered –

"And who's that other one behind you?" Brian turned. Nothing but the encroaching darkness.

"There's only us outside here," Brian said, laughing a little.

"Open the damn door. It's getting cold." Claudia said, not an inch from the lions head. There was another pause and then a small buzzing noise and unlatching sound. Brian pushed the heavy door open and felt the heat of the inside of the house escape into the night. Claudia shot him a stern look as she passed through the gap. Brian stepped in behind her and looked out one last time to see if he could make out a further person that had gone unnoticed by him. Seeing nobody, he closed the door behind him. He wondered however, what John had seen on the camera and why he didn't realise it was them at the door, and again what Hugo was so worried of to the extent of installing a new security system. Then finally, he wondered that knowing what the night had in store, if he could ever leave.

Chapter Three

Lust

Brian's jaw hit the floor as he marvelled the hall of the mansion. It was as though it had been built for the gods themselves, laboured over by angels for eternity, until every last detail is secured. He stood on white marble, the type only found in Roman Palaces and Holy Temples. Each paving looked different, each with its own unique blemish and pattern weaved into the stone as it spiralled from the edges to meet in the centre where a white statue made out of stone, of a woman stood, her sculpted hair falling over her shoulders as she held out her open palms out from her mid-section, a loose gown falling over her legs into the freshly planted flowers that sat at her basin, the red and blue petals forever staring up at the sentient beauty, always held together in timeless perfection. Its smooth face complimented its closed small lips, looking down lovingly at those who admire her. A modest statue placed in the centre of such a magnificent hall. To the edges sat on a curving staircase that travelled up to a landing, over looked by enormous paintings of nature and giants, encased in thick frames of gold and bronze, until falling again on its flank forming an illicit smile, its red carpet like a tongue projecting wonder and invocation for one to venture into its jaws and lead into the upper avenues of the house. The landing sat atop a high archway, crested in a wrapping of stone vines and leaves laced on its lip, giving way to what looked to be a large sitting room. 'This place looked like a maze,' Brian thought. His mind wandered further as Claudia fixed her hair in her hand mirror. 'One could easily get lost in either is hallways and rooms, or lost in its awe,

hypnotized by the diamond chandelier or pulled into the gaze of the many portraits, watery arms emerging from the canvas, and dragged you in.' He shook his head and snapped out of his daze.
"Quite a sight isn't it?" a voice called from the top of the balcony, as Hugo emerged dressed in a white fitted polo shirt, its collar open much further than a man of his age could justify. He was wearing light jeans, brown leather shoes that pointed at the ends, and his greying hair was slicked back, revealing his widows peak and his stubble freshly trimmed. His gold chain protruded out from his wrist that sat in his pocket, and his Rolex lightly clinked against the base of his crystal cut whisky glass, rocking a measure of brown scotch being smoothed by a single ice cube. Claudia rolled her eyes and leaned into Brian.
"He looks like an air brushed older model on the front of some dying fashion magazine". Brian smirked and then met his gaze.
"It's magnificent, Hugo." He looked around again, arching up his head to the high ceilings, and then whispering almost to himself, "Truly magnificent."
"It wasn't cheap I can tell you that much!" Hugo scoffed. He swaggered down the staircase, his hand loosely tracing the spiralling banister. She rolled her eyes again.
"Anyone would think he's in a fairy tale with that entrance."
"All he's missing is a flowery dress," Brian whispered. Both of them hushed a laugh, then moved further into the hall.
Claudia stood at the base of the statue. She opened up her hand bag and placed it on its base, crushing a small bed of flowers. She took out her makeup bag and was again readjusting her eyeliner. Brian laughed to himself and she shot him a look, but then got back to painting her face.
"You can put that away my love," Hugo called. "It's simply ironic how you do your make up next to a woman that won't age. Enjoy the curse of time, it's ours to bare. It's what makes us human." He reached the foot of the stairs and moved to her, then took her in his arms smiling. "It's what makes you so beautiful, that time will one day take you from me, so I must hold you now before it does." He closed his eyes and kissed her lips. She looked over to Brian, still locked with Hugo, almost pleading for help. Brian looked away from her and studied the statue. Again he thought of his crows' feet, and he again thought about getting more Botox. Hugo let Claudia breathe then shook Brian's hand.
"So nice of you to come my friend." He checked his watch. "I figured

you be here sooner?"
"Yeah, I thought so too," Brian said, thinking how he wasn't much later than was agreed. 'Then again' he thought, 'Hugo was painfully specific when it came to time keeping.' Hugo took a large drink of his whisky and placed the glass on the statue.
"Indeed. How was the track?" he said. Claudia quickly slammed her make up mirror shut, the clasp of the hinge clicking loudly in a protesting scream of "Let me make you beautiful." Brian was silent, only able to remember Claudia's delicious lips in the front of his car, and then her naked body lying on the hotel bed, and Claudia spoke before it became deafening. Trying to stay cool under the gaze of her husband. She stretched her words, almost finding them midway through saying them.
"We…", she paused. Then, the penny dropped. "Yes, the track. Yes, at the Verve. We had a great time, I managed to place a few bets and I won the odd one. I didn't come back with more than I took though. The joy of the track isn't to win, but to enjoy the process." Hugo furrowed his brow and Brian looked at her feigningly, as even he knew that sentence coming out of her mouth was complete bull shit. Still, he went with it.
"Yes Hugo," he laughed and slapped Hugo's arm half wanting it to affirm his lies, half not wanting him to see the sweat that would uncover them. "Claudia has an eye for the winners, however seeing as I would go often to the Verve track, she foolishly took my advice and we came back a little lighter than we went in." She smiled falsely and tilted her head to Hugo, like a puppy who wanted a treat of its master before they discover they have defecated on the kitchen floor. Hugo slapped Brian back with a wide smile.
"Tell me more!"
"Oh god where to start," Brian said. "We were three races up as Claudia had been on a good run, so decided to make the next bet and try to triple our winnings. Sadly, it came in dead last."
"Oh no!" Hugo laughed, his voice squeaking. "Which horse let you down?" Brian searched his head.
"The one with the green jersey. Lucky eleven or something?" Claudia blurted. Brian wondered if someone had turned the temperature up, his suit starting to stick to his back. Hugo lent back, and Brian felt he was going to collapse.
"Lucky eleven?" he said, his voice curious. "Who was the rider?" There

was that deafening silence again.
"McDermott I think?" Brian said, more confidently than he should. Hugo searched the air, trying to pick the name from it, mouthing it over again. Then, he clicked his fingers and pointed to Brian, and Brian felt like he had found gold.
"McDrummen!" he laughed. Brian and Claudia laughed with him, their rigid shoulders dropping an inch. "I told you not to go for that one. He's cost me more money than I would like to admit. I'll make some calls, see that he doesn't race anymore." He said with a wink. They walked towards the foot of the stairs, Hugo in front, still giggling to himself. "How did you find my booth?" He said, turning to Brian. His smile like a snake.
"Truly wonderful," Brian said, holding his best poker face.
"Oh good, how did you find the view?" Brian looked into Hugo, trying to read his facial expression. Was it one of implied delight, or one of discontent? He wasn't too sure. Like about to pull the trigger on a game of Russian roulette, with six chambers and five of them loaded, he spoke.
"Ahh," he said, "Brilliantly situated at the heart of the arena, you can really see the horses race furiously around the track of the verve as it came to life with punters." Hugo laughed at him and slapped him hard again on the shoulder. Brian felt a wave of relief, like he had fooled Saint Peter into letting him into heaven, while concealing the severed head under his robes. Until that is, Hugo spoke and his happiness tuned cold and concrete, like the sculpted woman who stood vacantly behind him, smiling as he writhed inside, hoping the ground would swallow him whole.
Hugo licked his lips, a slight glimmer of moisture sticking to his silver facial hair. "And the paintings? Tell me the inscription on it. I had it modelled after you, you know." Brian's heart beat in his head. He was obviously digging at something. He smelt a rat and was trying to flush it out. Brian began to feel his legs drain of blood and felt faint. Claudia stood next to him, desperately trying to come up with an answer, but in honesty, if she had such a thing, she drew a blank.
"We didn't really look at the art, what with the view and the excitement of the verve. The Horses, the music, the atmosphere." Claudia hurried. Hugo did not quiver, his gaze fixed into Brian's eyes which had widened considerably. Hugo could easily bury him and his career should he find out about him and his wife. Bring down his marriage,

relationship with his son, and set alight to his career until it was unrecognisable shards on the ground, harrowing laughter overbearing on him, while he scrounged naked in the mud and shit, desperately trying to piece it back together. Only then did Brian notice it. A hint of perfume coming from collar.

"Tell me about the painting," Hugo said, slowly. Brian's mind drew a blank yet raced at the same time, like a hedgehog caught in the headlights of an oncoming HGV, knowing certain death was getting closer, but unable to do anything about it. Suddenly, as if by a miracle, they heard a loud crashing noise of glasses shattering and steal clanging to the ground, clear bubbling liquid seeping into the cracks of the stone, hissing as it evaporated into the cool hall air. The three of them turned in shock. John was crunched over, desperately trying to pick up the pieces of champagne glasses from the ground. Hugo teeth clenched and his face turned red hot, throwing his hands up, marching towards his quivering housekeeper. "You idiot!" He raged, standing over him, pointing fortuitously at him. "Look at the mess you have made!" John splayed on the ground on his belly, the wet soaking into him, mixed with soil and flower petals, his foot ensnared by a fallen make up bag. Hugo screamed incoherently at him, his body animated, his eyes wide, arms flailing like a drowning man. "What the hell is the matter with you, John?! That's Mediterranean marble and a £500.00 bottle champagne!". Hugo gripped the back of John neck, pulling him upwards by his collar.

"I'm so sorry, Mr. Hugo, I didn't see the bag, I fell!" he pleaded, eyes wide with terror, like a monstrous beast was about to devour him in its menacing jaws. Hugo struck his face with the back of his hand, then threw him back to the ground and drove his foot into his stomach. Brian raced over to them, grabbed Hugo and pulled him away from John, like a silver back gorilla holding apart two flailing chimps.

"Hugo, calm down, it was an accident!" Brian shouted, gripping Hugo so tight his knuckles turned white. Hugo stood above John. His eyes still wide and his nostrils flaring, breathing heavily, red faced like a madman. John's face as white as his shirt. Claudia rushed over to him and crouched over, running her hand through his soft dark hair, his gaze unmoving, face fixated in shock, fighting back tears. "What the fuck has gotten into you!" Brian screamed at Hugo. Hugo's deep breathing began to shallow slightly, and he firmly brushed Brian's hand from him. He looked at John cowering on the ground, his wife comforting him, Brian's face of both terror and anger. He looked to the floor, the champagne pooling around his expensive shoes, marring into the marble. He crouched down, his back aching with the movement, and picked up the alcohol sodden rag from the ground, it still fizzing with the bubbling moisture. He did something he had never down in this house, or very much in his whole life. He began to clean up his own mess. He silently completed long strides around the flooring and cleaned up the splatters from the stone woman's base. He reached out his hand to John, who looked at it with fear, like a rattlesnake that wanted to give him a kiss.

"Mr. Hugo," John said, his voice shaking.

"Stop," said Hugo, raising a hand to him. He again gestured with his hand, which John studied for a couple of seconds, unsure whether he wanted to help him, or strike him further. He took his hand and Hugo pulled him up to his feet. John's back had soddened, his jacket sticking to his skin. "I'm so sorry." John wiped his eyes. Hugo went to put his hand on his shoulder and John moved back. Hugo continued and placed his hand on his cheek. He felt cold.

"It's okay, Mr. Hugo," said John, his voice shaking, the sodden rag in Hugo's hand creating another small pool beneath his feet. "The bag, I…". Hugo could feel his tense shoulders, and the eyes of Claudia and Brian on him.

"John, go and get changed and come back in an hour or so. I still need you for tonight. I'll continue getting the drinks ready for everybody for when the rest of the guests arrive." He pointed his eyes down to the floor and said "Do we have any more champagne?"

"Yes sir. I have a couple of bottles still open on the counter next to the buffet I have prepared. There's still plenty in them, and then there's more in the cellar I can fetch later." John looked at Hugo, then at Brian and Claudia, who stood there equally in amazement. Hugo had displayed something none of them had seen before. Empathy. John went to move away when Hugo took him in his arms, wrapping them around him in a tight hug.

"Don't ever embarrass me like this again," he whispered. He released him and smiled. "Now go on. Go clean yourself up." John felt vomit in his stomach push into his throat, then pulled it down again with a hard swallow, and then made for the stairs. The three watched as he slowly trudged away up the large staircase, pulling the sodden parts of his clothing away from his skin, still dripping lightly on to the carpet, before he disappeared into one of the corridors of the landing. Hugo let out a long sigh, crouched down and continued to pick up the shards of glass and crystal from the floor, carefully fishing them out from the cracks and edges of the stone. Claudia picked up her bag and looked at it in a twisted grimace at the damp leather. When the mess had been cleaned, Hugo took the silver platter of shards and splinters and walked with it through the hall, his shoes clicking on the floor, and entered into the kitchen. He walked over to a large metallic cabinet that cast a dim reflection of him from the strip lighting that lined the ceiling, pulled it open and emptied the contents of the silver plate there. He closed the cabinet and turned to see three open champagne bottles, each with about half a glass of liquid missing from them. The dark glass bottles wore bright gold and silver labels, written in a French calligraphy Hugo couldn't quite make out. The bottles stood next to a large display of colourful food, filled with bell peppers atop of lemon drizzled fresh salmon, wooden bowls of fresh rocket leaf and kale salads with cucumbers and mustard seeds, dried ham and poached eggs with a spicy chilli dressing, and vegetable kebabs and a plethora of other rainbow coloured foods, carefully hand crafted and designed to invocate taste, smell and pleasure. Hugo rinsed the large silver plate and dried it with a rag. He opened up several other cabinets before finding more champagne glasses and arranged them delicately, before lifting the heavy glass bottles and pouring the liquid into them, the liquid fizzing as it hit the cool surface of the crystal. He picked up one of the glasses and drank it, as his throat parched. He drank another two and wiped his mouth, his body feeling more relaxed as a quenched thirst he didn't know he had. He turned and rested his back on the edge of the counter and ran his hand through his hair. He felt unhappy. Come to think of it, he had felt this way for some time. He looked at his kitchen, his home and thought about his life and what he had achieved, but yet he felt so lost. Recently the medication had not been helping him. He was suffering greatly with headaches, insomnia and his blood pressure was through the roof. His hair had turned thinner and his body ached and pained, often finding himself vomiting unexpectedly or bed bound with horrific stomach pains. He had been the doctors about this but they had put it down to stress. Tonight was a big night after all, and he felt compelled to control the finest details, like a choreographer trying to direct the synchronised dance of rats. This time of year was always stressful and tiring. Tonight was the most important anniversary of his life as it was on this date that he had set up his first business as a young lad on the streets of Manchester, a small electronics store that sold second hand Walkman's and video players, among record players, vinyl and other parts and repairs. Since then, he had held the same get together of family, friends and business colleagues who he had met over the years, and let them eat and drink to his success. Partly a celebration of thanks and gratitude, of how he had benefited from them in one way or another, and how they have profited from him, again patting himself on the back. He looked into the sitting room and saw his latest unveiling covered in a white sheet, and if all went to plan, he would put his stamp on this world forever.

#

Claudia watched as Hugo vanished into the kitchen. At the sound of running water and chinking glasses, she finally let herself breathe. Brian shook his head.

"What was all that about?"

"I told you. He's getting worse." Brian moved to her, then checking the coast was clear, placed his hand on her waist.

"Is that what he's normally like?" Claudia nodded her head, holding herself.

"He's always been like that, from the day I met him to now." Brian looked at her intently, concerned wrinkles on his face.

"Has he ever…" he paused. Claudia studied his expression. Her face hard.

"No," she spat. "He's never laid a hand on me. I'd rip his cock off."

"But…" Brian looked at the smeared champagne pooling at the lip of the maiden. "He's so explosive, I still can't believe it."

"He's never touched me," she said, hard. "But that doesn't mean he isn't a bully to others." She looked up to the staircase and Brian followed her gaze.

"John?" he said, voice worried. Claudia nodded slowly. Brian held his head in his hand.

"He's done it before? Have you seen it?"

"You think I'm lying?" she spat.

"No I don't, but it's a serious accusation." She walked from him, her heel kissing the foot of the stairs.

"You just saw what he did to John, do you need fucking CCTV of it?

No, Brian. I've never seen him beat him before tonight, but the way he is with him, John looks terrified when he walks into the room, and he's always covered up."
"If that's the case, then why doesn't he quit?" Claudia pondered this a moment. Coming to no obvious answer, she rebuked.
"I don't know. But something isn't right." She turned to walk up the stairs.
"Where are you going?" he said, following her like a lost puppy. She turned and glared at him, her body tight.
"After all that had happened, after what we saw him do, after he interrogated us over a god damn painting at the races, you still didn't have the balls to follow through with your promise." Brian squinted his eyes and looked to the floor, shaking his head.
"What promise?" She laughed, a small bark that echoed up the stairs, hands outstretched like a confused scarecrow.
"You're kidding me right?" she stomped her heal with a thud. "That was the perfect opportunity to tell him about us, come clean that we didn't go to the fucking races. Hell, even make up something and tell him you can't work with an animal. Use your god damn brain." Brian breathed heavily, his body turning hotter.
"This was not the right time Claudia," he stressed. "I have a plan. Don't be so impatient." If Claudia's gaze could cut, Brian would be skinned alive.
"Well", she said, wrapping the leather strap of her handbag around her wrist, pointing at him. "You better do something quick." She stepped down onto the marble and strutted towards him. "Because if you don't grow a pair and tell him we are fucking each other, then I will. And believe me Brian", she leaned in close. Her once sweet-smelling perfume, turning repulsive like fermenting roses. "I can make it look like it was your idea." She kissed him on the cheek which left an imprint of thick dark lipstick on his skin. He hastily wiped it off and smeared it across his chin. He watched her as she smiled at him, and walked away, her hips swinging side to side as she strolled up the stairs like she was on a cat walk, before she vanished behind the lip of the landing. Brian stood there for a minute. He could hear Hugo in the kitchen, clinking glasses and moving bottles around. He wanted to walk in to him and spill it all out to him. He even took a couple of steps towards his direction, but then pulled himself back. He felt sick, realising he was in too deep, like he was on a broken merry go round

and couldn't get off. He need to do something, and quickly. If Claudia told Hugo, he could have no control over what was being said. His mind wandered to the darkest parts that you keep locked away. A place where only nightmares live. What if she said he raped her? Blackmailed her? He put his hand to his mouth, lost in his own mind. He looked at his wedding ring, and he felt a slam in his chest he thought he had been shot. The ground felt like it was filled with sharks, circling him ready to pull him under and tear him limb from limb. He looked up into the bright light from the chandelier, which burned his eyes, as if its radiance was pushing him further into his blackness. Clenching them shut, he stabled himself, wiping the damp from his head. 'Stuck between the devil and the deep blue sea,' he thought, trying to find a life ring out of his drowning mess. Brian heard the sound of footprints. The unmistakable sound of heels clicking on hard floor. His ears pricked and he followed the sound. They were too light to be Claudia's, so this intrigued him more. Ima? He wondered. He erected himself and put on his mask. He saw her walk through the archway through the stairs. She was a tall woman, maybe in her twenties. Despite the wide look of awe on her face, she looked like she was lost. Looking around the hall and Brian saw the same look of amazement in her eyes as he had had. She had wavy blonde hair that came to just below her shoulders. Her skin was a pale and she wore a tight black dress and bore a small tattoo of a lotus flower on her shoulder and high black heals. Her makeup was slight. A touch of black lipstick and a brush of eyeliner, and Brian's throat went dry at the sight of her, blood flushing his face. She was a stranger to him, but she didn't have to be. Just as he was about to say hello, and ask, how she was able to get in without pressing the intercom, certain he hadn't heard it, she caught his eye.

"Hi!," she said excitedly, like a child that has just met Santa Claus, and she hurried towards him, her small black handbag swaying loosely from her side. Brian's smile quivered, and he took a step back. Her eyes were wide and cheerful, her mouth hanging in a silent cackle. She stopped a few feet from him. Again, in the same tone. "Hi!" He studied her and she made Brian's skin prickle and an unsettling feeling creeped into his bones, like seeing a shadow dart across the room, which remains unseen when you try to find it. She held out her hand and shifted her weight to one knee, cocking her head to the side and smiling wildly. Brian took her hand loosely, and was shocked by how cold she was, like he was holding the hand of a corpse.

"Hello," he choked. He cleared his throat. "I'm Brian." She laughed, loudly, putting her hand to her face, her twisted smile protruding from the sides of fingers.

"I know you are."

"What did you say?" he whispered, his body beginning to tense. She continued to stare at him, either she hadn't heard him, or she didn't want to answer. Time seemed to stop as he became drawn into her deep blue eyes.

"I'm Precious. Nice to meet you." Brian continued to look at her as she turned around and walked into the open space of the hall. She held out her arms and began to turn slowly, looking up to the high ceiling, laughing to herself like a child playing in the sunshine, dancing around the mutilated family pet she had taken for a walk. Brian heard footsteps coming from the other side of the hall way. He heard Hugo's voice reverb through the air.

"Brian, come into the kitchen and have – "His voice stopped dead, lost in silence like it was never uttered. He saw her in his hall spinning insanely to a rhythm only she could hear. She stopped and turned to him, her head pointed down, her arms now relaxed by her sides and eyes fixated on Hugo. He felt his legs turn to concrete, and horror enter his soul. The shadow in his memories, the haunting woman in the glass.

"Hey there, Huggy bear," Precious said, arms outstretched to him. "Have you missed me?"

Chapter Four.

Gluttony.

Precious walked towards Hugo who stood there trembling. The reaper of his greed, the scythe of his gluttony. His body turned to stone as he struggled to find his words. How had she gotten inside his home? He had made this place impenetrable, and it was designed to protect him from the outside world, to keep his latest work away from the prying eyes of his rivals. But the real reason for his fortitude, which sat in the depths of his mind like a cancer slowly infecting him, and he had found himself installing dead locks on his doors and sealing his windows shut against the encroachment of hell. She drew closer, her black heals clicking on the hard flooring, which echoed into a torturous beat that made Hugo's ears feel they were about to haemorrhage. "Did you miss me Huggy Bear?" she said, elated, and the words ran around his head like a catchy theme park tune, which you quickly grew tired of until unbeknownst to the listener, had burrowed into your mind until you screamed it into your pillow at night.

"Precious." Her name tasted like vomit. "What are you doing here?" She laughed and slapped her hands on her thighs, like beckoning a puppy to come to her.

"You invited me remember?"

"That's a lie," he spat. "I don't invite creatures of hell into my home." He spoke with venom, wanting his words to be sharp enough to cut through her, and watch the shit flow out her body. Brian looked back from the stone woman, intrigued about this interaction.

"Interesting," he whispered to himself. Then, he felt the tickle of opportunity in his bones. He stood there for a while, calculating his next step. Precious again smiled, then reached into her hand bag a pulled out a small pink envelope. She opened it slowly, locking eyes with Hugo, whose fists were tightly clenched. She pulled out a small letter, which was hand written in calligraphy. She cleared her throat.

"Dear Precious," she said, projecting her voice which reverbed off the walls. "I would like to invite you to my annual meeting at my home. A night of drinks, food and company. A gathering of great minds and world changing ideas. A night of excellence and divinity. I hope I see you there. The address is listed below. Yours truly, Hugooooo." She looked back at him who seemed like a lost child in a busy street. He shifted in his stance, the blood draining from his legs. He rushed towards her and snatched the letter out of her hand.

"I didn't send you this," he snarled, studying the letter furiously, muttering it back to himself.

"Is that not your hand writing?" It was his hand writing, which made the cancer in his head pop and grow more tendrils. He thrust the letter back into her chest.

"Get out," he hissed. His body tense and rigid. She laughed in his face.

"Erm, no?" Her defiance of him, in his own house, made him fill with red hot fire. His beastly temper forcing its way through his body. His fear since evaporated and now she dare mock him in his own home, tonight of all nights? Her blonde curls hanging loosely over her shoulders, and he wanted to tie them around her neck and choke that smile out of her. "You invited me. I'm staying right here. In fact, I would like a drink." Hugo exploded as he lunged at her. He wrapped his fingers around her throat and slammed her back into the stone woman. Brian flinched out the way, horrified.

"Get out!" he screamed, spitting on her face with red hot fury. Brian rushed over.

"Get your hands off of her!" He tried to pry Hugo's hand from her throat. His eyes intent on pain, burrowing into hers.

"After what you did to me, you dare show your fucking face here? Here! I should tear you limb from limb you twisted bitch!" His teeth clenched tightly like a vice. His skin red with hate. Precious grabbed his hand as he gripped tighter.

"Just like Paris, Huggy Bear. I knew you liked it. You fucking animal. I like the beard. Did I leave marks?" She coughed. She dragged her nails down his chest and abdomen, and she fingered his belt line. Brian furiously tried to separate the melee, their shouts traveling through the corridors and halls of the home, desperation filled his heart, as Hugo gripped his prey like a rabid dog that hadn't eaten in days.

"Why the fuck are you here?" he seethed.

"To finish what I started." Precious forced her hands down his belt line and gripped him tightly. A burst of pain exploded from underneath, and Hugo released his grip on her and howled in agony. She lunged forward, gripping his slick hair at the back of his head with both hands and moved in to him, sinking her teeth into his bottom lip. Her mouth filled with the taste of copper. Hugo pulled back, hot liquid flowing freely onto his chin. He thrust her to the side, throwing her hard onto the floor where she landed with a loud crash, her bones and heals skidding on the ground. He stood over her, panting heavily, his shirt drenched with sweat. Brian gripped him.

"What in the Hell Hugo! You could have killed her!" His words moulded into a blur, a toneless drone that repeated in his ear and he began to shout. He shook him, and the monster of his body subsided and Hugo came back to the surface, like a man who was lost in a murderous fog of war, finally finds his way home. Hugo tried to speak. His body still shaking, tears running down his face. Brian continued to shout, as if speaking to stone. "Hugo! What's gotten into you tonight?"

"It's her." He mouthed. Brian looked over to Precious. She lied on the floor groaning in pain, her elbows cut, swollen and red, like a fallen angel forsaken from heaven. Hugo stepped back from Brian, keeping his head low and silent. He checked his watch and the arms ticked away mockingly. More were to arrive soon, and the devil was already here. However, Hugo was not sure if it was Precious, or him that the guests should be worried about tonight. He turned and walked quickly up the stairs, lowly sobbing to himself, not knowing what was happening to him. As he passed the brow of the landing, moving into the upper halls, he wondered if he would ever be the same again. Brian watched him leave, and he wondered if he really knew Hugo at all. He had seen him many times on the golf course, appearing happy and smiling under the bright sun, skin becoming a dark gold. Was it all a façade? What did Claudia have to endure under his roof? Had he struck her before? What else wasn't she telling him? Brian again wondered if there was more to this story. The story of Hugo and Precious, Hugo and Claudia. He was a man of ruthlessness and cut throat tactics when it came to business, and Brian wondered if this had bled into the other aspects of his life. Before tonight, he wouldn't think him capable of such acts, but seeing him with John earlier, Precious just now, and Claudia's desperation to leave him, made him wonder if Hugo's empire was literally built on the blood of those who opposed him. Precious groaned on the ground next to him, and he was brought back to the moment, back to the pounding in his chest, and the sweat dripping from his brow. He crouched to her. She was stunned, slowly writhing on the floor, staring up to the ceiling at the hanging chandelier lights.

"Are you okay?" he asked, touching her shoulders, sitting her upright. He ran his hand across her face, removing the blonde hair from her sweating forehead. She looked up at him, her eyes watering and blood shot.

"What's gotten into him?" Precious said, her voice trembling. "He was always so loving to me, so caring." Brian narrowed his eyes, still examining her for injuries.

"How do you know him?" he asked. "Are you friends?" She corrected her hair.

"Some might say more than that. We met a long time ago and we stay in contact every now and then, to meet up and get reacquainted." Brian's eyes widened. So that's why Hugo had been so enraged. Was he sleeping with her? Surely not? But then his outburst, and the pieces in Brian's mind came together, and he had the collages of betrayal complete in his head. And when he had invited all of his friends and business partners together, you didn't want the rotten apple ruining the fruit bowl, maggots and all.

"I see what's going on." He pitied her, and looking at her now, vulnerable and broken, he saw how beautiful she was. He took her arm and hoisted her to her feet, steadied her as she fell into his chest. "Careful," he said, catching her. Her legs wobbled like a newly born fawn. "Do you need to go to the hospital? Did you bang your head?" As soon as he said it, he wanted to pull the words back into his mouth. He could use her. She was more than just Hugo's secret. She was leverage. She looked up at him into his deep eyes, and she kissed him, wrapping her hand around the back of his head. He pulled away but she was strong, and he pried her off him.

"Whoa.." he said, pushing her away. She caught her balance again, wiping her lips.

"I'm sorry," she whimpered.

"No, its fine." Brian wiped his lips. No lipstick. Perfect. She stumbled and sat herself down on the maiden's base. "Are you sure you're okay?" he said, his breath hot with worry, his body flushing. She nodded.

"I'll be okay. I'm just a little shook up is all." She let out a long breath. "I just need a minute." She readjusted her dress that had ridden up slightly, revealing her long light legs to Brian, the only one around. "Do I have to go?" she said, feigningly. Brian noticed he was still looking at her legs, remembering the flash of black underwear he had seen.

"Not at all. You're welcome to stay the night." He looked around the hall. "Would you like a drink?" He said, gesturing to the kitchen.

"I would love one please. Get me something bubbly." Brian smiled, he looked as tears still escaped her eyes and again pitied her. He walked towards the kitchen then turned to her.

"I don't know what's happened to him tonight. But I'm going to find out. He can't get away with that." She nodded to him.

"I don't know either. But I know one thing." He voice firmer.

"What's that?"

"I'm not leaving." Brian tried to stop the smirk creeping across his face, then vanished into the dull hum of appliances and bleached surfaces of the kitchen. Precious held a face of pain until he vanished out of sight. Then, without missing a beat, she relaxed her face and pulled out a small mirror and lipstick and readjusted her makeup. She clasped the mirror shut and put it back into her bag. She popped her lips and dried the lipstick. She saw in the corner of the upper landing the peering eyes that had been watching her, hiding behind the corner, trying to stay unseen, before putting a hand to its mouth and rushing off into the halls.

"Perfect." she laughed to herself, and walked up the stairs to where Hugo had vanished off too.

Chapter Five

Violence.

The tarmac had turned a slick black as Francis sped down the winding road, his satellite navigation uttering orders, its robotic tone masked by an actress attempting to make it sound human, which despite her best efforts, failed miserably. A cheap thing off the internet, it had lost signal several times and Francis was certain he had taken the wrong turn again. Finally, swallowing what little pride he had left, he had to admit he was lost. He squinted through the clouding glass to make out any signs or road markings. All he could see however, were unlit roads, indecipherable from one tree to the next. A give way sign here, a left turn there, the odd traffic light, only to be repeated in the same order over and over again. His car struggling with the length of the journey. He looked at the car radio which read 18:02, which was the same time it had been for the past few weeks and Francis again had to admit that something else in his rotting aluminium cage was failing on him. He had spent the last part of his money to get the car heating fixed, which judging by the amount of condensation accumulating on his windscreen, wasn't quite there yet. He turned the heater to full and unwound his window. The cold air rushing into the inside of his car, sending a strong breeze through his long brown hair. It waved in the wind and he had to move it from his eyes. His satnav asked him to make a U turn after telling him to continue for another four miles after the last U turn it beckoned him to make, and he began to swear at it so much it would make a sailor blush. He was a man of the A – Z map books you would pick up from the local garage. At least they didn't lie to you, break when they didn't have any service or have an irritating robotic voice telling you how shit you are. He had had enough of that for one day. His mind was still racing from the encounter. His knuckles still tense. He looked in the mirror at his eyes. They were still blood shot and stung with pain as he blinked, desperately trying to make out the markings on the road. He wasn't sure if he was going the right way, let alone about to drive off the end of a cliff. "I'm not that lucky," he said, almost hugging the thought. He hadn't slept well in over a month. The days bleeding into the next, too racked with stress and worry that was eating him alive like a cancer. His skin had turned grey and his hair had turned thin and was starting to grey. He had bruises and scabs on his skin, where he would pick away at them unknowingly when it became too much, staring at the newspapers, his face all over them, in big red writing, "SCANDAL AT LOCAL PHARMACY LEFT TOWN IN SHOCK," and "DEADLY POISON FOUND IN PHARMACY SHIPMENT. POLICE INVESTIGATION CONTINUES." He remembers reading the latest bout of headlines a few hours earlier. He didn't know if it was morning or evening anymore, it was simply just, "today." He had never suffered with insomnia before, depression, anxiety, and all the other issues people seem to be having these days. A product of a sick world where we worship junk values and don't value each other. Where the desire of wanting overrides the desire of being wanted. Where Facebook and Twitter followers counted more than real flesh and blood human beings. Where views and likes could make you an instant star if you went 'Viral'. There's a reason it's called 'Viral' because it's a virus that infect those around you and when all is spent and the attention is gone, the virus turns inwards, and destroys the host. How many celebrities for nothing have risen to astronomical fame, only to plummet back to earth when people are just too sick of their bull shit or they're not the flavour of the month anymore. It's like a sick drug, Francis thought. A sick drug that promises everything you want, and all it will cost you is your soul. Christopher Marlow's Doctor Faustus came to mind. He gripped the steering wheel tighter, the ear splitting crackling of the engine almost deafening him. He closed the window and was again sealed into his obscured hot box that smelt of rotting takeaways and stale coffee. He licked his lips; they were getting dry again, and chugged the last of a six pack, before tossing it in the passenger footwell with its other discarded brothers. He savoured the taste that lingered on his lips, and couldn't remember the last thing he had drank that wasn't coffee or had a percentage marker next to it. He stared at the hypnotic lane dividers, slipping slowly into the opposite lane, before correcting his steering. He pushed back on the coils of the seat pushing through the fabric and into his back.

#

He remembered sitting there, in his local café, drinking his third cup of strong black coffee, his eyes wanting to sleep, but his brain denying him the peace. Even when he did drift off, he was quickly awakened by the sound of his mobile phone ringing, a knock of another "big scoop" journalist wanting a story, or the loud thumping in his head that pain killers just weren't touching anymore. He remembered how tight his grip was, scouring the latest article that had been written about him in the local paper. A picture of his face looking away as he walked through the streets with his black sun glasses on and his creased white shirt that came from beneath his long beige trench coat. The café was almost empty, other than a pair of wagon drivers who sat there in hi vis jackets, eating a cooked meal, and a man in a tailored black suit, short haired with thin rimmed glasses, looking into his computer screen probably plotting his taking over of the world. The white table was stained with tea and coffee marks that had engrained themselves into the painted plastic top and his chair was hard and creaked whenever he moved. He lit a cigarette and took a drag, the ashy taste mixing with the flavour of the bitter black that sat in a plastic cup. He studied the paper again, docked out the cigarette in the nearby glass ashtray that was already over flowing. His name was all over it. "FRANCIS WARD UNDER INVESTIGATION FOR IMPORTATION OF SCRYCHNINE." Indeed, it was true. He was under investigation, but as much as he pleaded with the police, the press and even family, nobody seemed to believe that he was innocent. He looked out the black windows of the Café, and he felt a glimmer of hope as he saw her walk up to the entrance, and enter the fluorescent lighting of the café. He caught his reflection in the window. He looked like death. Like a corpse left to rot and decay in the hot summer sun. His eyes sunken and they supported heavy dark bags that looked much puffier than the last time he had looked. He hadn't been home in over two weeks, showering at the motorway services and sleeping in his car. Watching his life unfold in the small television that played the news on loop that mockingly faced him in the top corner above the counter. The sound was always off, but when your face is on the news day after day, you don't need to hear what they're saying about you. He followed the familiar face. A woman dressed in a brown hoodie and light denim jeans. A red and black scarf wrapped around her neck which always reminded him of The Nightmare on Elm Street, both for the design, and the fact it was terrible. She walked in and Francis ducked his head behind his hand, covering the side of his face with the high red and white booths that wrapped around the tables, modelled like a candy cane that hid a sour secret. She walked over to the counter where a single waitress stood, wearing a red and white paper hat, a striped shirt and an apron that read "Ask me for anything!" and Francis always wondered how far he could push that. The lady behind the desk exchanged a few words with the woman, her greasy hair sticking to her ears and forehead, acne moving with her lips as she spoke. The waitress pointed in his direction, and he ducked his head again. He gripped the duffel bag he had on the seat to his right, sandwiched between him and the plastic wall of the booth stained with tomato sauce and dried spaghetti. She walked over to him and took a seat opposite, not saying a word. Her face was like stone. Her eyes almost black. She sat there, her dyed red hair pushing out brown roots, which were tied back in a tight bun, which sat underneath her black beanie hat. She had both hands on the table, fingers locked together in her black cotton gloves. She looked at him, unblinking, and Francis knew this wasn't going to be good news. He hadn't seen her in three days. Her face was unmoved. Emotionless. Done. Francis looked at his coffee away from her unmoving gaze, he studied the marks in the wood, anything to take his eyes away from her. The solid glare of a woman who believes she is looking at a failure, a liar, and a crook. He looked up at her finally, her eyes unwavering. Her lips pursed. He could hear his heart beat in his head, the recurring drum that hadn't left him in weeks, like a marching band on repeat. "Hi, Sarah," Francis uttered. His heart heavy. Sarah, still silent, reached into her jacket pocket and pulled out today's newspapers front page. She unfolded it, placed it flat on the table and pushed it towards him, her index finger pointing her chipped nail down at a picture of him. He was drunk in the photo, holding a cigarette in one hand and a pair of underwear in another hand. Pink and lacy. He still couldn't remember whose it was, or why he had it, but he felt the coffee coming back up to say hello. He took in a slow intake of breath. Sarah began tapping her finger that matched the rhythm of the ticking clock that hung on the wall behind him, and he realised how silent the café now was. "I know how this looks," he said, part hungover, part asleep, part pleading. He went to continue but Sarah lifted up her finger, and Francis fell silent, like a mean teacher catching you talking in class, knowing one more syllable would lead to your doom.

"Whose is this?" she said, again tapping on the pink underwear in the picture. Her voice painful and bitter. Francis looked at the photo, desperately trying to think of something, but he drew a blank.

"Sarah, I don't know. I wish could come up with something, anything. But I don't know why I had them. I don't even remember the evening." He began to well up. The stress of the last few months coming back into his mind.

"You said you loved me." Sarah said. Her voice was arid and dead. Francis reached for her hand but she pulled it away from him. His chest tore in two.

"Sarah, I swear on my parents' grave, I have not done this to you". He begged. "We were so happy. We can make this right, make it all better again. This will blow over. I promise." He was shaking now. "I love you so much. I'm so lost, I don't know what to do."

"You can admit what you have done." At first, he felt nothing. Then, like the botfly bites and waits, the larva of misery pushed out from him.

"Admit what I have done? What do you want me to say? Everything was going well, then in the blink of an eye, everything turned to shit so quickly. So goddamn quickly."

"People died Francis. I hope you wear that stain on your face forever."

"It wasn't my fault!" he shouted, knocking his coffee from the table. Sarah stayed still, her eyes not leaving his.

"You are a liar."

"I'm not."

"You are a cheater and a fraud. And you can't stop trying to dig yourself put of the mess you have made. The hole I'm stuck in with you."

"I never wanted this. Please believe! I…I can't go on like this. Without you… I'm done." Tears fell onto the table top. Sarah stuttered in her breath, a flickering of pain in her eyes, and then it was gone. "And I'm losing it all. Losing my mind." Silence had befallen them. Not like the silence in the café around them, or like the silence in their home when they had existed together like two shadows, but a new silence, and it was colder than the thickest fog. She stared at him further, her eyes burrowing into his mind.

"Francis." She sighed. She looked away from him, and that was even worse. She continued softly, carefully. Almost rehearsed. "For five years, we have built a life together. You were my one and only." Whatever hope Francis had left, was fading quickly like the heat from his coffee cup.

"Sarah, no," he choked, the weight of everything burying him again.

"We built up the business together, we were doing so well on our own, but you were so greedy." Her voice became raw. She fought her words as they came out. "But you let that man take over our lives. You let him sign his dirty mark on the dotted line of our future, for just a few more zero's in our bank accounts. And now what do we have to show for it? I can't show my face in public anymore. I can't walk down the street without strangers asking me questions and taking my picture. I can't even have a bath and feel anything but dirty." She wrapped her arms around herself, stoking her shoulders.

"It will get better, Sarah, it will. The papers, they've got it so wrong." Francis pleaded. Hot tears dripping onto the table, soaking into the grain. Sarah continued, like he hadn't spoken. His words falling deaf on her ears.

"You signed us away to him, that bastard. You thought it would help us. Strychnine, Francis?" Her eyes were wide now, she sat back mouth agape, hands pushing into her hair. "Strychnine! Do you know what that can do to a person?" His throat felt welded shut and it ached with pain.

"Sarah, it wasn't me, how many times do I have to tell you I didn't do this?"

"But it's only you that knew the passwords. Only you that had access to the accounts. Only you that placed the orders, organised the shipments! Francis, it's time to come clean, it must have been you! Our profits are down 60% this quarter, and overall sales are projected to be down 80% by the end of the year! Your greed has destroyed us!". She was shouting now, and her voice echoed through the silence. Francis held his head in his hands. "You never home anymore. When I do see you, you're always drunk. We haven't sat and had a real conversation about anything other than this shit in months." Her voice calmed. Like she had expended what little emotion she had left. Like she had given him all the love she had, and the well had ran dry.

"Hugo knew the codes," Francis whispered. Sarah pressed her tongue to her teeth and shook her head. She scoffed and leaned in closer.

"So, you're telling me our main investor and shareholder committed business suicide by selling fucking poison to people. Doesn't look very good for a pharmacy, does it, Francis?!"

"He's the only one who knew them. It must have been him. He's the only one who knew them. It must have been him. He was investigated when this whole thing happened. I saw it in the papers. Someone had sent information to them. But he managed to make it go away. Then his friends turned it around on me. The little man," his words pressing through his frustration. He had said this so many times to her but she would never believe him. He had said it even more to the press, but they wanted to pick him apart. Why would they go after Hugo anyway? This town was basically built on the wealth of that man. They wouldn't crucify him or throw him to the wolves, not when it was easier to pick the bones of the little guy. It made for better tabloids.

"You're a liar, Francis," Sarah said coldly. He looked up to her, his eyes bloodshot than ever. She tapped the picture of him holding the pink underwear again, like a tapestry of all his failures as a husband, a businessman and a friend. "A liar, and a cheat." She stood up from the table, not saying anything more. Francis continued to look down at the picture, not seeing her leave. He heard a metallic sound to his right, like a small coin being placed on to a counter. He heard the bell of the café door go and he didn't watch as she slunk away into the cold night air outside. She didn't see the tears appearing in her eyes from the hard decision she had had to make for the sake of her own future. He hadn't noticed her raw face untouched by the vanity creams, her eyes almost as baggy as his. All he saw was the picture of him holding a stranger's underwear, his shame printed in high definition for the world to see. His disgrace immortalized thanks to another drunken nights to numb the pain. He looked up to his right and saw it all in one on the counter. His failure, his defeat, his pain. A golden wedding ring. He sat there for a moment. Then another. His mind numb. He clutched his duffel bag again, feeling the weight inside it. He took it and put it over his shoulder and put the ring into his pocket. He put up his hood from his coat and his dark sun glasses and put his hands in his pocket and felt

the letter he had gotten in the post a week earlier. A letter he had read but hadn't replied too. Its calligraphic writing like taunting of curse words. An invitation from Hugo, inviting him to his get together of people he annually fucked over. He left the café and walked across the grey tarmac to his car that sat alone under a dim streetlight. He threw his bag onto the passenger seat and closed the door. Francis sat back, remembering the words what Sarah had said, all summed up into you are nothing.. He needed to do something about this situation. Something extreme. The police weren't going to believe the destruction of his company was due to Hugo. Neither would the press nor would anyone else. The only thing he could do was to confront Hugo about it and force him to come clean, hoping to make him pay for what he had done. He pulled out the crumpled letter from his pocket and punched the address into his sat nav.
"One hour away," he said to the robotic voice. He smiled to himself, and it was the first smile he had cracked in months.

#

He pulled into a lay by as his satnav decided to cut out. He looked at it with fury "You piece of shit!" he screamed to himself, thinking it would somehow make it come back on and work properly. He opened his door and stepped out into the night. The loose gravel crunching underneath his feet, his legs stiff from sitting down. He turned to the thick forest around him, and threw the small black screen and cable into its depths. "Bitch!" The rustle of the trees in the soft wind uttering no reply. He took out a cigarette and lit it. His lungs filling with hot ash fused air. He lent back on the wing of his car and looked up at the clear sky as he blew the smoke out. He saw the big dipper, Mars and Venus. He tried to count a few of them, but quickly lot track. He leaned over his front seat and unzipped his duffel bag. He took out a small plastic bag and undid it. He reached his car key in and held one nostril as he snorted a small bump of cocaine. He then did one more and licked the end of the key like a sherbet dip. He sealed the bag and stuffed it into his back pocket. One doesn't own a pharmacy if you can't enjoy its perks every now and then. He took another drag of his smoke, breathing in deeply as his brain orgasmed. His pupils dilated and he felt much better. The dopamine returning into his brain, and he realised this is what it's like to fight withdrawal. He sat back in his car and shut the door. He realised now that without his satnav he had literally no idea where the hell he was going. He put his key in the ignition, convinced that if he drove long enough, he would find a garage to either ask for directions, or to buy a map book. He turned the key and the engine clicked. "You must be fucking joking me." He turned the key again, then again, and finally again until the clicking stopped and there was just silence. He hit the steering wheel in frustration and held pulled at his hair, erupting a blood chilling scream into the night around him. He sat there for a moment, chest heaving. His mind consuming him. Torturing him. He clenched his eyes shut, and felt inside his bag. Without looking, he pulled out his instrument. Tears streaming down his face and mucus seeping from his nose. He clenched with both hands and put his finger on the trigger. He felt the hard, cold end of the barrel under his chin. He pulled the hammer back and heard the pistol cock. Just a little pressure and it would all be over. He thought of his life, how he had never had children. He thought of his business that had turned to ruins. He remembered his wedding day, and how beautiful Sarah had looked that day, her white dress flowing down past her feet, pooling at the bottom while the bridesmaids held her gown off the grass of the castle grounds. He thought of God, he thought of his soul being freed from his fleshy prison. He clenched his teeth and let out a loud groan as his finger pressed harder on the trigger. Just a little more, a little more.

Hugo. He thought of Hugo.

He relaxed the grip on the pistol and gasped, like through all the haze he had seen God, showing him the path to absolution. He was the victim of a greater evil, and he had to stop it from consuming others.

In the distance, he saw a pair of headlights coming towards him, like a glowing spectre passing through the forest, snaking with the flow of the road. He quickly put the gun into his belt line and grabbed his duffel bag. The headlights drew closer, and he could hear the faint music coming from its radio. The occupant of the vehicle, Edward, was on his way home from a christening. Designated driver for the night, he had shed his party of drunken family and friends and was on his way home, singing along to the radio, confidently navigating the familiar roads. He tapped the steering wheel to the beat of the song. His headlights kissed the bonnet of a parked car in a lay by to his right as he moved around the upcoming bend. He saw something in the road, and he slammed his foot on the brake, swerving and just narrowly missing the figure on the ground. His brakes screeched as he nearly lost control, bringing it to a sudden halt the side of the road, where the grass verge met the asphalt. He ran his hands through his hair, his heart beating out his chest. He opened up the car door, the thick smell of burning rubber finding its way into his nostrils. He stepped out into the cool night air, the brake light of the ticking car casting a long deep red glow into the night. He hurried over to the shape on the ground and couched down. His words lost in his throat, his eyes wide with adrenalin as they desperately tried to adjust to the dark. He placed his hand on the shape and found it to be empty. It's firmness did not hold his weight, but instead allowed it to passthrough. It was a long beige trench coat that had been throw into the road. He picked it up with his hand, the coat still warm and smelt strongly of sweat and alcohol.

"What the hell?" he said to the phantoms clothing. Then he heard the quick crunching of gravel and stone, getting louder and quicker. He heard a shout erupt into the silent air. He turned on his knees quickly and fear overcame him. He held up his hands and screamed as a shadow struck him hard in the face with a cold steel butt of a pistol. He fell to the ground holding his face, red hot blood pouring out of his head. He felt another strike and he screamed wildly with pain like a man being torn apart by bears, the blunt handle coming down on his hands that wrapped around his head, shattering them. "Take the car! Take it all!" the shadow made no reply, hitting him again and again wildly in his head and face. Edward heard the bones of his scull crack and splinter. He lay there unmoving, his eyes still open as the figure ceased its barrage. It lent over him, panting heavily. He drifted in and out of consciousness as the black pulled him under. The shadow pulled the coat from beneath him, it dripping with blood, his blood, and wrapped it around him. He watched as it ran to his car and heard the door slam, tyres screeching as it pulled away. The faint sounds of the radio kissing the night air. He felt the cold of the night pull him under the blanket of blackness, before eclipsing the moon and stars that cried above, and then all went black.

Chapter Six.

Precious Things.

Hugo hurriedly walked across the hallway into the bathroom and slammed the door. His heart was beating out of his chest and he was sweating heavily. He lent on the back of the door and squinted his eyes. His vision was becoming blurry and the soft lighting in his bathroom had become blinding. His face tensed in pain and he grabbed his chest. He wasn't sure if he was having the world's worst migraine, like he was having melted iron poured into his eyes and being shook about, if he was having a panic attack, heart attack or all three at the same time. He struggled over to the sink and bathroom mirror, clinging on to the side of the wall to keep him upright lest his ailment take him and send his scull firmly into the hard tiling. He reached the mirror, his face appeared gaunt and stretched out like a face torqued over meat hooks. His eyes were sunken into his head and his jaw hung loosely like the living dead. His breath was shallow, straining in his lungs like they had been filled with dirt, worms and beetles burrowing into his bronchia. He thrust open the cabinet and grabbed a bottle of medication. He hadn't suffered with a panic attack in a long time, but this one was back with a vengeance. He felt claustrophobic. Suffocating. The lights pulsed in his vision and he slammed them shut, fingering the medicine cabinet behind the mirror blindly. He gripped the brown bottle and went to take of the lid. His hand was shaking wildly and he popped the lid off clumsily, causing the pills to scatter on the floor in a sound of cascading rainfall. He winced and bent down to pick them up, squinting tightly. He managed to pick up two that lay next to his feet, put them into his mouth and swallowed them whole. He clambered back, again tightly gripping the porcelain of his sink basin. He lent over the white and vomited thick bile into the bowl which spluttered down his shirt and onto his face. He turned on the faucet and cleared the phlegm and spit from his mouth then drank thirstily, like a dying dog which had just found a freshwater source. The fresh water pulling him back from despair. He turned off the tap and stood in the silence, the blurry vision was slowly clearing and his heart returned to a steady pace instead of running like it was being chased by lions. He felt cooler and took a deep breath, the worms and bugs abated back into the mud. He collected the rest of the scattered medication and put them back into the brown bottle, and placed them back into the cabinet. He closed the mirror and she stood behind him.

The woman in the mirror. He jellied eyes and jaw hanging low.

Blonde wavy hair hanging just below her breasts. Her pale skin and tattooed shoulders. She bore a wicked smile, like a cat when it found a new mouse.

"Hey, Huggy Bear," she said cheerfully. Hugo turned around. The lions awakening his heart again.

"Get out of my home," he whispered. He held her gaze and slowly felt his body growing hotter, his legs again turning to stone. She stood up straight, feet together and hands behind her back, like a teacher's pet holding a gift for her favourite tutor. He clenched his fist, feeling the beast growling again. "Didn't you hear me? I said I want you out of my house!" Still she stood there unwavering, still holding her gift of joy behind her back. She looked like a porcelain doll. The kind old women hang in their living room to terrify their grandchildren. He peered to the side. "What have you got there?" he said, his voice going higher. Again, Precious did not move, did not utter a syllable. She just stood there. Hugo took a step towards her slowly, his hands primed to defend himself. He held one of them towards her. "Whatever it is," he said, his voice now shaking, "Give it to me. Give it to me and leave before I call the police." He took another step.

"You're not going to call the police." Precious said, the doll coming to life. "You don't want them digging up your business. You know they would lock you away to rot." Hugo took another small step. "You won't want them to find what you've been up too. You don't want them to know about Annie." Hugo felt the weight of her name hit him in his chest like a hard ball of ice.

"How do you know about Annie?" he whispered. His voice fading. Precious stopped smiling. Her face now bore a stern look. Her lips and eyes too like stone, burning their gaze into his. Her voice turned low.

"You ruined her life. Like you ruin all that come into contact with you. You speak lies and destroy people. You infect others with your charm before leaving them to rot alone, your memory imbedded in their head like a parasite they can't get away from." Precious took one hand from her back and dipped her head forward, grabbing a clump of hair and moving it to one side, revealing a large scar on the back of her skull.

"You got into my head," she said. Then her smile returned, as long and as horrifying as before. Her voice high and breaking. "I got so sick of you being in there, I tried to burrow you out." Hugo felt sick. This woman was sick. She was lying, she had to be? He stood in place, still noticing the hidden hand that sat behind her back, like a coiled viper waiting a few closer steps.

"You're insane."

"You liked it last time."

"What do you want from me? Money?" Precious laughed. Her voice bellowed from the walls and pushed into his head.

"No. I don't want money."

"Then what do you want?" he hissed through gritted teeth.

"I want to finish what I started."

"Get out of my house immediately." he spoke firmly. Precious cocked her head.

"But Huggy bear, we're not in your house." Hugo looked at her, confused. Then he followed her eyes as she traced the room. He looked up at the walls and was gripped by terror. His bathroom was gone. The grey walls were now dark brown, he looked down to his feet and he was standing on a soiled cream carpet. The room was no longer a gentle light but instead a dull flickering. He span around and could hear Precious laughing behind him, almost wildly, her voice pressing into his ears. He heard the sound of a loud drill and a crunching noise in his head, he let out a blood curdling scream as he fell on to the dirtied carpet, his knees soaking in the wet. In front of him was a large mattress, and he saw himself on there, lying helpless, naked and foaming at the mouth, eyes vacant, arms stretched out. He saw her on top of him, her naked body enjoying his. His face and body had been brutalized, and he was drenched in thick dark crimson. Precious was shouting like a hellish creature into the air as she ran her hands over her body with his blood. Across the room, he saw a metal table. A small body lay on top of it in the dark, the right arm and left ankle tagged. Features unrecognisable, like someone he knew but couldn't place. He turned on his back and saw a woman in the corner of the room holding a scalpel, dressed in a white night gown. She dug it into her stomach and began sawing roughly, screaming in agony. She opened up a large bloodied gash, ripped flesh and muscle hanging from the wound. She dove her hand in and pulled out a writhing infant, screaming and covered in blood and mucus. She held it into the air and pressed it into her bosom, whimpering in pain. He stood up, his mind not thinking, not believing, and not wanting to understand the wretched circle of hell he found himself in.

"What is this place?" he croaked. The sound of demonic laughter in his ears grow louder, mixed with the screams of the bloodied infant. Lightning pressed through the large suite windows and traced dimorphic shadows across the floor that stretched hideously. He saw Precious there, standing naked. His bloodied body lying on the bed. Her hair matted with deep red and face painted the same.

"You remember this place, don't you, Huggy bear?" she laughed.

"Is this Paris?" he whispered. His throat closing shut. Precious shook her head.

"Nope." She pounced on him, pushing him to the chest and he fell backwards. He looked to see an empty class of whisky on the floor next to him, filled with white powder, his reflection in the wardrobe mirror showing him covered in deep black bruises and cuts across his face and chest. She straddled him on the floor. She pulled her hand from behind her back, holding a large carving knife that shone in the lighting. "Welcome to hell." She screamed and his body erupted in white hot agony. Her thrashing as she drove the blade into his chest and stomach repeatedly, insanity blended into her wails and screams, opening him up and thick red blood burning his skin as it poured out onto the carpet. She leaned into him and kissed his cheek. "Let him be free." She hissed, before sinking her teeth into him. He lay on the ground, fading into the nothingness around him, eyes gripped on the self-mutilated woman that cradled the bloodied child, her eyes dead and vacant, as she moved to him.

#

Hugo screamed as he awoke on the bathroom floor, slumped into the corner holding on to an empty brown bottle. He took a sharp intake of breath and shouted again. He was drenched from head to toe, his clothes sticking to his stick, melting him into the ground. His body numb from the cold tiles. His mind was wrecked and racked and moving at one hundred miles per hour. He tore open his shirt to see himself unharmed physically. "It wasn't real," he said to himself in a hurried repetition, trying to catch his breath. "It wasn't real." He pinched his arms and slapped the walls to solidify his reality, before running his hand down his face. "It wasn't real." He buttoned up his shirt, hiding the feint scars under his chest hair. He quickly showered and freshened up before putting on a new set of fresh clothes. He cleared up the loose pills on the floor and unsure if he had taken them before his blackout, he took two more. He opened up a small cabinet that sat in the bottom of his sink basin and pulled out a small bottle of whisky, enough for a single measure. He had kept it there for when he and Claudia would have a romantic bath together, but that had never happened, so he figured now was as good a time as any. He twisted the cap and washed the pills down. His doctor would freak out if he saw this, but frankly, Hugo thought, fuck him. He stepped into the hallway and saw John stood there outside of the spare bedroom. His lips were moving quickly and speaking in a low tone, pacing on the spot. The door was slightly ajar and darkness emanated from its insides. Hugo walked closer to him. "John," he called. He turned his head and saw Hugo. He gripped the door handle and closed it.

"Mr. Hugo, I've been looking for you," he said quickly. He walked towards him, holding a small cloth and some anti-bacterial spay. Hugo looked at him and then to the closed door.

"Who were you talking too?" he asked, a confused look in his eyes.

"Nobody, Sir," Hugo shot him a look, and John knew what that look meant. "Sir, I wasn't talking to anybody, I was checking the interior making sure it was to your standards. Maybe I was muttering to myself checking all was in order, but not to a person, just myself Sir." Hugo walked over to the door, took the handle and opened it. His mind still racing from his nightmare. He turned the light on to see a well-made guest room. The double bed that faced the entrance was beautifully made, and the red linen sheets had not a single crease in them. A small lamp sat on a bed side table that looked free from dust, and a large painting of chaotic colour, with no clear purpose, hung above the head board. He stepped in and saw the cream carpet free from lint, and a small deep purple chair sat in the corner with a freshly puffed pillow on it. He turned to John.

"It will do" he said. John felt the familiar hit of disappointment in his chest. "See to it that the rest of the guest rooms are made up in this way." He looked him up and down. "And be sure to change your suit too." John looked himself over.

"I have already changed sir."

"Then change yourself again. And when you're done up here, be sure that the food and drinks are prepared on time, so that they are still hot and don't have flies in them."

"Yes sir."

"And once that is done, be sure to have fresh drinks ready for the guests as they come arrive. Be sure to have extra food on standby as well as more drinks, should people desire it."

"Okay sir." Hugo turned to walk away. "Miss Annie and Madam Edith have arrived. They are down in the kitchen now Sir". Annie. There was that ball of ice in his chest again. Hugo stopped and turned to him.

"Thank you, John, has Francis arrived yet?"

"No sir. I have tried to contact him but have had no joy. Should we wait for him?" Hugo looked at his watch.

"No. The night is running away and we have a party to start. Francis will understand. Please keep a listen out for him on the intercom." With this, he continued to walk down towards the staircase to greet the other guests, but stopped at the lip of the landing. "Did you let her in?" he asked sternly, fingers turning white as they pressed into the wall.

"Who Sir?." Hugo pursed his lips.

"Precious. Did you let Precious into the house? "John shifted in his step, pulling the cloth around his shoulder.

"No sir," he said. "I thought you did?"

#

Claudia sat in her bedroom on the mattress. She fingered the expensive duvet as she looked through her smart phone. She scrolled through pictures of her social media, holding a happy smile that was enhanced by a million filters, all wanting to scream to her followers "Look at me! I'm as happy as a girl can be!" She had amassed a large following since her clothing range was launched, inventively named "CLAUDIA." It was a prestigious line of women's clothing that hung on the hangers in the most prestigious of shopping outlets in Paris, Los Angeles and London. She had built a small empire of desire and greed. She looked through photos of her skiing in the Alps, working out in the early mornings thinking how good her ass looked in her gym wear as she did squats, and then she turned off her social media and went to her private photos. Some with her in clothing, some without. She had photos of her and Brian. Him holding her in his strong arms while they lied in bed, her face naked from makeup, him kissing her cheek while she rested her head on a pillow. Some out having dinner at fine restaurants, others in his home's Jacuzzi when his ugly wife had gone to Prague, or Vienna or wherever the hell she was from. She longed for him again. But she felt pain. What she saw in the hall, unseen by him, unseen by her. The blonde one. What kind of fucking name is 'Precious' anyway? She thought of her as an unloved child who has to steal happiness from others to validate her own self-worth. She felt sadness turn into bitterness, and then bitterness twist into pain. All she had done for Brian, all she was risking, as he thrusts himself into another's arms when he thought she wasn't looking. She felt like exposing it all. Exposing all the foul thing he had done. She could make it seem like he forced her into it. He pressured her into wanting him. Hugo would believe her. He wouldn't know the truth. As smart as he was, she was a better manipulator. She and Hugo had history, money, and influence, and they could bury Brian in the shit he had created. His whore wife would be homeless and their ugly child would go into care. Brian would be left ruined and penniless and she imagined driving past him begging on the streets in her limo, throwing rotting meat bones out the window to his starving feet. Her eyes burned like fire. Brian. That succubus. He knew she was vulnerable and he preyed on it. She began to delete the photos of him and her from her phone, wiping the memories clean from her storage. Swiping and clicking faster, seeing his face on there made her feel sick. How dare he? How fucking dare he use her like this? She stopped. It was a photo of another, and her heart plummeted. The morning in the Alps. Her last morning with Emmanuel. The thought of him again made the pain disappear briefly, and warm tears fell onto her legs that sat over the end of the bed. He wouldn't never take what she said, lightly.

#

"I want a baby," she had said to him on that crisp morning before his trip, as she straddled him on the mattress, their heat from their bodies holding each other closer.

"What?" Emmanuel said. The love vanishing from his voice. He moved from under her and she fell onto the bed. He walked over to the window and looked out to the milling people below, fake smiles on their faces. He rested his hands on the window sill, his bare back tensing showing off his defined muscles. He took out a cigarette from the carton that sat next to the window, cracked the pane, lit it and blew out smoke outside. "We've spoken about this Claudia," he said, heavily. "We can't have a baby. I don't want to be a father." His words hurt and she remembered this fight. They have had it before.

"That was back then," she pleaded, lying on the bed. "I thought you would have changed your mind?"

"Why? Because we have had a nice morning? Because things are going well?" He threw his cigarette out the window, leaving it ajar as the smoke fled the heating room. He walked over to a pile of clothes he had prepared the night before and hastily began to dress. Claudia sat up in bed looking at him.

"We were struggling then! But now, we have what we could ever want! We have money, we have a future, why not share it with another? Let us have a family, Emmanuel. I want a baby," she whined with frustration. He continued rushing to get dressed, hastily putting on his shirt and tie. "Are you even listening to me!"

"I don't want to be a father," he said bluntly. "Things are great right now, why ruin it with eighteen years of caring for another person when we have each other?" He picked up the pace, looking at the floor, half not wanting to explain himself, half wanting to get it out.

"But I don't know why? You say we're great which we are. We're married, happy, but is this it? I want to pass our love onto someone else. "I thought I had made myself clear about this last time, Claudia. I do not want children, now or ever, and you need to understand this." His tone was final. He put on his shoes and grabbed his satchel bag, before pulling his blazer and made for the door. He clicked the knob and turned to see Claudia staring at the floor. He was confused, but then his breath caught in his throat, and he wanted the world to eat him alive. Both were silent, as they stared at the pack of condoms that had fallen from his inside pocket. "What are they for?" she asked, swallowing hard, holding herself.

"It's not what you think." He said, moving to her. He touched her shoulders and she lept out of bed like he was on fire.

"Don't touch me! Don't touch me you pig!" she moved to the window staring at him, trying to push herself away from him, like his touch was acid. He moved closer to her.

"Baby, it's not what you think I promise. I didn't want to get you pregnant." She slapped him across the face, her nail cutting his lip.

"I'm on contraception and you know it. You think I would deliberately trap you? You make me-" Her head hit the wall as he turned and brought the back of his hand across her face. She fell into a heap on the ground like a bunch of crumpled clothes. He stood above her, his dark hair pinned to his sweating forehead. She sobbed and crawled after him as he walked out of the door and locked it behind him. She banged furiously on the wood screaming his name, screaming she was sorry. She heard fast footsteps down the stairs and then she ran to the bedroom window as he left, not looking back to her. She banged on the glass, opening the window and shouted after him until her throat burned and her tongue swelled. She watched as he got into his car and reversed off the driveway. She watched as he didn't see the oncoming HGV. She watched as it crashed into his car in a harrowing blitz of crunching metal and screeching tyres. She watched as the people flocked around him in his car holding their faces in terror, and she watched as rain fell on the glass of the window, as the paramedics told her that there was nothing they could do.

#

Claudia returned to the present. She blinked her vacant eyes, hot tears gathering at their lid. She walked over to the large mirror in the corner that sat on top of her dresser. She looked at her reflection, the same way a person studies a stranger, trying to figure out who they are. She highlighted the folder on her phone named PICTURES and took a sharp breath as she pressed DELETE. She exited her bedroom, and walked onto the hallway. She saw Hugo standing there, looking at her. He had changed his attire since she had seen him downstairs and he looked a little fresher, cooler, like he had shed his older self of bitterness and become a new, more relaxed version. He saw her and smiled, and walked towards her, not saying a word, and took her in his arms and kissed her. She smiled for a moment. "What is that for?" Hugo smiled at her, the smell of whiskey instantly driving away whatever little warmness she had suddenly felt for him, like the tide ruins a sandcastle, renouncing its existence.

"Can't I kiss my wife?" His wife. She couldn't keep this up much longer. She was like a dam ready to burst. She broke his grip and looked away, her eyes studying one of the paintings on the wall. She spoke timidly.

"Hugo, we need to talk." He moved in closer, putting his hands on her shoulders and kissed her neck.

"About what?" She again moved from him, his wet mouth leaving a trail of saliva on her neck, like a slug leaves its sticky trail of mucus across the kitchen floor.

"Do you ever really know someone?" she said, studying one of the paintings in the hallway. A picture of an old woman doing crochet.

"What do you mean my love?" She traced the painting with her finger.

"Do you ever really know someone? Their secrets? Their reasons? Their past lovers, their past pain." She felt tears pushing through again, the well of bitterness that they held behind them was starting to leak through.

"Is everything okay?" He put his hands on her shoulder and she took his hand in hers.

"If I tell you something, can we work it out?" He squeezed her fingers and felt a shudder of cold.

"Claudia, you're scaring me. What's wrong?" She moved away from him again, looking at another painting. This one of a vast mountain range encased in snow overlooking a frozen lake.

"Emmanuel beat me." His face dropped and he took her into his arms.

"You never told me." he pulled her into him, nestling her into his chest. "I'm so sorry." He ran his fingers through her hair. Then looked at her intently, studying her eyes like he had seen them for the first time again.

"He did it because I wanted a baby. He did it because he was unfaithful to me," She took his hand. "I need to tell you something."

"Anything my love." She paused and took a deep breath, looking him up and down. A small smile crept across her face.

“I’m pregnant.”

#

Brian stood in the downstairs hallway speaking to two new arrivals to the house. He was holding two glasses of champagne. One for him, and one for Precious who had since disappeared somewhere. He saw two women approaching, polar opposites to one another. One was tall, wore a flowery dress, high white gloves that came to her elbows and had long blonde hair and bright rouge made up, approximately fifty years old and spoke with an eloquent touch. She had said her name was Edith, and she was as lively as a box of lit fireworks, laughing loudly at Brian’s terrible jokes. The other was more subtle, she had a slim frame, short stature and had a wavy navy-blue dress with short mousy hair. She didn’t speak much but was still polite and smiled candidly in the right places. She held her arms across her body, holding the champagne Brian had gotten for Precious. This was Annie.

“And that’s when the minister said “Brian, you can’t do that to the water, it will give the children a reason to come back”!” Brian laughed and so did Edith. Annie smirked and took a sip of her drink. He was recounting a tale of when he was in South Africa, when he had gone on an aid mission to boost his profile with charity work. He had been installing wells in a poor area where African children were dying from water borne diseases, and he had been treating it so they could drink clean water and build a life there, until the local leader of the church group in the close by “White’s only” part of town had told him it was a bad idea.

“That’s awful,” Edith laughed. She smiled at Annie. “Don’t you think so?”

“I guess so yeah,” she said, holding a loose smile, taking another sip.

“Hey, I say, free water and healthcare for everybody,” added Brian.

“Well,” said Edith, “If you can bring something like that into fruition, as well as looking into more sustainable energy sources, and bring down the homelessness problem in the city, then I can see you going far,” she winked. “Then you have my vote, Mr. Mayor.” The three of them laughed to each other.

“Can I get you a drink?” Brian said to Edith. She looked at the bubbling champagne glasses in Brian and Annie’s hand and watched as they fizzed and sparkled in the light.

"None for me, thank you," she said politely, yet firmly, making it clear to Brian that she did not wish him to offer again. He nodded.
"I, however, would love a refill," said Annie, finishing her glass. Brian laughed and then drank his too. "It's not a contest."
"Even not playing the game is a form of competition, Annie," Brian said with a wink. He looked around and heard the sound of floating classical music coming from the lounge through the archway under the stairs, and heard the sound of the kitchen coming to life. Pots and pans, popping of champagne bottles and the chinking of classes. "So how do you know Hugo?"
"We are old friends." She tapped her glass with her nail. "Where can I get another?" Brian pointed to the kitchen.
"Just through there. There are tonnes of booze. Drink away. John, the house keeper should be in there." Annie smiled a thank you and walked to the kitchen. Brian watched her as she walked away. Edith tapped him on the shoulder.
"She's not quite herself yet. She just got out the hospital a few weeks ago," she said in a hushed voice, the same way a gossip spreads intimate details of other's lives as soon as they leave the room.
"Oh really?" he said, eyes widened.
"Yes," she leaned in closer. "She was a victim of a robbery. It was ugly. She was in the ICU for months. It's the first time she's been out socialising since then. If she seems a little, you know, 'off',' then don't take it personally." He looked back the way she had walked. Half feeling a warmth towards her, for her courage, half thinking how good the story could sell. He looked back at Edith.
"Her and Hugo?" She looked at him in a 'Don't ask too many questions,' way.
"All I know is she didn't really want to come, but I told her it would be fun and it would do her good to meet some new people. So she threw on some clothes and put a dash of eyeliner on, and here she is."
"What's the story between those two?" she laughed.
"Inquisitive little creature, aren't you?" He laughed.
"It's my job after all." Edith looked around, seeing they were alone other than the stone woman on the other end of the hall.
"I've asked her about it before, I think they might have had a thing going on a while ago, but she keeps her cards close to her chest, doesn't give much away." Brian again looked the way Annie had gone off few minutes ago.

"Interesting." He turned to Edith. "And how do you know Hugo?".
"I know him through work. I work in pathology, Annie was a surgeon."
"Was?" Brian asked, jumping in. Edith furrowed her brow, the way a mother would when her child had asked for another piece of cake before bedtime.
"It's not for me to say." Edith took out her makeup out of her handbag and opened up a small mirror and began to adjust her hair. "Anyway," she continued, "He helped me get off the ground, helped publish some of my work to get me more notable in the field. I and Annie went to a medical conference and Hugo was there, helping to spread my name and the rest is history," she clasped her mirror shut and put it back into her bag. She traced her gloves on her bare shoulders, her eyes flittering to Brian's champagne, then away again. He looked at the white gloves.
"Not often you see people wearing those these days?" he said, pointing to them. She followed his gaze.
"I prefer to keep it modest. Young women, these days, are so eager to show everything off straight away. Something as simple as covering up a bit of flesh can be tantalising to even the most dubious of spectators." Her lips went tight. "And I have always loved Cruella Deville." She said, trying to hold her smile from coming out. Both of the laughed.
"Puppy skinning and all?" said Brian. She tapped her nose.
"How else do you make clothing?" He looked at her bag with a slight alarm, and she shrugged with a smile and a wink. He heard footsteps coming from the top of the stairs.
"Edith!" They both turned to see Hugo and Claudia walking down the stairs, arms linked together. Edith's smile beamed at them and she walked to the bottom of the stairs to greet them. Hugo wrapped his arms around her and Claudia pecked her on both cheeks. Brian stood back, the image of Claudia and Hugo interlocked sent a hit of confusion in his mind, like he had just heard a cat recite Shakespeare.
"How wonderful to see you again. I'm so happy you could make it."
"I wouldn't miss it for the world Hugo." She looked around, wonder in her eyes. "I love the house, it's amazing."
"It wasn't cheap either." He and Claudia chuckled. Edith simpered.
"I saw the gates and the intercom? What are you trying to keep out?" He took her around the shoulder.
"Prying eyes my darling, prying eyes. I've got something remarkable to show you all tonight. John is preparing all the food and wine that

money can buy, and I expect you to eat and drink your fill."

"I hope you have water and lemonade!" Edith gestured to her empty hands. "Trying the Keto diet. It's supposed to make the weight fall off you." Claudia stepped forward and took her hand.

"My sweet, you look fantastic already." Edith, catching her accent.

"Tu teux toujours avoir meilleure mine." Claudia's eyes widened and so did her smile.

"Tuparle francais?"

"Oui un peu." Claudia wrapped her hands around her and laughed. She turned to Hugo.

"I like this one!" she laughed. "I've tried the Keto diet, dip in and out. It's great for shredding the pounds." She eyed Brian who stood behind Edith. "Keeps you looking good." Hugo moved past Edith and took Brian's arm.

"I see you met my business partner Brian? Soon to be Mayor Callahan?" Brian flushed and patted Hugo on the arm, like an arachnophobe stroking a tarantula.

"Business partner? Don't be so formal Hugo. We're friends." Claudia laughed under her breath. She saw how badly Brian was trying to act casual. He looked as uncomfortable as an ant trying to catch a tan under a magnifying glass.

"Is your wife coming tonight, Brian? I didn't ask earlier." Brian's stomach fell through his shoes, as he felt the eyes of Edith caress him, Hugo's smile at him, and Claudia's bore into him.

"Yeah Brian." Claudia said smiling. "Where is your wife tonight?" He felt like his collar was choking him alive, like a snake was wrapping around his windpipe.

"She's.." he cleared his throat, regained his composure. "Yes Ima. She's at home looking after our son Ivan. He's just started school so she's had her hands full with that sadly, so she can't make it tonight."

"Shame," blurted Claudia. Edith put her hand to her mouth.

"You have a little boy? How old?"

"He's six." Edith put her hand to her chest.

"Such a wonderful age." She held his gaze, and Brian saw longing in her eyes. Hugo burst into life.

"Well then, I say we get into the lounge," he gestured under the arch way. "Food should be ready in just a –"

"Brian's wife was a prostitute." Claudia blurted, tearing her arm away from Hugo. Brian gasped and Edith stood looking shocked. Hugo's

breath slammed.
"What did you say? "Hugo barked. Claudia stood in front of them, pointing at Brian.
"His wife was a crack addict who fucked for a gram. He met her at a women's refuge!"
"What the fuck, Claudia?!" Brian shouted, moving to her in front of the others.. "What in the hell is your-"
"Take one more step and I'll tell Hugo everything and you'll be fucking homeless by the end of the month." She hissed to him. He froze. He wanted to say more, he wanted to threaten to bring her down with him, but in war, there were no winners, and in this battle, it was about damage control.
"That's my wife you're talking about."
"I hope you treat her better than you treat your friends," she snarled. Hugo took her by the arm.
"Explain yourself now." He gazed hard. She looked at the prying eyes around her. This was it. She could expose it all.
"I thought you should know about her, about her struggle and how far she has come." Hugo's nostrils flared.
"Time and place Claudia. And for god sakes have some decorum about you. You can't go around show boating another man's business to people you have only just met." He pointed to Brian. "He has a reputation to uphold. He can't have all his dirty laundry hung out for all to see," he gestured to Edith whose face was fixated in alarm. "No offence my darling." She didn't respond, but instead made a confused guttural croak.
"Yes," Claudia rebuked. "Wouldn't that be a shame." She walked to Brian and he shuddered away from her touch, but she put her arms around him anyway. "I'm so sorry Brian, I don't know what came over to me." He patted her back, looking away from him, trying to laugh it off. She whispered in his ear. "I saw you with the blonde girl." He pulled away and looked at her confused as she held a smile then walked to Hugo. "I'm sorry, my love. I think I'm just stressed. Must be hormones." Hugo held her.
"Don't worry about it." He took her and they moved further to the archway where Precious was stood holding an empty glass speaking to Annie. John walked over and filled Precious' glass.
"Can I have one of those?" Annie said pointing to the bottle.
"Sorry miss," John said. "This bottle has ran out. I can get you one

from the kitchen." He dipped his head and moved away into the kitchen which buzzed and hummed loudly with appliances and extractor fans. The group merged together and there were hugs and smiles exchanged freely. Some given willingly, some given because it would look odd if they didn't. John made his rounds and filled up glasses freely and the group sank them quicker than he could pour them. Precious drank a light beer as she didn't like the taste of champagne, and Edith and Claudia stuck to water and soft drinks.

"Have we met before? Precious said to Claudia. "Before tonight I mean?" Claudia searched her mind for a moment, then shook her head.

"No I don't believe we have." Precious moved to shake her hand but Claudia turned to speak to Annie. They giggled about something incoherent and when she turned back to Precious, she saw her hand was still outstretched. Claudia grimaced quietly and took her hand lightly.

"I'm Precious."

"Claudia. Hugo's wife." Claudia tapped her glass, the barrage of sounds and voices droning in her ears. "How are you? From before? I thought you might have gone home after what happened?" She shrugged it off.

"I'm made of tough stuff darling. I don't scare easily."

"Did you not feel… ya 'know… unwelcome?" Claudia pursed her lips and tapped her heel. Precious smiled and moved her hand through her hair.

"If one person doesn't want you at a party, but the rest of them do, isn't that reason to stay?" Claudia thought about this for a second.

"How do you know everyone wants you here?" there it was. The assassin's smile again. Precious turned around to see Brian speaking to Annie. She tugged his blazer and pulled him to her.

"Well for one, I know Brian wants me to be here. He said so himself. Didn't you?" Brian felt the air was so thick he could chew on it. After a torturous pause, Claudia cracked.

"Well it's nice to know you two get on so well." She finished her drink and moved to the end of the lounge where Hugo was standing next to a large easel covered in a white sheet. She looked back to the pair of them as she walked, and then wrapped her hands around him and gave him a long kiss. Brian held her gaze and then looked away as she saw Precious still focusing on him.

"What's her problem?" she sneered to him. He shook his head.

"I don't know where to even begin." In the distance, they heard the sound of a bell ringing and the drone of conversation and laughter quietened down. They all turned to see Hugo and Claudia standing there, locking hands. It looked like a showman stood in the middle of an amphitheatre, before the lions and tigers emerged from the wings with the dancing elephants and monkeys in suits. This is the moment you have all been waiting for!

"Can I have everyone's attention please!" Hugo announced. He placed his hand on the sheet of the easel. "I have something to show you!"

Chapter Seven.

Anguish.

Hugo stood in front of his guests, chest puffed out and smiling ear to ear, his eyes focused on each person, drawing them into him. He stood holding a glass of whisky, a single ice cube clinking the double measure, in front a large fireplace overlooked by a giant self-portrait showing him on the brow of a ship, looking into a sunset. "'Thank you all for joining me tonight," he said. "Tonight, is a celebration of success, friendship and love. It has been a long road to success, but has not had its share of fear and terror along the way. Setbacks, poor ideas and complications have made the journey difficult. But through it all, and with each of your help, we have together navigated the forests of woe, to stand upon its hill in the blazing sun in triumph, suckling the delicious fruit of success!" A small road of applause seeped in his pause. "In thanks to your efforts and assistance in my own stature, I have rewarded each of you with power, influence and esteem, and as I look at your eager faces now, as I have done many times before," he raised his glass, "I bring you all together not for just a simple meetings of marvel and great minds, but to expand your influence, stretch your legacy into the difficult realms of your world. We have politics, science and industry all in one room before us, and I implore you all to take the opportunity to use this gathering as an opportunity to expand and feast on the richest fruit this world has to offer." Another round of applause. "Now, before I uncover the reason for our meeting tonight, other than the obvious benefits already outlined, I request that you all vow to keep this in this room." Heads nodded. "Then may ask you all to relinquish your escape to the outside world," Hugo dug into his pocket and took out his mobile phone, to which then John emerged from the back of the room with a mesh box and Hugo put the device inside it. "And I request that in the name of honour and privacy, and most importantly, trust," his voice went lower, like whispering his orders to followers. "I request that you all do the same, should you be able to tear your eyes away from your digital addictions for a mere few hours, so they may feast on a wonder never seen to mankind before." Hugo shouted dubious encouragement to the guests as they placed their phones inside the mesh box as John walked around them, them dropping in delicately like forsaken diamonds in a locked away box. Once he collected them, he moved away through the hall and the quiet thudding of footsteps were heard moving up the stairs. Eyes widened and goose bumps were soothed amongst the room. "Not to worry," Hugo called again, sensing the unease of the group. "You shall have your addictions back at the end of the night or once you wish to leave. Finally, as a precaution, the box with the devices shall be placed inside my study in a locked safe. That way you can be assured they are secure, and I can be assured that no unwanted prying eyes will ruin my unveiling." He turned to the easel and tugged lightly on the cloth. Claudia stepped in front of him, eager to see what he had been hiding from them. "Step back my love," he whispered. "This is not just for you." She felt like a child who had opened the wrong gift on Christmas day, giving back the shiny toy to receive an orange. The air in the room quietened as the group waited with baited breath. This is the moment you have all been waiting for. The room gasped as the sheet was stripped from the easel.

"What is it?" Edith stammered.

"That's… interesting," said Annie. Hugo turned and his proud smile quickly disappeared. It was not what he had expected under the sheet that greeted him, and he looked at it with a morbid wonder.

"It is a person?" asked Brian, taking a closer look. Indeed it was. It was a twisting of bulging vines that slithered around a wailing man who was clutched naked in its grasps. His mouth in a stretched horror and his eyes as black as coal mixed with a menacing sky that spiralled clouds of angry red and endless black that spread from the edges of the painting until they swarmed above the barren branches beneath it. Hugo stepped closer. The group following his wonder. He heard whispers coming from around him, low and indecipherable. And when he saw that no mouths were moving, he looked closer at the painted man, and found his to be. He studied him in a hypnotic gaze, as he felt pulled into his deep eyes of loathing. The painting began to shiver and creep, as the man's voice became raspier in Hugo's ear, as the vines quivered and choked him. He writhed and struggled to become free, but to no avail. Hugo called out to him, pleading with the vines to release him from their oily grasp, until he was pulled under the painting, the vines pushing him deeper and deeper past the edge. Hugo heard the sound of the bones clicking and breaking, as his screams ruptured into a hellish, violent rebuke. Hugo gripped the painting and let it fly, screaming incoherently at it. The guests gasped in horror as they watched the roar of maniacal torment grip their host, as he ran to the painting of sheer black, and began to stamp on it furiously. He fell to his knees and gripped his ears, the screams of the invisible soul growing louder and louder in his ears, until it was all her could hear, the taste of the vines pushing through his mouth, the writhing eels of black tendrils that bore from the canvas wrapped around him, pushing through his eyes and down his throat. He fell to the carpet, face pressed into the ground as it began to concave under him, tendrils and fingers of burning and smoke emerging from the ground, gripping and dragging him through its firmament, until he was falling, cascading into the hellish abyss of terror and anguish, and the world above him closed before his eyes, the faces of those he had tormented, loved and loathed were forsaken to his memory. The last thing he heard through the cackling of demons was a loud gravelling voice that vibrated through his bones. "Abandon all hope, ye who enter here."

"Hugo!" Claudia shook him. He was staring at the canvas. His head was thick with sweat, his clothing sticking to him. "Are you alright?" She put her arm to his shoulder and he recoiled. "What's gotten into you?" she laughed. He studied the expressions of the guests who stood in a quiet amazement, their eyes fixated on the sheet he was holding, awaiting the big reveal. He snapped back into focus, the echo of hell running through his mind, like a cold shiver one gets when a ghost whispers in your ear at night. His head felt hot and the marching band had begun to resurface, and noticed his hand was shaking, whisky tipping over the edges.

"Come on Hugo," Brian called, arms poised towards him. "You're killing us here!"

Killing.

"Sorry." He croaked, wiping his forehead. He sank the whisky and bit as his throat started to burn.

Burn.

He looked at the sheet and tried to steady his hand, his fingers gripped tightly around the fabric. What if he pulled it off and black eels pulled him into it again? His lip began to quiver and his throat ran dry.

"Are you sure you're okay?" Claudia asked, again moving towards him. He stared at the floor, and he heard the whispers of the painting in his ear, and then the sound of a screaming infant in the distance. He lifted his head and cast his vision to the end of the lounge, where the stone maiden stood. She was looking at him, holding a child in her arms. She was crying, and her tears were of blood. He shook his head and blinked hard. He looked again. The infant was gone. The maiden facing away from him. His heart beat slowed and he caught his breath.

"Sorry," he whispered again. "It's been a stressful week." Hugo took a deep breath, and in one swift movement, pulled the sheet away.

"What is it?" Edith stammered, moving closer to the etched lines and numbers on the canvas.

"It looks like plans of some kind?" Brian whispered. Precious moved closer, quietly to the flanks of the guests to get a closer look. Hugo stayed silent, not wanting to look at the canvas. He heard the sounds of wonder and intrigue escape the guests' mouths, like someone had just brought a new puppy to work. He turned and joined them in their childlike inquisitiveness, and the weight of fear on his shoulders was lifted. The easel was a dark blue, covered in sharp white lines and scribbling of math and golden ratios.

"It's the blueprints of a house?" Claudia said excitedly. "Are you building me a new home?" Hugo shook his head.

"It's a nursery?" asked Annie.

"A sex dungeon," said Precious, followed by a rumble of laughter. He tried to speak, swallowed hard, then tried again.

"It's blueprints for a museum I intend to build, right here in the heart of Manchester." The group shared a collective look of confusion.

"There's already several museums in the city, Hugo." Brian said, stamping on his tinder. He moved through them and took Brian by the shoulder.

"Indeed," he said, a hint of malevolence in his voice. "Don't you think I am aware of that? But this," he said, pointing to the canvas again, like it was a dog wagging its tail at a new tasty treat. "This is a museum dedicated to a new and upcoming artist," He stood tall, and his chest puffed out once again. The quivering of fear evaporated into the warm air. He moved through the group, projecting his voice to the paintings that stood around them. "He is the finest artist in Europe, dare I say the world. He is to come and work with me here at my home while the museum is in development, and then I will send his fame into the stratosphere." Precious' ears pricked up, and she studied him intently.

"What's this prodigy's name?" she said. He eyed her like a villain in a children's fairy tale, like she would steal his dreams should he utter them.

"His name is not important. What is important is the legacy I will pave for him, in the bricks and mortar of history. He is a man of fine artistry, and he is due to arrive in the coming weeks once the papers have been signed." Claudia went rigid.

"You never told me about this?" she said. "What about me?" Hugo laughed to himself.

"You're never home anyway. You're always out of the house. You would never notice someone else here!"

"And what about your housekeeper?" Precious interrupted. "Does he not get a say in this?" Hugo shook his head.

"John will be well looked after, I assure you. But I feel that he may need some assistance in the house to keep it up to my standards."

"Looks fine to me," Precious mocked.

"Well it's not!" Hugo erupted, throwing his glass against the wall, its fragments shining like embers of fire. There was that temper again, and the eyes of the world had a front row seat. He ran his hand through his hair. His features trembling. He looked around and the guests were stoked with worry.

"I think you need to lie down," Edith said, walking to him and pressing on his cheek. "You've never been able to handle stress very well. Is the medication helping?" The medication. The plethora of pill she had been given from his doctor. He nodded.

"It's been a hard week, with preparation, the pressure, and the investment." He began to well up.

"It's okay," she said and kissed his head. "It will all be over soon. I think it's a wonderful idea you giving some aspiring artist such a chance to make it."

"Yeah Hugo," Brian chirped up, moving to him. "It's good that you're giving a young lad a chance and making it. In fact, I think if you have him sent to my office, we could have an interview. You know, boost his profile and the launch of the museum?"

"I'll design the flower arrangements," Claudia shouted.

"And I'll prepare the food," came a voice from the other side of the room. The group turned their heads. It was John. He was standing with a silver platter of fresh champagne glasses and gesturing to the open kitchen door. "Dinner is served everyone. Please, drink and eat your fill, as per the wishes of Mister Hugo." Through the open door, everyone could see all the colours of the rainbow laced on plates and bowls. From bright pink salmon married with butters and salads, to rich red steak and bell peppers of all flavours. There were nibbles and finger foods, fruit and deli, all lined on a table, inter woven with a variety of spirits, liquors and wines. Hugo felt his stomach begin to rumble and he realised he hadn't eaten since morning. The group dispersed, moving into the kitchen and the sound of plates clacking and glasses clinking quickly followed. John moved and swept up the shattered glass from the floor and tended to the fire, quickly cleaning and mopping each crumb dropped and drink spilled. Spirits appeared high and jovial amongst the lot, far from the heavy atmosphere from which it bore. They reminded Hugo of a group of school children being called into the cafeteria after their hard studying. Some pushing to the front of the queue, and some sitting quietly awaiting their turn. The colour of the food broke the interior of grey and white in the kitchen, and Hugo felt a surge of pride as he saw it was all being lapped up, and a glimmer of pride crept into him, as he emptied whisky and wine, contempt that this was down to him, his success, and his ability to network. Classical music floated softly in the air as he saw John pulling out fresh glasses and pouring furiously as his guests drank heavily. He stood there with Claudia at the fireplace, the heat starting to burn the backs of his legs.

"Shall we?" Hugo said, kissing Claudia on the cheek. She looked confused.

"Shall we what?" He squoze her hand and placed his hand over her womb.

"Shall we tell them?" He awaited her reply with a smile. She flitted her eyes to him, and then to the kitchen, where she could see Brian eyeing her from behind his whisky glass. She laid her eyes on Precious, then back to him, and she felt wickedness slither into her bones.

"Okay." He hugged her and walked with her to the foot of the kitchen. He clapped his hands loudly and gestured to John, and the music began to lower. "Can I have your attention please!"

"Oh god, not another one. Don't nearly faint this time," Edith mocked. Hugo stared at her like a child and the group laughed.

"I have some wonderful news." He held Claudia tight in his arm and pulled her to him. "Were going to be parents!" The announcement was met with a gasp. John and Edith began clapping loudly, rushing to them and hugging both of them tightly, then pulling away from Claudia with delicacy, like they were hugging a balloon filled with razors. Brian moved to Annie and took one of her glasses and sank it, then clapped slowly, keeping eye contact with Claudia, who waved to him. He felt his world fall through his feet, and he took another glass of bourbon and sank that too. Precious soured, but lifted her glass to the happy couple. Annie sat quietly, stroking the empty glasses around her, her eyes welling up and dripping onto the stainless steel. The room resumed with the sounds of fresh champagne popping and Claudia drank juice, then ate some low carb pasta with halloumi and coconut. Brian walked to Hugo. He could smell the whisky on his breath.

"Congratulations," he said, and took Hugo's hand firmly.

"Thank you Brian," he replied jovially. "Cigar?" Brian's face went hard. "I need to talk to you." Hugo's smile began to fade. They went into the lounge and sat by the fire, John poured them a whisky, and left the men to their words.

#

Precious leant against the door frame of the kitchen, resting her heal on the wall, watching the two men in the other room, Cigar smoke mixed with the clinking of whisky glasses. Edith approached her.

"Such wonderful news, isn't it. A baby." She pressed her hand to her chest.

"I never liked the taste of anything fancier than beer." Precious said, ignoring Edith. She took a long gulp, then turned to her. "So why don't you drink?" Edith rapped her fingers on her glass of water. She shrugged the comment off, set her water down and continued to sample the lobster and pineapple.

"I don't like to drink," she said, covering her mouth.

"I thought you were on a diet?"

"That too." Precious held her beer in one hand, leaning against the wall.

"So which is it? You're on a diet? Or you don't like to drink?"

"I don't know. I suppose right now it's both."

"But it hasn't always been that way?" Edith was taken back.

"What are you implying?" Precious shook her head smiling.

"Nothing sweetie, but your eyes haven't left my glass since I poured it."

"I don't know what you're talking about."

"Sure you don't," Precious said. She winked. She pointed to Annie who was sat at the end of the table, four empty glasses in front of her, while sinking a fifth. Precious looked at them, somewhat impressed. "She's having a good time." Edith's lip went tight.

"Leave her alone. She's just got out of the hospital. She's nervous as it is."

"You tell every person you just met about your friend's intimate details? Or is that lobster getting to your head?"

"How disrespectful!" Edith gasped. Precious finished her beer and pushed it into Edith's chest and went to the large cooler in the corner of the kitchen, opened another bottle of beer, took a drink and sat with Annie.

"Damn you can really put it away," she giggled. Annie didn't answer, but instead stared at her distorted reflection in the array of glasses before her. "Hey," Precious tugged her dress. Annie startled and looked at her. She was sitting towards her, hands together, like a toddler welcoming a new friend to her nursery. Annie looked at her confused, and then at the glasses.

"They are having a baby together." She said, lifting another drink. "Congratulations I suppose."

"And aren't you celebrating." Annie shrugged.

"I don't drink often, so when I do, I sink it." Precious thumbed her blonde hair, wrapping it around her finger. She lifted her drink.

"To the happy couple." Annie didn't respond, instead she continued to drink and then pour a further glass. Precious leaned in to her. "So why were you in the hospital?" Annie turned, a look of pain on her face.

"Who told you that?" Precious tapped her nose then pointed to the lobster eating glove wearer near the doorway who was speaking to John, frequently looking back in their direction. Annie followed her finger then closed her eyes. "She can't keep anything to herself. Frankly Pearl,"

"Precious."

"Whatever. Precious. I don't want to talk about it." She rubbed her arms and Precious followed them as Annie traced her stomach, stood and moved to the empty seat on the other side of the table. The seat was cold, and it made her shudder. Precious looked at the sunken glasses, and she saw that they were dirty. There were remnants of what looked to be washing powder in the bottom of the glass. She had to squint to see it, but it definitely was there. She called John and snapped her fingers, and he came over to her quickly. She pointed to the glass and he nodded, collected them up, and cleaned them again under the faucet. Precious pulled out a cigarette from her bag and started to smoke. She turned to the maiden and looked at the front door. She checked her bag again and saw she had mud on her heals. She took a napkin, wiped them down and then threw it onto the floor. She stood and moved to Annie, who was picking at a bowl of cous cous with lemon and thyme and balls of spiced beef. She leaned over her, smoke making Annie revolt.

"Do you mind?"

"Don't you smoke?"

"I've seen the hearts and lungs of smokers. So not a chance would I touch one of those things."

"Oh," Precious laughed. "You're not pregnant, are you?" Annie spat her food out.

"What the fuck did you say to me?"

"I asked if you are pregnant, I just wondered-" Annie stood up, stumbled and then bellowed at her.

"What the hell is your problem?" John and Edith turned to look, the classical music in the background seemed to have faded, and now the deep breathing of Annie was the music in the kitchen. Precious looked around to the others now staring at her. Claudia turned from the corner as she poured a glass of juice, spilling it onto the floor. Precious took another deep breath of her cigarette and let the blue smoke collect around Annie's face.

"Can't handle your drink Annabelle?" Edith moved to them.

"What's going on?"

"Shut up Edith, you fucking gossip. You can't keep things private, can you?" Annie raged. Her nostrils were flaring, and Edith revolted at the smell of champagne on her breath.

"What have I done?" Edith cried, taken back. Precious took a bottle of beer from the counter and took a long drink.

"It was an honest question sweetheart," she looked at the empty glasses. "Either you're not pregnant, or with the amount you've drunken, you won't be by the morning." Edith gasped while Annie stood rigid, shoulders and fists tight. Precious took another long drag of her smoke. "Do you have any children?" she hissed. Blue fingers snaking from her nostrils into the air.

"What's your problem?" Annie muttered, tears filling her eyes. Precious set her drink down.

"I bet you have guys begging to get in your bra," she reached and tugged Annie's dress at her chest. She reacted like her hand was made of fire. She batted her away and Precious dropped her cigarette. John rushed and stomped on it as Annie began screaming at her, then she grabbed her bag from the table and hurried towards the front door, holding her face in her hand as eyeliner soaked through her finger tips. Edith looked at Precious with disgust, and Precious held a face of ignorance, with a small smirk creeping into the corners. Edith ran after her, her heals clipping on the marble.

"Where are you going!?"

"I'm leaving," she cried, striding quickly to the entrance. "I can't hold my head up anymore. I'm drowning in this shit." She stumbled and caught herself on the maiden, before continuing. Hugo rushed in and saw Claudia and John moving into the hall. Precious stood in the doorway nestling her drink.

"What have you done?" he seethed.

"Secret's out," she whispered. Hugo ran after Annie, his feet unsteady from the whisky. Brian followed slower. He moved to Claudia who took a wide birth to him.

"Annie, what's going on?"

Annie pointed to Precious.

"This bitch is what's wrong!" She turned and screamed at her across the way. "What you think you know me? What I've been through? I'll show you!" She lifted up her dress above her black tights. The murmur of whispers and concern fell silent, and all stopped their advances, and

Annie's tears hit the floor like the mouths of those who looked upon her. The scar was purpled and reddened, moving like a child's drawing of a crooked smile. Annie stood there, gripping her dress tightly, looking down at her mutilation. Her sobs echoing through the silent void. Edith approached her delicately, moving past Hugo and put her arms on her shoulders. Annie fell into her, gripping her flowery dress tightly, her running black mascara making the fabric roses turn like ash. The other guest held themselves in silent clusters, watching the house of cards topple before them.

"Come now Annie," she soothed, running her hand through her hair. "Come now, shush. Let's go sit down in another room and talk." Hugo moved slowly, and his heart began to rip open. Annie lifted her head, her dress now back to her feet, crumpled. She pushed Edith away and wiped away the tears and making a streak of black on her hand. She moved to the doors, almost silently, wishing to slip away in the night. Hugo ran to her, his mouth dry.

"We need to talk," he whispered, his words slurring. She turned and slapped him across the face, and his numbed lips reminded him he wasn't too drunk to feel pain. Her eyes were blood shot and fierce and his body went cold under their heat. His head felt woozy, the marching band coming back, this time with a full brass accompaniment. He felt his throat seal shut, and his eye begin to sting.

This is the moment you have all been waiting for!

"I'm so sorry, Annabelle," he croaked. Tears beginning to well in his eyes. Claudia watched from the far end of the hall. She studied the unfolding of him and she saw a flicker of humanity, and she saw his disgrace. Brian moved closer to her and whispered in her ear.

"Is it mine?" Her stone expression cracked, then the wall went back up.

"You'll never know." She felt the air as he moved away from her and she felt the sour fragrance of his aftershave in her nostrils and she felt guilt creep into her chest. Precious leaned on the railing of the stairs, not looking at the others, but instead fixing her gaze on the grandfather clock that ominously swung its pendulum in the corner. 'Almost time' she thought. Annie continued to sob.

"Don't call me that." Hugo moved closer, wanting to hold her, to comfort her, but she stepped away like her was made of snakes.

"Come here, Annabelle. It's alright. We need to talk about it." He drew even closer and Annie exploded in a fiery rage to him.

"I told you not to fucking call me that! You don't get to call me that Hugo!" There was life in the room again as the guests recoiled back. She spoke with hot venom. "You used me, I spent a year in the hospital because of what you made me do!" Edith rushed forward to the pair.
"What is she talking about Hugo?"
"Just shut up for a second," he ordered, raising his hand like he was scolding an interfering brat. He was disarmed now. His failings, his skeletons out the closet. Hugo saw the eyes on him, the ball now in his court, the laser sight fixed on his forehead, and lungs filled with air. Either to below in triumph, or to hold his breath as he drowned.
"I used you?" he seethed. "Look, I'm sorry about what happened. I really am, but you can't blame it all on me." he was pacing on the spot now. "It takes two, Annie. Two to create something. What was I supposed to do?" She swung at him again, hitting him hard across the cheek. She screamed in his face, every bit of her, every ounce of hate, guilt and pain, pushing its way through to him, as if to infect him with it, burn, and bury him under it.
"You ruined me in every way imaginable and you have the audacity to stand there and pretend you give a damn? You were supposed to be there for me. I begged and begged for you to help me. I sent you letters, phone calls. I even turned up to your office a couple of times, but you were always busy. You knew what you had done to me. What you had left me with. I had to do it on my own when you vanished. When you left me to fucking mutilate myself! I hate you. I hate you Hugo. You piece of shit. You fucking worm. How dare you push me to the brink where I turn my back on my career, my friends, my family and my god. I hope you burn in Hell for what you did to me. How many others have borne the weight of your sick touch? How many other women have you defiled with your body and casted them aside, leaving them to rot in the corner like dead leaves coated in shit? Fuck you Hugo. You despicable cunt. I hope you burn in Hell." Her pain reigned back on all below, hitting them hard, and the room was deathly silent in its wake. Her breath like acid, and Hugo returned in kind.
"Me? Me! Annie, it was one night! And to be honest, it wasn't even a great night. You want to talk facts? Fine. You were drunk, you liked that I was successful, and you were practically wet when I walked in the room." He leaned in to her, "You were easy." His voice trailed off and left her standing there in silent agony. She shut her eyes tight, not wanting to let her pain leak out anymore, the scar across her womb

pulsing with pain like it had done that night.
"I..." she croaked. "I just don't want to feel numb anymore." She crumpled onto the ground, falling within herself and she curled on the floor. Silent sobs dragging from her with staggered sharp breaths. Hugo felt sweat falling from his head, and Edith ran to Annie and held her again. He stood like a man lost in an airport, as eyes converged on him. He moved to comfort Annie, when Edith spat at him.
"Don't you think you have done enough!" She nestled her again into her bosom, as Annie buried her face into her, clinging onto her dress tightly, crumping it inside her white knuckles. Hugo moved to the door.
"John..." he called. "Get the car ready. We're taking Annie home. Party's over." A brief silence followed as he reached for the door handle. Then it was quickly broken as it gave way to the sound of rattling on the high windows that overlooked the unfolding pain of men beneath, their facades and fronts stripped away, revealing only their bare bones of secrets and lies. They heard the crack of thunder and the blast of lighting, and then they heard the wind howl through the opening front door, which crashed heavily as it shut. Francis stood there, dripping wet. His clothes filthy with mud and grass. He breathed heavily, his thin shoulders rising and falling under his sodden blood stained trench coat. The crowd looked at the intruder, the thick air of woe broken. Francis moved his wet hair from his face, looking around the hall, and his eyes laid onto Precious, who unlike the others, held a face of contentment, on his arrival.
"Go get 'em boy," she mouthed.
"Francis?" Hugo stammered, his voice drowned out by the crashing thunder and the heavy rain. "What happened to -" Francis pulled the pistol from underneath his coat and pointed it at him, nay a foot from his face. His cocaine filled brain rushing with adrenaline.
"Sorry, I'm late," he said, pulling back the hammer of the pistol.

Chapter Eight.

Treachery.

Francis looked in the rear-view mirror as he sped down the black roads, the driver's sunken silhouette disappearing from view. His knuckles wrapped tightly on the steering wheel as the engine screamed as the rev counter embedded itself deep in the red. He thought about stopping, giving it all up, running away and hiding in the woods. Then he thought about driving head long into one of the thick trees that blurred past him. He bit his lip and screamed at the dash board. His hands were shaking, his body was alive, tingling like he had taken the most powerful endorphin triggering drug known to man. He felt his manhood turn hard and he pressed on it, sending the sensation through his body and into his extremities. He had never felt like this before. He pressed the acceleration down harder, lavishing the popping of the exhaust and the roaring of the burdened engine. The excitement, the rush of it, the fucking terror of being caught, being chased down the winding road by police wails and flashing lights, and it made him scream again in wild laughter. Guilt began to creep into his mind, like a man who keeps drinking even though his liver is failing, casting the bigger picture out, keeping his conscience chained away. He would worry about that later. Right now, he just rode the wave of adrenaline. Finally he changed gears and cruised in fourth at a steady seventy. The engine jumped and he flipped it into third to stop it idling. He hadn't driven something this powerful before, and the engine needed stimulating. He slowed his pace for a few miles, and then pulled over in a layby. He got out of the car and the air hit his tingling flesh. He arched his back and screamed to the moon above, his arms outstretched, animalistic and primal, like he was defying the natural order of the world. Finally he could have some control. Finally he could have some say over his own fate, instead of it being dictated by others around him. He had committed a crime that would put him away forever, and he had never felt freer in his life. He took out a cigarette and smoked it quickly, followed by another. He took another bump of cocaine and rubbed the remainder of the bag in his gums, before throwing it into the dirt under his feet. He thought about calling his wife, telling her to get ready for him and he was coming home to ruin her body for the best night of fucking she had ever had. He felt like calling every person who had ever took the piss out of him, doubted him or told him where to shove it, and let them really know what he felt of them. Then, like a brick through his fragile glass of triumph, he thought about calling the police, and turning himself in. He shook his head at the last thought. No. He wasn't going to be caught. There was no way. He knew where he was going and it was a clear run to there. And once he had done what needed to be done, he wouldn't be sticking around to get hauled in front of the courts. He smoked a further cigarette and threw it into the bushes. He got back in the car and took a deep breath, then shut the door closed. He revived the engine and pushed it into first. The needle sped deep into the red as he pulled away with a wheel spin, kicking loose gravel and dust behind him. He followed the instruction of the satnav, continuing down the road for a further few miles. The blankness of the surroundings, a blurring black and the hypnotic allure of the cat lights, let his mind wander, it scratching its dirty finger nails against the inside of his skull.

I only meant to knock him out, drag him in the bushes, and take the car. He shook his head and focused on the drive. He turned on the radio and let it play. Some new upcoming band that were 'The best thing since the Beatles!' as the broadcaster confidently boasted, came playing through the speakers. Quietly at first, but then when the scratching in his scull got harder to ignore, he turned the volume up fully. Tapping away on the steering wheel, turning right down another country road, then jumping onto a dual carriageway after a poorly placed giveaway sign, he looked in the rear view mirror for the first time since leaving the boy lying on the road. He saw him there again, but this time he was behind him. His face drawn out and his eye hanging from its busted socket, membrane and brain fluid seeping out of the gaping hole in his skull. His tongue heavy and bloated, hanging loosely under his bent jaw. Francis' heart slammed in his chest and he felt his stomach drop into an icy depth. He quickly turned back to look at the monster that belay him, to find only empty seats with loose CD's and a church pamphlet with a small child on the front.

I left him alone to die. The sound of his skull. I can still feel his hair and blood on my hands.

He pressed the accelerator harder.

#

He drove silently for another few miles, not seeing another soul on the road, no street lighting, no break in the thick forest that flanked him to either side. The tingling in his muscles had now subsided, and the scratching in his mind had broken through. In the absence of adrenaline, a family feeling took its place, like an old friend that you didn't want to see but showed up anyway at your birthday party. Fear. He had never committed a crime in his life, and the looming possibility of now going to prison suddenly became a very real possibility. Surely they would have found the boy by now and they would have a record of the car. He began checking his mirrors, paranoid, like at any moment he would be under the giant spotlight of a police helicopter. He looked at the satnav and it gave an estimate of a little less than an hour. His attention drew to the fuel gauge, and a bright orange fuel sign taunted him. "Fuck." He cried. He had been running the engine hot and was now adding it to his collection of regretful things he had done this week. He slowed the engine down to an easy thirty. Then thinking that was too slow for a national speed limit road, he turned it up again to sixty. Then seeing the mile gauge drop quicker than he would have liked, he cruised at a forty five.

I'm going to break down, then its game over. Then in an unlikely turn of fate, through the crest of the trees on an upcoming bend, he saw the lights of a fuel station welcoming him with warm serenity, like an angel in the darkness. He sped up to it and pulled in. He checked his side mirrors to make sure he was on the correct side for the fuel gauge and found a pump that did both diesel, petrol, and would you believe it, gas injection. He was sure this wasn't an electric car or a hybrid, as it seemed too responsive for that. Or so he hoped anyway. He sat idle for a second, checked his eyes that went more blood shot than usual and cleared the cocaine boogers that had matted around his nostrils and turned off the engine, stuffing the keys into his coat pocket. He reached over the passenger seat, quickly stuffed the duffel bag under the passenger seat footwell and opened his door. He stepped one foot out when alarm struck him. His coat was stained with deep red blood across its side, and his mind wandered back to the boy. He felt panic grip him and drag him back into the car. He took the keys out of his coat, scrunched it up and put it into the footwell too. Checking his reflection in the rear-view mirror, he tried to look as casual as possible, and then stepped out under the artificial light. He filled the tank with petrol and then walked across the forecourt into the store to pay. As he entered, he caught a sign saying "Smile, you're on CCTV." He dipped his head down and looked at the floor. His hands stuffed into his pockets trying to look as normal as possible in the view of the black circular balls that hung from the ceiling, the eyes of the cameras watching. He waited to pay laboriously as two others were before him. A blonde woman in a dark dress with tattoos on her shoulders directly in front of him, and an elderly man that had the world's worst comb over and a red jumper who paid with coins and was indecisive when the cashier obligatory asked him if he wanted some chocolate at a reduced price. Francis tried to hold his nerve before barking "Just pick one, will ya." His voice cracked the quiet store and the blonde woman looked back to him, along with the old man and the cashier who secretly thanked him for the outburst. The blonde woman had fair skin and was lightly freckled, and Francis thought her quite attractive, albeit out of his league in his dishevelled state. She smirked subtly before turning her attention back to the old man who had finally made his mind up and was now paying, freshly bought chocolate in his hand. She stepped forward, bought a pack of cigarettes, paid promptly and then left the store, before giving a passing glance to Francis. He caught her scent, like that of lavender. He pointed to his car and the cashier read the amount. He pushed his hands into his front pockets, then his back, and realised he had left his wallet in his coat. Francis apologised to the half-asleep cashier, who had obviously been dicked with the night shift, heavy bags under his eyes, empty cups of coffee stacked on his desk. As he turned to walk back to his car, his heart pulsing in his throat, he saw a police car pull in, and two officers stepped out. They were parked next to his vehicle and peered at it curiously. It was a sleek black sports car with bright alloys, its hood raised in a diamond shape to fit the modified turbo engine inside. Francis stopped in his tracks and went back to the cashier. If he went to the car and looked in his jacket, surely the police officers would see the blood on it. "Can I come back and pay you later? I left my wallet at home." He tried to sound cool. The cashier looked at him blankly.

"If you don't have money, I'll have to tell those two officers." He pointed to the forecourt. "We've had three drive off's this month and I've been told not to let anyone leave without payment." Francis let out a nervous laugh and his mind turned a blank. He rapped his fingers on the counter, trying to not look to desperate. He spoke again, trying to refrain from pleading. The officers entered the store and waited behind him, looking through the confectionary that stacked to the side of the counter.

"Come on man, look I'm good for it. I can be back in an hour or so, give me a break." He felt his shirt collar going damp. The cashier shook his head and waved to one of the officers who stepped forward next to Francis. His black body armour giving way to his heavily tattooed bulging biceps. The officer had a bald head and a thick brown beard, and Francis knew if he tried to run, he wouldn't even make it to the entrance.

"Is everything okay sir?" the officer said. The cashier pointed to Francis.

"He won't pay." Francis looked jittery and the officer eyed him up and down.

"I will pay," he said, trying to keep calm, keep his composure from cracking. "But I have left my wallet at home. I said I would go get it and be back soon." The officer rubbed his hand across his face, his patience wearing thinner than Francis' hairline. The officer turned to Francis, his shadow bellowing over him. He looked a mess, and he was concerned if she should be driving at all. Francis' throat grew dry as the light above his eclipsed under the shadow of the officer. He was easy six seven and built like a truck. Finally, as time dragged across broken glass, he coughed, "I've just finished a twelve-hour shift, I just want to get home to my wife." The officer caught the quivering in his voice and continued his gaze, thinking he recognised him but not sure where.

"Pass me your details, you can be on your way, and if you don't come back then I know where to find you." The officer pulled out his notebook. "Do you have some ID please sir?" Francis remembered how to breathe.

"No sorry, that's in my wallet."

"Okay, then is that your car?" he pointed his pen out the window. "We'll do a check on it and get your details that way. So, what's your name and date of birth?" There was that heat again. Francis felt like he was stuck in a vice. If he told the officer his real name, he might recognise him from the news. Even worse, the car wouldn't come back to him, and they would find the blood stained coat and the pistol. He would be handcuffed and locked away for the rest of his life. He uttered a strange sound, sort of like a sigh mixed with a dying animals croak. The officer tapped his pen on his notepad, no doubt near the end of his shift. "Your name, sir." The bell of the entrance to the store went off, and a hit of cold pushed into the store. All looked to see the blonde woman from before walk towards Francis quickly, holding out a purse.

"I'm so sorry, officer, my husband has forgotten his wallet."

"You know this gentleman?"

"I do yes, he's my husband," she grabbed Francis' arm and kissed him on the cheek. She turned to the cashier. "How much?"

"£87.90." She opened her purse and swiped her credit card. The till buzzed and she was handed a receipt. She looked at the officer who was still holding his notepad, wrinkles appearing across his shaved forehead.

"Can we leave now officer?"

"Not yet." He said. "I still need your husband's name."

"Why?" said the blonde woman. The other officer, female and smaller but much easier on the eyes stepped forward.

"Your husband has committed an offence of making off without payment. So therefore we need his details to establish-"

"I think you'll find his bill has been paid, and he hasn't 'made off' from anyone." The officer pointed out the window, her voice shaking. The blonde woman smiled. She was a rookie.

"Well under the road traffic act, I can ask details of any person driving a motor vehicle."

"But he's not driving it." The two had a staring match. Who blinks first loses. Eventually, the big tattooed officer broke the silence, putting away his pen and pad.

"I suppose you're right, ma'am." The younger officer shot him a look, and the blonde woman took Francis by the arm.
"Have a good shift, you two." Francis, still not knowing quite what had just happened, walked with the stranger. He was sure he was done for, but yet here she was, his guardian angel, saving him from absolution. He walked with her as the two officers watched them go. She stood with Francis next to his car and she looked at him to open the passenger door so she could get in. Francis was unsure what to do. Who was this woman? Why had she helped him? He looked through the driver side window at the sleeve of his coat poking out from under the seat. He fingered his keys and she looked at him eager to get in the nice hot ride.
"I'm getting cold darling. Unlock the car." He looked at the two officers watching from the window, then at the bloodied coat once more.
"Yes okay.." he pressed the car fob and it unlocked, the LED headlights bringing the face of the steal horse to life. They got in the car and the cops looked away from them, and finished paying for their goods. She climbed into the passenger seat and looked through her hand bag. He whispered to her in the silence of the cab, afraid even in here he would be caught out. "Who are you?"
"Just drive," she said firmly. The warmth from her voice vanishing like it was never there. Without asking any further, he pressed the keyless ignition and brought the beast to life, cranked it in first, then cruised out of the court yard. The two officers watch them leave, the powerful engine rumbling loudly into the night.
"Did you get the registration plate?" the bald one said to his colleague.
"Sure did." She smiled. "I'll run it through."

#

The pair drove in silence for a few minutes. The blonde woman lit a cigarette and she pressed the window down, the roar of the exhaust growing louder mixing with the wind that was picking up.
"So, go on then," Francis said, finally breaking the tension. "Who are you, and why did you help me out back there? I had it covered." She took another drag of her smoke before throwing it outside and closed the window.
"You didn't have anything covered. Those cops were on to you and

were a second away for arresting you, Francis." His head turned to her so quickly he thought he gave himself whiplash.
"How do you know my name?"
"Please, everyone in the fucking country knows your name. Your face is everywhere." She opened up her purse and passed him the receipt. "You owe me big time." Lost for words, he repeated the question again.
"So, who are you and why did you help me?"
"I recognised who you were, and I know about the case you're involved in with Hugo." The sound of his name made his teeth clench.
"And?"
"And I believe you." The weight of her words, this kind stranger, saying she believed him, his protests, despite the slander and the marring of his reputation and his name. Believed him over the papers and the press. She didn't even know him, only what she had read about him in so many distorted and lying tabloids. Such a simple phrase spoken, but the gravity of it hit Francis hard, and his eyes began to redden again. He had a moment and then whispered, his voice ragged.
"Thank you." It's nice to hear somebody finally –"
"Shut up," she interjected, cutting him off. "I'm not here to be your best friend and I'm certainly not here to jump into bed with you."
"Then why are you here?" he barked, the certitude he had felt for her out the window with her cigarette butt. She looked at the glowing satnav that perched on the driver's side window.
"You're going to that party tonight, aren't you? You got an invitation?" Francis nodded. "But you're not going there to drink fucking whisky and dance like the rest of them, are you?"
He remained silent, watching the road. She leaned in to him. "I saw your coat as I passed your car, and the pistol poking out the duffel bag. You're lucky I saw it and not the police or we wouldn't be having this conversation." Francis eyes widened and his body ran rigid, remembering how close he had come to getting caught. He looked in the rear view mirror again, and wondered about the boy, and wondered if at any moment the black behind him would grow with bright blue and red. He pressed the acceleration harder. She continued. "I pulled in shortly after you did to the fuel station. I saw you and I recognised you. And a car as nice as this," she ran her hands across the dash board, "doesn't go unnoticed. I'm guessing it isn't yours?" Francis raised his hand to speak, but his voice squeaked then fell quiet, and that was

enough for her. "Your hesitation tells me no, so please don't say any more. I'm already in too deep already helping you." Finally, Francis croaked.
"Helping me with what?" The blonde woman looked at him stupidly. She pulled out a fresh cigarette and played with it in her hand.
"I'm going to help you kill Hugo."

#

The pair drove further up the ever winding roads in silence. Their position on the satnav growing closer to their destination. After a long while, the satnav pinged and Francis saw a large black gate that set back into a large wood, illuminated by welcoming floor lighting. Seeing this, she spoke. "Don't pull all the way up to the gate. Slow down and there's a small clearing in the forest." Francis did as she said, his accomplice clearly knowing more about his plan than he did. He pressed the brakes lightly and crawled at an easy 5mph.
"Why do we not go through the gate?" he asked. She looked at him in a 'Stop asking so many question' kind of way, however, seeing he was clearly a fool, she explained. She pointed the edges of the gate.
"The front gate has cameras and it is a part of a sequential locking mechanism. Some new fancy security system he's installed. Stop here," she barked. Francis pulled the car to a stop at the side of the road. "If you trigger the gate, the front door locks. If you bypass the gate, the door stays open. There's a break in the trees just over there," she pointed to a small gap in the wood that one could easily miss if you weren't looking for it. "Give me a couple of hours, and then follow my way in. After that, he's yours." She stepped out of the car. Francis put his hand out and held it open before it shut. Trickles of rain now starting to spot on the windscreen.
"You really believe me? That I had nothing to do with the poison shipment? That I'm not responsible for all those poor people dying? That that bastard Hugo used my company to transport it? That I had nothing to do with it all and he let me take the fall for it?" The blonde woman crouched down, her hair blowing gently in the pacing wind.
"Do you honestly care if I do?" He released the door and let the question go, and the heavy door which closed with a thud. He looked down at his coat and duffel bag. He put on his coat and pulled out his weapon, nestling it under the leather. He killed the engine and sat there

quietly, savouring the moment, like a calm before the storm. He heard a knock at the passenger window, as for a moment he thought it the police and it startled him, gripping the gun with urgency, he turned to see it was her again, her hair blowing in the wind. He leant over and opened the door a crack. "It's Precious, by the way," she said through the gap. She moved away without saying another word and saw her vanish into the trees, disappearing into the night. He let his mind wander about her. Her prowess, her determination, and her explicable ability to manipulate those around her. Time creeped by as Francis' anxiety peaked and trothed. He was struggling to hold his nerve. He would sit and stare at the vacant road, occasionally seeing an owl flit by to snatch up a passing rodent, open it up before carrying it away bloodied and wriggling. He thought of what he was here to do. Was he capable of murdering a man? He thought again of the crunching of the boy's skull and it appeared to Francis that under the right circumstances, pushed hard enough and backed into a corner, he was capable of anything. Hugo had torn him limb from limb and was denying any knowledge of it. It had started well, him, a master of medicine and pharmaceuticals from the University of London, graduating the top of his class, he had been promised greatness from day one. He hadn't struggles as a child, in fact he had had quite a good childhood. He was always in fine clothes, always branded, his shoes have never seen mud and his belly never rumbled from hunger. As he grew older, his hair was always neatly combed and his skin always clean, as he cruised through school with several friends. He was the envy of the bullies for his smarts and envy of the nerds for his looks. All the girls wanted him. Looks that had since eroded away like fine art work left outside in an acidic downpour. He had never truly known what it was like to struggle as he was younger, love and wealth were always in abundance, and he always had doors open for him, and never really had to knock too hard to open a difficult one. He thought of Hugo and his background, a man who had struggled through life over broken vodka bottles and stone like affection from his parents, how he had grown up and needed to learn to fight in order to survive. Always committing petty crime to feed himself in the winter when the dying apple tree close to his home had relinquished its foul fruit. Hugo was a saviour, a man who had literally walked over shattered glass and rotten shit to get to where he was today. Perhaps, this was why he was able to bounce back so well from catastrophe, whereas Francis, a man of a silver spoon, hit the bottle when things got hard, unskilled in hardship. Hugo had explained his humble beginnings to him over a dinner they had had, him and his wife Sarah.

#

Hugo boasted his success by ordering the most expensive thing on the menu, and when the bill came at the end of the night, he would casually swipe his credit card without looking at the total. "So, we've discussed terms, I can assure you this is the best anyone is going to offer you," Hugo had said, wiping his mouth with the felt napkin, expensive candles creating an intimate light as the three of them on the large round table covered in a white cloth. Francis and Sarah both looked over the contract, Sarah, a newly qualified in business and management, gripped Francis' leg under the table unable to believe the offer he was giving them. They would receive £500,000 initial investment to start up their Pharmacy business, then Hugo would leave them to it and let them run it themselves. He was merely a silent partner and a shareholder, the contract was for five years and he would make over two million in return. What Francis and Sarah would make was up to how hard they worked at it, and given the figures proposed by Sarah, they would double Hugo's return for themselves in that time frame. All being well of course. They shook hands and accepted his offer and then the plans began. Hugo gave them some advice and injected the funds into the business, and the Pharmacy chain took off and within two years, it was the fourth largest chain in the UK. Things were going well, Hugo had his investment returned with the promised capital, and Francis and Sarah would sit by the beach in the Maldives with their laptop open, watching their empire grow. The downfall of his company was soon to follow however, and he never saw it coming.

He and Sarah argued ferociously the next few months, as their stock plummeted and their bank accounts were stripped and their assets seized by police. A local woman, Tracy Ringer, had bought cough medicine for her daughter Jasmin from one of their stores and gave it to her as directed. However, her fever worsened, and her body began to fit and convulse. A ride in the ambulance later, she was pronounced dead on the operating table. She was just seven. An investigation was launched by police and the bottle of "Happy Hippo" cough medicine was recalled, examined, and found to have high levels of the deadly poison Strychnine. Upon further investigation it was found to be in large quantities of many other products, and a shipment of goods for the business was intercepted by customs from over sees coming into the UK. Forty units of the poison were inbounded for the pharmacy distribution centre. The press got a hold of it and Francis and Sarah were arrested. Of course, they couldn't prove it was them, so they didn't face criminal proceedings, but his empire was now aflame, along with his marriage and his life. Hugo denied all knowledge, but it wasn't his wife Sarah that had destroyed both of their lives, so it must have been him. He took his money, then he felt threatened on seeing how well Francis was doing, ordered the poison knowing it would be found, and left him in ruin. Another bottle being sank, another bump of cocaine, and another night with whoever's underwear he woke up holding, his life was well and truly cast into oblivion while Hugo hid away and watched him burn. The remembering of this chain of events enraged Francis.

He was going to kill Hugo tonight. The man who claims to want the success, the wife, the family, the house, the expensive holidays, the £3000.00 suits, the £400,000.00 cars, the diamond watches and gold plated art work. He was the real villain in all of this, and he had built his success on the broken backs of others. His time had come, his judgement from above. Francis rummaged in his coat and found another gram of coke and took another bump from his car key, swelling in hatred. He was less man now than he had ever been, his humanity lost in his pain. He saw a car pull into the gates with two women inside, one middle aged wearing white gloves, one younger, maybe mid-twenties. They had drove by quickly and had missed him sitting there. The rain began to fall heavily, the light freckles of rain drops on the window screen now an obscene smear. The air grew warmer and the wind picked up as heavy blackness coated the sky and banished away the stars. He waited another few minutes, the hours had passed since Precious had left him. The car now returned out the gates now shy of the two women. Francis watched as it pulled away, until its headlights had disappeared, then stepped out into the wet and disappeared into the trees.

Chapter Nine.

Judgement.

Hugo held his hand up in terror, the barrel of the pistol staring into his face. "Whoa, Francis, what the -"
"Shut up! Just shut the fuck up!" Francis screamed, his body trembling, rain pooling around his feet. "Don't fucking move! I'll blow your damn head off!" A crack of thunder and shot of lighting enhanced his fury. The windows rattling from the heavy downpour and howling winds.
"Francis, whatever this is about, please, we can talk about it, just please, put the gun down."
"I said shut up!" Francis said, and hit him across the face with the butt of the pistol. An explosion of pain erupted in Hugo's mouth, his teeth cracked from the force, as he fell to one knee holding his mouth, blood seeping through his fingers. Brian tried to run over to help Hugo, and Francis pointed the gun at him. "Don't fucking move!" Brian froze and held up his hands. Edith and Claudia stood terrified, watching this unknown stranger, eyes wild and manic, holding them at ransom. John took cover behind the stone woman in the centre of the room unseen by Francis, as he peered from the woman's base and watched the madness. Precious still lent on the side of the stairs, smiling to herself, her presence almost forgotten as the rooms attention was on the man holding the gun, changing his target wildly, should anyone dare to step into his line of sight. It was like a game of chance, and you better hope your lucky stars you drew a good card. Hugo coughed and held up his

hand as he yearned back to his feet. The barrel of the pistol shaking as the blood drained from Francis' hand, his eyes darting from one person to the next.

"How does it feel, Hugo?! How does it feel to have your life in the hands of another? Knowing at any minute it could all end!" His voice was ragged, trembling and fierce. He spoke quickly, like he was saying his words before he had even thought of them. He was running on blind adrenaline and amphetamine. "You fucked my life up, and you can't even admit it." Hugo spat blood onto the floor. "You took my life! You took everything I had built, you destroyed my world, my marriage and my livelihood." Hot spittle gathered around his mouth like foam, like a rabid dog gone crazy with rabies, his eyes deep blood shot red, and his face drained of colour. He looked like a corpse that had been denied death. "I can't sleep, I can't eat, and I can't even take a fucking shower without somebody trying to take a photo of me. You have created a putrid web of lies and lies that follow me, capturing my every move. I close my eyes and I see the flash from the cameras, the microphones thrust into my face," Francis was crying now. "You tore out my soul and fed it to hell, while you kept getting richer and richer, sitting on your ivory tower pissing down on me, boasting with your trophy wife, your new jewellery and your happy fucking existence. I begged and begged you to help me, but you just spewed out lies and lies and nothing but rotten putrid shit! You have destroyed everything I have, I'm ruined!" He thrust the pistol closer to Hugo, pointing it to his forehead, and he felt power of ensured annihilation upon him, like the grim reaper had stood on his side, about to take his hand and lead him away into the blackness of death "I'm going to make you pay, you bastard." Hugo slammed his eyes shut, sure that annihilation was sure to follow. But it never came. In a moment that felt like eternity, he reopened his eyes and saw Francis still there, crying onto the floor. The gun still shaking fiercely, had lowered to Hugo's chest, his breath rapid. He took a chance, and he spoke softly, like trying to talk a man with nothing to live for off back onto the right side of a bridge.

"Francis," he whispered delicately, like speaking to fragile glass, knowing the slightest wrong tone would cause it to shatter, and the flame of his life would be extinguished with a little more pressure on a pistol trigger. He gulped, his throat dry. Annie slowly moved away like walking on shells as Hugo took a step towards Francis, and then another.

"Stay there," Francis barked, lifting the gun back to Hugo's face. He did as he was told and lifted his hands, palms out, subordinate, vulnerable.

"Whatever you think I have done, we can work through it." His nostrils flared. His words like a red rag to a very pissed off bull.

"Don't try to play this off as my fault." He seethed. "I see you for what you are and I know what you have done." He announced to the room. "He used my company to order fucking poison." A confused gasp and exchanging of worried looks followed behind Hugo. "That's right. Poison, Hugo! You have killed so many people and pinned it on me. Tonight, me and you, this is for them." Claudia shouted from the back of the hall to Hugo, not believing what she was hearing.

"What's he talking about Hugo?"

"Go ahead, tell them. Tell them about Jasmine Ringer, aged seven. Tell them about Chris Owen, age five, Ronald Williams, age eight, Sapphire Scott, aged fucking three! Tell them about me and Sarah, tell them about the police, the papers, the destruction of my entire god damn world. Tell them! Come on!" Hugo waited before he answered. It was only a few seconds but it felt like much longer, the grandfather clocks pendulum slamming into his mind. If he admitted it, he would be lying, but he may live. But in doing so he may lose his wife and friends, and god knows if he was being recorded. He could lose it all by admitting to something he hadn't done. However, the other option was telling the truth, tell Francis that he had gotten it wrong, and he would have a bullet between his eyes, and none of it would matter anyway. "Answer!" Francis barked. "Answer your wife. Tell her and everyone else what you have done." Hugo, pushing away the lump in his throat, spoke.

"I will not admit to something I have not done." He puffed out his chest and dropped his hands. The lion in him was not ready to submit. "If you are to shoot me, then go ahead and do it."

"Hugo, no!" Claudia shouted. Francis lowered the gun and then quickly raised it again.

"You think I'm fucking bluffing, Hugo? I'll blow your head off!" his voice was wavering more now. Hugo reopened his eyes and shouted to him. A voice that did not croak, a voice that fathomed no head of trepidation, but a voice of defiance, triumph, and power.

"If what you're saying is true Francis, why would I invite you to my home tonight, knowing what I had done to you."

"You wanted to rub it in my face!" He said through fresh tears. "You're a sick man, you wanted to see me on my hands and knees as you rested your feet on my back. You use people, the same as you've probably used everyone in here," Francis looked over to the back of the room. "Isn't that right, Precious!" Precious suddenly felt all eyes on her. She froze. This wasn't how it was supposed to work. She thought. I didn't think you wanted theatrics and me to be a supporting role. Her lip quivered and she let out a howl, forcing tears to stream out of her eyes, a skill she had gotten quite good at.

"No! Hugo is a good man, we've had our differences yes, but he wouldn't do this. Not what you're saying! How do you know who I am? I've never seen you before!" She buried her head in her hands, mascara turning her fingers muddy like a child playing in met mud. Hugo's eyes narrowed to her and he didn't join in the worried looks of the others. Then, a realisation struck him. The intercom hadn't gone off. She hadn't come through the gate. He saw the slither of mud on her heels which she hadn't cleaned off, and he wanted to take the pistol from Francis and deliver her a bullet himself. She knew another way inside. But how? Francis looked pained, in shock. He thought back to the fuelling station of how she had just "Happened" to be there at the exact same time he was? She had just "happened" to notice his car and him and know where he was going? Come to think of it, he didn't even see her drive in or if she even had a car in the first place. He moved the barrel towards her.

"You lying bitch! You used me! You led me here, you told me how to get in!" Hugo saw the anger well up in his eyes, like pits of fire and his finger squoze the trigger. He rushed Francis, pushing the gun to the ceiling as it went off, broken shards of brick and paint scattered off the roof as the blast from the barrel caused an ear shattering bang. Hugo gripped the pistol and it went off again, and the two struggled in a war of might. John grabbed a plant pot and raced from behind the stone woman and crashed it on top of Francis' head, opening up a deep gash that filled with soil and shards of terracotta. Brian joined the affray, rushing into Francis with his shoulder, knocking him to the ground along with Hugo and John. The gun went off again and Annie screamed and ran away into the kitchen, followed by Edith. Precious slunk away to the upper floor of the home, and Claudia stood there frozen, watching her husband and her lover battle. Hugo punched Francis twice on the face, opening up his nose and cutting his eye with one of his rings. John wrestled the gun out of his hands while Brian held him down and tied his hands behind his back with his blazer. The three moved back and stood atop of him, him screaming into the floor, sweat drenching the three of them.

"Is everyone alright?!" Hugo shouted. Brian and John nodded, both gasping for air. Brian looked at Hugo and pointed to his stomach. A deep red patch swelling under his shirt.

"Hugo, your…" his voice trailed off as he pointed to the red. Hugo looked down and he saw the blood. His legs went numb and his head felt filled with helium. The colour fled from his face as he lost his balance and crashed to the ground. He coughed up deep clots as blood pooled onto the floor. Claudia rushed to him, tears in her eyes. Brian and John knelt to him. Brian pressed on the wound shouting to Hugo as John looked around frantically, like a soldier fresh out of training in the middle of a gunfight.

"Call an ambulance!" Brian shouted.

"We don't have our phones!" cried Claudia, her make up smearing around her eyes and lips. She held Hugo's face and stroked his cheek as Francis screamed in the corner.

"Don't die baby, please don't die! Our baby! Don't die!" Claudia whimpered. Hugo raised his hand to her and touched her hair, thick blood matting it. She looked and saw her dress was drenched in dark red. A large pool seeping under her knees which felt warm and sticky on her bare legs.

"Check him!" Brian called. "Check him for his phone!" Claudia pulled away from him, driving her hands into his trouser pockets. She pulled out a couple of bloodied bank notes but nothing else.

"What's the code to the safe, Hugo! We need to get you some help!" Hugo's face was now the colour of snow, his lips were turning blue and his eyes were sinking into a white hollow as he fled this world. He whispered to her but she couldn't make it out. John rushed over to Francis and dug his hands into his pockets. He rummaged around and found empty bags of white powder, a receipt for fuel, and finally. A mobile phone.

"Got it!" he shouted, showing them the phone. "It's got three bars of signal and a lot of battery life." He quickly dialled '999' and spoke as fast as he could to the operator.

"He's just been shot! I need an ambulance now!" he gave the address to the call recipient who told him that help was on its way. "Hurry, he's going to bleed out!" The person told him as fast as she could on how to slow the bleeding. John relayed it to Brian who took off his tie and stuffed it into the bullet hole, then put all his pressure on it. "Turn him over, he might have an exit wound!" Brian did so, and there it was, flowing freely from his lower back. Brian took out a handkerchief from his pocket and stuffed it in there too then rolled him back onto his back and put pressure on him again. The blood flow reduced, but Brian wasn't sure if it was because he had been clogged up, or if there wasn't much left in him to flow, like a smashed juice carton that haemorrhages onto the kitchen floor, and stops as you pick it up, the damage already too far gone. John hung up the phone and placed it in his pocket. "Go get a first aid kit, there's one in the bedroom! He'll need fresh bandages. I think there's a clogging agent in there too. Go get it me," Brian stared at him panting heavily, frozen in place. "Go! Go now before he dies," John ordered. Brian stood up and ran up the flight of stairs. "Claudia, go help him. He'll get lost up there without you," She didn't ask any further questions, seeing the sight of all the blood had made her feel sick, she stood up and ran after Brian up the stairs, disappearing over the lip of the landing. "It's going to be okay, sir, we'll get you some help," he said to Hugo, him passing in and out of consciousness. Francis crawled off his stomach and then sat with his back to the front door. He watched Hugo as he saw the life draining away from him, the tight bounds of Brian's blazer cutting of the circulation to his wrists. He watched as John held him, his expensive suit and white gloves matted with red as he pressed on his stomach. He saw the pistol sticking out from his waist band. He wondered if he could undo the binds, take the gun and finish him off and take his own life away with it before the police arrived. John felt the hot begin to slow under the weight of his hands and Hugo's breathing become shallower. He was fading away. Hugo tried to speak.

"I didn't do anything wrong, John," he whispered.

"Don't worry about that right now, Mister Hugo," John soothed. "Everything will rectify itself soon. You'll be okay, I promise. Help is on its way." Hugo smiled weakly.

"You have always been a good friend to me John, I'm so sorry for hurting you," he said, reaching his hand to his face. John took it with a free hand, still pressing on the wound with his other. His face wet with cooling blood. He smiled at him warmly. "You're the reason I'm here in the first place. You've given me the opportunity of a life time, you gave me shelter, skills and taught me how to how to love my work. I love you like a father Hugo," he ran his hand through his hair and leaned into him, Higo's breath growing fainter. His eyes were turning paler, the life flitting from them, as the reaper held him, pulling him closer to the other side. John heard whispers. The whispers from behind the door he had heard before. This time they were closer. He looked above him further into the hallway. He saw a dark silhouette, scratching loudly at the railing of the stair case, its long fingers digging its talons into the wood, arms jittering as it moved unnaturally, vanishing then reappearing rapidly, morphing its outline in a blurred frenzy. It moved towards him, its presence that of death. It moved to Hugo and John felt a strange feeling. Warmth, like a welcomed stranger. He felt happiness and sadness take hold of him as the being moved closer. It moved airily, not touching the ground, floating towards them like a phantom. It couched down, it had no scent, no solid form and John wondered why he could see such a creature. Despite its menacing and evil form, it was something to be welcomed. An agent of death, which arrived to take those away when it was their time. It lent down to Hugo, its face featureless, just a blank canvas of black. It held Hugo at the side of his head and then traced its hands around his jaw. It moved its head into his, like it was giving him a kiss on the forehead, like a mother would saying goodnight to her child. John felt at peace as it took Hugo from him. He did not feel sadness, or pain, however he feared that one the being had gone, they were sure to return, no longer anesthetized by the phantoms strange beauty. It seemed to pay no head to him, as it lifted its head and Hugo let out a long exhalation of breath. His body convulsed tightly in a sharp controlled fit that was short lived. The creature stood atop of them, overbearing as tall as a full extended grizzly bear on its hind legs, its form long stretched, arms and fingers like wire. John looked down to Hugo's eyes and he knew he was gone. His mouth was closed and he looked relaxed, like a blanket of peace had fallen over him, wrapping him tightly like over a freezing child on a winters night. John ran his hand across Hugo's face, still numb from the spirit. Why had it showed itself to him? More so, why was he not afraid of it? John gently closed Hugo's eyes, awaiting the lights of the ambulance to come shining through the windows of the hall, it's siren to creep over the surrounding hills and valleys. He stood up, his hands still red with the fresh blood of Hugo's wound. His legs were stiff and his arms ached from holding down the pressure, now albeit in vainly. He turned to see Francis. He looked horrified with his eyes wide, they fixed on John. His face was twisted in a fixed glare of horror. His teeth bared, his mouth wide, and a scream caught in his throat. He released it to John, a harrowing shriek that shook his bones. An unnatural scream, one that came from a place of innate terror and instinct. John held up his hands and rushed to him, his feeling of tranquillity granted by the soul taking spirit now gone, returning his emotions of pain and sorrow to him, like a smashed widow rushes in the wind of a violent storm.

"Get away from me! Get away from me!" Francis howled to John, his feet kicking wildly on the slick marble floor, his shoes slipping and sliding in all directions as he pressed up against the wooden door, almost trying to push himself through it. His arms and shoulders were tort, trying desperately to free himself from the binds of Brian's tightly knotted blazer. John crouched to him and tried to hush him. He turned and saw nobody rushing to his aid, nobody had heard his shriek, and John thought for a second, he had imagined it. Maybe he had imagined the whole thing? The fury of emotions in the night playing tricks on his mind, making him see and hear things that weren't there. But the look in Francis' eyes said otherwise. The man was beside himself with terror, inconsolable. John put his handover Francis' mouth, to try and muffle his terror.

"Shush," he hissed, "You have caused enough tonight. You deluded fool. Wait until the police get here." He would not call for help, Brian and Claudia still looking for the first aid kit they think could save Hugo's life, Edith and Annie racked with fear in the kitchen, and Precious who has slunk away in the halls clearly as guilty as the bound man before him. Francis' nose dripped wet mucus onto John's bloodied gloves.

"Keep your voice down!" John barked..

"Y... you...you!" he repeated, unable to finish his full sentence.

"Did you see it too?" John released his hold on Francis' mouth, allowing him to answer him. Francis held his eyes to him, the blood matting around his face as he struggled. His chest rose quickly and John pressed again hard on him as Francis let out another muffled scream. "Control yourself! You have caused enough death tonight without making more of a scene, and I shall not let Hugo's memory in his friends mind be destroyed by them rushing in here seeing him dead and bloodied on the floor. They will see him in the hands of the paramedics, and not lay on the ground like a sagging corpse devoid of life. Do you understand?" Obeying his demands with urgency, Francis slowed his breathing and repented his howling. "Now I'm going to take my hand from your mouth, and we're going to talk?" Francis nodded. Still needing to know what had happened with the spirit, he asked again, more for his own mind and less for Francis'. "What did you see?" His eyes, still wild, flitted to and fro, unsure of how to answer. He opened his mouth, his lips babbling silence, a meek noise squeaking out his throat. John heard shouting coming from upstairs, followed by a loud bang and a crash that came from the back of the house. He had to hurry, should the madness of the night take another person, should Precious be walking around the house silently with a butchers knife.

"I saw…" Francis croaked.

"Yes, go on, you saw it too?" John said, his voice eager to hear it, that it wasn't just him, that Francis too had seen the spirit from the other side. He looked at John unsure, confused.

"You and Hugo…"

"Yes, go on, did you see it"

"See who?". John's spirit dampened, his response raising more questions than answers, and a flare of irritation enter him.

"You saw death take Hugo, the spirit from the other side. It was so peaceful, did you not think?" Francis shook his head. John's heart sank. "I saw you kill him." John's eyes went wide, then narrow. This couldn't have been true, he wouldn't kill Hugo? He would have no reason too. This man was mad, insanity had consumed his body, clouded his mind like thick bleach and lye in drinking water. Poisoned him, rotting him from the inside. John had a flash of a thought. What if he told the police that? He was covered in Hugo's blood, and all the witnesses had left the hall leaving just him and a bound mad man. Nobody would believe him. John gripped Francis.

"You're lying! Tell me you saw it!" he slammed him against the door. "Tell me you saw it" Francis reeled his head back and thrust it into John's nose. He fell back and held it as it exploded with blood, pain and cartilage, shooting up into his forehead, racing around his skull and down his neck. He lay on the ground dazed, staring up at the ceiling. He saw Francis erect above him, his presence towering over him, unbound, a psychopath on set free. He reached down and took his pistol from John's waist band. John hung on to consciousness as long as he could, as Francis pulled the hammer of the gun back and pointed it to John's face. Then all went black.

Chapter Ten.

Trapped.

Brian rushed upstairs through the long snaking halls. He turned erratically, quickly losing his way. He had never been to this house before and now he was expected to navigate it blindly while a dying man depended on him finding his way. He ran into one room, thrusting open the door. It was a small cleaning closet, filled with brooms and mops and cleaning chemicals. He tried another door, a small guest room, another, a large study with bookcases and a giant fireplace, that pulled his attention to the devils and angels carved into the wood. He turned and looked either way down the halls, bright lights hung on the sides above paintings of animals and people, which appeared to smile at him. He felt the hallway beginning to spin and a pain rise in his stomach. He wasn't himself, his panic was tearing his insides apart. He took a deep breath and bent over to his knees. He was no good to Hugo if he lost his nerve and collapsed from a panic attack. He heard a familiar voice come from the end of the hallway.

"Brian?!" It was Claudia. She sounded alarmed. He thought she had stayed downstairs with Hugo. He saw her appear at the foot of the hall. She turned frantically on the spot, like she was also lost in the maze of lights and doors.

"Over here!" he shouted, catching his breath. She rushed over to him, she tripped on the carpet, stood up, and thrust off her expensive heals and caught up to him. She placed her hand on his back.

"Are you okay?" she said with haste. She pulled him into her, his damp shirt sticking to her skin and kissed him hard. Brian looked shocked, and confusion pulled into his mind. What was she doing? She was to have a family and soon, he could be free of her. Then he thought she must be terrified, the thought of losing her husband and the family they were to start, so she was falling back into him, her safety net. Then a more chilling thought crept into him. Unless the baby is mine after all?

"I'm fine," Brian said, pushing away the thoughts of betrayal for another time. "We need to get to the bedroom." She took his hand and they raced down a further array of halls and down some small steps that could easily trip you if you didn't see them and continued down to a large door which she burst open. Brian looked in astonishment at the magnitude of it, it was certainly fit for a king. He had no time to admire the details however, he quickly got to work throwing back the chairs and the draws, sifting through them and looking for the kit. Claudia did the same, however less ferociously than Brian. She appeared cooler about it. Slower, calmer, until she stopped all together and stood, looking at him. He was on his knees, pulling items from under the bed, half empty suitcases of papers and clothes, desperately trying to find what was needed. He looked up and saw her, she stood there with her arms folded.

"What are you doing, Claudia? Help me look!"

"We could let him die," she said, coldly. Her face absent of expression. Brian's eyes widened. He held her gaze, mouth hanging loose.

"What did you say?"

"Or at least wait until the ambulance comes." She said hastily. "Town isn't too far from here, they should be here in a couple of minutes." She pulled out a carton of cigarettes from one of the draws next to a giant wardrobe, its long stretching mirror reflecting Brian's amazement..

"Claudia, shut up and keep looking. I can't believe you." He slammed the suitcase shut and began to pull further items out, his eyes flitting under the large bed. He found a case tucked right underneath and had to sprawl to reach it. It was large, violet and zipped up tight. As he pulled it, he noticed it was much heavier than the other ones. He got it out, undid the zipper, and found it to be filled with women's clothing, jewellery, fragrances and documents. He opened up one of the papers which was small and bound in dulled red leather. "Claudia Bouvier," He studied her tiny photograph and read the word 'PASSEPORT." She crouched next to him, her dress opening up between her legs, showing off her underwear. She ran her hand down his face and traced his strong jaw bone.

"I see you found my suitcase." He looked further into the case. He saw bindings of money, plane tickets, and the papers from an estate agents in Cote d'Azur, in the south of France.

"Claudia, what is all this?" He said, studying the papers. She moved closer, taking his hand.

"If he dies, we can be together." The words made him feel sick. "You said to me, tonight is the night we do it, we run away together, what better opportunity than right now, while its chaos? If he survives, Hugo won't even remember it, and nobody will see that we've gone." She blew smoke in his face, almost teasingly. Brian put the papers down and closed the case. He took a heavy breath.

This is the moment you have all been waiting for.

He took hold of her arms and looked into her eyes pleadingly, and then eyed the burning cigarette. "You're pregnant with his child. You can't expect me to do this." She put her hand over her tummy.

"I and Hugo haven't been passionate in weeks. He's too caught up in himself to realise that." She stroked his hair. "But you," she said tugging at his collar. "You couldn't keep your little paws off me." He recoiled from her, her touch burning him.

"I can't, Claudia. I can't do it." Her smile held but was pursed with confusion and shock, until it left her face completely.

"But you said tonight we would be together. Are you going to leave me to raise a child on my own?" She looked into Brian's eyes and he felt his heart beginning to crack. He did adore her, and he had loved her, but it was misplaced.

"Things aren't that simple, Claudia. I have Ima. I have my son Ivan. I love them. I can't leave them." She stared at Brian for a moment, then he continued to look for the kit, still kneeling. He was moving slower now, deflated, awkwardly. She held her eyes on him, and she felt hatred rise in her.

"You were using me all along, weren't you? Using me to get closer to Hugo for your own profile?" He stayed quiet, sifting through the boxes under the bed. "You told me you loved me." she spoke with bitter pain now, her proud front forcing back her quivering lip and her developing tears. "You would rather have Ima, an ex-crack addicted whore than me." Brian stopped looking and met her gaze. Moments ached by, the unsmoked cigarette still lit, its smoke filling the room. He began to breathe heavily, her words of truth cutting though his thick web of lies and deceit.

"Ima is my wife." He hissed. "Me and you.." he continued to sift under the bed.

"Me and you what?" she said.

"Nothing." He batted her off flatly, ignoring her. She stood over him. "Say what you were going to say Brian. Me and you what?"

"We were just a mistake." His words cut into her. She had been right all along. He was a wolf in sheep's clothing. Mr good deeds with a soul as black as coal. He saw someone who was hurting, promised her the world and after he'd had enough of getting his dick wet with her, when it came to her wanting something real, he was going to throw her away like a cum stained tissue.

"You fucker," she bit. "Are you fucking the blonde girl now?" He snapped his head to her.

"Claudia, me and you shouldn't have ever happened. I wanted to break it off sooner with you and not let it go this far, but…" he pointed to her tummy and shook his head, not knowing what to say, his shame of the affair clouding his mind like someone was stuffing cotton wool down his throat. "I didn't want it to end this way. I didn't want to do it because of Hugo."

"What? Because you knew that if Hugo found out you were fucking his wife, he would skin you and your family alive? Expose you as a fraud and not the god damn hero you pretend to be in the papers?" her voice was firm and rising quickly. Her eyes growing wider with hate. A woman scorned. "You love Ima. Were you loving her when you were inside me? Were you thinking of your wedding day when I was sucking your cock?" He recoiled at what she was saying, as he knew it was all true, and she was shedding his skin away with her words like a sharp sword that cut without drawing blood.

"I'm sorry, Claudia." He whispered.

"Stop apologizing, you pitiful worm!" Her chest rising and falling rapidly. "No Brian, you don't get to do this. I saw you in the hall earlier with Precious, leaning her over and ramming your tongue down her neck, now all of a sudden you don't want to be with me? Or is it because you don't want your baby?" He laughed.

"You've got it all wrong." He stood to her, towering over her. "You're messed up in your mind. You concoct these stories to fit your own agenda, you do mental gymnastics to make the square peg fit the round hole. Your husband beat her, like he attacked John. I saw the whole thing. She was upset and I comforted her and she kissed me. What was I supposed to do?" She scoffed.

"Yeah right," she said. She leaned in close. "I don't believe a damn word that comes out of your mouth. How long have you been screwing her?" Brian grabbed a lamp and threw it across the room and it exploded against the wall.

"It's not like that!" he yelled. "I will not stand here and have some money hungry harpy make me out to be something I am not!" Claudia howled in bitter laughter.

"The truth hurts.." She looked at the smashed lamp on the floor. "And it looks like you're hurting a lot right now. Go back to your whore wife." He bit his fist.

"And you derogate my wife? Because she was a victim? What's your excuse? You hunt after men with money and use them as a stepping stone for your next round of fancy jewellery." The smile quickly left her face. He turned from her, holding his head in his hand, his head pounding, the anger keeping the fear at bay.

"I will support the baby and I will be a part of its life in one way or another," he turned to her again, as she stood in front of the wardrobe, with arms folded and face like stone. "But you can't expect me to drop everything I have, all I have worked for and built, to run away with you in your little fantasy. I just can't. I'm sorry."

"You're a manipulator. You used me and when it finally comes to taking some action, some damn responsibility, you cut and run like a moth that hides from the light." His nails dug into the insides of his palms as his fists turned like white rocks.

"I used you?" he scoffed. "Hugo gave you expensive clothes, round the world cruises, hobbies and connections, money and notoriety and it wasn't enough so you seduce one of his friends? You live off the wealth of whatever poor soul you leech onto. I was stupid enough to fall for it. You are the user, Claudia, and you have never felt anything close to love, a family. You told me about Emmanuel, how he left, how he was cheating on you? You're both the same! You thought that you would tear my marriage apart and if I hadn't have come to my senses sooner, you probably would have. I was your ticket to a new wardrobe and more pictures in the newspaper, you Claudia, were never anything more than a warm mouth to me." His words, deep and cutting into her made her loose her mind.

"You wretched human being. You don't get to do this, Brian. Not to me. Lie about loving me, making me fall for you, compelling me to dream of having something better than this shit existence with a man I loathe, and then you openly take advantage of another woman when I'm not looking and then say I've got it all wrong. Fuck you Brian, I can't wait to tell Ima everything and bleed you dry for the baby you will never ever see!" His eyes flew wide and he grabbed her by the throat and thrust her into the wardrobe, it shook with the impact and a box of perfume fell from the top of it, leaking on the ground. He bore his gaze into her, his nostrils flaring, the veins popping out of his neck. Her head hit the wood hard and she was dazed a moment, her body pulsing with adrenaline. This is the beast in him, the beast she wanted to see. Shed away from the suits and ties and cameras, morality gone, that which he loves threatened by one who can destroy it.

"Tell my wife about this, and I will fucking kill you," he seethed, teeth bared like a wolf pinning a rabbit. She began to cough, her breath heaving through his grip.

"I'm going to ruin your life." She took his hand with hers, gripping just under the joint of his thumb. She twisted it away from him and his wrist went tort. He yelped in pain as he was forced over, and his face was met with a sharp knee. He recoiled back, holding his nose. She brought a fist up into his jaw and he fell to the floor in a heap, holding his face.

"Don't ever put your dirty paws on me again." She hissed, holding her throat, catching her breath. She stood on the burning cigarette on the floor and composed her hair. She opened up the wardrobe and took out a long leather jacket and a designer black handbag. She turned and looked at Brian, who moaned on the ground, his shirt marred with deep red as he held his nose. She blew him a kiss, "Au revoir Brian." She put her coat and bag on, and then took a pair of sun glasses from the bed stand and exited the room, slamming the door closed behind her.

#

Precious had slunk away from the chaos of downstairs and had begun exploring the upper section of the house, keeping herself hidden. Her involvement in Hugo's murder was surely outed by Francis' outburst. She was a good actress when she needed to be, but given how deranged he was, it was a 50/50 chance of whether she was to be believed or not. She checked a hanging clock on the wall and saw she had a little bit of time. She walked through the halls, looking around corners and off the reflections of glass ornaments and the frames of paintings to see if she could spot anyone coming her way. She slunk around the house like a fox in the night, undetectable, inconspicuous. She could get a mobile phone out of the safe, it shouldn't be too hard to crack. Also, she hoped to find a gun in there that she could use, should anyone tried to pin this whole thing on her. She thought about how the police worked, and she hoped they would go for a man bound red handed with the smoking gun, than his deranged outburst of her involvement. She could call the police and tell them everything, after all, why would an accomplice to murder call the police and ask for help? She entered one room and found it to be empty, nothing more than a small guest room. It looked delightful, its bed freshly made and a small bed side lamp on, casting a small glow that invited a sleepy head into its embrace. The room was cool like the rest of the house, and Precious felt the urge to lie on the bed and say goodnight. She saw herself lying on it, nestling her head into the fluffed pillows, and then the blankets snake around and suffocate her. She shook the image from her mind and closed the door. She had begun to feel nauseous, and felt like there were insects crawling under her skin. She caught herself on the wall as she slinked over until the feeling passed. She breathed heavily, wondering what the matter was with her, her head was sweating and she was breathing heavily. She heard loud shouting and a sudden bang come from down the hall towards her, followed by silence and then, the sound of a door closing. She heard the faint muffle of footsteps on a carpet. Thinking she was soon to be discovered, she walked quickly to a nearby door, which she opened and slid into, its darkness cloaking her as she peered through the open crack. She waited, until the muffling had stopped and she saw nothing. The cessation of the phantom footsteps abated her nausea and burrowing mites under her skin. Her breath slowed and her temperature cooled. She stepped back out into the hall, unknowing what had come over her, like a wave of ill that had fallen back again. Maybe it was the fear of being caught before her plan was complete, maybe it was a feeling of uncovered guilt being excavated by her conscience. She continued down the hallway less cautiously than before, moving more quickly, opening rooms and peering in, some nicely made up for a sleeping guest, some as black as a dead fish's eye, looking for the security room. She continued down her path, looking over her shoulder repeatedly. She turned a corner and saw Claudia standing there alone, looking at herself in a wall mirror, puckering her lips as she applied lipstick, a deep black, like she was preparing for a funeral. She was wearing a black hat and sunglasses, a small black leather jacket a top of her white dress. Her heals were black and high, and Precious wondered how she could ever walk in them without toppling over. Precious moved around the corner of the hallway. She would have to turn back as there was nowhere else to go, as there were no more escape rooms on this part of the hall, which bent at a right angle, her on one corner, Claudia on the other side. A voice broke the silence.

"You can come out Precious," Claudia said into the mirror, finishing her makeup. "I know you're there." Precious put her hands on her face and forced out the tears again, pressing her finger tips into her eyes to make them red, and when she was happy with it, she stepped out into view.

"I can't believe he's gone," Precious said quietly, wiping her eyes. Claudia snapped her make up kit closed and put it into her black bag that hung from a golden chain over her shoulder. She fought back tears, making her quivering lip rigid.

"I know. He's gone for good."

"Why are you not down there with him?" Precious asked through the river of crocodiles.

"I and Brian were looking for a first aid kit to help him. Brian is still in there looking, in the bedroom. John called an ambulance, we were trying to help him while he took care of him downstairs." Fear passed through Precious, breaking her show for a split second, like an actor who had forgotten her lines on stage. Someone had managed to call the police already? Francis must have had a phone she thought.

"Oh, that's great news, we should go and be with him." Precious said. "When I saw the gun and the fight, I ran, I panicked I didn't know what to do. I got lost up here, this place is like a maze." Claudia held her gaze to herself in the mirror. Precious' words not cracking her stone look.

"It's horrifying I know. I was so worried about Hugo." She said, checking herself in the mirror. "Why did Francis say that downstairs to you?" Claudia turned to Precious, who was still wiping away her fake tears. Claudia wasn't fooled by the show. She knew a charlatan when she saw one. Claudia fished a comb out of her handbag and held it in her hand.

"I just can't believe what happened. He's going to die, isn't he? Hugo? Wonderful Hugo. He was so sweet, so kind, so loving."

"Stop avoiding the question," Claudia barked. "Why did Francis mention your name downstairs?" Precious took her hands from her face. Her eyes were red, but her cheeks were as dry as arid slate. Her gaze cut into Claudia.

"Why are you looking so pretty and freshly made after your husband's just been shot?"

"Why have you not called the police if you were so scared?"

"Why have you not run out of the house screaming to get help?" Claudia smiled, her face cracking. She leaned into Precious.

"How do you even know Hugo? He's never mentioned you before. You're not one of his business partners, you're not family, and your certainly not one of his friends. Who are you to him? To us? To this house?" Precious leaned into the mirror and puffed out her hair to just the way she liked it.

"Why were you fucking Brian behind his back?" Claudia's eyes widened. How could she have known that? She bit her lip and shuffled in her stance. Precious smiled at her. "Gotcha".

"Did you tell Francis to kill my husband?" Claudia hissed, squeezing the comb tighter.

"No," she said blankly. Her face was cold. "I just got him in here." A tight smile creeped across her lips.

"I'm going to call the police and have you arrested. An accomplice to murder."

"Hugo died the moment he met you bitch. You fucked him way before Francis arrived tonight. Don't pretend you give a shit about him now. You've been thinking of this day for a long time. If you actually gave a shit about him, you would be down there right now holding his head and whispering into his ear how much you love him and crying onto his face, not up here preparing your make up. Speaking of which," Precious looked past her down the corridor. "Where is Brian? Have you broken him too?" Claudia felt anger grow in her veins. She wanted to smash her pretty face into the mirror and bounce her head off every wall in the house.

"You stole him from me," Claudia said, moving closer to her. Precious laughed.

"I stole him? Jesus you really are a spoilt brat, aren't you?"

"Were over now, anyway. You can have him." Precious flicked her hair.

"I don't want him. I just like knowing he doesn't want you."

"You're insane. Who even are you? Why did you come here? What have we done to you?" Precious took a step back and held out her arms.

"I'm the devil, sweetheart, and I'm here to make sure you all pay for your lies." Claudia moved to her again.

"Even if you tell Hugo what happened, he won't believe you. If he lives, he will take my side. I'll tell him I was coerced, blackmailed into it all, and he will help me bring down Brian, and shred you to pieces." Precious opened up her hand bag and sifted through it.

"You sure about that?" She pulled out a small bundle of papers, wrapped in an elastic band. She waved them to Claudia, who snapped them out of her hand. Precious didn't resist, like she was willingly giving someone a rope to hang themselves with. Claudia's eyes turned wide and the blood drained from her face. They were photographs taken of her and Brian. She knew where they had been from. They were taken a few weeks ago, when they had gone to one of Hugo and Brian's golf games at the local club. They had rented the course for the day as they played eighteen holes. The pictures showed Claudia and Brian in the golf cart driving to the next hole, the shade from the roof protecting them from the harsh sun. It had been a hot day, and Claudia and Brian were both wearing white. Him in tight polo shirt, her wearing black shades and small shorts. He was resting his hand on her inner thigh, away from the glance of Hugo who was driving away in his cart, a bag of silver clubs sticking out the back. Another photo was them stood in the club bar, Brian's hand on her butt, and the third photo made her feel sick. It was through the window of a hotel room, a large bed filled with lush pillows on the floor, empty bottles of wine and her underwear hanging from a lampshade, with Claudia naked on top of Brian under the bed sheets.

"Where did you get these?!" she shouted, her voice cracking the silence of the halls. Precious laughed quietly and tapped her nose.

"For me to know and for you to not. There's one thing you didn't think of, however." Claudia didn't answer, she continued to hold a mortified look as she peered at the pictures. Another of her and Brian in a jacuzzi, another of them eating dinner at a restaurant, another them out shopping holding hands. "When Hugo dies, what influence will you have to keep you safe from Brian?" Claudia threw the pictures at her and they scattered on the ground, the photo's falling face up, staring at her.

"Who the fuck are you, bitch! Why do you know so much about me? Why are you obsessed with my husband and my life?" Precious looked down at the photos. This must be how Francis felt when he saw his face in the newspapers, his debauchery uncovered.

"You really don't remember me, do you?" Precious said. Claudia's response got caught in her throat and she drew a blank. For once in her lives she was lost for words. "I met you and Hugo in Paris. About six months ago. You had been to the music hall and were sitting outside in one of the busy cafes eating god knows what, it stank whatever it was, and drinking expensive coffee." She began to walk around Claudia, like a vulture about to consume a dying animal. "I had seen you first. I sat just in the peripheral of you both, watching. I was there on holiday. I had finished some work on profiling killers for the UK police and took some time off." She moved up behind her, placing her hands on her bare shoulders. "I joined you and we drank coffee. You were too preoccupied to notice me, you were just happy to be back in Paris, and you were showing all your Instagram followers how lucky you were, capturing the Eiffel tower through your camera, putting filters on it to amplify its already amazing beauty. You didn't notice me putting it into your drink, a little something I picked up at the drug store, and when you finished your coffee, when I had finished suggesting to Hugo's subconscious that we go back to your place, you were already out of it, but you liked what happened next." A blurry vision came back to Claudia's mind. It was fractured, fragmented, like watching a broken slideshow that jumped and flashed on a dusty projection screen. She remembered the busy streets of Paris, sitting there under the overcast sky, drinking a coffee while she smiled at a woman sitting with Hugo, her face, once a blur was now forming and features appearing. It was Precious. She had joined them and was stroking Hugo's back and arms. The pair newly married, he hadn't quite gotten used to the idea of it just being them and no one else. She remembered feeling loose, heavy and weak at the same time. She remembered Hugo laughing saying she must be drunk, and Precious kissing him and looking at her, touching her naked thighs under her dress. She remembered getting into the taxi, them both sharing Hugo on the back seat, biting his lips and kissing each other too. She remembered the large bed, the velvet sheets and the sweat on Hugo's chest while Precious was on top of him. She remembered seeing blood come from his lips as Precious bit into him as they continued to merge into one, blurring together. She was below her now, Precious' lips between her legs. She gripped the pillow in ecstasy as Hugo was behind Precious, his hips moving slowly, groans that stretched out and echoed around her mind. Precious ran her hands down her back. Claudia began to feel sick. She had awoken the next morning in bed with Hugo and the room was otherwise empty. There were empty beer bottles and lines of cocaine on the glass table at the end corner of the room. She had wondered what had happened as her head pounded and her body was numb. She remembered trying to make Hugo from a deep sleep, and saw his eyes to be vacant, his body cold and he had large wounds on his chest and face. She had called for an ambulance and he was given CPR and after a roller coaster ride of wails and screams, the defibrillator brought him back after she had begged the paramedic to give him one last shock. Now she realised she had known Precious long before she had realised, and she had let her into their lives, her and Hugo had both welcomed this monster into their home. Precious leaned into her, whispering into her ear, bringing her hand down to her breasts.

"I can have you again, tonight, one last time." Claudia snapped out of her trance, bringing herself back to the moment.

"Go to hell," she snapped, she turned and pushed away Precious. She nearly lost her balance, but regained her posture. A smile on her face that stretched from ear to ear. "You a sick woman. You crawl under people's skin like a parasite, infect their brains with your presence, until they have served your purpose and then you drop them." Precious laughed at her mockingly.

"I'm the whore? Honey, everything I do is for a reason. I am a slave to the cause unlike you, little miss brat face spreading your legs for fur coats and jewellery, and when you get bored of that, you latch onto someone new. I'm a whore? You're a parasite, a leech, you suck the blood from those you touch until there nothing left and your fat and dripping." Precious moved closer to her, manic with rage. She gripped Claudia by the hair and pushed her against the wall. Claudia spat at her and bit her hand. Precious shouted in pain and released her, panting heavily. Claudia brought the sharp edge of the comb down onto her but missed by a hair. She swung it side wards, and Precious stepped out the way again. Precious grabbed a painting from the wall and hurled it at her, knocking her to the floor, the sharp comb falling from her hand. Precious ran to her and picked the comb up, flying at her, the sharp edge glistening in the light as it cut through the air towards her face. She kicked out and stuck Precious in the stomach with her heel, before rolling over to her knees and bolted forward like a sprinter on a 100m dash. Precious gripped her hair wrapping it tight in her hand and dragged her backwards. Claudia felt her back crack and click as she was brought down. Precious wrapped her arm around her neck and they fell backwards onto the floor. Claudia kicked wildly, trying to scream out for help, but nobody came running to her aid.

"Who's going to help you now, Miss Leech?" Precious hissed in her ear as Claudia scrambled on the ground, flailing her arms back, trying to catch her with her nails. Never give up your back her Jiu Jitsu instructor had said. If you give up your back, it's game over. The lights in the hall began to fade in Claudia's eyes, and the walls began to stretch and warp, as the faces in the paintings looked down on her and laughed hysterically. "Hugo loved you irrefutably. He wanted to spend the rest of his life with you, and you used him. Then you latched onto Brian, and used him too. Who's next on your list?" she tightened her grip around Claudia's neck and Claudia heaved for breath, her flailing becoming slower. "I've got big plans for you and your friends, shame you won't be able to tell anyone from inside the Morgue." She clenched harder and Claudia felt her strength leaving her. She heard loud foot steps behind her, moving quickly, running across the carpet. She heard Precious scream loudly into her ears, and her grip was no longer trying to choke her, but cling onto her. She felt Precious being pulled away, her screams fading away as she was dragged off of her and pulled down the corridor. Claudia then heard a loud heavy thump, and Precious stopped screaming. Claudia crawled on all fours, coughing heavily into the carpet, blood spattering and soaking into its white. She put her hand around her neck and rubbed her skin. She cleared the tears from her eyes and they remained blurred, the corridor still swaying as the air returned to her lungs. Her chest was on fire and it retched red hot when she breathed in, like the air was coated in razor blades. She looked up to where Precious had been dragged away. The corridor bent at another right angle and she had been taken to an unseen section of the hall. Had Brian come to her aid? Had John stumbled across them? Had Francis taken his next victim? Or what about Annie and Edith? Whoever it was hadn't made themselves known to he, like an unseen guardian, but Claudia wasn't sure if it was an angel or a devil, and if she would be next. She stood up, her legs wobbling like Bambi on ice, and she trudged slowly to the end of the hall, where she would try to run down the stairs and out the door into the howling night.

Chapter Eleven.

Fraud.

Annie stared at Hugo with fiery rage that felt like it could tear the heavens into two. Her muscles were tense and sharp, like rough diamonds. Her eyeliner had streamed down her face and was dripping onto her dark dress, smudging into the fabric. Everything that had happened, all decisions she had ever made in her life had led her to this moment. She had forsaken such thought of destiny, fate and even faith a long time ago, but this was a reckoning of some sort, a build-up of the pain and hate forced headlong into present time. Her confronting him was the only thing on her mind, and the extent of pain he had caused. She went to speak further, her eyes red with tears and fury. She heard the door go and a dishevelled, muddied man came in from the outside storm, and as much as she had wished for death since her life was cut out of her by her own hand, the sight of the pistol and death in his eyes made want to live, like something reborn from ash and mud of a fallen empire. She remembered the shouting, the popping of the pistol and a melee of bodies. She remembered being dragged away and pulled into the kitchen by Edith, who was now shaking with terror, the melee in the hall since gone quiet. They both dared not look out to see the result, and Annie, noticing the door was still open through the cracks in her fingers that pooled her blackened tears, rushed and slammed it shut. A false sense of peace and safety fell over her, but she knew that they were still in danger. She didn't know if the gunman had now been subdued or if he was currently stalking those left in the house, so Annie ran and grabbed a steak knife from the knife rack and put it into her hand bag, to protect herself. Edith was sinking a glass of champagne like a dying man in the desert who has stumbled on an oasis. Her famine now gone in a gulping of flavoured bubbles. Edith slammed the glass down. "So," she said, the champagne still tingling her lips, as she stared at her reflection in the dark rain speckled kitchen window. "We have to get out of here." Annie sat on a stool, her bag close by, the handle of the blade protruding out.

"We need to call for help," said Edith. Annie laughed.

"How do we do that? We gave up our damn phones to John and they are in a locked safe in a room we don't know how to get to, in a house that has a psychopath walking around it." Annie took a half empty bottle of champagne from the counter and took a long swig until the bubbles burned her throat, she took a breath and then did another. Edith deflated, rapping her nails across the counter, frequently checking the kitchen door from the hall, and the archway from the lounge.

"Well, we can't stay here. We're sitting ducks."

"We should wait for the police to arrive, or wait until the others come and get us. I'm not looking through that door. I'm not being added to a body count."

"What if we run to the door and get out of here?" Annie smirked and ran her finger around the top of the bottle.

"I don't know what it is, but you know when you walk into a room and you feel like eyes are on you when there's nobody in there? Like you're being watched?"

"You're imagining things," Edith whispered.

"In the time we have been here, have you seen another passing car?" Annie said like she was speaking only to herself. "Have you heard a single bird or bit of wildlife? Have you seen any other house for miles? Not to mention the damn storm outside. Were up shit creek without a paddle. This place," she looked around the room. "This place is wrong. I can just feel it."

"Annie, I think you've had too much to drink."

"Stop making me out to be imagining things. Since we arrived here, things have gone from bad to worse. It's like everything you hold inside yourself unravels like peeling skin from a sunburn. Layer after layer of putrid lies coming out for the world to see." She turned to Edith and bit at her. "If you want to live, stop coming up with fantasies of running out the front door into the arms of the police and start coming up with actual solutions of how to see the sunrise tomorrow."

"Hey, this isn't my fault." Edith stammered, taken back. A silence fell between them and Annie didn't wish to break it. Instead, she traced her arms with her finger nails and began to fall into herself, and she cursed herself for beginning to cry again. She couldn't remember the last time she had been happy. Not crack the odd smile or felt satisfaction, but felt truly happy. Since that night, she had felt nothing but numb, and she welcomed this feeling of fear in her heart, that a gunman could burst into the room and empty a clip into her and Edith, casting them both into oblivion at any moment. She would rather feel fear and pain, than feel nothing. It was like a constant white noise that only you could hear, and after a while, you forget what it's like without it. She looked at the knife sticking out of her bag. It was sharp, sharp enough to cut through flesh with ease. Her thoughts wandered to the dark places human beings have in the deepest recesses of their mind. Edith saw she was tracing the blade around her forearm, red stripes following the path of the blade. Annie's eyes were closed, lost in her darkness. She quickly stepped towards her and took it out of her hand and placed it on the counter behind them, like a mother who had just found her child playing with a lit firework.

"Don't even think about it Annie." Annie looked blankly at the work surface in front of her where she sat, her tears now dried on her cheeks.

"I don't want to be here anymore, Edith." She spoke with a coldness only seen in those that commit to jumping head first off the top floor of a building, that when they have run the idea through their heads a hundred times, no longer have the fear of taking the final step into annihilation. "He's dead, I know it. Now I feel nothing. He was my anchor to this life, in a sick kind of way. My hatred for him, my fucking loathing for that human being is what kept me going. Now he's gone, I just feel cold." Edith took hold of her palms. They were so cold.

"You are much more to me than you think. We have been friends for years, Annie, and I love you. After you were attacked and put into hospital, it's only natural to feel the way you do."

"Hugo is the reason I was in the hospital Edith." Edith nodded.

"You blame him for the attack. I understand. You two went to the races together. Hugo left you on the way back to your car you were set upon by a group of thugs. A passer by found you and called for an ambulance." She rested her head on her shoulder. "That man, so quick to get back to his own business he let a vulnerable woman walk back to her car alone." She locked her eyes with Annie." But he couldn't have known what was going to happen to you. He couldn't have known, and you couldn't have predicted it. It's just a horrific thing that happened and nobody could have predicted it." Annie stared blankly at the counter.

"They were never caught." Edith nodded into her. "They never found finger prints. No witnesses. No weapons."

"Such a sad thing to have happened and those bastards to never see justice. We could re-open the case? Try to find out who did this to you and get some closure on the whole thing." Annie shrugged her away.

"We can't."

"Yes, we can." Edith took her shoulders and stared into her eyes, like convincing her best friend that doing a séance in a graveyard on Halloween was a good idea. "It's been a long time yes, but we can ask the media, put some pressure on the CCTV company to dig up the footage of the night. Put out appeals to witnesses." She was talking fast now, almost forgetting the silence they had to keep, should the psychopath walk through the kitchen door. "Annie, there's so much we can do! We just have to contact the police and ask them to re-open the case."

"There never was a case." Annie spoke, her voice hushed.

"What do you mean? You mean they were never called?"

"Sort of." Annie looked away from her, focusing again on the knife handle. "The police were never called because it never happened. I lied about the whole thing." Edith was confused, her mouth open in a stunned half laughter, half silence.

"What are you talking about?" she croaked. "You told me that's what had happened and why you were in the hospital for so long. You told me that your liver was ruptured and they had to go in through the front to get to it, which is why you got the scar."

"I'm sorry."

"No, I don't believe you. It's okay to block it out, Annie, it really is. We can get you someone, I know a really good counsellor who deals with things like this. I think you have PTSD, and after what you told me in the hospital, about how savage it was, I don't blame you!"

"I don't have PTSD. I don't think so anyway." Annie took another

drink from the champagne bottle. Then realising it was empty, she grabbed a half open bottle of beer that Precious had been drinking. It tasted sour and flowery at the same time, but Annie sunk it anyway.
"Annie," Edith took the bottle from her, no empty. "I sat by your bed side in the hospital and listened to you tell the police about what had happened."
"They were only there because you called them." Annie looked at Edith, whose face was growing deeper with wrinkles by the second. A realisation crept into Edith's mind, and her body began to tighten.
"But your scar?"
"You saw it before. Does it look like a surgeon did that? In a hospital with nurses and assistants helping them? Does it look like it was done with sterile instruments, iodine and anaesthetic?" Edith shook her head.
"I can't believe what I'm hearing. You must be more deluded than I thought. What with the shock, the alcohol."
"I'm not delusional!" Annie shouted, breaking their vow of silence. "You're a pathologist. You know that a ragged scar like this is self-inflicted." She shut her mouth before she had finished speaking. Wanting the words to be pulled back before they hit Edith's ears. There was the silence again, but this time it was long and stretching. Annie stood up, and Edith felt the urge to grab the knife from the counter. "I did it to myself Edith. I opened myself up. I put myself in the hospital. And it was all because of Hugo." Edith didn't know what to say. She was both confused about what Annie was saying, angry that she was lying and upset that if it was true, she had been driven to do such a thing to herself.
"You're drunk, Annie, you don't know what you're saying," she said.
"Don't belittle me Edith." Annie threw her hands into the air. "Me and Hugo hooked up, after we met at the medical conference you invited me to, last June, you were promoting some book or something. I and Hugo met, we fucked and he left." Edith's eyes went wide.
"You wouldn't do that," she shook her head. "You've always been a strict Catholic. You go to church, you wear a damn crucifix around your neck. You wouldn't…" For the first time in the night, Edith had had a moment of clarity. She looked at Annie in front of her, her shoulders tight and her hair sticking to her face over her tears. She saw her neck devoid of jewellery, and she saw a look in her eyes that she hadn't seen in a long time. Honesty. The realisation of the dark tale she

was telling came to fruition, like when you realised who the murderer is in a plot twist of a movie.

"I fell pregnant with his child. He took my virginity because I thought, hey got to lose it sometime! It's the 21st century, and who the hell lives a strict religious life to the letter these days anyway?" She was pacing on the spot now. "I tried to call him, I tried to reach out to him, but he avoided me, never returned my mail and my calls. I even turned up at his office a couple of times until security threatened me with being arrested for harassment. So, I continued in my work with all this going on, a baby in my body I didn't want, to a father who didn't care, under the loving eye of a God that forgets about you when you don't scream his name." She moved to her and Edith froze. Her eyes flitted again to the knife. She slammed her palms on the table, leaning into her. Edith could smell the stale booze on her breath. "I nearly killed someone while they were under the knife."

"Oh my god," Edith gasped. "They lived?" Annie nodded painfully then stepped away. She was smaller now, her body like that of an old woman ruined by rickets and arthritis.

"Just about, but I was suspended from surgery until further notice, until I got my head sorted. So now I had no income either, and bills were piling up and my reputation was in flames. I couldn't go to my family, they would disown me for having sex with a man I had just met. I disowned myself, I turned my back on my God for letting this happen to me after a lifetime of strict devotion, and I couldn't go to an abortion clinic and sit with all the other unwanted children, I just couldn't. I took a scalpel and some utensils, and I performed the abortion myself. The baby could have lived had I waited a few weeks, but it was dead from the moment I pulled it out. But I had cut too deep, and I nearly bled out. I managed to dial 999 before I passed out and I woke up in the hospital." Annie sat quietly as Edith stared at her in disbelief. Her mind wandered a moment, as a memory she had buried away in a locked box crept open, dead hands creeping out of it, scratching at its wooden lid. Her blood ran cold.

"How could you do that Annie? That poor baby didn't deserve that!" Edith was enraged. "You denied a poor child a right to live because you saw it as an inconvenience?" Edith began to cry, speaking through a swollen throat. "You knew about Oscar, my little angel, how he had died, and I came to visit you in the hospital and you had the gall to lie to my face about some bullshit attack, when it was you all along." Edith was shaking, the locked box now fully open, and the bloated face of her baby boy peeking over the lid, covered in sand and river weed.

"The reason I never told you the truth was because of Oscar and what you went through. I didn't want you to be ashamed of me, like you are now. I knew you and Hugo were good friends. I didn't want to mar your view of him."

"Oh, such a diplomatic answer, Annie. You didn't tell me the truth because you were ashamed of yourself, not because you were sparing my feelings. Don't make this out to be doing me a damn favour." Annie began to well up again.

"I'm so sorry, Edith, I shouldn't have lied to you about it! I came to speak to Hugo about our child, to get some kind of closure. But then he declared him and his wife were going to have a baby themselves, I lost it." Edith screamed at Annie.

"You're a fucking murderer, Annabelle! How could you do such a thing! You robbed it of every chance it had of life and potential! I would have never thought you would go to such lengths to save your own skin!" Annie felt herself crumbling, the walls she had built around her crashing into the deep blue abyss.

"I'm so sorry, Edith," She begged." I'm so sorry for what I did, I'm so sorry for your little boy, I'm so sorry for lying, I'm so sorry for everything." Annie rushed to her, wanting to hold her, wanting to plead with her. Edith moved back, not wanting her to touch her, like to do so would burn her flesh and bleed her eyes. She stepped onto the broken shards of glass and slipped on the wet flooring, catching herself on the counter. Annie moved in closer to her. She saw in her mind her boy, skin puffy and filled with water, skin slippery like an eel. His blonde hair matted with river bed, and a sweet rapper sticking out of his mouth. She fell onto the floor, sliding down the counters, pressing her back into it and weeping to herself, quietly at first, and then howling. Annie put her hand on her gloves and saw the fear in her eyes. She pulled her in to her and Edith let the dread spill out onto her shoulder, it sinking in and she absorbed it willingly. She fell next to her. She held her tightly. Annie cradling her like the baby she could never have. The baby she had taken away from her, and she felt the numbness subsiding.

"I don't want to die," Edith cried. Annie ran her fingers through her hair and kissed her crown.

"Were going to be okay," she whispered. They started as a loud bang came from upstairs followed by a barrage of muffled voices, then followed by silence, then further screams and banging, and then nothing. "No gunshots," Annie whispered, taking hold of Edith's white knuckles that wrapped around her dress. That was in some way comforting. They then heard the quick sounds of footsteps racing down the stairs and across the hall. They heard panicked screaming as the front door rattled over and over, desperately trying to be opened. Annie stood up, and Edith gripped her tightly.

"Don't go." Annie continued and she stood up, taking the knife from her bag and crept to the door of the kitchen. She opened it just enough to see through into the hallway. Claudia stood at the front door, yanking and banging on it wildly. The ground was painted red with pooled blood, and Brian's blazer sat abandoned on the floor. There were no bodies. Maybe Hugo had survived? Maybe the police had already been and gone, paramedics and all? Where were the others? Another harrowing thought crept into her mind. Where was the gunman? And was he taking aim at her right now?

"Let me out!" Claudia screamed over and over again, like a caged animal gone mad with terror, as the executioner inside the abattoir drew closer with his meat cleaver hanging loosely from his belt. She turned to look at the kitchen and Annie placed the door shut. The less people know they are in here, the better. She walked to Edith and helped her to her feet.

"We need to find some car keys or something. The gunman must have come here in a car, or Hugo will have a car in his garage. I'll steal a damn horse if I have too, but tonight, we are getting out of here." Annie spoke with a renewed determinism, and Edith felt safe being with her. She was a strong woman, much stronger than she had given her credit for. Given what she had been through, she had almost unconsciously trained herself to fight for air when life tried to suffocate her.

"Okay," Edith whimpered "What's out there?" Annie looked back at the closed door.

"Nothing. And that's the worst part." She moved but her bag wrapped around her ankle, fell onto the hard flooring, make-up brushes, paper and coins spilling in front of them in a shattering cascade of brilliant tap-dancing. The pair of them grabbed at the fleeing items and stuffed them in Edith's bag. Annie picked up a green slip. Before she could make out the words, Edith snatched it out of her hands like a starving beggar who had found a fresh bread roll. She stuffed it deep into her bag and continued to pick up the rest of her belongings. "What's that?" Annie asked, taken back by Edith's urgency.

"Nothing, just.." she paused. "It's just a prescription for some medication. I struggle sleeping sometimes. It's just personal that's all." Annie didn't answer. Instead she nodded to Edith, her eyes still looking into the bag.

"Ready?" Edith hurried, as she fought the urge to crawl in a hole and wait for them to be rescued, or worse. They turned to exit the kitchen, gripping each other's hands tightly, like two schoolgirls planning to run away to New York waiting at the train station, Thelma and Louise against the world, before they fall headlong over a cliff. They heard the handle of the kitchen door begin to rattle. Edith stopped breathing and she took cover behind Annie, who was already holding the knife outstretched towards the phantom danger that lurked on the other side. The door swung pen, bouncing off the wall. Claudia stood there in front of them out of breath, panting wildly. Her hands were loose by her side and she looked as white as December snow.

"Help me," she said, she rushed in and slammed the door behind her. Annie and Edith looked at her cautiously. If she knew they were in here, who else did?

"How did you know we were in here?" Annie said, the knife shaking in her hand, the tip pointed at Claudia, who pressed against the door.

"I didn't, but I can't find a way out. All the windows, the doors.... They're all locked tight. Hugo had them reinforced with thick glass so we can't even smash them. We're trapped." These words of dread fell onto Edith's ears as the thin film of courage she had quickly evaporated into the air as he lips went tight and her eyes began to swell again. She squoze Annie's hand as she felt her legs shaking.

"Maybe there's another way out?" Annie routed. "If we find keys to one of the cars, I mean Hugo must have a garage or something right?" Claudia nodded.

"It's on the opposite end of the house though, and he keeps everything locked in the study in his safe."

"But you know the combination?" Claudia shook her head.

"The only people that have access are Hugo and John."

"Where is Hugo?" Annie's words fell onto a thick silence. Nobody dared break it, and that told each of them enough. "Look," Annie finally said. "We find Hugo and John, arm ourselves, and get to the study."

"Why won't the doors open?" Edith blurted. Claudia paced on the spot.

"It's a ridiculous system he's installed. I told him he should wait for them to work out the fine details first before buying it but no, he had to –"

"Why won't the fucking doors open, Claudia," Annie spat, patience growing thin. "I don't care about your marriage issues, I want to know how I can get out of here outside of a body bag." Claudia looked stunned, but then, continued.

"The house has a panic button in the study upstairs. Once its activated, the house goes into lock down, nobody goes in or out and you monitor the grounds from Hugo's computer. It sends out a message to the emergency services." She held her head in her hands. "Somebody must have pressed it when everything went to shit. It's supposed to keep people out. The cameras and the gates outside as warnings of something coming, so you can lock the place down before hand."

"So either John or Hugo has flipped the switch?" Edith said, clinging to Annie.

"Must have. I know I didn't." Claudia said.

"So the police are on the way?" Edith said, a hint of relief on her voice. Claudia nodded.

"If that's what's happened, then the police should be notified and be on their way."

"So," Annie said. "If we find John or Hugo, we can either reverse the system, grab some keys and get out of here, or the police get here first, and we let them in."

Claudia didn't look convinced. She was trembling, her humanity showing through her exterior of vanity and prowess. She was human after all, and she showed primal fear in her eyes. Annie tapped the knife on the counter, pondering their next move.

"Precious is dead," Claudia spoke, the words hitting a wall of silence that had befallen them.

"The blonde one?" Edith whispered, putting her hands to her gaping mouth. "Oh dear, oh no," she collapsed her hands on the counter behind her. "Oh, dear god no."

"How do you know this, Claudia?" Annie said. Claudia ran her hands through her hair, gripping it tightly at her crown.

"I don't know what happened. She attacked me upstairs. We were on the floor and she began to choke me. Then something, someone dragged her off me and I haven't seen her since. I just ran." Edith continued to sob whereas Annie's eyes narrowed. She raised the knife back to her.

"So, you didn't see what happened?" Claudia shook her head, her eyes closing tightly. "And you don't know who took her?"

"No," her voice meek.

"And you got away unharmed? The lady of the house, heir to the estate, the only real tie to Hugo, the focus of the gunman's rage? He let you live over a stranger? A stranger the gunman named in front of everyone?" Claudia opened her blood shot eyes and pressed her hands into her chest.

"Do you think I'm lying to you?" her voice now firm. "I was attacked and someone saved me, I didn't see who it was. Maybe it was John or Brian? I didn't stick around to find out." Annie drew closer to her, cautiously, the tip of the knife shining in the overhead spot lights.

"If it was one of them, they would have announced themselves to you, if it was the gun man, he would have surely shot you or shoved your face in. You're lying to me and I don't know why." Claudia's eyes began to dart around the room, breathing rapidly. Annie moved in to take hold of her, desperate to uncover the truth. Claudia stepped back and grabbed a cork screw off the counter which sat next to an array of empty bottles. She held it up to Annie, them both now separated by a large kitchen work surface that stood alone in the centre, over looked by hanging pots and pans that were shaking slowly.

"I had nothing to do with any of this, you bitch. I don't care if you believe me, but I am getting the fuck out of here with or without your help." Claudia threw the cork screw at Annie and she batted it away with the knife. It flew back and stuck into one of the surrounding cabinets with a 'Thunk'. She picked up a heavy pan from the hanging array in front of them and threw it at Annie who again just managed to dodge. It hit Edith in the knee and she heard it buckle and crack. She let out a large cry as she fell onto the ground, holding her bent knee with both hands, shouting wildly in agony. Annie rushed to her aid, then remembered the danger she was in, she picked up a handful of broken bottle shards from the floor and threw them at Claudia who was running from the kitchen. Some shards stuck into the door, some fell loosely on the ground, but two managed to stick her, one in her upper thigh and one in her upper shoulder. She cried out in pain and caught herself on the door frame as she lost her footing. Annie rushed over to her and pushed her into the open door, her body ricocheting back from the impact. Annie caught her mid fall and went at her with the knife. Annie fell atop of her, Claudia now gripping the knife with all her strength.

"You killed Precious. You're a murderer. I'm not going to let you take me and Edith too!" Annie hissed to her, mad with rage. Claudia writhed under her, her fight or flight engaged, she was of slim build but she mustered all of her strength and managed to push the knife away from her and twisted it in Annie's hand, releasing it, tossing it across into the hall. She grabbed Annie's hair, tearing out a small clump, and then bridged her back making Annie lose her posture. She isolated one of her legs and threw her onto the ground next to her. There, she scrambled across the ground to the discarded blade and took in into her hand. She turned on to her back and saw Annie was moving towards her. She slashed insanely at her, cutting through the air with swift, deadly strikes. Annie clumsily grabbed for the weapon, which Claudia sank it into her wrist and pulled the blade back out again. Annie shrieked and fell back pressing on the gash, thick blood spurting out onto her dress and face. Claudia stood above her, the knife dripping with red, it pooling beneath her.

"He'll come for you next, bitch. I'm getting out of here." Claudia ran further into the house under the archway of the stairs, ignoring the agony in her thigh, before disappearing. Annie lay there a moment and saw Edith at the kitchen opening, her knee had swollen to twice its size and was turning bright red and purple. Annie crawled to her feet, and held her wrist up above her head. She gave herself indirect pressure, pressing firmly on the artery that sat on the inside of her bicep below her arm pit. She moved past Edith and hastily looked through the cupboards and cabinets. There, she found a large kitchen towel and tied it around her arm in a make shift tourniquet. She gripped it with her teeth and secured the knot firmly. Then, she managed to find a small needle in a small sewing kit that sat under the sink in an opaque plastic tub. She pulled out a wooden spoon from a collection of utensils next to the oven, put it between her teeth and bit into it firmly. She roughly stitched her knife wound shut, rinsing it repeatedly with cold water which stung like acid was pouring onto her body. She let out a series of muffled screams as her teeth indented the wood of the spoon. She finished her stitching and tore off the loose fabric. The blood slowed and stopped, and she unclenched her jaw and the spoon fell onto the floor with a light rattle. She saw Edith standing watching her do the procedure, somewhat in awe, but mostly in shock. She couldn't believe what she had seen in Annie. The built-up rage and fire inside her had been released once again onto another, her desire to live and fight. Annie turned to Edith, her leg was shaking violently. Without speaking, she pulled out a stool and sat Edith onto it and she crouched looking at her knee. It didn't seem to be broken, just maybe some tendon damage or a ligament had torn. She wasn't out of the game yet. Her body would react with a lot of swelling in an attempt to barricade the wound from further harm. She would hurt like hell while walking, but she would live. Annie quickly rummaged further in the array of draws and cabinets that lined the kitchen, not trying to be quiet or cautious, their position surely now well known to the gun man. She found a small box of pain killers which were prescribed to Hugo and thrust a small handful of them to Edith.

"Take them," she said. Edith took them in her hand.

"What are they?" she asked, wincing through the pulsing agony of her knee.

"It's Oxycodone," She urged, like it mattered right now. "They're a strong Opiate. It will take the pain away until we can get you to a hospital." Edith wavered.

"I know what Oxycodone is, Annie." She pushed them back to her. "I won't take them, Annie." Annie flustered. She pushed them back to her.

"If you don't numb the pain fast, you're not going to be able to walk, and you'll either go into shock, or you'll get a bullet in between the eyes." Annie grabbed a glass of half drunken champagne from the counter and popped the pills into it. "Now take the damn painkillers." She spoke with a cold certainty, not giving a damn about how Edith felt about the drugs, her urge to get the both of them out of this house away from wrapped in a black body bag, taking priority over her feelings. Edith took the glass, the white bundles of numb fizzing in the amber liquid. She sank them back as the drugs entered into her. She gave the glass back to Annie.

"Done." She said, like a problem child that won't take their medicine from the doctor.

"There," Annie whispered. "That wasn't so hard was it?" Edith pursed a small smile, her eyes looking back at the open container of remaining pills on the counter.

"No. Not at all."

"Grab your things, we're leaving. We're going to find John, get those damn keys and get out of here." Edith nodded. She stood up, the strong pain killers already taking effect, and she managed to stop herself from collapsing. She knew she would have to take it easy, and hoped to god she didn't need to run.

Chapter Twelve.

Hydra.

Brian stared into the mirror of the en suite bathroom. His face was a mess of smeared blood and he was sure he was getting a black eye. The white sink basin was covered in blood and a huge stack of bloodied tissues lay discarded in a small waste bin to the side of the sink. He took out a fresh role of tissue paper, the blood now slowing. He rubbed and clogged his nose one final time. His shirt was surely ruined. He washed his hands in the en suite sink. The dried blood pooling in the basin as it disappeared in a gurgling down the drain. He went into the bedroom and opened up the wardrobe and took out a polo shirt from a hanger and squoze into it. It was tight around his neck and his arms, but it's all he could hope for at the minute. His nose throbbed painfully, and his mind raced even more. What had he done? His wife and his son. Was it all going to be over like that? And what of his career? His chances of becoming mayor? What would he say to the papers when they come knocking on his door, shoving cameras in his face and digging up every part of his dirty laundry. His heart picked up its pace. He would be ruined. He would be homeless and disgraced. He wouldn't see his son again, his little blonde boy who he had promised the world too. He wife would take him to the cleaners, as all his money would go on trying to salvage his reputation so he would be left penniless to fight for his assets in court. The worst part of it all, he knew Claudia would be sitting there in the back of the court room smiling at him as he was tore into pieces. She would be in the newspapers, slandering him. Telling everyone how he used her, how she was taken advantage of. Ima's past would be dug up and she would be dragged through hell and back again, having to relive all she went through over and over as it was slapped on the front pages of the national tabloids. His friends would abandon him, and all he had built up in his life would crumble and burn at his feet. What had he done to himself? What had he allowed himself to succumb too? He was so happy before he met her, before he met Hugo and Claudia snuck under his skin. He'd found himself extending his business trips so he could spend time with her. He took out assets and investments to buy her jewellery and fancy nights away. He had lied to his wife's face when she asked why he didn't take her to bed anymore, that he was just tired or stressed. Why he didn't take his son to the park as much, or why they didn't go out often as a family. It was because of him. It was because of her. He felt himself growing hot under the collar, as he paced around the room muttering to himself, cursing her, cursing every last hair on that bitches head. She knew what she was doing. She actually believed that this was forever? That he was going to leave and abandon everything for her? She was the villain here and he was the victim. But they wouldn't see it that way. Nobody, would see it that way. He saw his refection in the wardrobe mirror and punched his fist through it, it shattered and he saw the reflection of a broken man staring back at him. His true self now revealed, forgone the façade of a virtuous man of love and charity, but instead one of rage. He pulled free a piece of shattered glass and clenched it into his hand, his blood smudging across it as it bit into his palm and whitening fingers. Claudia did this to him. She tricked him. She caused this. He stared at the shard of glass. He would end it tonight, and Ima would never know the truth. The slut had to pay, and luckily for him, everyone had seen a mad man burst in with a gun, who was still tied and being held downstairs. He could take his gun, and failing that, he could stick the glass in Claudia's neck. He knew how the press reported things, so he knew how to make it look. He threw the bedroom door open as it bashed against the wall. He moved quickly, his footsteps loud. His eyes fixed on the end of the hallways. He remembered the way, looking into the oil paintings that gazed with deadeyes as he moved. He stopped. He saw a mess on the floor. He moved closer and crouched down. He picked up a scattered pile of photographs and he held back the urge to scream. They were of him and Claudia. Had she been planning this all along? Had she been aiming to blackmail him all this time? She must have had them with her all night, in her bag maybe. Then after their fight, she threw them on the ground either for him to see or someone else. Maybe Hugo had seen them, which was why they were scattered on the floor like this? Or maybe someone else had had a look through. Maybe there were more copies. Claudia was manipulative and definitely not stupid. She had left them here for a reason, and if Brian was going to blackmail someone, he wouldn't leave the only leverage he had unattended and out in the open. She must have more. He ripped the photos up into tiny pieces and then stuffed them under a small table. He would come back from them later, but for now he didn't want anyone else, not even him, looking at them again. He continued on, his footsteps meeting the carpets with a series of heavy thuds. He remembered the turns and twists of the hall and found his way to the foot of the stairs. He put the shard of broken glass in his beltline and covered it with the shirt. He looked down into the wide hall to the foot of the stone maiden. Hugo was gone, the gunman was nowhere to be seen and his blazer was strewn on the floor covered in still coagulating pools of dark thick crimson. Had he been too late? Had the ambulance arrived and taken him away already? Or had Hugo died and the gunman gotten loose and was walking the halls? Was Claudia alive? Were any of them still alive? His rage abated as he felt worry pass through him mixed with explosive paranoia. Was he being watched right now? Was he on the end of a barrels sight, the trigger about to be pulled? He hurriedly ran down the stairs and pulled on the front door. I rattled wildly but didn't open. He kicked it but still it didn't budge.

"Fuck," he cursed. He looked across the hallway, the maiden still holding a stone smile back at him. He saw that the kitchen was open and there was a small pool of blood on the floor and broken shards of a champagne bottle. He heard the faint muffle of footsteps, a slight shuffling of cautiousness, dragging the soles of their feet, like a wounded dear struggling across a country road after being hit by an oncoming car. He took cover behind the maiden and heard the sound grow louder. He saw two women from before, Annie? he remembered her name, and she was supporting the other woman Edith?. She was struggling to put pressure on one of her legs, and they were sinking further into the house, Annie struggling to support her as she held her up under her arm like a human crutch. Brian took another look around the room. No gunman in sight. No Claudia either. He moved from behind his cover. "Hey!" he called to them, as he ran to take Edith's arm.

#

John opened his eyes as he laid on the marble. He squinted hard as the burred ceiling came more into view. His head ached with pain and a strong pulsing ran from the front of his forehead to the back of his neck, and everywhere in between, like someone had cracked his head open and had stuck a pneumatic drill in there. The bright lights in the hall had become a dimmer shade of grey, and as hard as he tried to clear his vision, they continued to spread into their surroundings, like looking at them through smudged glass. He sat up and his head erupted again. He touched his forehead. He had a patch of dried blood there which stung when he ran his fingertips across it. How long had he been out? Was everyone okay? Where was the police? The ambulances? He wondered if he had been forgotten by the emergency crews and the remaining guests, or if he had been out for so long that none of them had made it out alive. But that raised another question: If Francis was still stalking the halls, why had he let him live? He took to his feet, momentarily losing his balance and caught himself on the maiden. He looked up at her, wanting to see her solemn smile looking down on him, telling him he would be okay. But instead of a stone face of warmth, he saw a distorted face of malevolence. Its smooth features were contorted and her eyebrows frowning down at him, and her smile, once loving and welcoming, was now stretched and her eyes wider. Her hands where she was holding herself, still remained at her waist, but now she had long protruding fingernails. He saw that the lush flower garden was dead, and withered black roses were meshed atop of themselves at her feet. He turned and found the blood stains on the floor now gone, and the hall was cast into an ash grey. He heard nothing, only silence accompanied by the beating of his own head, the drill speeding up in his temples. It reminded him of a crypt at twilight, a place of death and eternal rest, a tomb in not quite living, but not yet dead. He felt fear creeping into his stomach. He went to speak, but his voice uttered a shallow whimper, which echoed loudly and stretched out into the walls, which bended ached with the noise. He took a step, and then another. His black shoes tapping lightly on the stone below him. He moved to the staircase which now laid a dim red carpet, like the tongue of a dead dog. "This place," he whispered. "I've been here before," as he studied the twisting walls and the grey light, that in some harrowing nightmare he had indeed visited this place, and he had tried hard to forget about it ever since. He moved up the stair case, holding on to the rail. He felt a deep complement to continue upwards farther into the house. He moved onto the balcony and turned into the halls. They shifted and swayed as he walked, the portraits that hung on them contorted into sinister poses, leaning out of the canvas as if to grab him and drag him into them, their faces a pale grey, the animals turned to living bones. He heard a faint laughter moving through the house, and he felt icy finger tips crawl up his neck. He turned rigid, darting his head around as the laughter eluded him. Again, it came, but this time he saw a figure at the corner of the hall. He called out to it, "Hello?" The figure was dark like shadow, and it flitted in and out of sight while standing still. It was the phantom from earlier. Why was it here? Why had it followed him to this place? John did not feel the warmth he had felt when he felt when he encountered it earlier, if this was indeed the same apparition as before. He felt uneasy, he studied its body made of flitting black wire and it studied him back. It moved out of sight, further into the house. "Wait!" John shouted, the walls aching loudly. He ran clumsily along the hallways, the eyes in the paintings following him. He turned the corner and saw it fading again around another turn. He continued to pursue it, demanding answers from it. To tell him the fate of the others and if it had taken them too. He turned and saw it disappear into a room as he heard the door slam closed. He stopped and took hold of the handle but paused as he heard the faint floating of classical music come from inside. His breath caught in his throat. He opened the door slowly. The room elicited a bright and warm glow, it was not of dullness and blurred like the rest of the house, but it was how he had prepared it earlier. The bed was nicely made and the bed side lamps where lit inviting him inside. He saw a small record player in the corner spinning a black vinyl. He stepped inside and closed the door, A figure sitting on the corner chair, its face concealed as it read a large book. "Divine Comedy," By Dante Aligheri.

"All hope abandon, ye who enter here," it said, its voice broad, harsh on the vowels, almost grainy and broken, like one who has smoked too many cigarettes.

"Who are you?" John spoke, his voice quiet like a trembling mouse. It turned a page.

"Quite fitting under the circumstances, don't you think? Or how about this one, "There is no greater sorrow than to recall happiness in times of misery."" John took a step forward. It continued to speak. "Midway upon the journey of our life, I found myself within the forest dark, for the straightforward pathway had been lost."

"Who are you?" John said again, more firmly. His wonder disappearing and impatience taking its place. He stopped. "What are you? Where am I? What the hell am I doing here?" It uttered a low laughter.

"Hell," it whispered, "Is an illusion of mortal men, one subjects of hell is different to another's, and one punishment for all doesn't seem quite right, does it? This is why I love this book, it takes every sin, every blight and act of treason, and casts them all into its own circle." He moved closer, hand outstretched. The figure wore black, a tight suit. Its hands under white gloves, gripping the book as it sat lowly into the chair. "If you are blind, then you cannot see, deaf, you can never hear the sounds of your screaming, but pain. Yes, even when you have all of your flesh stripped from your bones, your brain will still give you agony, like an amputee gets a phantom scratch it can never suffice." John tore the book away from the figure and dropped it to the ground where it laid open, the divine text looking back up to his harrowed face. It was him. He was looking at himself, looking the same as he did this morning, but he appeared colder, firmer, harder. It crossed its gloved fingers within themselves and crossed its legs.

"It can't be?" He said, as he moved backwards only to be met by the firm wall behind him. He reached for the door but it had gone. The figure spoke.

"You looked astounded, Johnathon?" it said.

I'm dreaming. I have to be." John said, slamming his eyes shut and then opening them again to the creature still with him.

"I can assure you, Johnathon," it said, "You are not dreaming." It let out a low rumbling laughter.

"Who are you?" John said, his body trembling. It parted it hands.

"Isn't that obvious? I am you. Or at least part of you." It stood up and walked to him. John moved away towards the spinning music disk, like a creature of death was encroaching on him.

"No, no, it cannot be." John ripped the vinyl out from the player silencing the music with a sickening scratch. He held it up to warn the creature away. It laughed.

"John, you have never been one to fight. To defend yourself, you stick up for yourself. Hence why I am here. Hence why you created.... Me." It took a bow, almost mocking him. "I have been with you always, Johnathon, I am you and you are me. We've been brothers since the womb." It waved its hand to John, like it was about to perform a magic trick. "I was there when you first met Hugo, in Scotland. I was scratching behind your eyes while you busked in Edinburgh square. I was there screaming in your skull when he offered you a job, and I was there burrowing in your brain when you singed your life away on his work contract. You were weak, and it seems like every part of assertion, anger and strength you had, was pushed deep down into your mind as you openly bent forward and let him fuck you over and over. You had dreams that you have forgotten. You took shitty job after shitty job, working all hours and being treated sub humanly from that man, every shit filled toilet, every beating, every humiliation. You took it all, and pushed all of your resentment backwards. While Hugo made you weaker, I grew stronger. I was there when you first thought of getting revenge. You and Catherine, getting revenge on him." John cocked his head.

"How do you know about Catherine?" he croaked. The beast smiled wildly.

"I know everything about you, John. I am older than time itself. When mankind was crawling from the mud and finding its feet, I was there when Cain bashed Abel's head in. The blade that cut Caesar, and in the hearts of all men that wish to do harm." It tapped its head. "I was there with you when you looked into his computer. I was whispering in your ear when you selected orders from Francis' company. I guided your fingers while you locked all the windows and doors." It leaned in closer, took the black disk from Johns and threw it away from him. "And I was there with you when you murdered Hugo." John began to whimper.

"You're lying," he cried out. "I couldn't do all that! I don't know how to work computers, make orders! I haven't killed anyone! I haven't done this so stop lying right now!" his voice was harsh, like a spouse wrongly accused of cheating as their significant other packs their belongings into black bin bags and tosses them into the rain. The creature moved closer to him as John began to cry into his hands. It whispered in his ear. It's breath smelling like dried blood.

"I'll show you what you have done." It gripped John's head with its gloved hands. He felt a surge of screams and rupturing his vessels through his head. His eyes turned white and mouth fell agape, as the creature laughed maniacally, as the acts flashed before his eyes. He was in the study, crying on the floor. His head was hot and his body ached. He saw red on his hands and tears falling from his cheeks. He could hear the sound of shouting, and turned to see Hugo moving away from him rolling down his sleeves. He lay on the carpet and sobbed, holding himself as he curled into a ball. He felt the brush of fingernails on his face, caressing him like a caring mother. He looked up and saw the fire place in front of him. The eyes of the wooden angels and devils boring into his. Whispers. Whispers in his mind. He touched the base of the mantle, and he remembers screaming. He was on a large golf course, the sun was warm and the lush grass that had been freshly cut. He saw Hugo sitting in his golf cart far away, and Brian and Claudia in the cab behind him, his hand on her inside upper thigh. He felt a heavy metal object in his hand and he lifted it and captured their affair through its lens. The scene pushed itself into another, a dimly lit hotel room while Claudia rode atop of Brian. It twisted more, he was in the house now, speaking to himself in the guest room. He had been talking about the system, how it was to be exploited, how he could trap them all inside. He closed the door as Hugo approached him and he threw his comments off. He thrust open the door to see a well-made room, his spectre only visible to him as it sat in the arm chair smiling back to him. He went to the study, to work on Hugo's computer, as he saw the dying embers of the fire, him tapping in the codes on the lines of binary, to exploit its flaws, and to seal it tight from the outside world when the time was right. He saw himself in the kitchen while he prepared champagne and when Hugo and Claudia declared they were going to be parents, and as the crowd cheered, he tipped the strychnine in the bottles of champagne and over the food. He saw himself fall onto the ground next to the maiden, the champagne smashing on the stone. Hugo beating him, his face red with pain, the beast watching him in the corner of the hall. Again as he moved silently pouring poisoned drinks. He cried out again, as the last scene came more vividly into his mind, pushing away what little strand of absolvent he could wish to have. He saw himself after Hugo had been shot, his feeling of fear and adrenalin returned to him.

"Go get a first aid kit, there's one in the bedroom," he called to Brian, who blurred up the stairs away from him. He called to Claudia to help him, his voice stretching out and her face like a melted oil painting. He looked again into Hugo's eyes, they were black as coal as he saw thick branches crawl from out the ground and wrap him in John's arms. John whispering to him, the light around Hugo fading as the branches coiled under his body.

"You have always been a good friend to me, John," Hugo stretched. His features were like through dirtied glass.

"You're the reason I'm here in the first place," John said to him. He held his gaze, as he fell into his darkness. He saw the beast in him, and as he turned to look around the hall, the room was silent and still, the lights dim and a sinister macabre fell over him. He saw himself. He saw him move to him, fall into him, and rage fill his body like a forgotten lover. He felt stronger, braver. He felt like a fool that had been ridiculed too long, like one awakens from a bad dream where they were laughed at by all around them, to awaken and want vengeance on all those who taunted and teased him. The beast was a welcomed friend. It was like watching the replay of a forgotten dream, and for the first in a long time, John felt clarity like nothing before, like a fish that slips into crystal clear water, after a life time in the murky sewer. He remembered the hurried calls and cries from upstairs, hoping an ambulance would come from the phone call John had never made. He smiled warmly at Hugo, and then his face turned to stone, and leaned into him. Taking the pressure off his wound and letting the life drain out of him again. Hugo let out a gasp. He whispered in his ear. Remembering the fights with lawyers to be set free, and all the pain that had been brought with it. "You're the reason I could never leave." He began to choke Hugo. His face turning swollen and red. His eyes bulging and his tongue falling out of his mouth like a wet sack. His legs thrashing on the floor, his shoes skidding across the marble. John heard the crack of his windpipe and Hugo fell limp, his dead eyes looking into empty space. John looked at him and saw the beast next to him, nodding its head slowly.

"Vengeance," it whispered in his mind, "Comes to us all." John looked at the beast's hands and saw them to be dripping with blood, as were his own. John looked back to the beast, but it was gone. The room returned to normal, his fractured self now whole. He saw Francis cowering in the corner. John walked towards him. Francis began to cry. He knelt to him and pressed a finger on his lips.

"Shhhhhhh," he hissed. Francis looked at John, like the way a small child stares in terror when he finally sees the boogie man. John spoke in a voice that was not his own, hard on the vowels, grainy like he had smoked too many cigarettes. He wrapped his hands around Francis' throat, who struggled and gargled until the life left his eyes, the last thing he saw was the beasts harrowing face staring back at him.

#

John fell to the floor as the beast released him. His breath shallow, his body drenched. His mind much less clouded than before. The beast looked down to him. It took out a Glock from its belt line and handed it to him.

"I didn't do this. I didn't want this," John said, weeping onto his lap. The beast knelt before him. It's eyes now solid black, its mouth stretching cased in thin pail lips.

"But you did," it hissed. "You called for me. You asked for my help long before you knew you wanted it. And now I am here. Let me help you, John." The way it said his name made his heart break, like everything he had ever wanted he could have. He could have his freedom.

"You aren't real." He whispered. The beast rumbled a low laughter, and it ran its long fingernails down John's face.

"I am as real as hell itself." The beast said. "And you called me here. You remember the fire place?" John held the monsters black gaze, and he remembered being in the study earlier in the night, hearing its whispers as he closed the dying flames under the fire. He remembered studying the wooden cut outs of tortured souls, and how he had heard the beast talking to him. He remembered seeing him again in the shadows of the guest rooms. He remembered the scars, the bruises and the beatings. And he remembered his pain, and the beast drank it.

"Don't you want Catherine again?" John slammed his eyes shut. The mention of her name opened an old wound that had been covered in flaking bandages. He savoured her name, like cradling barbed wire.

"What do I have to do?" John said after a moment, looking at the gun. "Do you want my soul?" The creature flung its head back. Its gaping jaws a hellish abyss as it roared a bone chilling laughter that warped the walls and creaked the ground.

"Your soul was sold long ago," it whispered. "But you can feed me more." John dropped his head as he sat on his knees, his hair falling onto his face. He felt the nails run through his hair. He felt warm breath on his face. He felt the fear and pain fade like melting snow, kissed by warm spring sun over a meadow. He saw her, just the way he had seen her on that day. The rumbling of the engine next to them and the bustling street in the background as he said good bye to her. She moved into him and kissed his lips, and they held each other for a lifetime in a moment. He didn't feel her skin grow cold and black. He didn't hear his screams as eels pulled from the ground and popped though his skin and bones. He couldn't feel his fingertips as he adjusted his cuffs. He looked in the mirror, watching behind his own eyes as the beast stared back at him in the bathroom mirror, its teeth bared and its jaw hanging low.

Chapter Thirteen.

Heresy.

"Hey!" Brian whispered, unsure of who or what was lurking within earshot. Annie felt alarmed and turned, brandishing the knife at him. Brian stopped and held his hands up, staring on the knife. "I'm not going to hurt you. What happened?" Edith winced in pain as Annie studied him cautiously. Where had he appeared from?

"Claudia," Edith winced with pain, holding on to Annie's shoulder. The pain killers were working, but were not quite there just yet, but they had to move. They couldn't afford to sit around waiting for the pain to fully abate. Brian heard Claudia's name and his body went tort. He noticed the half open wound on Annie's wrist.

"She did this to you?" Brian asked, pointing to the gash. Annie lowered the knife and looked at her wound.

"I fixed it. But yeah, she did this. I think she killed Precious. She came out with some bullshit then attacked me and Edith, when I called her out on it."

Brian didn't know what to say. He didn't think Claudia was capable of such a thing, but then again, it seemed she was capable of anything. He saw Annie struggling to hold Edith under her petite frame and he quickly took himself under Edith's free arm.

"Thanks," Annie said, letting out a deep breath.

"Where's Claudia now?" he asked.

"I don't know," Annie said. "She said there are car keys in the study

somewhere but only John and Hugo know the code to get into it."
"Where is Hugo? Did an ambulance come?" Annie shook her head.
"We haven't heard anything." Brian looked around the hall, seeing the smeared blood on the floor, and his jacket strewn near the front door. "Then where is he?" he looked around, studying the halls and the landing above him. "And where is the gunman?"
"I don't know." Annie whispered. Edith began to sob silently again.
"It hurts…" The two of them carried Edith through the arch way to the study where Hugo and Brian had sat having a cigar and a whisky, and talked about business. Brian wanted to talk about more, but wasn't able to bring himself to do it. As they walked into the dimly lit room, a single lamp illuminating a small portion, they heard the faint sound of a piano playing. Not a recording with crackles and levels, but a real piano. The sounds were defined, rhythmic. They saw a spectre dressed in black sitting on a dark stool facing away from them in front of the piano in the corner of the room. It pressed the keys and they watched silently, unseen by the spectre, as it appeared lost in a melody of macabre and melancholy, smoothly pressing its white gloves over the ivory of white and black, hitting the sharps and flats and stringing together a treble cleft in common time, while accompanying its bass clef in a three four, like a twisted waltz for the dead. Edith recognised it as the first movement of Beethoven moonlight sonata, and it hypnotised her for a moment, suspending her worry and fear and transporting her to another place of love and contentment as the soft notes filled the air. It was John. He sat there, his body flowing with the keys as he played, his long dark hair tied back.
"At last." he spoke. His Scottish accent no longer apparent, instead it sounded deeper, more defined and dark. "Like flies flock to the decomposing sack of meat, our brave wanders crawl forth into the darkness by the sound of soft music." He didn't turn to look at them. He appeared in a trance with the music. "I haven't played in so long," he said, "but it's just like riding a bike. Muscle memory. Hugo never let me play the piano so I never did. But now, I have all the time I like to practice again." He slid up the keys and began to increase the rhythm of the song, the pianos powerful tone echoing into the still room, as the three of them watched him mesmerised. Brian let go of Edith and Annie took up the extra weight again. He walked towards him.
"John," he croaked. "Where is Hugo? Have the medics come for him? Where is the gunman?"

"Music is such a strange thing, isn't it?" John whispered. "Why does it feel so warm to us? Why does it want to make us make love, get ready to fight or evoke such emotion into our hearts?" He stopped playing and looked at Brian. He looked the same but he was not the same man. He appeared, different, and Brian felt afraid. John stood up and Brian moved back a step. The large fire place was burning and it crackled into the quiet. "I wasn't able to get through to the emergency services sadly. Francis' mobile phone had no service." Brian cocked his head.

"But I heard you? I heard you on the phone to them? You called for an ambulance for Hugo?" John shook his head. "Then we can use my cell phone? We can get them out of the safe and call for help. We can even get some car keys, use my car outside and we can get out of here. Drive to a police station, tell them what has happened." Brian gabbled, becoming more animated. John stood unmoved, his eyes giving a steady glare into Brian's eyes. Brian began to feel nauseous again, much stronger this time.

"I don't think that's a good idea," John said. Brian's mind's wrecked.

"What? It's not a good idea? John, what's gotten into you? Where is Hugo!" he was shouting now, the stress gripping his throat. "Tell me what's going on right now."

"You really want the police digging into all of this? Digging into everyone's past? Everyone's secrets?" This last syllable slithered out of John's mouth as his face turned hard and lips widened into a crooked grin, teeth bared, the glow from the fire dancing on his face.

"What's he talking about?" Edith barked. "What's he saying?" she was sitting on a small couch now caressing her bruised knee. Annie stood opposite, unsure whether to run, looking over her shoulder into the entrance hall, the maiden growing huge hellish black wings and stretching out skeletal arms with daggers for fingers, and then back to normal again. Brian slowly slithered the glass shard from under his cuff, feeling much more on guard than he had before. John looked at his sleeve, the small protruding glass reflecting the dancing yellow and reds.

"I know all of your secrets," John hissed, stepping to Brian. "I know all of your sins." Brian felt hot, the feeling of nausea nearly making him buckle over and crack in two. "How was your food? Did you enjoy the drinks?" Brian's stomach plunged as a feeling of dread came through him. He turned to Annie and Edith, both of their eyes red and jaws dropped in horror.

"What have you done?" Brian whispered. John laughed, his mouth stretching wide and black.
"I added something. But don't worry. That's the least of your concern right now. It's already too late for everyone else. But you, Brian," He gestured to him, like a magician about to perform his biggest trick yet. "I have something better for you." John moved his hand towards the fire place. Brian followed it and he saw a small bag burning on the fire, unseen before. He looked closer, squinting his eyes through the millions of dancing fingers that wrapped and caressed the brown sack in blue and yellow flames. It was their phones and car keys, and he vomited on to the ground.
"What have you done?" Brian cried. "What have you done!" Brian brandished the glass shard, moving towards John quickly, rage gripping his heart. John pulled out the Glock from his belt line and pointed it to Brian's chest. He froze like a badger caught in the headlight of an HGV.
"Whoa.." he rebuked. Edith held her mouth in terror. Annie's eyes flitted to the large bronze lamp to the right of her on a small table, her legs like coiled springs. The pair studied each other. John's eyes boring into Brian. Brian's eyes staring into the black barrel.
"Did you find my photos?" It took Brian a second to think what he meant, him unable to think of anything other than the gun pointing at him. Then he remembered the bundle he found in the corridor.
"You took them?" John tapped his nose.
"I don't kiss and tell." He let out a low laugh. "One thing I will say to you," he ran his hand through his hair, cool and calm. "Everyone in the world will now what you are really like Mayor Callahan. They weren't the only copies and by the morning, the papers will know and so will your wife."
"What have you done?" Brian croaked, eyes now bleeding tears.
"Congratulations," John hissed. "You're going to be your paper's biggest cover story yet." Brian saw John's eyes turn black. "Abandon all hope, ye who enter here." He emptied two rounds in Brian's chest. He flew back and hit the ground hard. The sound of the gun shattered through the silence, galloping through the house on hooves made of death. The bullets cut straight through him and exploded the lamp, casting the room into a hellish black, the light from the fire casting wicked morphing shadows onto John, as it bared great wings and tall horns. Edith screamed and covered herself and Annie stood there

motionless, eyes wide and nailed to the spot. Her ears ringing. Brian laid on the floor coughing and spluttering thick red blood that now leaked down his neck and mixed with the large pool on the floor beneath him, its red soaking into the carpet. John stalked over him. Brian held up his hand, begging for mercy, the glass shard laid to his side.

"The mind sees what it wants to see, and you are no different. You see a vulnerable house with a wife yearning for better, you see a messed up blonde girl aching at the feet of a mighty man, you see a mad man racked with vengeance in his eyes, and you see me, withering and writhing under the feet of giants, not seeing me tie the rope around their feet to pull them down." John reached down into Brian's trouser pocket and pulled out a small set of car keys, with the word "Bentley" on the side. "Tell me Mr. Callahan, what should I do with your car once you die?" and threw them into the fire which ate them hungrily. The fire roared, burning with hellish ferocity. Brian's vision dipped in and out of focus as he tried to cling on to the land of the living. Annie followed this, the ringing in her ears faded, now replaced by the gargling of Brian's death thrall, and the whimpering of Edith as she shook with fear.

"Claudia is pregnant," Brian coughed. "We're going to have a child." Annie's honed into this. The buried scream creeping out in a low whimper. She was so confused. Maybe Precious had attacked Claudia upstairs? Annie felt sick that she had thrown her calls for help back into her face. It made her remember her own situation, her own past, when all she wanted was someone to help and no one would listen to her, and she had done the exact same thing to Claudia in her time of need.

"You didn't care for your own child," said John. "And you don't care for this one. You want me to let you go so you can make amends? No. It doesn't work like that. You had your chance." John smiled. It was long and filled and a flicker of black crept into his eyes like ink poured on still water. "I do the laundry remember. So consider it a lucky escape." John winked. Annie saw a pile of items in the fire, a set of car keys, a mobile phone, then another and then another, all burning and cracking in the heat. She felt claustrophobic, but managed to supress the burgeoning scream in her chest. "Hugo was never very good at keeping things locked away. Ironically he installed a security system built that was designed to imprison rather than keep its occupants safe from harm. At least if you know how to move data and code around anyway. When you and Hugo were out golfing, while you were fucking his wife."

"She was lying, wasn't she?" Brian heaved. "You knew all along and you let her break me." John laughed.

"It doesn't really matter anymore, does it?" Brian's breath went shallower.

"You bastard, how could you do this? What have I ever done to you?" Brian coughed. "What have any of us done to you?" John again laughed at Brian.

"John, you don't have to do this," Annie called. "If you let us go, then, then we can forget about this. Forget all of this. Hugo was a despicable man who has trampled all over everyone he knew." she moved closer. Edith tried to grab her dress, like a protective parent does when they see their child wanting to stroke a rabid dog.

"You must have been treated the worst of all, and the fact that you never left him, must mean he had a tighter hold on you than anyone else." Annie drew towards him, hands facing John. For a second, the black moved from John's eyes. But again it fell back into them, and pointed the pistol at her.

"Nice try." he said. He reached into his jacket and pulled out a small vile. The word "Strychnine," written in bold under a skull and crossbones. "You have drank a considerable amount of this since you got here." He waved the bottle at her, tutting like she was a misbehaved child. Annie felt hot. Her feeling of shock and nausea now mixing with a feeling of dread, like her insides were rotten. She realised she was sweating heavily, and her heart was racing. "You framed him? You planned all of this!" Edith called through her tears. "It was you! You ruined that poor man's life!" John again laughed.

"I also discovered a lot about you Ms. Edith McGrath. Did your boy really die so tragically in the pond?" Brian coughed loudly on the floor and John saw he was trying to crawl away from them. John moved over to him, knelt down and gripped his head, pulling him back with the barrel pressed into the back of his skull. Brian yelped with pain. Annie moved closer to him, seeing her chance but John span the gun around and pointed it dead at her. "You're all filth. All of you. Mr. Hugo got the biggest dose, and he would have died slowly if Francis hadn't have shot him. You're all murderers. Fraudsters. You have all wasted your life pursuing shit." He looked back down to Brian. "Now

Callahan, lie there and die." John pulled back the hammer of the pistol. Annie, in a sudden surge of courage in the face of death, ran to him and grabbed the back of his hair and pulled back with all she had. John let out a scream of pain and Brian with his last might of strength, grabbed the glass shard and swung with it wildly, narrowly missing John and nearly cutting Annie's throat. John kicked out to Annie, catching her in her stomach, knocking the wind out of her. He stood up and emptied another round into Brian's back, and he fell limp on the ground. The gun shot screaming into their ears again. Annie lay crumpled on the ground, pushing herself away from John as he drew closer to her. He raised the pistol to take another shot. Edith screamed at him and lunged up from her withering state and threw herself into John. The gun let off a round as they both fell into the mouth of the fire place, like the inferno of hell was trying to drag them both into its immolation. Edith thrashed at him, her gloves catching fire as she struck him. He screamed wildly and went to shoot her but in the frenzy, he missed. He buried the gun butt into her face as she fell backwards in an explosion of blood and fire. Annie quickly threw herself onto her, patting down the flames before they managed to consume her. John thrashed wildly, taken over by the fire. He threw himself onto the floor, howling in agony as thousands of tiny fingers licked his suit, hair and face.

"Can you run?" Annie shouted. Edith nodded, her face black with smeared coal. "Then move!" Annie and Edith ran from the hall, John's screams following closely behind them, which had now turned to chaotic laughter, bellowing out into the house, chasing them as they ran into the hall and raced up the stairs thrusting themselves into one of the guest rooms before slamming the door behind them.

Chapter Fourteen.

Mutatis Mutandis

Four Years Earlier.

John Bachman woke up with his third hangover this week. He knew he needed to stop drinking after his shows in the city, the Edinburgh music festival "Performer," badge still around his neck. But when everyone pays for your drinks after you had finished your set, it was rude to say no. You never knew when the person you refused a line of coke from, was your ticket to that all-time record deal. So for now he was an open vessel to be abused by chemicals and amphetamine. He scanned the room through his one half opened eye, the morning sun too much to fully commit too. He reached to grab a glass of water he kept by his bed, but instead his fingers felt lacey fabric. He squinted as he saw he was holding a bright pink thong, and behind that, a giant poster of The Smiths. After realising he hadn't gone insane and become a Smith's fan, and his taste in underwear hadn't suddenly changed, he realised he wasn't in his studio flat. He saw his acoustic guitar propped up against the cracked white dry wall on the opposite end of the tiny room, next to a closed door that hung a photo of some band he had never heard of, above a pile of ruffled clothes and a half-eaten box of pizza, empty beer cans and bottles stacked in a leaning tower. The bed was itching him, and he realised he was naked. He heard soft breathing coming from next to him and noticed tucked under the thick duvet was a brunette woman. Her skin was light and

smooth. Her shoulders and back pointed in a 'V' shape, and John knew that she clearly worked out. He tried to place her name, hell even to remember her face would be a bonus right now through his haze. He ran his hand down her body, hoping they had already passed the 'holding hands,' stage. Her skin was lightly freckled, and he traced the outline of her back and ran his hands down to her buttocks, tracing over them like they were an exotic fruit, then down her legs and back up again. She stirred and she turned around and nestled her face into his bare chest. He felt a pulse of electricity through his skin. Whatever he had said to her to get her into bed, or as it were, she get him into bed, seeing that he wasn't at home, he hoped he could capture it again and make a love song from it. She was way out of his league, and he savoured every part of it. He ran his hands through her waving hair that was like silk and he glided his digits through with ease, like brushing his hand through fine mist. She wasn't wearing makeup, and she was still the most beautiful woman he had ever seen in his life. She opened her eyes and they were deep green. John thought maybe she was from South America, maybe Latino or Brazilian. He wasn't sure.
"Morning," he said, as he kissed her forehead. She reached up to him and kissed him on his lips, the faint smell of cigarettes on her breath, slightly more dominant smell of pizza and beer on his.
"It's afternoon actually," Her accent was eloquent, floating. She was English alright. John wanted to ask her why he was here or what had happened last night, however considering that he couldn't even remember her name, he thought this to be a little rude. He remembered he had a spot booked in the city centre in this evening, where he would play for commuters near the gardens on their way to and from work. It was his favourite spot, where the attention was plenty full, and people finishing a hard day at work could unwind and listen to him play while they threw money in his guitar case and got a coffee from the local bistros.
"What time is it exactly?" he asked. She kissed him again.
"Do you have to go?" He was going to say yes, but seeing the deep yellow of the sinking sun through the bedroom blinds kissing her body, making it outlined in gold, he shook his head and moved towards her. They made love together then, it was like a harmony of bodies perfecting a dance practiced for a millennia. He didn't know this woman, but he felt like he had always known her. He didn't believe at love at first sight, but he felt like he had been with her in another life,

in another form, and they had been brought together by fate, destiny or whatever else you might call it. She knew his body and he knew hers, He made her quiver and tremble in bliss and she to him. They lay there afterwards, the bedsheets soaked in hot sweat. She traced his chest with her fingers and laughed. "I still can't believe you shave your chest. It's so strange." John giggled. It wasn't the first time he had heard this, but he was led to believe that it's what women liked, and since doing it he had never heard anyone say that they did. He kissed her again.
"It irritates me. It's easier to manage this way."
"You look ten."
"Does that mean you're a kid fucker then?" he said boldly, his dark humour testing the waters. She laughed at him and smiled.
"It means you need to man up and get some chest hair. Or if you rather I can borrow you one of my lady razors, seeing as you are intent on fighting your genetics." John laughed again. He stood up, his naked body standing still firm. His tight chest and shredded abs showing themselves off to his new playmate. He half stretched, half flexed his body, showing her that he too works out. She sat up, her breasts revealed atop of the duvet. She reached into her black hand bag next to the bed and pulled out a cigarette and began to smoke. "You know, you would look pretty hot if you weren't standing in your own puke." John looked confused at her and she pointed to his feet. There he saw he had stepped into a cold pile of vomit, filled with booze and half eaten pizza toppings. "You should really chew your food," she mocked.
"Fuck sake," he cried. He stepped out of the cold bile and moved onto the carpet, spreading the mess that was stuck to his foot and between his toes. "I'm never drinking again, I'm so sorry." She blew out a blue cloud of smoke to him.
"We've all said that before." she pointed to the door. "Showers through there to the left. I'll be with you in a minute."

#

John dried himself off as the girl stepped out of the shower with him and they shared the same towel, taking turns doing each other's backs and behinds. They walked into her bedroom and she pulled out some fresh clothes from a small wardrobe, him putting on last night's underwear and shorts. "I suppose you have to leave for your slot now, right, John?" He finished getting dressed, again embarrassed he couldn't remember her name.

"Yeah, hopefully I'll do well today. Come watch me?" She smiled, still half naked.

"I can't sorry. I'm working late then I have to prep for an exam tomorrow." John remembered she had mentioned this to him last night, flashbacks occasionally coming to him in a slide show of booze and dizzy heads. He remembered seeing her pull out her driver's license to prove her age to a barman, and it said 'Jessica Milby.' Her name, finally. Jessica. Maybe. John felt like he was trying to remember a song he had heard once on the radio when he was four. She was at the university, but he didn't know what she studied. Mid-twenties, managing to afford a small house on the outskirts of Edinburgh with part timework at one of the Baristas on the gardens where he played.

"I could come by later on, when I've finished my set?" he pressed. She put a coat on and handed him his, a black leatherjacket that was coming apart at the seams. She didn't answer him. She picked up her bag and stood there waiting for him to pack up his stuff and leave the house with her. They walked into the cool autumn air, her shutting the door behind them. She lived on a row of terrace houses directly outside a main highway that ran through the city, black cabs and people in duffel coats moved through the busy air. It was already dark, John figured it to be about six in the evening. He checked his phone and saw him to be right.

"I thought you said you lived on the outskirts? This seems near the centre?" He asked as they walked.

"I do," she said, looking at the ground. "That wasn't my place, it's my friends. He's away for a week."

"Does he know you're staying there?" she looked at him, her green eyes hypnotising him.

"Do you care?" John stopped as she continued to walk, confused and intrigued all the same. He caught up to her.

"Can I see you again? I had so much fun. Can I give you my number Jessica? I could play for you again, one to one this time and not as part of a show? I mean, I would love too, only if you wanted too, though. I think we should see each other again, or I could still come by tonight and help you study? Maybe I could test you for your exam? Or I could show you how to play guitar? Do you like piano? I can play piano. I learnt when I was a kid. I tried the violin but that was too tough. It

doesn't have frets you see, so it's all about the ear. I have a good musical ear, but. I'm rambling aren't I?" She shot him a look through the corner of her eye. "I'm sorry, Jessica." He said, heart beating like a jackhammer, his throat like a vice. She laughed. That sound. It made the hammer stop and the vice loosen, and his legs felt like warm jelly.
"I'll see you around, I work at the bistro next to where you play. Don't sweat it, I'll see you again soon." John wanted to step over a grid and let his jelly legs make him fall through the cracks. He had blown it. He felt like Hansel and Gretel lost in the woods, and she was giving him breadcrumbs to keep him on her path, hoping it led him back to her and not into the witch's oven. "This is you," She said. She stopped under a black street lamp, which glowed a soft white onto the cobbled ground. They had walked a couple of miles deeper into the city; he was where he needed to be and he felt like he had floated there.
"I'll see you around, Jessica." he said. He smiled at her and she didn't return one, he felt like he had blown it, his desperation for her attention had messed up his chances of seeing her again. He doubted she even worked around here, and that it was just a soft way to let him down. He turned to walk towards the gardens, his heart heavy, and his guitar pressing down on his shoulders.
"Hey," she said. He turned and she pulled him towards her. She was around six feet tall and didn't need to move much to reach him. She kissed him hard and took his hand. He felt endorphins riding lightning chariots stampede through him and he had to anchor himself to the ground to stop him floating away. She moved away from him. "Come by, tonight." she said smiling. "My address is on there and my number." John looked at the piece of paper she had slipped into his hand. His brow furrowed and he flitted his eyes back to her. "Jessica is my sister's name. We look alike and I took her ID." She blew him a kiss and moved away into the busy streets and gave him a small wave. He watched her go before she disappeared in the milling of bodies. He looked again at the paper, made a note of the address and typed the number carefully into his phone.
'CATHERINE.'

#

That night he played the best set of his life. He sang with a crisp tone which was envied by on lookers, his guitar singing perfectly blended chords that flowed into the night air. Passers-by gathered until there was a crowd around him around six or seven rows deep, like he was a rare attraction that you just had to stop and see. He counted his earnings when he was done and he had made easily over five hundred. He was amazed with himself, and ecstatic at how well he had performed. His fingers that would normally be numb, now tingled with electricity. He packed away his mic and guitar and was going to set out home, when he was approached by a large man wearing a plethora of thick jewellery. He outstretched his hand.

"Good show," he said. John looked up at him. He was middle aged and had sparking white teeth which were clearly fake. He wore a grey shirt which was cut finely to his shape, showing off his sagging muscles. He had a brown leather jacket with a fur lined collar, and John thought he looked a bit like a world war one fighter pilot.

"Thanks," John said.

"Looks like you've earned a good number tonight," the man said, pointing to his money. John studied the man and his body went tort. He had been robbed before. The man laughed, almost like sensing a cute dog that was about to bear its teeth. He held his hands up. "Hey, it's not like that. What's your name?"

"John Bachman." He closed his guitar case and placed the money into his jacket.

"Hugo Black," he said, again holding out his hand. John took it and squeezed it firmly, holding Hugo's gaze, showing he was not one to be fucked with. "John, how about we go for a drink. I would like to know more about what you do."

"Look man if you're looking for someone to fuck, I'm not interested."

Hugo laughed again loudly, his belly bouncing up and down like a five-year-old on his new space hopper.

"No, god no! A young man like you has talent, and is trying to make a name for yourself, am I correct?" John nodded cautiously. It didn't take a genius to figure out he was tired of playing to passers-by in the street, hoping they would stop and listen to him. "So then, let's talk. Just a coffee, that's all I ask. We can go to one you choose." John scanned around the square, and he saw the small bistro where Catherine had said she worked. She should be working tonight too. He could go there. Don't refuse an offer by someone, just go with it. This could be your big break remember? He pointed to it and Hugo smiled. "Fine choice, John. Let's go." They walked across the square together, exchanging awkward small talk. John didn't say much, he was still trying to weigh Hugo up. The way he walked, the way he spoke, and the clothing and jewellery alone he was wearing was probably worth more than John would ever see in a single lifetime. Hugo said he was in town on business, finalising a new pharmacy chain with an up and coming entrepreneur couple that lived in the midlands and had some other business things to attend too. John quickly switched off. His business was music, not spreadsheets and tax loop holes. They entered the warm Bistro and sat down at a small corner table. The place was quiet, intimate. Plastic menus boasted a range of food from paninis to designer cub cakes, and the air was filled with the welcoming scent of fresh coffee beans. John looked around trying to find Catherine, but he couldn't see her anywhere. Maybe he had gotten it wrong. He felt a feeling of disappointment in his stomach, like a small child that wanted a puppy for Christmas, and he got everything but. Hugo took off his coat and pulled out a small black diary, flicked through it a couple of times and then put it back in his pocket. John sat there impatiently, wanting to know what Hugo so eagerly wanted him to talk about.

"So," Hugo eventually cracked. "You want to make money yes?"

"Obviously."

"Well today is your lucky day. You seem bright, talented and a hard worker. Am I right?" John nodded, his eyes shifting around the coffee shop. "I'm going to guess that you make what, one hundred and fifty a week, if you're lucky?" John shifted in his seat, his fingers pausing the rattling on the table top.

"Sometimes," he bit. Hugo leant back and cracked his fingers. John winced, the sound going through him like nails on a chalk board.

"I have just moved into a new estate off the outskirts of Manchester. I am looking for someone to help me to run the place while I tend to my work. Is that something you would be interested in?" John thought about this for a second. A very brief second.

"No. Sorry, I'm not interested in being a maid. I want to play music, not wash dishes." John stood up but Hugo held out his hand and John, seeing how thick the gold chain on Hugo's wrist was, sat down again.

"John, I'm going to be honest with you. How long have you been grinding the busking scene? You are very good, which is why I noticed you tonight. I want to give you the opportunity to fulfil your dreams of stardom. But how long do you think you can stand out in the cold for? How long before you give it up and move to more affluent areas where the opportunities are greater but the competition is much fiercer? And how long will it take you to save the money to even do that?" John knew Hugo made sense, however he didn't want to admit the truth. He had been busking and playing for a couple of years now. He was mediocre at best, tonight was a fluke.

"I can move to London," John said, defiantly.

"London is great for music, but it's so saturated. Without any backing behind you, you'll just get lost in the mash up of upcomers and the ones who have retired their dreams and hung up their instruments to gather dust." Again, John felt the annoying realisation of Hugo's words, and they cut into him. "If you come work for me, I will pay you well, you will be able to live on site, and when I get more settled and you're ready to move on to greater pastures, I will back you and help you to get that record deal." John thought about this for a second. He pulled out a guitar pick from his pocket and ran it through his fingers. "But this place is my home."

"I understand that," Hugo said, almost with compassion. "But we all move on. Do you have family here?" John shook his head.

"They died when I was young. I lived with my aunt until a few years ago when she passed too. Cancer." Hugo let out a deep breath.

"I'm so sorry." John stared at the counter for a moment, sinking into his buried woe. How could this man come into his life, lure him into a coffee shop and then open him up like a can of dry food and let the contents spill out so easily. He was dangling a carrot in front of him and the more he tried to ignore it, the less reason he had not to take it.

"How about a girlfriend?" John thought about Catherine, how he had arranged to see her. He figured he could make it work long distance; if she had anything about her she would understand. Maybe they could even move down together eventually, once Hugo had fulfilled his side of the agreement.

"No," John said. Hugo held out his hands.

"So what's stopping you?" As they were talking a waitress came by and asked for their order and apologised for not seeing them come in. Hugo apologised and pulled out a large bundle of twenties, which caught John's attention. There was that carrot again, he thought. He asked for a latte, Hugo a black coffee and he handed the waitress a twenty.

"Keep the rest," he said, and she smiled back before disappearing behind the counter and began pressing buttons on the coffee machine.

They continued to talk about terms and what this entailed. John was to work at his home for as long as he felt fit to do so. He would complete small maintenance, prepare food and clean the house. He would be paid well for it and then once his work was done, Hugo would represent him and support him in his music career, the conditions of this to be drawn up at a later stage. Eventually, weighing up the pros and cons, John decided to take a chance.

"I'll do it," he said. John shook Hugo's hand and they arranged to get the contract drawn up tomorrow morning, and to leave promptly the following evening.

#

The next day John met with Hugo at his office in the centre of the city. It was a tall spiral shaped building with more windows than bricks, entwined with steel girders and reminded John of something you would see in a science fiction novel. He told his name to the receptionist whose hair was a light shade of auburn, and she nodded him through and gave him a visitor's ID badge. There he took the elevator that played classical music, a piece he had never heard, and rode it up to the 14th floor. He exited and sat in an open plan reception area, looked through various magazines and twiddled his thumbs waiting for his name to be called. He closed his eyes, did some meditation which quickly laid a blanket of calm over his anxiety, and then bought a can of sprite from the vending machine. A tall middle-aged woman wearing a blazer and pencil skirt and thick rimmed glasses came out of a glass door leading into a room that was filled with computers.

"John Bachman?" she called. John thought this to be funny as it was only him in the waiting area. He waved to her and he stood up, he shook her hand and she said her name was Rita. He acted like he was interested and he made a small joke about the weather and it fell as flat as an elephant that jumped off the 27th floor. She walked him through the office, the sound of key pads going resembling the tiny shoes of a million miniature tap dancers. He walked into a large office and saw Hugo standing up behind a large desk in front of a huge glass window overlooking the city. Rita followed him in and closed the door behind them. They greeted each other and Hugo pulled out a small bundle of A4 papers and handed them to John.

"It's essentially a working contract." Rita said. "All the terms of employment are included inside. I can give you a hard copy or email you one, if you like. Have a read and sign where it says, please." John skimmed through it as best as he could, not wanting to look like he was scrutinizing it too much when he was being offered a very good kick start to his music career. He signed on the dotted line and that was it. He and Hugo shared a small measure of whisky between them, and Hugo recounted tales of going to operas and his knowledge of classical music, while John educated him on more up and coming artists. They drank some more and Hugo bid John goodbye.

"I'll pick you up from the bus station tomorrow at 09:00. Make sure you're all ready and packed. Say your goodbyes and tell them you'll see them again when your name is in lights." It all seemed very surreal to John. This whole thing. He felt a mix of happiness and sadness however, as he hadn't been to see Catherine last night like he had promised. He had messaged her but she hadn't replied. He punched in her number again and the phone rang while he walked back to the bus stop to go home. The phone rang several times and John's chest was tight until finally, she answered.

"Hello?"

"Catherine, it's John, from the other night?" his voice was trying not to sound too eager.

"Oh, hi John. How are you? You said something came up? It's okay, I was working late anyway." John then went through the events of the night and spoke to her in detail about his future plans. They had agreed to keep seeing each other. Catherine would try to visit him when she could, and he would do the same on his days off. They would send emails and talk on the phone often and make plans for the future. She even joked about being his manager.

"What do you know about business?" he laughed, as he put his key in the door of his small flat.

"What do you know about cooking, pizza boy?" She teased.

"More than you about business, or is that what you're studying?" He said, trying to remember.

"Psychology, actually. It's amazing to look into people's minds. I've recently started looking into serial killers too. Bundy, Gacy, Gein. You know, all the good ones." The good ones. It's cray to think that such psychopaths are viewed in such a way and have a following.

"You're fucked up." He laughed.

"Think what you like, but they will be famous forever. That's the reality of it." They continued to talk more about the future, and John asked if she could come by and spend the night before he left to go work for Hugo. She agreed. That night she came by with a couple of bottles of wine, and after they made love, John sang to her with his guitar the love song he had wrote. He thought it was cheesy, creepy and way to quick considering they had only been dating about 48 hours, But she loved it. She listened intently with a glass of wine lying naked on the bed. She stroked his hair and kissed him over and over until they fell asleep in each other's arms.

#

In the morning, she helped John pack his belongings and they walked, holding hands, to the bus station where they saw a large Rolls Royce sitting with its engine idle. Hugo got out of the driver's seat and popped the boot and helped John with his bags.

"I was never one for having someone driving me around. I find it lazy and ridiculous. If you want to go somewhere, make the damn effort I say." Hugo said. He greeted Catherine with a smile, though they didn't make a direct eye contact, and sat back in the car, observing the two young lovers say goodbye through his rear view mirror. He had the heating on and sat quietly thinking of his latest investment. A house keeper and hopefully a fine one at that. John took Catherine's hand and he saw tears coming from her eyes.

"I don't have to go, I can stay here with you?" he said. She smiled, her beauty pushing away the cold.

"No," she wiped her eyes. "It's only for a little while, and you're only a phone call and a train ride away. It's a great opportunity." She kissed him. "I'll see you soon." John's heart felt heavy, like it was about to burst. His words got caught in his throat, the things he was dying to tell her. Eventually, he coughed.

"I love you, Catherine." Her eyes widened, and the moment seemed to never end.

"Really?" she said softly, interrupting his brain going into a complete meltdown.

"I feel like I've met you before. Somewhere, I don't know. I'm sorry, I shouldn't have said that. I know it's so quick and I'm sorry if I -"

"I love you too," she said. He held her there in the cold in a moment, the hot exhaust from the Royce pooling around them, in a moment he

never wanted to end.
"You're so Precious to me." He said, nestled in her dark hair. She squoze him tighter, their hot tears pooling onto each other. "You're so, so Precious."
#
John looked at her as she stood in the bus station watching him drive away. Hugo patted John's thigh.
"She's a pretty girl," he said, checking her out in the rear-view mirror, trying to get a look at her face, covered by her hair. John shifted in his seat. He didn't say much for the next half an hour, once they had gotten out of the city and were on the motorway down to Manchester.
"So how long will this ride take?" Hugo seemed to be lost in his own world. He was watching the steady traffic weave in and out of lanes as the Royce cruised at a stead 75mph. Again John asked, "Hugo, how long will it take to get to your place?" Hugo took his eyes off the road and looked at John. He no longer looked jovial or sincere, but now his face looked cold, hard like rock.
"A couple of hours or so, depending on traffic. Did you get a solicitor to look over the contract?" John studied his expression and Hugo returned his eyes to the running grey of tarmac in front of them.
"No," he said. "I didn't think I needed one." Hugo let out a narrow smile. They drove another few miles when Hugo spoke.
"John?"
"Yeah Hugo?" Hugo slapped John hard across the face. He lay against the passenger window holding his bloodied mouth, tears in his eyes, looking in the side mirror, watching his home disappear further away.
"It's Mister Hugo from now on. And don't ever forget that."

Chapter Fifteen.

Blood.

"How badly are you burnt?" shouted Annie, grabbing hold of Edith's arms, her white gloves now charred black and her dress holed with disappearing embers. She continued to pat her down.

"I don't think it went through the fabric, I think I'm okay," Edith said, wanting to believe she had some good luck left. She didn't feel in any pain, which meant one of two things. Either she wasn't burnt, or she was so badly burnt, it had gone through her skin so deep that it had burnt away her nerve endings. Annie checked her over, looking for any bubbling, stripping, or reddening of flesh.

"Here let me take these off and look at your arms," Annie said. She took hold of the top lip of the white gloves that ran up to Edith's elbows. She pulled away quickly.

"I'm fine, Annie." She was holding her arms towards her chest, like she had gone to pet a friendly puppy which had then bitten her hand.

"I need to see if you're okay," Annie protested, again stepping forward to check the gloves.

"I said I'm fine, Annabelle," Edith bit. Annie was caught off guard by the use of her full name. Edith was one of her longest friends and even she had never used her full name. She felt like she was a school girl being scolded by the head master whenever somebody mentioned her by her full name.

"Just let me check your arms, for god sakes, Edith. I know what I'm doing. I'm only doing this so we can tell the hospital the extent of the burns when we get out of here." Again she stepped forward. Edith stepped further back away from her, the puppy bearing its sharp claws moving closer, its fur standing on end, foaming at the mouth.

"I said no!" Edith snapped. Her voice silenced Annie's worry. Edith sat down on the bed. "I'm sorry. But I'm okay. I don't need you to undress me to see that I'm fine. I'm not hurt, the fire didn't spread. Maybe singed a couple of my hairs but that's about it. I'm fine. Honestly. I'm fine." Edith continued to repeat this under her breath even when Annie moved over to the bedroom door and put her ear to the wood. She listened carefully. The demonic laughter from the lower section had ceased, though she worried about John. She hoped he was so badly injured by Edith's brave but stupid surge of courage that he couldn't follow them. But she also feared if it had made him loose what little of his mind he had left. The pain in her stomach from where she had been kicked by him grew, like an inflating balloon. She hoped it was just transient and at most she would have a bruised rib. Then a more insidious thought crept into her mind. What if it's the poison slowly killing me? She had drank a lot since being here, her guilt, shame and always present pain making her consume alcohol to numb it, when in reality it was literally killing her faster. Typical, she thought. She heard nothing from behind the door, it's cold and grainy texture tickling her ear. She looked at Edith, who was staring into the carpet, focusing on a single spot. Annie wondered how much she had drank too. A couple of glasses at most. Maybe she would be okay. At least to survive long enough to get out of here. Maybe long enough to watch Annie collapse onto the floor, begin to fit uncontrollably and foam at the mouth while her eyes rolled to the back of her head, mouth fixed in a scream of agony, while it made her muscles disintegrate and her brain and eyes haemorrhage. But she was older than Annie, by at least twenty years, and Annie wondered again exactly how long they both had left to live.

"I can't hear anything from outside the landing. If we move quietly, we should be able to find a way out of here," Annie whispered.

"How are we supposed to get out, Annie?"

"I don't know. I think John threw all the car keys in the fire along with all of our phones. There's got to be some way we can leave, but sitting here won't get us out. How's your knee?" Edith flexed her leg a couple of times and winced.

"It'll hold for now. The swelling's getting bad though." Edith stood from the bed and walked to Annie. Annie cracked the door and looked out into the hall. She couldn't see anyone and all seemed quiet. She opened it more and slipped out into the hallway. The hall stretched both in front and behind them, and she knew they had to move quickly as they were sitting ducks. They moved swiftly but quietly to the corner of the hall. They looked further down the hallway. They saw another room a few meters away where they could gather their bearings and thoughts, Edith clung to Annie's dress, and although Annie held a brave face, she too was terrified of seeing John step around the corner, with a gun in his hand. Annie froze. At the end of the hallway was a figure staring back at her. She tried to speak, but her throat was arid and a sinister fear ran through her, like someone had tipped ice down her neck and shook her. It stood tall, maybe around eight feet. It was black, featureless. It was unmoving, its naked, black featureless body facing her.

"What is it?" Edith whispered. "Why aren't we moving, come on!" Annie turned to Edith who looked worried. But she was looking at Annie, and that was much, much worse. Annie turned to look at the thing again. It was still there, and Annie felt like she was going to cry.

"Come on!" Edith urged, tugging at her dress. "We need to move, what are you waiting for?" Annie turned back to Edith.

"Don't you see it?" she said, her eyes swelling with tears.

"See what?" Edith said, looking over her shoulder. "See what, Annie?" Annie heard the clicking of bones in front of her. She slowly turned her head. It was above her, hanging from the ceiling. It's black jaws open wide, its wire frame clinging poised over them ready to pounce. A long sliver of saliva dripped down onto her shoulder as its head twisted, clicking and cracking. She remembered its laughter, low and growling, and then its rows of sharp white teeth falling to her face. She let out a scream and fell backwards, thrashing wildly at the monster. It had her. She could feel it gabbing hold of her, trying to pull her into itself. She tried pushing it away, delivering alternating punches, in pain. She opened her eyes and saw Edith on the ground holding her face. Annie quivered, looking around the hallway quickly. The beast nowhere to be seen. She crawled along the carpet to Edith who lay there groaning quietly.

"Did you see it? Where did it go!" Annie cried to Edith, holding her head.

"What the fuck?" Edith moaned. Annie saw the blood on Edith's face, and then smear of blood on her hand.

"Oh my god," Annie said. She hugged Edith tight on the floor. "I'm so sorry, Edith… I…" she tried to find the words, but drew a blank instead.

"You just flipped!" Edith moved away from her, backing into a corner, her eyes wide with fear. "What's gotten into you? Stay away from me!" Annie crawled to her but Edith cowered further. "Don't come any closer!"

"I'm sorry!" she said, over and over again. "I'm so sorry, I don't know what happened. I saw something, a creature. It was black and thin. Its teeth," she held her head in her hands. "Oh my god, its teeth! It had no eyes, it was black and naked!" Annie was hysterical now. Words moulded into one, crying wildly into her hands. Edith went to her slowly and put her arms around her, the pain in her knee growing bigger, like a balloon was blowing up and about to explode.

"It's okay," she whispered, stroking her hair. "It's okay." Annie looked into her eyes and Edith's eyes were a deep red. Tears falling from them onto Annie's dress.

"We need to get out of here, don't we? I'm losing my mind." Edith didn't answer, but she kissed the crown of Annie's head and they helped each other to their feet. They locked hands and continued to walk down the hall way.

"Annie?" Edith said. Annie turned to her. She was staring at her shoulder. "What's that?" Annie followed her gaze. She muffled the scream as her mind dissolved at the sight of it. Her dress over her shoulder was ripped over and over, like a shark had sank its teeth into it, and began thrashing its jaws. Annie stared back at Edith, whose face was white as snow. Then all went black. Panic gripped them both. "What's happened?" Edith cried.

"I think the power's gone out," Annie said, pushing the fear into the back of her mind, where all of the locked boxes were kept. Annie squoze Edith's hand and looked around. She couldn't see the beast, if it existed at all. But there was another monster walking around with a loaded gun, and that she knew, was definitely real. She moved again, pulling Edith with her. They heard a whimpering, soft, quiet, but definitely there, coming from inside the guest room in front of them, the door still ajar.

"Do you hear that?" Edith whispered, clutching Annie's shoulder, her fingers digging in deep, pushing through the tenseness of her muscles, like massaging brimstone.

"Yeah, I do."

"It could be Claudia? Or Precious?" Edith went to move but Annie stopped her.
"It could also be,"
The beast, it's wide jaws ready to eat your soul.
"The gunman, John, or whoever is in here."
"Well, we can't stay out here in the open." Edith urged. Annie took a deep breath, her adrenaline spiking, fused with her fear. She had never liked the dark, it reminded her too much of the time she laid bleeding alone in her bathtub. There had been a power cut that night, which was the reason why she had botched it. And again, the dark had descended on her in her time of desperation, and she did not trust it.
"Come on," Edith moved past Annie who tried to grab out to stop her, but she moved through the door towards the whimpering. Annie followed her, half expecting the silence and the dark to be split with a flash of white light and a bellowing of gunfire, and she have to find her way out alone. But the flash of death did not come. Edith sat in the corner, running her hand through a figures hair that was curled up in a ball, knees tucked below her chin, like a terrified child in the middle of a lightning storm. It was the blonde woman, Precious. She moved closer and heard Edith whispering to her, soothing her soft moans of pain with loving delicacy. Annie drew closer to her warily. Claudia's cries in her mind. She tried to kill me. Maybe she had made the whole thing up? Maybe Claudia was in on the whole thing and she had beaten Precious to a pulp and left her for dead. Where was Claudia? Was she hiding in the dark, waiting with a blade to cut their throats? The rain splattered bedroom window occasionally breaking soft moonlight that fell onto Precious' face. Her face was badly bruised. Her lip was cut and she had what could easily be confused with a ligature mark around her neck, but Annie knew they were consistent with finger prints. She was missing a heel, and her hands were tarred with dry blood.
"What happened sweetheart?" Edith asked, still running her hand through her hair. It was clumped together and Annie figured she had a hematoma to her scalp which was possibly still bleeding. Precious looked at her. Tears falling from her face, pooling onto her knees.
"I don't remember much," she said, her words cracking. Annie crouched to her, moving in closer to inspect her injuries. "After that man came in and shot at us, I ran away, into the house. I tried to find a window, a phone, anything I could to call for help or to get out of here. All the doors were locked and none of the windows would budge.

I went to Claudia for help, I saw her upstairs in the hall. I don't remember much else". Her blue eyes shining like wet crystals in the moonlight, then disappearing under a black cloud of rain.
"Did she do this to you?" Edith placed her hand on her leg, tracing up Precious's shin. Precious nodded.
"I can't remember, I remember her grabbing me and pulling me to the floor with my hair. My shoe came off and she just went crazy, hitting me over and over again. I thought I was going to die, so I just went limp. I gave myself to her, my life in her hands. I thought I was already dead when I passed out," she made a downward motion with her hand to her head. Edith wrapped her arm around her and kissed her on the head.
"You're safe now, sweetheart, we're going to find a way out of here." Annie checked her hair and saw there were shallow cuts on her scalp which had begun to swell. She didn't appear to be bleeding but she couldn't be too sure in the poor lighting. The heel, if that's what had really happened, had pierced the top and back of her scalp several times. It looked much worse than it probably was. She would be fine, maybe need stitches, but fine. Precious suddenly became alarmed, like she had just remembered she had left the food in the oven as she got into bed.
"The power outage! The system might be offline! We should be able to get out!" Precious stood up, using Edith and Annie to push herself to her feet, her legs stiff from being in a ball for so long. She walked towards the bedroom door, devoid of fear. "Come on!" Precious took Annie's hand and she pulled back.
"Hold on, I need a minute to think," Annie stammered. Edith moved with Precious.
"Annie, no time to think. If the place isn't secure, then we can walk right out of here?" said Edith.
"Wrong." Annie said firmly. "If someone turned off the system, then they obviously know how to work it, and if they know how to work it, then they are probably standing right near the exit, waiting for someone to run down head first into a bullet." Precious and Edith looked at each other, walking hesitantly towards the door.
"If we stay here," Precious said, moving closer to Annie, "Then we are going to die." Annie knew even if they held out long enough to not be blown away, time was against them as their insides were slowly rotting. It was between the devil and the deep blue sea. Sit and die, or run and

possibly live. Well, when you put it that way…
"Okay," she said, biting her lip. "Let's go. Quietly. Any sign of John, then we run, okay?" Both looked at her, and they agreed without saying a word.
"Wait," Precious said. "I have an idea. If we can get into the system, we could turn on the power but leave the doors unlocked. That way, we could trick whoever is messing with it into thinking we're still trapped."
"How would we do that? We don't even know where this system is?" Edith protested. Precious looked confident.
"It must be in Hugo's study. Where else would it be? He must have a computer, a laptop or something? Something he works on. I saw a room full of books and other fancy shit earlier, it's not far from here."
Annie narrowed her eyes. She wanted to speak but Precious, not waiting for an argument to cloud her bravery, left the guest room and disappeared out the door into the black. Edith took a step and Annie took her arm.
"I don't trust her." Annie said. Edith moved towards the door.
"We don't really have a choice." Annie waited a moment. Then she took a deep breath and held Edith's hand and stepped out into the hall.

#

The three of them moved quietly, peering around corners, clinging to the wall at the slightest sound. At one point, they thought they heard footsteps and darted into a side room. They waited there, holding their breath, as the invisible stalker disappeared into the sound of rattling windows and howling wind, then, the footsteps unseen, the three of them continued to look for an item that might not exist, in a room they couldn't be sure where it was, to achieve an impossible goal. Escape.
Precious moved through the halls quicker than Annie and Edith. She recognised certain landmarks which helped her navigate. An exotic plant here, a self-portrait there. Annie and Edith moved slower, more cautiously behind her. "She said she's never been here before right?" Annie whispered to Edith.
"I think so. She must have a good memory," They moved, crouching low, stepping lightly. Edith turned her head frequently, checking for shadows and monsters. Precious pushed herself through a set of double doors with a golden handle. She closed it behind Annie and

Edith and moved quickly to a corner cabinet, rummaging through it loudly.

"Quiet!" Annie urged. "Someone will hear you!" Precious continued to search, smashing glass ornaments on the floor, pulling out books and ripping their pages from their spines. Edith stood and watched, shocked. She rushed over to Precious to get a hold of her, to stop her manic search before they were discovered. Annie watched her. She moved but she heard something crawling near her foot. She looked down and saw a small bundle of flesh writhing in the dull light. It moved on hands and knees, a bloodied rattle in hand and a soiled diaper dragging behind it. Its face was cold. Its skin dark purple and green. Annie looked away, then looked back again. It was gone. Like it had never been there in the first place.

"Ahh, here we are," Precious said, pulling something out from under a small table next to the fireplace of devils. Her face lit up with a bright white light and Annie realised she had found a laptop. Precious balanced it in one hand and typed furiously with the other. "And… Done." with one final click, the lights began to flicker and warm, until lighting up again. Edith breathed a huge sigh of relief. Nightmares are less frightening in the light. Edith walked to Precious, who had now put the laptop down on the small wooden table and was looking at them, her face full with glee. Annie looked back at where the bloodied child had been. Just empty space where it's jellied eyes should be. She saw the smile on Edith's face as she supported her step with the backs of furniture, hobbling to Precious on her bad leg. Annie felt betrayed by her own presumptions. Maybe she had been wrong about her? She began to relax a little. But not for long. Edith moved towards Precious, her arms out, ready to give her a giant hug, like a wife misses her child after he hadn't been seen for three days, not realising he's covered in mud and wet leaves, brains ticking out of the holes in his skull.

"Precious, you did it, I think we might actually-" Her words were cut short. Precious took a large wooden ornament from one of the shelves and brought it down on her, crashing it into her nose. Edith fell back onto the floor, her nose gushing, dripping hot and thick onto her dress and it sinking into the cream carpet below. Annie let in a sharp intake of breath as she watched Edith fall to the floor onto her back, the back of her head clipping the hard wood of the fire place. She laid there still, and Annie didn't know if she was conscious or breathing.

"Oh my God!" Annie howled, her voice tearing the silence. She rushed to Edith, but Precious raised the ornament again over her, its mantle still dripping.

"Not another step," she barked. Annie abated, eyes flitting between Edith's still chest, and Precious's weapon. "Move, and I bash your fucking head in too." She lifted the laptop and punched in more codes. Annie heard a loud rumbling and then a series of clicks around them. "There we are. System, disabled." She laughed mockingly.

"Why are you doing this?" Annie's fear had left her, like a well that had been drained of water, revealing the bones that had laid unseen for so long. Now, she just felt pain. It was bursting through her skin, her body shaking like withdrawal. This was her drug. Misery, and she had become an addict for it. Precious flicked her hair back, like she was getting ready for a night in the town. She threw the laptop across the room, crashing it into the book shelf, knocking thick hardbacks onto the floor, smashing the screen until it lay on the floor flickering black and white. She reached into her bra line and pulled out a pack of cigarettes, put one in her mouth, then pulled out a match and scraped it along the depiction of tortured devils and valiant angels mangled into the fire place. The match hissed as it came to life, then she lit her smoke, took a drag, and threw the dead match to the floor. She laughed again, Annie confused, leaning towards Edith. Precious span around in a circle like she was listening to insane chime of a merry go round, singing a tune that never seemed to reach an end, "La da deee, la da doo, la da hooo, la da deee." Annie shuddered. The rage spilling out, her eyes fixed on Edith.

"What the fuck is going on, Precious! I need to help Edith!" She continued to spin like a deranged woman, eventually slowing. The bloodied statue in her hand had painted a blood-spattered ring around her feet, turning brown as it mixed with the air.

"Rude," she said, taking another drag of her smoke. "I never liked this colour," she said, running her fingers through her hair. "I was never one for the blonde bimbo look. I had to keep on dying it. Do you know what peroxide does to your hair if you keep going with it?" She clicked her fingers. "Snaps like hay." Her voice was floating now, like a woman who was in a dream world, dipping her toe in the sea of clouds and fairies. Her head fell back and she pinched her eye. She took out a small clear piece of lens that had a slight tinge of blue in the light. She did the same with the other and blinked hard. "Those have been killing me all night." Her eyes were now a deep green, like the sun-drenched leaves of a beautiful, yet deadly plant.

"Please," Annie croaked. "Let me help her," Annie went to move, but Precious screamed at her.

"Not another step!" Annie froze. She looked closely at Edith. She couldn't see her chest moving.

"Who are you?" Annie whispered through her tears. Precious took another drag of the cigarette. She pointed behind Annie.

"Why don't you ask him?" She heard the door creak behind her, and she felt like a rat trapped in a box with two vipers. She turned to see John standing there. His face cracked and red, marred with black. His white shirt was badly burnt, the flames eaten away large patches of it, showing charred flesh underneath.

"Thank you, Catherine," he said. She finished her cigarette with another long drag before stumping it on the fire mantle. "I knew you could do it. You truly are Precious to me." John and Catherine set their eyes on Annie, murderous and wide. It wasn't John's retched appearance that made Annie start to cry, or that when he looked at her, his eyes were filled with hate, his mind relinquishing her to nothing. No. She began to cry because when she looked at his waist, she saw he still held the Glock in one hand and a large kitchen knife in the other.

Chapter Sixteen.

Wolves.

Catherine stepped over Edith and moved around Annie to John. She placed the ornament on a small table and she took hold of him, sharing a long kiss. Annie's eyes followed her as she watched their sick love unfold.

This is the moment you have all been waiting for!

She turned to Edith on the ground, her chest still not rising. I could make a run for it? She wondered. But could she? How far would she really get? Could she outrun a bullet? She had never been in a fight in her life. Not a real one anyway, where there's more on the line than playground respect. She thought Edith was dead. Or if not, she would be soon. She wondered if she could quickly check her pulse, while the two vipers weren't looking, and were still busy swapping venom. She dared not move however, her feet cemented into place. Catherine released John, flakes of charred flesh around her mouth. The peeled away skin revealed a bright pink under layer on John's face.

"How do you want to do it?" John giggled. Catherine stoked his chest and traced her hand down to the knife. It's pointed edge shining in the study light. They turned to Annie, a smile creeping across their mouths.

"What did I ever do to you?" Annie crocked. "What have any of us ever done to you?"

"It's nothing personal," Catherine said in a matter of fact tone. "It's what you represent."

"What I represent? What the hell does that mean?" Catherine took a step towards her, and Annie a step back, nearly tripping over Edith. "My poor baby was held here by Hugo. He made him weak, beat him and trapped him. Promised him the world and John was so destroyed by this that we vowed to get our revenge. So I worked on Hugo. "Chance encounters, you'd be amazed what slipping a little something in a drink on a warm afternoon in Paris can make someone do. We talked, we drank, we fucked. And then when he was numb and couldn't move on his bed, I beat him. I let all of my fury out on that son of a bitch," she was laughing now, gripped by fury, but savoured it too. "I took his money and his cards. I called his clients and got codes for his computer. His accounts. He took my soul mate away from me, and I made sure he paid. I followed him, sent him letters, phone calls, took photos of his whore wife being unfaithful, all waiting for today. Tonight. When I could finally do justice on him for what he put John through. They say human slavery is dead," she shook her head. "It's very much alive. But instead of chains, we have contracts. Instead of executions, we have solicitors. Tonight was about undoing the wrong that had been done. You're just another shit stain we need to clean up. No offense." Catherine walked to the tall windows in the study and looked out into the black. Her reflection staring back at her. She fingered the window frame and tapped the thick glass. "That's why it was easy for John to persuade him to up his security system, knowing that one day, we could trap him and everyone else inside it." Annie stood in a shocked horror. Both of them were clearly insane, but in a twisted way they saw what they were doing as justice?

"What about the gunman? Francis? You destroyed his life. How is that 'justice'?"

"Gotta crack eggs to make an omelette," John laughed from behind them. Annie saw him in the door way. Teeth bared like a hungry wolf. "That man was tied to Hugo. He was in his pocket. If you cut off the head of the Hydra, more will grow. Francis was just another head sprawling out of the vile body that was Hugo Black. Now the body is dead, we have to take care of the heads that are still clinging for life." Annie looked at them both.

"Why didn't you just leave? Why did it have to take all of this? Why couldn't you have just gone to the police?" John and Catherine howled a sinister laughter, like Annie had just told them geese shit rainbows.

"Hugo treated me like a slave," John said. "I was too much of a pussy to fight back. I did try a couple of times through legal routes to get out of his contract, but you should always read the fine print. Especially when it's written by a monster. I jumped at the opportunity to have a better future. I was promised a kick-start to my music career. And in the four years I have been kept here, I haven't played a note until tonight." Annie saw a flicker in his eyes. A snap of black and then back to blue. "I tried to leave, but it was impossible. I tried to catch a train, to run, to burrow my way out if I had too. But Hugo's grip spanned further than just my neck. The more I was here, the more I was being crippled by the debt he was bestowing onto me. Charging me extortionate rent, utilities and food. I had to 'work,' to pay it off. Not only could I not leave, but even if I did, I would be ruined. It's like asking someone in a violent relationship why they don't just 'leave.' The simple answer is because after a while, it no longer becomes an option."

"Why did you poison the food?" Annie blurted, noticing her skin was beginning to feel much hotter. Catherine picked up a glass vase from the fire place and eyed it curiously.

"When you run a bath, you always have an overflow plug to stop the damn thing flooding." She threw the vase which exploded against the wall. "Not only would it destroy the confidence Hugo's business partners would have in him, for allowing such a thing to happen, but it would mean there was motive for someone to murder him. In the event that went to shit, which it did, we had a backup."

"Who did you get the poison from?"

"Inquisitive little bear, aren't you?" John said. He closed the door in the study. Annie felt like the walls were going to grow arms and choke the life out of her. He grabbed a handful of vinyl from the book case and began stomping on them, shouting over and over again. Catherine threw ornaments and overturned furniture. She emptied books from the shelves and tore paintings from the walls. She picked up a large candle stick and turned to the fire place filled with devils and angels.

"Morbid piece of shit." She reached her arms back, holding the hard block over her head, like she was at affair grown with a giant hammer, trying to hit the bass just right to make the lights dance and the tickets spew out. John screamed.

"No!" Catherine startled, nearly dropping the block on her head. She turned to John, meeting Annie's terrified eyes on the way. He was heaving, his eyes wide and his face of worry. "Do not touch that." He said, his arm outstretched, trembling. "Not the fireplace." Catherine studied him and drew her eyes back to the wood. The devils and angels woven into the wood seemed to call to her, and she heard their screams in her ears. She put the wood down and stepped away. She seemed lost in her thoughts. Looking into the eyes of the wooden beings. John drew closer to Catherine. His face was softer, and she looked at him, his eyes into hers. They smiled. "I had to look at that every day, cleaning it over and over." He put the Glock in his waist band and ran his fingertips over it. "I want to break it. Not you." Catherine nodded. "As you wish." They shared a kiss, and Annie tried to think of anything else than Somebody please help me. John and Catherine turned to Annie and moved towards her, circling around her like hungry sharks waiting for her to slip below the surface.

"The police did nothing to help him. I begged them to help but they fobbed me off. Told me I was crazy. "This thing never happened in real life," is what they said. That night they contacted Hugo. That night, John was beaten so badly he tried to cut his own throat with a razor blade. Thankfully he called me before he did and I talked him out of it."

"Why me? Why any of us?" Annie panicked. The sharks growing impatient, tired of her thrashing and will just drag her below the surface themselves.

"Hugo kept everything on his computer." John hissed. "I know what you did to your child. For that, you're just as sinful as him." Annie felt like she had been punched in the stomach. They knew. They had always known. Her terrible secret. It was out for the world to see.

"You don't understand. I tried so hard to get Hugo to help me but he never responded. He threw me away when he was done with me and left me to rot and suffer alone."

"Correction, Annabelle." Said John. "Hugo didn't leave you to be fed to the wolves. All of his messages and phone calls came through me. He never heard a single one of your cries for help." Annie nearly collapsed. Hugo was innocent in this. He had never spoken to her about what had happened because he had never known that she was suffering. John had made it so he never knew a thing.

"Oh my god…." Annie whispered, her eyes bloodshot with liquid pain. "Why would you do such a thing? My baby… Hugo would have had a baby."

"You were needed. We needed your rage, your pain Annabelle. We needed you to hate Hugo, to show the world what kind of man he was."

"But he was innocent! He never knew what I had been through!"

"He is far from innocent." Catherine hissed, an inch from Annie's ear.

"What about Claudia? Brian?"

"Brian and Claudia were just an extra piece of the puzzle that grew organically." John said. "We could have stopped it from happening but we figured Hugo's friend and wife having an affair was simply a sweet turn of fate. You can't ignore Karma."

"So you fucked Hugo's life in every single way imaginable," Annie shouted, her voice raw. "You turned everyone he knew against him, dug up all the dirt you could find on everyone he knew and used it to destroy him? And for what? Fucking revenge?" Annie felt a hand grab her shoulder, then an explosion of pain deep in her stomach. She felt the brushing of blonde hair on her cheek, and a whisper in her ear.

"For love." Catherine stabbed her. Annie collapsed to her knees, pressing on her stomach as red pulsed out of her. She saw the lights start to turn dim, as she began to fade away. She held on to reality as much as she could, like instinct, remembering her training on knife wounds. She tried to breathe normally, which was a near impossible task, while she tried to keep shock from taking hold of her. Catherine and John stood in front of her. John laughed as Catherine passed the bloodied knife to him. He crouched down in front of her, his smile wide.

"You murdered your child and then lied about it to your friends. You cut your baby out of you and destroyed its chance of life to save your own skin. Its time you closed your eyes for good and paid for what you have done." He raised the knife to her chin, taunting her with it. "Consider this me reuniting you with it." Annie spat at him. A think mix of blood and phlegm spread around his face. He swung his hand back and the back of his knuckles hit her across the cheek. She fell on her back in front of Edith. She felt warm air on her face. She was alive, but only just holding on. John stood over her, proud and mighty over Annie as she tried to get to her feet. She wasn't ready to die yet. Not here. Not now. She pushed through the pain and got to one knee. John grabbed a fistful of her hair and retched her head back, her neck stretching out. Annie let out a scream of pain.

"You fucking bitch. You and Edith deserved to die here. You're both fucking child murderers." She heard Catherine laughing, clapping her hands jumping up and down on the spot.

"Kill her, baby!" she howled. John slammed Annie's down into the rug, rubbing her face into it, the fibres tearing her skin as she let out a muffled scream. John suddenly let go, as Annie heard shouting behind them. She heard a large thump, then another, followed by more shouting, the explosion of a pistol, then felt hands on her back. She looked up and saw Claudia, shouting in her face, her mouth stretched and the words sounding muffled. They came clearer, then pushed into her ears like a bull horn.

"Can you run!?" She pulled Annie up by her shoulder. She crawled to her wobbling feet, dress drenched with blood. Claudia caught her and stopped her crashing into the ground. "Don't fucking die on me now, Annie, we have to get out of here." Annie looked around and saw Catherine on the floor, a large bloodied gash to the back of her head. John laid next to Edith, he was groaning lowly on the ground. She saw a wooden ornament matted with hair and shards of broken bone. John was rising to his feet, still holding the pistol. He raised it at Annie and Claudia as they ran, her arm draped over her shoulder, the other pressing on her knife wound. John let off a pop, it went flying past Claudia's head and smashing a light bulb as they ran down the hall way. They heard a huge cry of anguish below through the house, bouncing off the walls and it followed them as they reached the front door, like a howling beast from hell. Annie reached for the door handle. "No!" Claudia shouted. "It's locked. Follow me!" Claudia pulled Annie like a rag doll. Annie watched the door vanish away, like being dragged back into oblivion. Her only escape but finger tips away. Claudia led her into the lounge through the arch way. She sat Annie on the sofa next to the piano. Claudia trampled on the embers in the fire place, a mash of coal and dust melted into the carpet at its base. She ran her hands under the lid of the fire mantle until Annie heard a soft click. The back of the fire place moved. "Come on!" Annie tried to get off the sofa but her legs failed her. She fell to the floor in a heap. "Don't you dare!" Claudia urged. She picked up Annie around the waist and pushed her against the wall, slapping her face. "Come on, it's not that far," black coal smearing on Annie's face. Claudia took her under her arm again. She turned and she dropped to her knees. Annie fell like a crumple on the floor, reunited with the carpet that licked her face. Annie's vision blurred and she grew colder. She watched as Claudia crawled on all fours to the body on the ground behind the sofa. She hadn't noticed him in her panic, but now, all she could do was wail.

"Brian!" Claudia called, stroking his waxy fac. His dead eyes looking back to her. "Oh no! Oh god please no!" Claudia held Brian's head in her arms, cradling him. She kissed his cheeks and his limp lips. Annie had seen pain in her time on this planet. God, she had experienced her fair share. But she watched Claudia tear into two. She shook wildly, thumbing at his clothes like she was looking for the on switch of her favourite broken toy. She fell into him, her face on his chest soaking in his dried blood. Her hands were covered in thick sticky red, and her knees curled under his arms, painting them. They heard footsteps coming down the stairs. Annie lifted her head and saw Catherine. Her face painted like a school kid who was let loose with the red paint. She stumbled to the front door and rattled it. She held the back of her head and her hair was matted in thick clumps. Her heels clicked clumsily as she stumbled to them, reaching the maiden. She rested on her base and eyed Annie on the ground. Claudia didn't notice. She couldn't have. She was stuck in the in between, the void between earth and hell where all pain still exists, but you feel as dead as stone.

"You ruined my hair," Catherine hissed. Annie saw her lift the Glock. It wobbled in the air, like it was a jet being flown by a drunk pilot. She let it go, and Annie buried her head into the carpet, like an ostrich that chooses concrete over sand. The bullet went wide. Cutting the air and burying into the piano that cried an explosion of broken notes. Catherine raised her arm again, trying to stumble forward. Annie pushed through her wooziness. She moved to Claudia, crawling over Brian. She tugged her dress and Claudia relinquished her grip on Brian. They scurried to the opening in the fire place.

"Get us out of here," Annie cried wearily to her. Claudia didn't say anything. Her eyes as she lost sight of Brian as they passed through the opening said more than enough. Another pop of the pistol and Annie heard the crashing of stone behind her. She looked back through the dark tunnel as they moved, hunched over in the black narrow passageway. Catherine's face poked through the gap, like a monster looking at its victim over the top of an open well. Annie heard soft whimpering coming from Claudia as they turned a corner. Catherine's face no longer there, but firmly imprinted into the back of Annie's eyes. Claudia opened a small dusty trap door above them. It was wrapped in cobwebs and dead spiders. A burst of wild air hit her and she felt relief like never before. Heavy rain drenching them as the black sky streaked with ferocious lightening, like heaven itself was about the crack into two. They crawled out into the mud. The trap door hidden amongst branches and thorns that dug into their hands and knees as they crawled from it. They got to their feet. Claudia stumbled as they moved through the brambles towards the front of the house. Urgency hit Annie, mixed in the wind and howling her name.

"We have to get Edith!" Annie screamed into the night. "She's still alive!"

"We can't go back there," Claudia cried. Her face was numb. She stumbled again, this time meeting the ground. Annie summoned her last bit of flitting strength and heaved her to her feet. "We need to get you to a hospital," said Claudia. "You're going to bleed out!" They continued down the snaking drive way, supporting each other in so many ways. The trees stretching over them like withered skeletal hands, about to grip them and drag them back into the house of hell. They reached the gate and it swung open as Claudia and Annie pushed themselves through. They continued down to the road. There was no one to be seen, no passing cars to ask for help, and the closest hospital was over three hours away on foot. The ever stretching black highway before them and behind them. Annie's legs finally quit. She collapsed to the ground in a puddle of dirt, mud streaking up her body and into her fingers as she tried to get up, her strength leaving her body, being sucked out by the storm. Claudia shouted over the bellowing rain and wind, her hair flying crazily across her face. Her body was going cold as she desperately tried to pull Annie to her feet. But then, like a sickness taking hold of her, pushing what little adrenaline she had left, she fell backwards at the road side, her eyes still open looking at the black sky. The rain pummelled their faces and cold wrapped its hands around them. Both left to annihilation in the dark, unseen and unheard. Annie took her soaking hand, and gave herself to the realisation that this was it. The angel of death coming to carry them away.

"I could have saved him." Claudia broke. "I loved him so much." She whispered into the wind and her words were carried away. Annie turned into her. Together in their agony. "I could have gotten him out. I was so angry. I was so selfish."

"You came back for me." Annie stroked Claudia's frozen face. A trickle of warmth pushed through Claudia's misery and their eyes met. "You came back for me. I'm sorry I didn't believe you. I'm sorry for everything." Claudia touched Annie's wound. The blood starting to slow on her stomach. They lay there a small moment as the wind

howled through them.
"I don't want to die," Claudia broke. Annie smiled solemnly to her and she held her. She kissed her hair and closed her eyes. A feeling of serenity crept over her. This isn't so bad, Annie thought. Her mind falling away from her, to that place of peace you rarely ever find. At least I will be with you again. Annie's eyes snapped open. Claudia began to convulse, she began to whimper and cry, then breathe quick and shallow. Her muscles cramped like tight bundles and then relaxed. She tried to scream in pain, but hot thick mucus drowned her wail. Annie saw blood creep out of her eyes, her ears and her nostrils. Annie tried to help her but all she could do watch. Watch as her body gave itself to the poison. Shock wrapped its arms around her. Claudia was gone. Annie finally broke. Like a dam that can only hold back the flood water for so long. She howled into her vacant eyes, running her hands over her face, mixing the blood, rain and mud through her finger tips. She stroked her face.
"Thank you," she mouthed over and over to her. "Thank you for coming back. Thank you for not leaving me in that place." She closed her eye lids as her heart rate started to drop. The rain and wind seemed too slow, and there was a brief moment of peace and silence as the storm grew still around them. A peace that she slipped away too, holding Claudia in her arms.
"You're both fucking child murderers."
His words slammed into her mind again. Pulling her back from her tranquillity and throwing her back into the fire. She mouthed the words again as the wind picked back up, rain flickering her skin. She turned onto her front. Her body was numb and ached. She looked down at Claudia. Her body at rest. Annie crawled on all fours to the lip of the iron gate, it's cold steel hinges creaking. She pulled herself back to her feet and held herself in her arms. She wanted answers. Claudia had come back for her and Edith was still in there. She forced her legs to move, crunching the cold stone under her feet as she began the painful walk towards the foot of the house.

#

Catherine laid on the ground next to the fire place. Her head was pounding and her skin was burning. She heaved and coughed into the mixed coal on the ground. Thick hot bile gargling and slapping onto her legs. Her vision swooned like she was looking through moving water. She saw him standing above her.

"My love," she whispered as she grabbed at his suit. He moved away. She coughed again. Blood. Thick blood mixed with green and black. She reached for him again and her finger tips traced his trouser leg. She looked up to his face. It was red and burnt. He leaned down to her and pulled her hand into his chest. She felt cold. "We did it." She tried for a smile, but it fell loose like a dead worm. "We can be together. Our plan worked. They drank it. Those greedy pigs. They drank it all and it's only a matter of time." She heaved again. Her chest and throat like razor blades coated in barbed wire. He took her face and leaned into her. He kissed her and licked his lips.

"They did indeed," the beast said, as it pulled out the knife and slid it across her throat.

Chapter Seventeen.

Phlegethon.

Annie tumbled through the hot air. Wind rushed through her finger tips and face. She tried to catch her breath but couldn't. It was trapped inside her as she plummeted down and down beneath a thick grey sky that was being destroyed by a bombardment of ferocious lightning, the cracks of thunder mixing with the deafening wind as she plummeted past giant barren mountain of red rock. She hit the ground with untold agony. She writhed on the ground moaning lowly to herself. She caught her breath finally, heart thumping through her rib cage. She dragged her finger tips through the dry dirt, the fine ground cutting into her naked body, turning her the colour of muddied ash. Struggling to her feet, she cleared her eyes. Through the pain, she looked around. She had no idea where she was, but the sight of her surrounding bore a new fear in her, a fear she had never experienced before. She looked up to where the ground moved to a lip and moved closer to it slowly. Her goose bumps growing as her legs wobbled and lips quivered. Over the lip, she saw an open stretch of desolate land. Mounds of sand dunes and dead branches poking out of the ground. She caught the scream in her throat, suffocating it with her muddied hands. The harrowing sight of so many people, wrapped in chains walking in single file towards the mouth of a giant black gate surrounded by high walls of bone. The bone bars twisted and wrapped amongst themselves, jagged points holding large fiery torches where human heads lay impaled still screaming. The thunder cracked again, and she felt a strong push of hot wind lurch her forward. She lost her footing and tumbled down the dune. She coughed as blood stained filth poured out of her mouth. Scrambling to her feet, she walked closer to the gate, almost compelled to do so. She looked down and saw that the dead twigs of withered plants were in fact fingers trying to grab at her. The sounds of screams of pain grew louder as her feet crunched closer to the gate. The naked people linking in chains were being followed by large beasts that dragged giant talons on the ground, stained a browning red. Their heads bore large horns that had rotting entrails hanging from them, and their mouths oversized bearing row upon row of serrated teeth. She saw one man fall to the floor, and the ground suddenly protruded writhing black eels that wrapped around his head, popping her eyes and cracked through the back of his skull. His body writhed in agony as they opened him up and spilled the contents onto the ground. He went limp and was absorbed into the dirt. She heard footsteps behind her, and there he was again, a man in his late twenties, heavy with stubble, a chain already around his neck as he appeared from nowhere and re-joined the line of pained lost souls. A revolving cycle of agony he would never be set free from. Annie saw behind the gate, the sky was a deep blood red mixed with black, carved into pieces by fierce lightning. She took a step across the threshold from the wasteland behind her to the hellish realm. Wooden barrels of boiling water where people were being submerged in by monsters, their legs kicking wildly as they re-emerged as skeletons with loose skin clinging onto their stripped bones. She saw the crushed bodies of people under huge boulders, still kicking, unable to die. She heard a low growl behind her and she froze. Then a snaking black eel move over her shoulder. She tried to run, move, fight back, but she was already constricted by more of them, flailing out of the ground, wrapping her up tight and she felt her bones begin to break. She tried to scream as the eel writhed in her mouth and forced its way down her throat further into her, before pushing out of her stomach in a bloodied red pop. The dirt was up to her knees now, as she was dragged screaming and crying. She was fully covered now. Both suffocating and mutilated, her bones cracking and popping as she was pushed deeper in the harrowing blackness below.

#

Annie shot up as a breath of cool air filled her lungs. She screamed and patted her body. She saw no creatures, no dirt, no finger tips grabbing at her ankles. She felt the earth and it was wet and cold, mud mixing with the dried blood on her dress. She was outside the house again. She turned to see Claudia, eyes reopen, looking at her like empty windows. She checked her knife wound. The blood had stopped. But she knew, deep in her heart, that she had visited the other side. A taste of what was to come, like an old lover who leaves dead flowers at your front door. It was more than a nightmare. It had been real, and Annie had been lucky to be spared from it. She didn't know what to think, her mind was racing and every part of her hurt. Her joints ached and her skin was numb. She slowly got to her feet. Her vision was shaky like her legs, but she held it together for a few steps before falling. Edith. She remembered Edith. Was she still alive? She remembered the eels. Was that what was awaiting her? Was it a warning of what was to come if she didn't try to absolve herself? She had been rescued, so she had to repay her debt. God knows what John was doing to her. Annie looked back into the night as she reached the main entrance of the house. Her feet pushing through the gravel as she clung on to what strength she had left. Claudia had completed one last bout of heroism in her final hour, when Annie was in her time of need. And she felt ashamed for ever doubting her. Her misplaced trust tasted like sour milk in her mouth. As she touched the hard wood of the front door, she pressed her ear to it and tried to listen. She couldn't hear anything. Her mind wandered back to the eels, writhing through her body. She shuddered. That place. The pain. The suffering. How long she had been gone for? She hadn't died, or she would still be there, but she hadn't simply fallen unconscious either. No, she had gone somewhere in between. The place in the middle. A space between Earth and Hell. Was it too late to save Edith? She remembered Claudia's shuddering body and foaming mouth. Had the poison worked itself into Edith too? Or had she suffered a worse fate? She needed to know. At least to try. Annie tried to push open the heavy front doors. They didn't budge. She moved under the thick tree line and retraced her steps as best she could through the mud and dark. Finally she found the small doors embedded into the ground. She took a deep breath. The storm had passed over her and she took one last look at the star filled sky, before slipping into the black, not knowing if she will ever see it again.

#

She came to the fireplace that sat ajar. She peered around its base and saw no monsters ready to eat her. Carefully, she slipped through the gap onto the soiled carpet. She kept low, moving behind the couch next to the piano, should someone be watching her. Then a thought struck her. A realisation she never wanted to have, but couldn't ignore. Where were the bodies? She remembered Brian's hanging jaw as Claudia cried into his skin. He wasn't there. She didn't see anyone around her, living or dead. There was a large pool of blood under the piano from where he had been laid, but after that there was nothing. Nothing obvious anyway. She looked into the entrance hall. Silently, she tiptoed to the maiden, keeping low to its base. She waited quietly. This house was huge, and one would easily be lost in its labyrinth of halls and rooms. She waited for something, anything that could help guide her where she needed to be. She heard nothing distinctive, only the faint creaking of the pipes and the sound of loose bricks falling after being dislodged by stray gun shots. The marble, at first glance, was clear, but at a closer inspection, you could make out the outline of roughly cleaned up blood. They streaked towards the maiden, who still stood there holding a warm smile. She moved closer to it and followed the red trail which stopped at its feet. She ran her hands over the cold stone where the blood vanished. She saw the faint grooves of what looked like an opening that led into the belly of the stone. A rush of fear gripped her.

"There's a shaft under it. It's a tomb," Annie whispered to herself. John must have moved the bodies. Hugo, the gunman and Brian were down there. That's why they couldn't see them when they had cowered in the kitchen. Why Claudia hadn't shrieked at the sight of them as she fled down the stairs. Annie feared that Edith was down there too, crying in the dark as hands touched her. She fingered its base. Inspecting it like it was a shining diamond, looking for a tiny flaw. She couldn't find any. If it was a chamber of some kind, then she wouldn't figure it out here. She heard something. She wasn't sure what it had been, so faint like it was never there at all. She listened again, hoping it wasn't her imagination. She heard it again, louder this time, more clearly. It was coming from below her, through the stone.

"Help…." The voice echoed, drenched in weakness and sorrow. "Heeelp meee." Annie pressed her head to the stone, and she felt a

slight draft coming from the creases. The ghostly whimper came again. "Help me....". Annie pressed on the groove.
"Edith?" she listened as her words fall flat in the silence. A couple of seconds went by, and she heard the groan again. Annie wondered if it actually was Edith making the noise, or if it was someone else luring her into the belly of the house. She pushed her fingers into the flower bed, desperately trying to find a hidden switch of some sort. As hard as she tried, she didn't hear a click or a buzz, and the shaft didn't open. She went back down to the hatch.
"I can't get it open, I'm going to find a way down. I'm coming." She had to find a way to get down there. Maybe it was a cellar or something. A hidden room used for hiding out, should shit hit the fan. Maybe some kind of panic room? She moved quickly across the hall and stepped into the kitchen. She thrust open a drawer and took out a large knife and held it in her hand. She had seen hell, and the only fear she had left was the fear of being reunited with it. It was like that place, this house, were bleeding into each other. She smelt the faint aroma of burning wood, and the walls flashed black and burnt then moved back to normal. Moving through the hall, Annie caught a glimpse of a writhing eel from the corner of her eye, only to vanish when she focused on the spot. The ground would blend into burning embers and barren rock and then back to marble and red carpet. She moved through the house, quietly checking locked doors and peering into open ones. The house was much larger than she once thought. There was the kitchen, the study, a gym, an office, another study, a small sauna, another bedroom. She turned through the labyrinth before realising she was helplessly lost, like a child on its first day at high school. Annie pushed through a small door which was set back out of the way. Easily enough to miss. She had to push hard on the door which scraped across the flooring in a loud crunch that split the silence. The room was poorly lit. It was cold in here and smelt of musky. She saw cobwebs in the corners of the ceiling, and dirty sinks and cabinets lined along the edges. It looked like a kitchen of some kind and judging by the thick brown stains in the sink, it had been out of action for a while. Annie stood there with the knife held ready, expecting a creature of the night to descend on her and drag her back to inferno, but the creature never came. She heard the faint groan again, coming from deeper in the room. She moved along the hard floor with trepidation, the knife held up by her face. Her shoes clicked down a small flight of

stairs as she passed boxes of plates and chipped glasses. She stepped over several mouse traps and rat droppings that had long forgone this place. Aching floor boards groaning under her weight. The stair well was narrow and was lit by a single light that dangled above. She saw another room come into view, smaller, which descended further into the house. The desolation of this place spat in the face of the rest of the home. She was in a dimly lit bedroom. The walls were grey granite, there were broken wooden chairs in the corners, and a small bedroll with a heaped pile of black pants and white shirts. "This must be John's bedroom," she whispered into the cold. "Oh my god." There was a faint smell of urine and bleach. It reminded her of something you might see on a charity advert, where a rich celebrity stands above children living in squalor, asking the public for donations. "That poor man." She walked quietly across the stone floor to another door that was open slightly. She heard the sound of metal dragging along the ground, coming from the open door, which welcomed her with a black she had only seen in the darkest of nights. She studied the small room and found in the dust and cobwebs, something to be a miss. She hit her foot on a small bundle of papers that had been wrapped together in a red ribbon. She set the knife down, still close enough to grab at a moment's notice, she held one of them up and strained her eyes in the poor light.

"Johnathon,
I can't bear to hear that you are suffering so horrifically. I wish I had stopped you from leaving. I wish I had grabbed you by the scruff of the neck that day when you got into that pig's car. We've tried the police, we've tried everything. I hope he doesn't find these letters. He'll hurt you even more. Not long now my love, we know what we need to do.
I will always love you, I will always be your Precious –
Catherine. Xx"

Annie looked through the letters, there must have been at least fifty of them here, all of the same nature, all from Catherine. She put them down and saw another small bundle, just sticking out from under the bedroll. She crouched down and picked them up. It was a small book filled with loose notes and newspaper clippings. Some of Hugo and his latest investments, a list of bank transfers from Hugo's account into

John's, thousands of pounds being taken out of John's account every month labelled "RENT" and "FOOD" and only a tiny amount being put into his labelled "WAGES." Hugo was paying John for his work, but was taking much more from him for his living here, which he had no choice to do. A feeling of empathy crept into her heart. What man will be driven to do when he has no other option? Her knife wound tinged and throbbed, and the feeling slowly melted away. Annie looked further. She saw newspaper clippings of Francis and his Pharmacy going to shit, she saw hotel tickets for a stay in Paris for three people in the presidential suite. She saw photographs of Claudia and Brian together, holding each other in hotel rooms, Jacuzzi and one on a golf course. She flicked through the pages furiously, John's diary of treachery, saving it all up as a justification for his actions. She saw her name in there, the letters she had sent to Hugo begging him for help. A log of her phone calls to him, detailing the voicemails she had left him. Annie felt like she was going to be sick. He had studied and captured her misery in rough print. She saw a newspaper clipping of her hospital suspending her after botching a surgery when she was under stress, and another, a copy of the final letter she had sent to Hugo, spilling it all out to him. She turned the page again. It was a list of codes to various accounts, one of them named 'PHARMACY.' and next to that was a list of names and ages. "Keely Emerson, Age Nine, Happy Hippo Cough Medicine. "Josh Rowlands, Age Three, Happy Hippo Cough Medicine, Gareth Young, Age Six, Happy Hippo Cough Medicine." The list went on. Next to the list was a title in thick bold letters. "KILLED BY SCHRYCHNINE." Annie's tears fell onto the ruffled pages. "Those poor souls," she whimpered. "You evil bastard." Then she saw something that made her grip go loose and drop the book onto the floor. Her mouth quivered and she shook her head in her hands. She reached back down and picked it up, hoping it wasn't true. She saw a photograph of Hugo and Edith, shaking hands at some sort of dinner, posing for the cameras. She then saw a cut out of a newspaper article, with a picture of Edith and a blonde boy, no older than six.

"Tragic Death Befalls Local Medical Pioneer.

Manchester's own 'Edith McTavin' has suffered a tragic loss of her only son 'Oscar' this week. The Pathologist and visionary

in medical science and biology discovered her child lifeless on the grassy verge of 'Clay Hole' pond after they had been out for a picnic on Wednesday afternoon. McTavin made little comment stating 'I can't go on knowing that this happened so unexpected. He was my life, and now I have nothing left.'
Condolences from all over the world from medical personal and high-profile friends and family of Edith have poured in. Her home address in Manchester has been inundated with flowers and sympathy cards.
Local born Hugo Black, a long-standing friend of Edith released this statement – 'It is with a heavy heart that I have to do this but Edith does not have the strength to speak to the press right now, Edith contacted me when she discovered that her son had drowned. I attended to her aid immediately and I held her and comforted her all night. The police and ambulance arrived and deemed it was death by drowning, which is backed up by the pathologist report and coroner's inquest. I urge the press to respect Edith's privacy during this difficult time.'"
Signed – Brian Callahan

Brian Callahan…. His name was like a pinball in her head. Had he known all this time? What was his role in all of this? Had he reported the story to get close to Hugo? Annie felt pain in her eyes. Edith must have been destroyed when this had happened. Annie never got to hold her child, but Edith had spent six years devoting her life to hers, only to have him suddenly taken away from her by a cruel twist of fate. That poor boy, flailing in the cold water, his lungs filling up until he sank under the surface. Annie wondered how such a thing could have happened. Had she been distracted with work or something? She was a remarkably busy woman, and she was sure it could have been a phone call or some other distraction that took her attention away for those vital couple of minutes. She whipped her eyes and continued to look through the scrap book of misery. John's book of black, his memoir of pain. She turned the page, and saw again another note. It was a copy of an email addressed to Edith.

"Dear Miss McTavin,
Thank you for completing your five weeks of residential

rehabilitation. This is now the first step to the rest of your life. We advise that you do not partake in any risk-taking activities for the short while you are out of the centre. We also strongly advise you try to remain as stress free as possible, for example a highly stressful work environment, as you are fragile at this time and any adversities can easily cause you too relapse.
We would also like to thank your sponsor, Mr. Hugo Black, for placing you with us and covering all the costs required to help you in your road to recovery.
Should you feel that you are struggling and may feel the desire to use again, please call us urgently.
The very best of luck –
Moiré Bates – Consultant."

Annie stared at the email until the words blended into one on the paper. This had to be a mistake? Edith was in rehab? Had she totally gone off the rails once her son had died? And Hugo knew all about this too? It couldn't be right. But Annie read it over again, and the message didn't change. Then she remembered when she had been offered wine and champagne throughout the course of the night and she had refused. She also remembered how hesitant she was to take the pain killers for her knee in the kitchen, and how she had only had a drink when her life was threatened by the shooter. Then she realised that Edith wore long white gloves, and even when they were burnt and charred, she refused to take them off and became extremely hostile at the thought of doing so. There must be marks under her arms. Had she been using needles? Annie dared not let her mind focus on the thought that was creeping into her mind but it pushed through and demanded her attention. Had Edith been high the day her son drowned? Had Hugo helped her cover it up? She was a pathologist. Had she forged her own son's report to make it look like a definite accident? A child wandered off too far when his mother wasn't looking, or was it that his mother was incapacitated through her own drug habit and he had wandered off, or if not that, had he possibly taken some thinking it was food, and he was placed in the water to stage an accident? Annie's mind raced and she was sweating heavily. Her attention, so focused, so concentrated on the conspiracy unfolding in front of her, the world could end around her and she wouldn't notice. The book had one page left, and she turned it over not wanting to see what it had to offer. It was another email, between Hugo and Edith.

"Hugo Black – Edith I helped you stay out of prison. I need you to do this for me.
Edith McTavin – Hugo I can't do that. Do you know how heavily this stuff is monitored?
Hugo Black – I don't care. I have a way to transport it, through a pharmacy chain that I partly own. If we get discovered, it's on me anyway.
Edith McTavin – Why do you need it?
Hugo Black – It's none of your concern. If you do this for me, I won't reveal what really happened with your boy.
Edith McTavin- How could you even say that? Okay Hugo, I will. I'll pretend that everything is okay and do as you say. I'll organise a new order and send it the way you explained.
Hugo Black - Good. Let me know when you have sent the Strychnine over to me. Regards."
Annie gripped the pages tight and then threw the book across the room where the papers fell across the floor. John's voice rattled in her skull. "You're both fucking child murderers."
It made sense now. The berating of Annie for having an abortion. The deep longing in Edith's eyes when speaking about children. Brian and Claudia. Francis' rage. Catherine and John. Secrets will spill over no matter how deep you bury them. She again heard the faint moaning and calls for help again. She wondered if there was more to the story she didn't yet know. And the only way to find out was from the horse's mouth. She stood up, dusted off her knees and grabbed the knife, before walking deeper into the vaults of which she found herself entwined inside.

Chapter Eighteen.

Scars And Secrets.

The groaning became slowly louder, stretching out with brief pauses. Drips of water trickled down the beams of wood above that cased over the cobblestone walls and as Annie descended the stairs, she felt a slight breeze creep across her face. She peered around the bottom of the stair well, where the last few steps met the hard ground. She saw several shapes in the dimly lit room. A small lamp cast a shy glow over them as it sat on a small wooden table in the corner. Next to it was a wooden work shop table, which had a variety of tools on top. Drills, screwdrivers, a rusting vice with cobwebs wrapped around its handle. The room was otherwise bare, other than a broken wooden crate in the corner about the size of a large dog, and Annie also saw four or five large jerrycans that sat under the table, a small dark puddle flowing around them and smelt the unmistakable fumes of gasoline. She heard the sound of creaking wood and shifting of weight, followed by the groan again, but this time it was higher, more of a whimper, like a small puppy that had been locked away from its owner for the night. Annie saw a woman sitting in a chair, next to the lamp facing away from her, her charred white gloves pulling at their binds.

Edith.

Annie's first instinct was to rush in, untie her and escape, but now she had other ideas. If Edith was here, tied up, then surely John wasn't too far behind. She took a step into the room, treading lightly, sticking to the corners, in the shadows. She couldn't see anyone else in the room, nor hear the sound of a phantom stalker. She believed it was just the two of them. She peered to her and saw another wooden door that was closed, and Annie wondered what secrets awaiting her on the other side. She moved cautiously towards Edith, still unaware of her presence, as she weakly pulled at her binds. Annie kicked a loose screw on the ground, which clinked and rolled along the concrete. Edith began to pull more frantically at her binds, uttering muffled screams like a person stuffed into a coffin and buried alive. Annie rushed over to Edith. She grabbed her shoulder and she turned to face her, her eyeliner like a stream of smeared coal under her eyes. She was gagged, a wet cloth stuffed in her mouth and a loose bit of duct tape that flailed from her cheek. She saw Annie and her eyes widened. Annie saw hope and fear in a split second.

"Shhhhhhh," Annie whispered holding her. She put the knife on the table and peeled off the tape and pulled the ragout of Edith's mouth. Edith began to cough. The rag was soaked in gasoline. Edith retched, gasping for air.

"You came back for me," Edith gasped, a smile cutting across her tortured face. "I thought I was going to die."

"You're going to get out of here Edith, I promise," Annie began to examine the binds. The ropes were double knotted around her wrists and her ankles merging her to the chair.

"He… he was going to burn me alive, he was going to destroy everything, all the evidence, all the bodies, and then disappear. He's not normal, Annie. He's not ordinary. His eyes. Such black in his eyes. We need to get out of here, we need to get help. Hurry before he comes back!" Annie felt sweat dripping from her forehead and was drank by the dry wood of the arm chair, ready to feel the sharp edge of a blade sliding between her shoulder blades, her shadow creating a frantic dance on the wall. Annie heard the sound of a door swing open, followed by a chirpy whistling. "Quick!" Edith urged. "He's coming!" Annie grabbed for the knife and began to saw the rope. It was thick and tough and the thin blade of the knife made it difficult to cut. She would need more time, she needed more time but there was none. The whistling grew closer, the clicking of firm footsteps in dress shoes moving closer towards them down the stone stair case.

"I'll come back," Annie hushed quickly, re-stuffing the rag into Edith's mouth. Edith began to panic frantically, her hope disappearing as Annie moved across the room and tucked herself through the small wooden door. Annie stepped in to the black, pressing her head against the wood. She could hear Edith muffled and crying hysterically. She knew if she didn't stop, John would know something was amiss, he would find her and kill them both. Annie waited with baited breath as the footsteps grew closer and the whistling continued. Edith had calmed, no longer pulling on her restraints but had now resumed to a low sobbing.

"Help…" she cried. The footsteps were in the room now, not ten feet from Annie. She looked down at the knife in her hand. She couldn't see it as she was in darkness, but she knew it was there. She could run in and end him once and for all, she had the element of surprise. But then what? Her and Edith have a nice talk about self-preservation? Or, would she run out to John, and he blow her away with his pistol. Annie couldn't even be certain that Edith wasn't in on this whole thing. Annie clutched her stomach suddenly, it felt like her intestines were trying to burst out of her, like the black eels, and her body turned hot like fire. She managed to hold back her scream of agony, clenching her teeth like a vice, as she buckled over, her legs went weak and she grabbed out for the wall but missed, falling head first into the black. She landed on the ground further into the room. The poison. It was killing her.

"Hush little baby don't say a word…" she heard John sing. Edith let out a loud scream, as John pulled the rag out of Edith's mouth. She let out another barrage of loud coughing and splutters for air.

"What do you want!" Edith screamed. John didn't answer. He continued to circle around her, picking up a drill and let off a rev. He then placed the clunking tool on the table, tracing his fingers over the other tools and opened the tool box and started to move items around.

"Momma's gonna buy you a mocking bird…." His voice was soft and floating. Annie reached out and tried to pull herself to her feet. She didn't have much time. Expecting John to start drilling into Edith's kneecaps at any moment. She felt the ground, then something soft, followed by something damp. She grabbed hold of it. She felt soft fabric and then cold, like she was touching raw meat. Her fingers continued to trace the shape. A tight bundle of hair, a break in the fabric for more cold. John stood opposite Edith as she repeated her mantra of harrow and tears. His arms folded, smiling to her.

"What do you…what do you want?" John leaned into her, putting his hands onto hers. His cracked and red fingers pulling the white gloves from her arms. "Don't…" she begged. He paused and locked eyes with her. They flitted black and then back to normal. Edith stopped whimpering for a moment. He slipped them off. She clenched her fingers in a vain attempt to keep them on but they came away anyway. She looked at her scarred arms.

"How old were you when you started doing Heroin?" he said. Edith collected her thoughts, mouthing the answer. He pulled out a bottle of water from his back pocket, unscrewed the lid and held it to her mouth. He gestured her to drink and she hesitantly pushed her lips to it, watching him. "Don't worry, it's not poison. You've had enough of that. By my counts, you have about ninety minutes to live anyway." She drank from the bottle, swirled the foul taste from the rag out of her mouth and spat it to the floor. "So how old?"

"Thirty," she whispered.

"Why so late?" Edith turned her head away from him.

"I hate you."

"You hate yourself." He took a drink from the bottle. "Why so late?"

"I don't want to talk about it." She fought back the tears, clenching her fingers tight.

"You don't have a choice. This is your only chance to get that weight off your chest." Edith bit back. She bit her lip and clenched her eyes shut. She shook her head.

"I don't want to… I don't want to talk about it." John leaned in closer to her. His breath on her cheeks. His eyes turned a deep black. He grabbed her head and her eyes flew open. She cried loudly, began kicking wildly at the floor and pulled at her binds.

"Tell me what he did to you," said the beast. He let her head go and it fell onto her chest. She breathed shallow and quick. A moment passed and she looked at him again. He was leaning on the table, drill in his hand.

"I was raped." Floods of tears burst from her eyes, dripping onto her dress in the cold silence. Annie stared into the black, listening to every word. She put her hand to her mouth.

"Oh my god…." John walked around the room, sipping lightly from the bottle.

"Who violated you," he said. Edith carried on talking, staring at the floor, like she lost in a world of her own, taken back to a place she had tried so long to hide from.

"I was at a party. We got really fucked up. Drink and weed mostly. I could hardly move. He pressed on to me. I tried to get him off but..." her voice was shaking. "I tried to call for help but I couldn't move from being so out of it. I laid there helpless while he violated me." Edith finished the last sentence in a whisper. Her eyes glistening with pain. John lent on the work table and folded his arms, waiting for the rest of the story. "So rather than call the police, worried about them finding out about my drug use and it destroying my reputation, I shut it away. I started injecting, not a lot at first, just enough to make the pain pass. But then it was more and more. Before I knew it, I was a full-blown addict." John rapped his fingers on the table with a rhythmic thud.

"Who did this to you?". She shook her head and clenched her eyes shut.

"God it hurts."

"Who was he?"

"He was a construction worker. He lived in a small place with another girl who was on the gear. He would have his friends over and we would all take drugs and get fucked up. I think the girl that lived with him would have sex for drugs in the end. It was a horrible place. He was from Prague. His name was Xavier and the girl was named Ima. I heard from the local press that the place had been raided by the police a few months later. Xavier was dead and the girl had been taken away. I don't know what happened to her. I found out I was pregnant not long after that."

"But that didn't stop you?" John lent forward again, his blue eyes unblinking looking into hers.

"No," Edith said, biting her lip.

"You killed your boy, Edith," John said coldly.

"No! He drowned!" Erupted Edith. All her pain, all the bottled-up emotion was now spilling out to him. "Oscar drowned at the park. I fell asleep! I was tired from work and I nodded off for a second. It was an accident!" she began to rattle against the restraints. "Let me out! Let me out!" her voice nearly breaking as her vocal chords burned at her screaming. "Let me fucking go!" She stopped screaming and panted heavily, looking at him. Even now, when all was out, she was trying to run from her past. John held her pause, like a high stakes poker game of who blinks first. "It was an accident…."

"You don't have to lie to me. I'm much worse than the police. I know all your sins, all your lies, I know you inside and out."

"What?"

"I was unsure what you were to be in this whole thing. But now I know. You are Pride."

"Nothing about me is proud."

"But yet, even when your bound and being forced to absolve your secrets, you still scream your innocence. You were attacked, and I'm sorry. But you had a choice, Edith. You decided to save your own skin rather than go to the police and leave that predator to continue making others' lives a misery. You could have ended the misery for so many others, but instead you chose not to report it. Then, you continued to descend into your guilt and your shame, and you took chemicals to supress the pain. Not only that, you then found out you were pregnant and continued to take your drugs. When the baby was born, you were a functioning drug addict. You enjoyed success and notoriety in your field, but you still couldn't put the needle down. You covered them up with long sleeve clothes and high gloves, to create this façade of success and single motherhood triumph."

"Stop…" Edith cried. John walked around her, circling her, his words, the truth, tearing into her.

"You Edith, did not fall asleep that day because you were tired. You took a hit and you passed out because you were high. Your poor boy then ate some of your fucking stash because you kept it in colourful bags so nobody would suspect a thing."

"Stop it!"

"And when your boy was dead next to you, when you finally came round, you called for help from Hugo, because you knew he could make it all go away provided you were able to make the cover up stick, so you put on a sad face, a mourning mother, and you put your baby boy on a cold slap and forged the report to satisfy the coroner. All to save yourself." Annie's ear was glued to the door. Her suspicions confirmed. How could she do such a horrible thing? "You finally stopped taking the drugs and went through the rattle yourself, but when I emailed you from Hugo's account, asking for strychnine, it was a test. A test to see whether you would willingly destroy the lives of others to again, save yourself. You're sick, Edith. You're sick with Pride, which has ultimately led to your self-destruction." John picked up a jerry can and opened it. He splashed gasoline on her and she begged and coughed for him to stop. He splashed it around her and emptied the can around her feet. Edith thought he was going to light a match and cast her into oblivion, but he stopped. She continued to spit and spatter, her hair drenched with fuel, it stinging her eyes and she blinked furiously to clear them. He came into focus through the blur. He was stood there again, arms folded. "The man who raped you, he was a disgusting human being. But you bore a child from him. The woman who was taking drugs too, Ima, she took the correct path. She got clean and she met Brian, Brian who was here tonight. They had a child, who would have been your boy's brother. But as much as he had the golden road to virtue and morality set out in front of him, he strayed into the arms of Claudia. You see Edith, everyone is connected in so many ways, ways we don't even know about. The person you pass on the street could marry your relative, or could have killed their unborn child. You can't escape karma. Sin will tempt you away and consume you without realising it. We are all connected. You are Pride, Annie is Heresy, Brian is Lust, Claudia is consumed by Greed, Francis is the violent, Hugo, the wrathful. Even my own Catherine, my Precious, is fraud." John looked into the dark, alone for a moment with his thoughts, his emotion turned heavy.

"So what are you?" Edith croaked. John righted himself.

"I, I am treachery. The worst of the hellish circles, sitting at the side of Lucifer himself. And I was driven to it by every other circle of hell that has befallen me." Again his eyes flitted black. "And he asked for me long before he needed me. And I am here to collect what I am owed." It studied its body. The tight biceps and the smooth hair. "I like this one. I think I will stay a while."

"What are you?" Edith whispered. "Who are you?" The beast smiled, its teeth seated and brown.

"I am the collector." The beast traced its finger nails across Edith's face. "And you are all mine."

"I…I'm sorry." Edith cried. "I'm sorry for what I have done, for what I am." The collector shook its head.

"I'm not the judge, Edith, I am just its courier. But you'll be meeting him soon." The beast reached into the tool box and pulled out a green rectangular component with an aerial and two buttons, one red, one blue. It looked at Edith and then over to the wooden door where Annie was hiding. It smiled and Edith's eyes went wide. It knows she is in there. It had known all along. She shook her head to him, pleading him not to hurt her, to leave her believing she is unseen by him, to let her go home and live in peace. The beast winked at Edith, and she knew her silent plea was useless. It pressed its thumb onto the red button and smiled to Edith.

"So, the flames spread quicker." It pushed the button and there was a quiet buzzing noise, as above them, the hatch from the stone maiden pulled open. Annie felt a large draft swoop down into the room she was in, as well as a cast of light onto her, and there she saw them. It was the gun man, his mouth open wide and eyes jellied staring into the void. His waxy skin and his arms were curled into his chest, his fists sealed tight. His fingers and where he laid were a dark purple and yellow, as stagnant blood pooled by gravity swelled. Annie had seen death before, but nothing as horrific as this. She saw another, Hugo, his face contorted in a permanent scream. By her side was Brian, dead finger tips reaching out to her. Annie didn't remember screaming. She didn't remember clambering to her feet and bursting through the door. She didn't remember the beast grabbing her. But she remembered its eyes. The eyes of a soulless black as she swathe eels writhe in them, staring into hers as hands wrapped around her neck.

Chapter Nineteen.

Flames.

Annie felt the hands of death closing in on her windpipe. She clutched at the collector as she fought for her life. She kicked out wildly as it straddled her on the ground. Edith screamed helplessly behind them, thrashing in her chair, watching her friend be murdered. The beast's teeth were bared and clenched, a blue vain protruding from its forehead as its hair stuck to his forehead with sweat. The beast's eyes were insane, a two soulless vessels of hate, Annie's soul thematic wished to reap. Annie grabbed out at its face, catching its cheek and nose with her finger nails drawing fresh blood as she dug them in. The creature howled in pain, then reeled back its fist and buried it in her cheek.

"Bitch!" the beast growled, spit hitting her. She gargled and choked, falling limp and dazed. Her head fell to the side and she saw the dead faces of Hugo, Brian and Francis staring back at her, their gaunt faces laughing at her in the shadows. She routed, grabbing the beast's fingers, Annie clamped her teeth shut as hard as she could. It wailed in pain and she heard the crunch of bones as her mouth filled with red. The beast recoiled back, grabbing its hand looking at its missing index and middle finger.

"Break me all you like," The monster hissed, "I will simply wear another. You have kissed the soil of hell, and I like you." Annie scrambled to her feet, and seeing the blade of the kitchen knife glistening on the ground, she lunged for it, knowing she had only a few seconds. She heard hurried steps of dress shoes behind her, and fingers wrap around her bare ankle. She was pulled back under him, fist coiled to deliver the knockout blow when Annie kicked out, smacking him hard in the stomach. He folded in two with a loud cry. A second blow caught him in the jaw, and he fell backwards knocking the tool box off the wooden table. Annie scrambled again for the knife, she looked up and saw the dead faces in the other room smiling at her. She clenched the handle and crawled along the concrete to the beast, the rough surface shredding her elbows and knees until she was a top of it.

"You think this is it, Annabelle?" The monster snarled, its mouth bloodied with missing teeth. It grabbed a hold of Annie's bare arm as she howled in agony as its touch seared into her skin, like hot acid being poured onto ice, sizzling and all. "You will be mine." Annie headed no reply. She drove the blade deep into the monster's chest, feeling the sternum cave as the blade severed its lungs and heart. The beast wailed. Thrashing its arms and howling an ear shattering wail. Annie slammed her hands to her ears, as the sound ricocheted around her mind like a cannon ball in a hall of mirrors. The ground begin to shake and the table and chairs rattled around her. Dusty photo frames fell to the ground and the light bulb flickered madly. The creature's face shark around its bones turning gaunt, and its eyes swelled as black gas evaporated from its stretched mouth through the door and up to the open shaft. Eventually, the shuddering stopped. Annie watched as the gas melted away, and the figure before her now returning to normal, looked peaceful. Its face was a warm pink and its ragged hair now smooth and silk. Annie held the figure's gaze, as she saw a flicker of life in them. She watched as the hate and fury faded from his face, and a softer expression returned. One of sorrow and regret. John tried to mouth something before death took him away, but the reaper came too quickly, and left him collapsed in a forever half spoken word. Annie fell onto her back panting heavily, staring at the blank ceiling and single steady lightbulb.

"You did it," Edith whispered, staring at John's lifeless body. Annie crawled onto all fours. She heaved loudly and vomited a mixture of foaming bile and blood onto the ground. "Annie, don't fail on me now," Edith called, pulling at her binds. Annie's head spun as she looked at the mixture on the ground. A soup of ill.

"It's just the effects of over exertion, exhaustion and adrenaline." Annie said. "If it was the poison, I would be bleeding from the eyes and having seizures."

"How do you know that? Are you sure?" Hurried Edith. Annie wiped her bile on her arm.

"Yes," she said, looking at the smear on her roughly stitched wrist. "I've seen what happens from strychnine poisoning." She got to her feet, steadying herself on Edith's chair.

"We can get out of here, me and you. We can explain everything to the police, get to the hospital and expose the truth about tonight." Annie watched as a thick string of mucus dangled from her arm and fell into the wet pile of poisoned waste. Even now she thought, through the banging of the drum inside her head, Edith McTavin was still trying to save her own skin.

"What would you say to the police?" Annie said.

"What? Annie, untie me please, you don't have long left! Untie me and we can get out of here!" Annie studied her, and through her pleading she knew she spoke only lies.

"How do I know you wouldn't blame me for all of this?"

"Don't be ridiculous, Annabelle. We're friends! Please, Annie, untie me and we can go." Annie reached over to John's body, hoping to find something useful. As insane as he was, she didn't believe he would kill them, then commit suicide. He didn't have the gun with him, he mustn't have thought it necessary seeing as he would have thought it was only him and Edith left in the house, a miscalculation on his part. She didn't find a weapon, but she found something even better. She dug into his clothing and pulled out a car key from inside his trouser pocket. It looked it belonged to sports car of some kind. Modern. She placed it inside her bra. Edith watched as she did this, a light of hope in her eyes. "We can leave! Oh my god Annie, oh my god we're saved! I can drive us to a hospital, I feel okay, so long as we can get there soon, I think we'll be okay. I didn't drink much so I should be okay, were going to be okay Annie, me and you! Cut me loose, we can leave and get out of here!"

"How will you drive if you hurt your knee? You could barely walk before."

"I know Annie, but the pain killers you gave me, they must have kicked in. I begged John for another one when we were down here, he must have slipped me one maybe in the water. To keep me from passing out. I don't know. I'll be okay though, just cut me free. Come on, help me." Edith pulled on the binds again. Her wrists were cut with rope burn, bruised and inflamed. Annie reached down to John and pulled the knife free from his chest, which released with a crunching of bone and John slunk to the side with a heavy thump, eyes still wide open. She stood in front of Edith, the blood dripping from the edge of the blade and onto the floor, down her legs and feet. "Come on, yes Annie, help me please." She saw Edith's leg was still badly swollen. Annie reached over to her binds with the knife. "Oh thank you Annie, god bless you, sweet child god bless you." Annie stopped. She pulled back, again fixing her gaze on Edith, whose feigning smile had now completely left her face. "What are you doing?"

"I know about your son, Edith." There was a pause. An ear splitting pause that dragged with broken nails.

"What?"

"I know about Oscar. What happened to him! I heard you talking to John. I heard you tell him everything." Her voice was low and cold.

"No, no, Annie, you have it wrong. It wasn't true, none of it was. I told him what he wanted to hear. I knew you needed time and you would come and save me, I knew –"

"Shut up!" Annie barked. Edith's words fell dead in the air before moving past her lips. "I know what you have done, Edith. I can't believe even now you're lying to me about it. Me! Of all people! You had the audacity to lecture me about what I did to my child, but I am not a bad person and still am not a bad person." Annie was pacing now, like an enraged animal. The tight ball of pain in her gut coming loose and flowing from her. She felt herself getting hotter, her body shaking, and before she knew it she was screaming at Edith who sat there silently, lapping up what she was saying, whether she wanted to hear it or not. "I messed my life up and nearly killed myself doing it, and I suffer every day. I don't try to cover it all up and lie so much over and over again that I actually start to believe it. Maybe John, or whatever that thing was, had a point. He, in some way, was trying to do some good. To rid the world of filth like us." Edith was quivering. Fresh tears coming from her eyes.

"I'm so sorry, Annie. I'm so sorry. Please, I can be good, I can be better," Edith begged.

"No, Edith." Annie said, her voice calm and cool. Devoid of emotion. "No, you can't." Annie placed the knife on the table and picked up the sodden gasoline rag. Edith screamed as Annie stuffed it in her mouth. She reached under the table and pulled out a jerry can. She opened it and poured it over Edith, who screamed wildly, rocking and racking and shaking in her chair, pulling at the rope so hard she opened up her wrists until they were wearing down to the bone. Annie threw the rest of the half-filled jerry can around the room. Edith's muffled screams broke through the rag, as she inhaled more and more fumes. Annie figured it would be a small blessing. She would be nearly passed out when the flames ate her alive. She rummaged through the scattered tool box on the ground until she found a pack of matches. Annie felt her body turn numb. She peered to the laughing faces of the dead and to the whimpering eyes of the living. She spoke coolly, feet together like a child reciting her morning assembly. "And so the screams will lament as the tumbling of souls descend, down and down into the earth. Through the howling winds the sinners will burn" Annie struck a match. "And from the ground you bore, to ash you will return."

"No!!" Edith screamed from behind the rag.

"Abandon all hope, ye who enter here," whispered Annie. She flicked the match to Edith. She watched as a thousand tiny fingers ran up her and around her. Edith wailed and screeched as the flames buried into her scalp and her face, popping her eyes and ravaged through her body as an explosion of reds and yellows danced across her, leaving her to become the legacy she left on this earth. Just ash and dirt. "Now burn." Annie ran from the room as the flames snaked across the ground like ethereal lava that chased her feet, the flames like snaking eels on the walls liking her feet as she raced up the stairs as the bare bedroom filled with thick black smoke. Floating embers pushed their way up the stair well and set fire to the bedroll. Annie stopped quickly and remembered the book of clippings and newspaper articles, like it was the key to her freedom, the chalice of truth. She grabbed a hold of it, it beginning to burn quickly. Desperately she shook it, but the book was already ablaze. Its secrets devoured in a river of red and blue. The flames spread further up the wall and onto the dried wooden beams that lined the top of the ceiling above her. She heard the cracking of wood and a flaming beam fell next to her. She watched as it tumbled down and she recoiled in terror, like a lost fawn in a forest fire. The flames from the book spread onto her hand and she cried out in pain, waving it around and patting it furiously, tossing the book into the hungry inferno. She raced through the hall ways, desperately trying to remember her way out, while spectral hands reached out of the burning walls and tried to grab her, melted oil paintings spilling down the walls. She dodged past them, holding her head low under the thick gathering smoke. Her eyes stung and her throat burned. The place was crumbing at her feet and if she didn't find a way out soon, it would collapse around her. She passed through one corridor and then another, moving past flaming curtains and cracking vases. Through the orange and red, she saw the hallway leading from the main lounge where the secret exit in the fireplace was. A sick twist of irony, the wheel of fate trying to correct itself. She ran through the flaming halls, the exit growing nearer. She saw a shadow darting across the room as she passed the door way to the kitchen. She stopped briefly for another look and knew she must have imagined it. But then she saw it again, the silhouette of a person standing upright cast onto the wall as it moved in and out of focus from the surrounding inferno.

"Hey!" she shouted, looking into the kitchen. She covered her mouth with her hand. She heard the sound of windows around her shattering, which caused an implosion of fresh oxygen mixing with the fire. The broken piano popped atonal notes and melodies, like a broken nursery rhyme. She saw a figure standing in the corner of the room. Was it a guest she hadn't met? Precious? Had Claudia survived? It stood there with its back to her. It was a woman in a white dressing gown and long flowing dark hair with its back to Annie. She looked to be nestling something in her chest, looking down at it calmly singing a soft lullaby.

"Hey!" Annie screamed again, coughing violently. "You need to get out of here!" It reached its head up and stood firm. It turned around and Annie saw it. It stood bloodied and mutilated. Its face was twisted and bore a hideous smile. Its eyes were dead and its lips a shade of black. Its skin was a dull blue and it was naked, the open gown falling past its breasts and legs. In her hands an infant writhed bloodied and red, mouth full of clotted mucus and bile. It was Annie. The creature moved closer to her. Annie fell backwards from it. She crawled on the ground. Her eyes fixed on its. It shuffled to her, holding out the dead writhing infant to Annie. She could smell rotting flesh mixed with burning wood and ash. She saw black spectres crawling out of the walls on all fours scurrying like cockroaches. The woman in the gown spoke, her voice like a roaring beast and a woman moulded together.

"Hold your baby one last time." Annie felt the grip of hell around her, touching her, dragging her under again. Her lungs filled with smoke and the sounds of the crying child moved farther away, until muffled and faded. Her body was hot and her breath thick like tar, as she tumbled and fell into nothingness, until all went black.

Chapter Twenty.

Absolution.

Rain.

Heavy swelled raindrops that poured around her. A brief thought crept into her mind. One of confusion, dissolution, like she was meant to be somewhere else, had been somewhere else. But the thought flew away no sooner than it had arrived. She didn't wish to find it again, for she could remember nothing else before this moment. She knew her name yes, and that she was a human being. But everything else other than that didn't seem to matter. Why she was under the rain didn't bother her. Instead she accepted that this was where she was, this was where she had found herself. And for some unknown reason, she had the most powerful feeling of this was where she was meant to be. Right here, right now. Within herself. Inside her own mind. This was the beginning of the rest of her life. She ran her hands over her face. Her eyes softly closed. Her lumps and dried blood had gone. Her skin was sooth and softer than it had been in years. Her deep wrinkles had smoothed out, and her eyelids no longer puffy and sunken. She traced her hands across the rest of her. The stitches in her arm where gone, and she couldn't think as to why they would be there in the first place. The more she tried to think of such things, the more the thought was pulled away. For the first time in a long time, she felt wonderful. She didn't hurt, ache, or feel anything but deep relaxation, as the rain pummelled her head and ran down her shoulders. Rested, calm and at peace. The rain was warm and lovely, she felt it sink into her skin and wash all of her hate, and bitterness away. She felt lighter, like her anguish had been weighing her down for so long, she had forgotten how it felt to be without it, like a slave who is finally set free from a lifetime in chains now able to run in the sunshine for the first time. Gently, she opened her eyes, as she heard the distant cracking of thunder that tiptoes through the drone of the rainfall. Pink and electric blue lighting danced through the dark clouds above her. She held her hands out, her arms wide open, staring at the clouded sky. The air was hot and thick, but yet refreshing, as a soft breeze blew through her hair and made her body tingle. Annie felt the tickle of grass between her toes and for the first time saw she was naked. She looked around her and saw nothing but lush dull meadows overlooked by dark sky. The rain stopped suddenly, like it had never had fallen and she could feel her body now dry and cool. She felt nothing but happiness, a feeling that appeared to have always been inside her, hidden away and locked in a box wrapped in angry black chains. The tightness in her muscles now gone, like the rain had cleansed her of her black and the wind was injecting serenity into her, rejuvenating her with every breath. Destroying anxiety, depression and pain, and replacing it with beauty and contentment like she had never felt before, like her body had been a dead arid garden, and now large colourful flowers were blossoming from her kissed by warm sunlight, all the colour of the rainbow and then some. She saw a figure across the way, on the lip of a hill walking towards her. The figure was small and had flowing dark hair that blew gently. Her frame was thin and she was holding a small paper windmill that spun in the warm wind. She wore a small white dress and was barefoot. Annie walked towards the child, almost guided with a gentle push from the breeze under her step. She saw the sky was changing. No longer dark and gruelling, but now a dark blue and then a dull green, to a light crimson and finally sky blue, the clouds now completely gone. Around her budding flowers opened in a sea of deep reds, wild yellows and intoxicating blues and purples. The little girl moved closer And Annie saw she bore a beaming smile. The girl began to run. Running as fast as she could and Annie did the same. She didn't think as to why she wanted to or who this girl was. She just wanted to be with her. To hold her. To wrap her in her arms. The wind picked her from her feet and she leaped through the air to her. She landed a few hundred yards from her and ran faster. Faster than she had ever ran in her life. Arms wide open and laughing pure joy. The girl was shouting something. Annie tried to listen but the wind in her ears was too great, her thumping footsteps too loud to make out the exact words. They were cheerful, happy and excited. Annie leaped again and the wind carried her further, pushing her closer to the girl. The girl's voice became clearer as she got closer and closer. Annie's body nearly fell apart when she heard her voice clearly, sweet, cheery and oh so innocent.

"Mum!"

The girl met Annie next to a bed of bright roses. Falling into each other. Annie wrapped her arms so tightly around her, she thought she would break her, but the girl returned her mother's love, and squoze Annie so tight. So very tight indeed. The girl felt Annie's tears soaking into her cheek, and Annie held her there as it all spilled out onto the girl. Annie pulled away and held her daughters head in her hands. She ran her fingers through her hair and stroked her face, kissing her over and over again. The warmth of her skin on hers, and Annie realised she had been freezing her whole life.

"I'm so sorry baby," Annie cried. The girl, no older than seven, smiled at her and stroked Annie's face. She took Annie's hand and placed it on her chest. She then placed her hand on Annie's chest.

"I'm in here," the girl said. Her voice was soft and sweet. As pure as one could ever be. She was beautiful and precious. Innocent, untouched by the stresses and turmoil's of life. She had never felt the sickness of disease, never the torments of bullies and never the stomach pains of hunger. But she had never been held, sang to sleep at night or ran around for hours in the local park climbing trees and trying to touch the sky with her fingertips on a high swing.

"I love you so much sweetheart." Annie cried again onto the girl, who held her silently stroking Annie's hair, the windmill humming next to them. Annie pulled away, running her fingers through her soft hair.

"What's your name?"

"I don't have a name." The girl said smiling. "Nobody has names here. We don't need them, were all together here, not separate." Annie looked around.

"There's more of you?" The girl nodded and then pointed to where she had come from, further across the hill. Annie followed her finger and then fell back into her deep eyes and in a moment, somehow she understood. Like trying to hold on to pain in her mind was fruitless in this place, wherever this place was, trying to ignore the message it held was like trying to hold fire. You just couldn't ignore the burning. It was a bizarre idea that everyone could be part of one thing completely and not have their own unique identity. But then she thought about it further, in that we are born from the elements of the stars, and life is recycled into the earth and the wind, and everything that has ever been or will ever be is a collection of all that has come before it. Identity is a formation of the individual, the ego, when in the grand scheme of things, we are all part of the same thing. There is only This, and there is always, will always, and has only ever been just This. While thinking this, she got a flicker of something else. Another memory. And for the first time since standing under the rain, she felt fear again. The other place she had visited, filled with anguish and fire. The naked man in chains she had seen being mutilated and dragged into the ground by the eels had reappeared in the endless cycle, because he was the cycle. He was not an individual so he could never leave, and so because nothing could be born from his death, no new beginning coming from his end, he was to be relived it over and over again. She felt the girl tugging on her shoulder, as she fell back into her gaze, away from the screams and pain of her memory. She saw that she was no longer naked, but instead she was wearing a yellow flowery dressed that flayed at the bottom, like something one would see a sixties model wearing. Surprised, she touched herself and her hair which was now tied back in a bun and a red rose pin. She was wearing small black dolly shoes, and she could hear the sound of children playing in the distance. She stood up and looked to her daughter who was standing by her side holding her hand, and she had never felt such a gentle touch in her existence. She pointed to the brow of the hill she had emerged from.

"Where are we?" Asked Annie. The girl held a tiny smile.

"This way, mummy." She led Annie to the brow and she could see a vast playground, filled with hundreds of children, all playing, running and singing songs under the bright sun. "This is where we wait."

"Wait for what?"

"We wait until we can go away. Sometimes boys and girl don't stay long and they go up," she pointed to the sky. "And sometimes they stay here for a long time."

"Why do they have to stay?" Asked Annie.

"Because they can't go yet. They haven't had the water." The girl made a sign of the cross on her forehead and Annie knew she meant baptism.

"If you haven't had the water, you have to stay here until someone can take you up when they are done." Annie looked at her confused.
"What do you mean, done?" The girl laughed.
"You talk a lot," she said smiling, which Annie returned. "If you can't go up, then someone can take you up when they are okay to go up, from being good in the other place." Annie thought she understood.
"So…" Annie began, crouching to her, stroking her face. "If a child hasn't had the water," she made the sign of the cross again. The girl laughed and copied her. "Then you need someone who has been good to take you up so you can leave?" The girl nodded and squeezed her mum's hand, a look of hope in her big eyes.
"Are you good?" she said, a smile on her face. Annie felt sadness for the first time since being in this place. She was good, or at least she had been. She was the reason why her daughter couldn't move on, because she hadn't given her the chance to live and hadn't had her baptised, as she had turned her back on God after everything that had happened to her. And after the events of the night, sending Edith to the beyond, wherever she may end up, more than likely with the eels, she had denied another person the right to life. But she had not been cast into hell when she closed her eyes in the fire, instead she was here, in between. So she was not without salvation, not without chance of redemption. If the stories of heaven and hell were true, which given her experience, she was becoming more of a believer by the second, she had not yet been judged at the gates of heaven. So she figured there was more for her to do. Even if that meant spending the rest of her life in prison for what she had done, she could repent and come back here, and walk into the golden gates of heaven holding her beautiful child and be with her forever, until the moon turns black and the stars burn out. Until endless time. Annie shook her head, and the girl's joyful expression dropped.
"I'm so sorry sweetheart, but I have not been good." Annie said, trying to fight back the tears. Even here it would seem, one cannot escape their guilt as it chased them over the stretching hills, marauding chariots with flaming swords and rabid dogs.
"But you're here," the girl urged, her arms wide. "You're here and not down there!" She pointed to the ground, her voice with a hint of fear.
"I know sweetheart." Annie hugged her again tightly and pulled her back, still holding her shoulders looking her in her eyes. She studied them, hoping that if she returned to the land of the living she could

remember them, or should she be damned, they would guide her through the shadows. "But I can be, I will be, and I promise I will come back for you and we can go up there. Just a little longer." The girl moved away from her with her head low. She sat on the grass and picked a dandy lion from the ground, twirling it in her fingers.

"Why didn't you want me?" Annie's heart felt like it had been hit with a truck. It was the question she had been dreading. She went to speak, but her mouth uttered no noise. She crouched next to her and held her again. She turned to face her and Annie eyes began to well. A million excuses came into her mind. She was scared, wasn't thinking clearly, stressed, it wasn't the right time for her? But no matter how many times she justified it to herself as she cried herself to sleep, now didn't seem enough as she stared into the child's eyes that she never allowed to open. She pushed through the ball in her throat that was swelling by the second. She saw the clouds appear in the sky and pull closer together, blotting out the sunlight, casting a grey shadow over. Annie ran her fingers through the girls hair, the paper wind mill laid abandoned on the dulled green.

"I don't know baby," she said. Now face to face with it, it was the honest truth. Now all her reasons had fallen flat, she simply didn't know. She had no excuse. She had no reasoning. Tears fell onto the grass and she held the girl in her arms, worried she would float away or turn to dust. Like this was all a test and failure would mean the very thing you craved and desired would literally turn to ash in your fingertips. But she stayed firm and solid, and she looked at Annie with a small smile.

"Thank you for being honest with me, mummy. I didn't want you to lie to me. You've done some bad, but I know you're good." The girl again put her hand on Annie's chest and she took it into hers, wrapping her fingers around her tiny digits. "Close your eyes." Annie did. She felt the warm tiny lips kiss her gently on hers. She felt the girl's breath in her ear. "Don't let the shadow man take you like the others." Annie's eyes snapped open. Her daughter was gone. She looked around the meadow. She no longer heard the laughing of children or the songs of innocence. The rain came down again heavy and warm, drenching her naked body once more. The wind picked up and she was filled with panic.

"The Shadow man?" Annie looked over the crest of the hill to the empty playground. There she saw it. A tall wiry frame that stood motionless amongst the swings. Its face blank, pointing a long bony finger to her. Before she could react, the wind grew stronger as it started to flow through her. She lifted from the ground high into the sky as the figure grew smaller as she drifted from it. It's eyeless face watching her as she began to change, turning transparent, dissolving her in the wind and rain. The Shadow man. Her daughter's words ringing in her ears amongst the whirling wind. She pushed away fear as best she could and held on to the sound of that sweet voice. She closed her eyes, not knowing what was next, but whatever was to come, she would face it. When it got too painful, she would remember the soft touch of her child's hand and kiss, and let her beautiful brown eyes guide her through the challenges, knowing that when she was done, she would be able to walk with her again. Annie heard a faint shouting and she felt hot, sweating, the blanketing downpour of rain now turned into a thrashing chaotic stream that hit her from all directions. She couldn't feel a warm breeze, but only hot fire and thick smoke. She could smell charred wood and heard the popping of glass. She opened her eyes again, and saw a gas mask in front of her, her refection in its black face and thick yellow gloves grabbed hold of her. She lifted from the ground, not like she had been before by the wind, but this was rough, hastily and powerful as she was placed over the shoulder of a large man. Thick grey fabric rubbing against her. She drifted in and out of awareness as she saw the study being doused by giant streams of water that roared its fury on the dying flames. She then saw the bright red and blue lights flickering on the exterior of the house, as a woman with long dark hair wailed wildly, being held back by police as she tried to run into the flames, screaming someone's name and grabbing at the hot air. Finally, she saw the bright overhead lights as paramedics laid her onto her back on a small bed and put a mask over her face and plugged her into machines. A woman with short red hair talking to her through muffled sounds as Annie began to fall away and she tried to fight it as long as she could. The last thing she remembered was the wailing sirens of the ambulance, and the hard pressing of hands on her chest.

Chapter Twenty One.

Deliverance.

24 Hours Later.

Annie held the detectives gaze for a few seconds, her head still spinning. Murder? Arson? "I want a solicitor," she said again. "I need to speak to someone about all of this." The detective stood with a stone gaze. Finally, she opened her mouth.

"If you want a solicitor, then that's perfectly fine. Under the current legislation, you are entitled-" Annie cut her off.

"I don't care why I am allowed one," Annie snapped. "I just said I want one. Now if you don't mind, I'm tired." Annie laid down and closed her eyes, wishing she could instantly drift away to sleep. She could feel the detectives' eyes on her. A thick silence in the room. Eventually, the nurse spoke.

"It has been a lot for her, detectives."

"It's Sergeant. We'll leave her with you, we'll have someone from uniform come and watch her. She is under arrest, so until she's out of your care, we'll be here with her."

"I understand, detective."

"I said its Sergeant."

"I know." The nurse stood up and picked up the notes from Annie's bed. "I heard you the first time. Now please let the girl rest. Whatever she's done, she's under my care and until the day comes she isn't, I will look after her. Now please." The nurse held the curtain open and smiled at the Sergeant. She sighed and exited the curtain, quickly followed by the pink shirt detective who scurried behind her. The nurse came back to Annie and stroked her forehead. She felt hot and the nurse checked her readings.

"I'm getting a fever," Annie said, eyes still closed. The nurse looked down at her, almost offended.

"How do you know that?"

"I have severe burns and I have been poisoned. My immune system is in the toilet. It's probably a mild Pseudomonas Aeruginosa at the minute, but given my injuries, I'll need some anti-biotics before it becomes something worse. Simple Penicillin should suffice. Failing that, hit me with some cephalosporins. That should do the trick. I'll need my fluids and electrolytes checking every three hours, and I'll need a bucket and bedpan for the vomiting and diarrhoea." The nurse tried to hide her impressed grin. She detached the fluids and put on some new ones. She changed the dressing on Annie's burns and took notes of her readings.

"How do you know all this?" she said, putting the disposed bandages in a bio waste bin.

"I was a surgeon in a past life. Now please, get the drugs. It's going to be a rough ride for me."

#

Over the next few days, Annie deteriorated quickly, descending deeper and deeper into illness, narrowly avoiding full blown sepsis twice. She would howl and scream at night as her bones ached and her skin was both on fire then ice. Her bedsheets were changed every four hours sodden with sweat. She would cough, vomit, shit herself and then do it all again. She had to be fed intravenously, and had a permanent nurse on standby, who would press the big red button on her monitor when she would fit and even flatline. By day four, she had had two blood transfusions and all the fluids in her body cycled three times over. Thank god the UK had a national health program, or she wouldn't have made it past day one. In the darkest depths of her illness, Annie would let her mind fall back to the sunny hills and the heavy rain where she held her daughter. She came to her like a memory she had never had, from a place she had never been too. When she had first returned from that place back to her body, her mind had been hazy, still piecing the fractured memories together from what had happened. The amnesia was her mind's way of coping with the trauma of that night. She remembered now though. She remembered it all. The gun shots, the fights, the treachery, the inferno and Edith. However through her pain, she remembered her daughter's beautiful brown eyes and the way her hair blew in the soft wind overlooking the playground on the hill. The Shadow man. What had she meant? Who was the Shadow man? She tried to push it out of her mind, but as much as she tried, she remembered seeing him on the hill staring back at her.

"I can be, I will be, and I promise I will come back for you and we can go up there. Just a little longer." The eternal promise she had made to her in the land of the in-between rang in her mind, like a burrowing maggot that had imbedded in her skull. It was down to her to make it blossom into a beautiful butterfly, and not into a black moth with hundreds of larva eating her alive. As much as she didn't like the two detectives, she had given them to her ticket to freedom. If she admitted her crimes to them, yes she would go away forever, never to walk on hills and spend time in the outside world again. Maybe, she would even be sent to a psychiatric hospital, given the tale she could tell. But that wouldn't the truth. She would tell them about the woman in the fire, the insanity of John, the self-preservation of Edith. But what if they wanted to pin all the deaths on her? If she admitted that then what would happen? She would be lying yes, but she wouldn't be believed anyway. Not with a major crime investigation landed on a reporter's desk, and her eyes lighting up with the prospect of promotion on the horizon, the only suspect telling a tale of spectral women in flames and the real killer entwined in a plot of fraud and deception, violence and betrayal woven so deep it resembled a ball of barbed wire, all who try to unravel it left with the deepest scars. And what if she told them of the other place? With the black eels that pop out your eyes and rip out your belly? This wasn't going to end well for her, but remembering her promise again, the alternative was much worse. Annie spent the last week having her bandages changed. She saw several uniformed officers by her bedside, day after day. Some officers were happy to talk about anything other than work, and other officers were too busy typing on their portable laptops, finishing investigations, thankful for the respite to actually get some clerical work done which they had been falling behind on. Today however, she wasn't sure which day as they all seemed to bleed into the each other, only discernible by the changing dinner menu and the content on the small television which was mounted on the corner of the wall in her ward, an officer had been brought into the hospital and was put in a bed and was being seen to, by nurses. He was a large man, bald on top with a thick beard and he had more tattoos you could shake a stick at. Annie had spoken to him, as the officer who was guarding her, the same one for during the day for the past three days, had gone to check he was okay.

"I'm fine," tattoo said. "I was hit by a car a couple of days back." The officer who was guarding her was stocky and square looking, and he had short blonde hair and a rounded face and reminded Annie of a Lego man.

"Jesus," said Lego. "How did that happen?" Tattoo folded his arms, obviously embarrassed about being a patient at the hospital he had guarded people at.

"I saw a woman and a guy at a petrol station on Windemere Road. The guy was all twitchy and was struggling to pay for his fuel. When a woman, blonde, tattoos, black dress came in and paid for it. They then left in a fancy car." Annie's ears pricked up.

"Fuck man, so what was up with the car?" Lego said.

"We ran the car through, and it came back to a young lad in his early twenties. The kid had a picture on our system, as he had been done for being drunk and disorderly a few months back. The kid wasn't the same guy driving the car. Given how twitchy he was, and wouldn't give us his name, knowing it wouldn't match up to the car, we figured it had been stolen. We did an area search and checked ANPR, which came back negative so we knew it couldn't be far away. Anyway, we found the car ditched outside of the giant house on Windemere. Fuck me, it was ablaze." Annie held her breath. They were talking about the house, Hugo's home. They were talking about Catherine? Precious or whatever her name was? Had she stole a car? Annie listened closely, straining to hear what the officers were talking about, half hearing, half lip reading. "I called it in, and then we got a call from a patrol that the owner of the car had been found lying in the road not too far from the motorway services."

"Alive?" Lego said cautiously. Tattoo shook his head.

"Head smashed in. The weirdest part is, there was a second abandoned car parked up in a lay by next to where the kid was found. Forensics did a swab on it after it got seized, and it was the guy from the petrol station, apparently he gone off the rails since his company fell to pieces. The house that was on fire? That was his main investor." Annie tried to stop herself from gasping as she lay here pretending to not be listening. Francis? The gun man? Were the police were thinking he was behind the whole thing? That he caused the fire? That he stole the car and killed someone to do it? Annie's joy quickly vanished and her old friend pain settled in. She hadn't known about the boy having his car taken. Another life lost in this horrendous ordeal. No doubt innocent, as innocent anyone can be anyway. Annie faced yet another dilemma. Does she say she was completely innocent, now that the police potentially have a suspect, albeit dead and burnt to dust by now, but they have someone with motive, placed at the scene and a violent crime behind their name? Or does she explain what really happened to her, what her involvement was in this whole thing, and hope that they believe her that she wasn't responsible for everything. Francis didn't start the fire, she did. Francis didn't kill Edith or anyone for that matter. Annie can't say that, and if she blames Francis, then John and Catherine would have gotten away with it. Even from beyond the grave, the dead were still making her life a misery. Annie toyed with the idea while listening to the two officers talk about their grim discovery. "So I found the car of the poor guy that had been beaten to death and left to die in the road." Tattoo continued. "So as I'm checking it out and call it in, I was hit by a drunk driver. Thankfully, I didn't suffer any more than bruising and was able to go home after a day or two, but I started being sick and passed out, so they brought me back in to do some more checks on me. God bless the National Health Service. If I had to pay for my treatment, I would have been left for dead, or me and my family would be bankrupt and twenty-three years in the job would have been for nothing." Lego patted him on his shoulder.

"Here here mate." Tattoo nodded to Annie's direction, and she turned her head away towards the wall so not to look like she was listening in.

"Who's she?" Lego turned and saw Annie in the bed.

"The fire and job you're on about? She's the main suspect." Tattoos eyes went wide.

"Fuck off man really?"

"I know, right".

"But, but she's tiny? Surely she couldn't have done all of that?"

"I don't know. She's an odd one. Doesn't talk much. Doesn't move much. Just sleeps a lot and prays." Annie caught herself muttering herself into the covers. She remembered everything now, the injuries and cloudiness had lifted during her stay in the hospital. But she had remembered something else without realising, she had forgotten to remember, that even though she had renounced god, she was still a part of god, and him a part of her, and even when she hadn't realised it, she had been praying to him. Not for her, as she felt she was on the verge of damnation. No. Instead she was whispering to the great father into the fabric for her daughter. Her nameless child she had never met. But here she was, noticeable by those watching her, if not noticing herself, that she had been silently praying for her child to be held by the hand of god, and to be kept safe in his love until the day she can be reunited with her, no matter how long that may be. Lego bid Tattoo a farewell and a get well soon before returning to Annie's bedside, opening his laptop and continuing to work on the amassed case files in his work load. Due to her risk, she had been deemed to need two officers at all times watching her, however that had been downgraded to one.

"What's going to happen to me?" she asked Lego as he typed so fast she thought his fingers might catch fire and the sprinklers were going to go off. She hadn't spoken to him much and they had hardly exchanged anything more than a 'Hello' and 'Goodnight' when he was relieved by the end of his shift by another officer. She liked when he was around, despite his resemblance to a children's toy of building blocks. He closed his laptop which Annie liked. He had her attention, which was a rare quality in these days. People putting away technology to actually speak to each other.

"Well," he said, taking a sip of water from his flask he kept under his plastic blue chair. "When the doctors say you've healed enough, then you'll be taken into custody and you'll be interviewed over the allegations. From there you will either be charged and remanded, charged and bailed, released under investigation when there are still more things to look into or," he scratched his head, "you will be free to go and there will be no further action." Annie could tell from the look on his face that the last one was a fool's dream, or either of the last three of four options for that matter. They obviously had a lot of evidence to put at least some of the incident on her. She was sure they had done extensive digging into her background, they no doubt, by now, knew everything about her and her life, which included the stress and her dismissal at work, her medication she had been given to help cope with the anxiety and to help her sleep, and maybe even the hospital report from when she had been a victim of a 'robbery'. "An insane woman finally cracked," she could see the headlines now. The detectives laughing back in the station at how they had solved the case.

"Okay, so when will that be? Will I go to prison?" Lego shifted in his seat, more from discomfort of the question rather his arse had gone numb.

"That's not for me to say. But I'll be honest with you, I don't think you'll be free to leave custody anytime soon."

"Why is that?"

"I'm sorry, Miss. Jones, I can't discuss the details of the case with you as you're under investigation. I'd have to report on any significant comments you make." Annie looked at Lego who was now reaching for his laptop again. She fingered her blanket and looked up to the bright light above her in the ceiling and the gap in the curtains that Lego had left when speaking to Tattoo. She saw him lying in bed, a broad man with large arms and a heavy rising chest. She felt sympathy for him. She felt sympathy for Lego. How much money was she costing the tax payer with what she had done? Innocent people were paying their wages for her to have a police officer sitting with her in a bed she felt she had no right to be in. The money could be spent much better elsewhere, to people who actually need it. Not only that, she didn't want the detectives sitting there in the office concocting a tale to send her down. She took a deep breath, and hoped god would forgive her.

"Pull out your notebook officer," Annie said. "I'm going to tell you everything."

#

Annie spent the next two hours speaking in immaculate detail about everything that had happened. The officer stopped her on several occasions reminding her she was still under caution and if she wanted a solicitor to consult with. "It's okay," she said, shaking her head. The officer continued to write in his notepad until that was full, then requested a small pile of lined A4 paper from the nurses that came in to change her drip and her anti biotics, and then would ask for another few pieces, before just asking for the entire pad. She told him about her relationship with Hugo, how they had met, about Edith and what she had said and done, about John, oh dear lord she spoke about John. How he had stabbed her, beaten her and tied up Edith as well as all of his other crimes against the inhabitants of the house. She told him what she knew about Brian, Catherine AKA Precious. She told him about the Strychnine, the money John had been taking from Hugo, his plans to move away. Lego stopped her on many occasions and stretched out his hand from writer's cramp. "Why don't you use your laptop?" Annie asked. Lego winced as he got blisters on the inside of his fingers while holding his pen.

"Because it's not evidential on there, it has to be in my pocket notebook," he said, holding up a small brown note pad with his name and number on it. "PC Darren Harper." He turned over another piece of paper. "I'm going to have to transfer all of this into a fresh note pad," he said laughing sympathetically, listening to Annie's incredible tale. She continued on, telling him she knew nothing about the stolen car, nor anything else that happened outside the house. When asked why she didn't call the police, she explained she thought John had done that, only to find it to be a lie. She told him about Francis, his gun and that he had tried to kill them in the hall and how Brian had tried to subdue him and Hugo had died. PC Lego stopped writing and put his pen down. He leaned into her and stroked her face.

"You have had so much go on Annie. It's no wonder you did what you did in the end. You were clearly not thinking right. The courts will see you as a woman in a desperate state, and they will look fondly on you. What, with losing your child, with the betrayal? You'll be okay. You have my word." She smiled at him, wanting it all to be true, wanting to believe him, wanting him to take her away and stand in the docks with her and scream to the jury that she was innocent, that she had not done what was being accused of her, that the mitigating circumstances should all be considered and she should be free to live out the rest of her life in peace. She wanted to hold him, drawn to him by her unleashing of the burden she had carried, and him intently listening to her, writing it down and making it immortal. That's what she wanted to happen.

That was what she wanted to tell him.

Instead, she admitted to everything. She said she had been stressed out of her mind from work. She told him that she wanted to hurt Hugo and that she had arranged Francis to bring her a gun because of how he had treated her. She told him that she had poisoned all of the food and drink at the party, and had even stolen a car and beat up the owner in order to get there undetected. She said she knew the layout of the house, the stone maiden and its hidden shaft. She told the officer that she had done it all. The murders, the fires, the poisoning, the secret passageway to make her escape. She ignored his pleas to seek legal advice. She ignored him as he asked her to consider what she was saying or he would have to activate his body worn video camera to capture the evidence as well as writing it down. But she continued anyway. She admitted to it all. When she was done, he said "Is there anything else you would like to tell me, Miss. Jones?" She thought about telling him about her daughter. She thought about telling him about the woman in the flames holding the writhing foetus. The black smoke from John as he lay dying, or the desperation in Edith's eyes as she begged her for her life. But she didn't. She sat there in the bed, looking at her face reflected in the small screen in the video camera on his chest.

"No," she said, tears falling onto the blanket. "That's everything." He put his pad away and switched off his body camera. As he did, Annie's heart filled with terror. Her refection in the tiny black screen. A tall black figure stood behind her. She turned quickly, nearly jumping out of her skin, hoping to not see it. Not feel it. Not believe it was there. The black shadow with the vacant face. Her heart slowed. It wasn't there. Only tulips of different colours in a flowery vase.

"Are you okay, miss?" A voice said behind her.

"Yes," Annie whispered, wondering what she had seen. She turned to the officer. "I thought I saw some-" It was there. Standing behind him. Teeth bared, wrapping its hands around his throat. Annie screamed and fell backwards, pointing to the spectre. She wailed loudly, trying to push herself away from it. The heart monitor blaring loudly. Her cannulas coming out. Blood flowing from her flailing arm.

"Behind you! Behind you!" she screamed. The officers turned quickly, arms up in front of him ready to fight. A blue apron pushed through the closed curtain. A flash of greying hair and tired eyes.

"What's going on in here?" said the old nurse. The officer stood to her staring at her blankly. His open mouth lost for words. The nurse shot him a worried look, then she rushed to the end of the bed, wrapping her arms around Annie's crumpled body on the floor. Her sobbing loud and her tears drenching her gown which played on the floor in front of them. "What happened pet?" Annie's lip shook underneath tightly closed eyes. Her hand was shaking as she pointed to the officer. "It's there…." She cried. "It was right there."

#

A few hours later Annie awoke in her hospital bed. Her head hurt like hell and her vision was shaky and blurry. It started to clear the more she blinked her eyes, like trying to clear a plastic film from her vision. She heard the tapping of keys next to her. She looked and saw it was Lego sitting there. This time, however, he had another officer with him. They didn't notice Annie sitting up and looking around. She saw the plant pot had gone and the faint remains of dirt were engrained into the grooves in the floor. She tried to touch her pounding heart but found herself to be handcuffed to the bed rail. She began to panic again. The vision of the monster coming back into her mind like a nightmare she couldn't run away from. A hand touched hers. It was cold but soft. She looked up to see the other officer holding her. She was maybe sixty, tanned and hand neck length blonde hair with brunette underlay. Her eyes were a deep blue, and her face was calm and relaxed.

"Try not to move so much," she said soothingly. "You took a nasty bump to the head before you were sedated." Annie looked and saw Lego had stopped typing and was watching her cautiously. His handcuffs gone from his belt.

"Sedated?" Annie whispered. The lady officer nodded her head.

"You were quite upset. We had to put you under to stop you from breaking anything. Annie looked where the vase had once been. "It's okay," the officer said. "I preferred roses anyway." A faint smile crept across her face.

"What's your name?" Annie asked timidly, still coming around.

"Sharron." Sharron sat down and Annie and she exchanged small talk. Apparently, they were just waiting on the nurse to come back with her notes and she would be released from the hospital. Swept away to custody where she would be spoken too by the detectives from earlier. The thought of them left a sour taste in Annie's mouth.

"How long will that take?" Annie said, clearing her throat. Sharron looked at her watch.

"About fifteen minutes or so. How are you feeling?"

"My head hurts and I need a drink." Lego looked at Annie and then again back to his computer screen. Will you stop typing away? It's like nails on a fucking chalkboard. Annie thought. Irritation pushing through the drumming her head.

"Well I can't give you anything for the pain," said Sharron. "There's a nurse in custody you can speak too. I can, however, get you a quick drink of water if you like?" Lego didn't look up. He just carried typing away. Annie felt her teeth brush the inside of her lip.

"That would be nice," Annie said with a strained smile, watching Lego on his computer. I am going to bash that damn computer over your head until brains decorate the vinyl flooring. Sharron smiled.

"I'll be back in a minute." She said to Lego, as he didn't so much as lift his head to watch her leave the room. The two of them sat there in silence as he continued on his computer. Annie felt the blood rise in her. The more she tried to ignore it, the hotter she became. Tap. Tap. Tapafuckingroo.

"Will you stop with that fucking noise!" Annie howled, splitting the silence, knuckles white as she gripped the bedrail. She held her hand to her mouth, amazed at the outburst. Lego looked just as shocked, his eyes wider than his hanging jaw.

"What did you say?" he croaked.

"I'm…I am so sorry," Annie started. "I don't know what came over me." She fingered the itchy blanket. "I don't know why I said that. You've been very nice." The officer studied her and Annie saw he was looking at her handcuffed wrists. They won't save you. She thought. In a mental voice that seemed alien. For a moment Annie wondered if she could make a break for it before he could call for help. Lego looked down and continued on his laptop again. A silence fell between them. Every silence before this had been one of peace and quiet, but this once was heavy and thick with tension. He had one eye on his work and the other one on her, his legs twitching. Annie felt the creeping in her throat again. "Do you think if I got out of bed and sank my teeth into your throat, you could stop me before I crushed your wind pipe?" The officer stopped taping on his keys. They locked eyes and electricity filled the void. Like a cowboy showdown at dawn, fastest hands wins.

"I know about your father, Darren," Annie said. Her voice gravelly and low.

"What did you say?" whispered Lego, a quiver in his voice. Annie

leaned forward, turning to him. Head cocked to one side.
"How many times did he touch you before you finally put the glass in his food?" Annie pulled her wrist and snapped the cuffs. She jumped from her bed, arms outstretched and in an instant she was upon him. She grabbed him and they toppled over from the chair. She was atop of him, fingers wrapped around his windpipe. He called out for help, eyes wide with terror as he locked them into Annie's, hers turned solid black. The officer struck her to the side of the head but she didn't relinquish her grip. She foamed at the mouth through her bared teeth. The officer grabbed hold of her hands and emptied the can of irritant spray into her face, which filled the room with a hot noxious gas. He lay there choking, screaming for her to let go of him as his legs thrashed wildly squeaking on the floor. The gas had blinded him and he heard hurried sounds of footsteps coming from the distance and the loud blaring of an alarm. A whispering through his ears that blocked out all the insanity around it. A voice that chilled his bones and made his skin tight and cold. "I am the thing that makes men quiver. I am the beast that lets eels slither." An excruciating pain exploded into the side of his cheek, as teeth cut through him and met in the middle. The teeth pulled away and his face swelled with red hot fire. The fingers around his throat dragged away, nails dragging across his skin as he heard her wailing, screaming like a banshee. He slammed his hand to his face and forced his eyes open. He had never seen so much blood before. He saw through the stinging blur a large bald man with tattoos and Sharron pinning Annie to the bed, limbs flailing like an octopus drenched in acid. Her wails of anguish and screaming indecipherable other than one fractured sentence repeated over and over again.
"Its eyes! Its eyes! It has no eyes!"

Chapter Twenty Two.

Between Earth And Hell.

Three Weeks Later.

Annie sat alone looking out of the small window in her cell. It was morning and she had had yet another sleepless night. The howling of the wing she was on had kept her awake from lights out to sun rise. The inmates around her were taunting the new arrivals from the upper decks, projecting their foul promises of pain and misery to the new bunkers that sat in the lower parts of the wings. Annie had kept quiet through her time being here. She hadn't said so much as a whisper to anyone. It was better than the other place she had been. After the hospital. She didn't remember much of it. But that apparently played into the psychosis she was diagnosed of. Once the officers he had taken a chunk out of, had finished having plastic surgery, she had another charge added to her rap sheet. She had initially been deemed "Criminally insane," by the hospitals psychologists. She remembered screaming her innocence to him, that she wasn't herself. Something had come over her. She told him about the Shadow man, and fuck it, she told him about her daughter, the black gas out of John's mouth and how she knew that whatever it was it had somehow moved into her. She told him about the eels, the hill under the clouds and the woman in the fire. He nodded, said he understood and continued writing in his book without so much as asking her to elaborate once.

So she was put in a mental hospital for a couple of weeks and then, once she was re-evaluated, she was deemed of sound mind. She remembered sitting in the court room. The hard benches digging into her back. The cuffs hurting her wrists as she had to sit there like a good little egg while other people she had never met decided the rest of her life. With a bang of the gavel later, she was found guilty of all charges and then swept off to this dear little place. As Annie looked out into the blank landscape and the barbed wire lined high walls, it would seem that if god had a plan for her, then he must have forgotten to write this part out and was obviously winging it trying desperately to rectify his plot holes. Annie felt however, that in God's great manuscript of her life, that he had given up half way through chapter five and gone to work on other projects. She felt like a character in a book who loose ends had never been tied, and she would drift forever on an endless page until her tale was lost in history. Either way, she figured, it would end slowly and without a definitive conclusion. She had noticed some of the more seasoned prisoners had begun to watch her with an intriguing eye. Most new comers she had seen either broke by the end of the first week, or had gained some kind of friendships by the second. Annie however had stayed mute, only speaking to the prison officers which walked around the perimeter above the wing atop of the suicide netting, like hold guardians patrolling in black ties and white shirts above the spiralling cauldron of wasted human potential beneath them. And even then, her words were brief and uninteresting to anyone listening. She mainly grunted, or gave a "Yes Ma'am," and that was as far as she went. Some of the prisoners had grown resentful of her, challenging her and intimidating her during free roaming time, where Annie would mainly stay in her cell and read.

"Fuck, you reading?" one woman had said. She was a frail, twitchy woman, hair pinned back so tight it looked like it was the only thing holding her face onto her head, her black teeth snarling, and her crow's feet and wrinkles so deep they looked like they could be used to plant flowers. Annie named her "The Wretch," as she reminded her of something that should have died a long time ago but still clung on to dear life beyond all odds. She had faded black tattoos on her hands and forearms, one which said "Fuck Police," and "Luv Familie," Her tattooist clearly as illiterate as her. She had leaned into her door way and walked over to Annie leered above her as Annie read a book. A withered copy of Doctor Faustus by Christopher Marlow, which appeared fitting in Annie's current state. "I said, what you reading, Mute." Her breath smelt like something had crawled into her throat and died. Annie had felt tense, like a school girl that just wanted a bully to leave her alone, no longer reading the tale of the man who sold his soul, but now just staring at the page. The Wretch pushed Annie to the side of the head making her neck crack. "Answer me, freak!" Annie then did something she regretted later. She shut the book, clapping its firm hard back cover together, and swung it into The Wretches mouth and nose, colliding with what little specs of black teeth she had left. The Wretch recoiled holding her mouth, her protruding ribs rising and falling quickly under her white T shirt. Annie put the book down onto her desk, reopening it and pretending to read again. What little bravery she had mustered, had now flitted away and was replaced by fear. Fear of what would happen now, and worse, tomorrow or the next day. The Wretch spat thick bloodied phlegm on the linoleum flooring and barked something before scurrying away. She had stood up for herself this time, but there were only so many novels she could thrust into the faces of the living dead, before they came to her during the night and devoured her alive. Three days later, The Wretch now sat alone on a steel bench across the hall, eyeing her as she stood in her cell watching the prisoners mill around talking about why they were inside, how long they got and how innocent all of them were. She locked eyes with Annie and Annie felt a twinge of pity towards her. She was a loner just like her, but instead of using her time to be productive and to get herself away from the life which had landed her in here in the first place, she wanted to dominate those around her, showing herself and her deflated ego that she wasn't weak, she was strong and powerful and wanted to become the head bitch of the wing. Annie looked away and reopened her book. "Dorian Gray," by Oscar Wilde. She knew as she began to read that The Wretch was still staring at her. She could feel her eyes burrowing into her skull and it made her skin crawl. She didn't see The Wretches crooked smile. But Annie knew what was happening, and like a few days earlier, she again felt fear for her safety on the wing.

#

The next night, Annie hardly slept again. As soon as she closed her eyes, it came to her. Its long arms and legs. Its serrated teeth and blank face. Reaching out its hands, black eels sprouting from its mouth. She woke up, sweating. She looked around the room and saw her to be alone. She laid back, her heart racing. Was this her punishment? Not only was she chained to these walls, but was her mind to be tortured like this until the day she died? A creeping thought came into to her mind. It had been embedded in there for some time now, deep inside it. And now, as she stared into the black, she felt its rotten seed sprouting vines and withered leaves blossomed under its black petals. I could kill myself. She buried the thought no sooner as she thought of it. To kill herself would be self-murder. And it would be cheating the divine system. To end it in that way would push her further away from her daughter and not bringer closer to her. Tears began to appear on her eye lid. Her daughter. She hadn't thought of her for a while. She had always been present in her mind, but given the insanity of things she hadn't had much time to sit and think of her and the promise she made to her. What had she said to her on the hill? Annie squoze her eyes tight, pulling the blanket into her chest. Don't let the Shadow man take you like the others. "The Shadow man," she whispered to herself in the darkness. She was letting him in. And if she let him take hold of her, then she would become like John. Then where would she be? Would she be damned to never see her child again? What if he was already in her? Annie remembered what she could from the hospital, it was coming back to her in flashes. One moment, all was fine and she was asking for a drink, her lips dry and parched. The next, she was screaming, the taste of hot copper in her mouth. It was like watching it through someone else's eyes, like she want in control of her own body anymore. What else was she, it, capable of? Had John committed those crimes or had it been the creature? And if it had been then what allowed him to take hold? Annie thought back to the wolf pit. Where she had been cornered by Catherine and John. Catherine had been smashing things up, John too. Breaking everything they could get their hands on indiscriminately. Ripping wall paper from the walls and breaking ornaments and shattering glass.

"No!" John had called to Catherine mid rampage as she held up a weapon to bring it down on to the fire place carved with angels and demons. "Do not touch that. Not the fireplace." Annie remembered how fearful his eyes looked. The fireplace. Maybe that had something to do with it? Was the creature bound to it? A conduit of some sort? Then why would it want to burn the house down? The gasoline in the cellar. It didn't make sense. Then as Annie watched her memory unfold in front of her, her limbs growing stiff, she remembered the fires of hell and the souls that were trapped there, and a grave realisation grew in her soul. "Oh god," she whispered. "It's feeding the conduit with souls. Fire releases it." That's why she had burnt the house down. That's why she had such a strong compulsion to burn it all down. Fire was the secret. Fire let it escape to feed on more souls, and Annie had lead it straight out of its confines and into the greater world.

"Annie…" she heard something whisper in a creeping voice. She stuffed her head under the covers like a cowering child afraid the bogeyman was coming to get her. She listened again but couldn't hear anything. Her bones became icy as she laid under the blanket fearing the Shadow man was in the room with her. Hiding under her bed, ready to drag her under and push eels through her eyes. That if she dared drift off to sleep then she would never awaken again. Her thoughts again fell into that dark place where only the tormented dare venture.

I could kill myself.

Annie didn't sleep at all that night.

#

The next morning was the same as the repetitive rhetoric that had come before. The morning bell rang at 06.00hrs as Annie stared at the deep orange sun creep over the horizon, banishing the night away, she heard the sounds of inmates rousing in their cells. Annie blinked her dry eyes and trudged to her cell door where the guards let her out. She stretched and let out a tired yawn.

"Sleep well?" one of the guards said. Annie feigned a smile. She was led into the wash room where she then brushed her teeth with the bitter tooth paste, before rinsing with water that tasted like perfume. She dressed into her grey joggers and grey T shirt, before then going for breakfast in the communal hall. She sat alone. Inmates talked around her as the tucked in to stale cereal and burnt toast. She heard a call for the guards for a cell extraction in ward E due to an inmate threating to kill themselves and to fight anyone that stopped them. A minute later, she saw a string of guards on the balcony above her running towards E block in full PPU gear. Helmets, body armour, platted legs and arms and large shields, running in single file like ants to an unknown cell to see and unknown lady with fuck knows what else. Annie tucked into her bitter porridge with her sour 100ml of ml 'Fresh' milk. A couple of forced chunks down, she picked up her tray and walked to the canteen area and placed it down with a rough 'Thunk'. Annie turned and saw The Wretch standing behind her, veins pulsing out of her arms, collar bone exposed like a thin strip of leather draped over the engine of a monster truck. She was shaking, looking at her with burning eyes.

"Disrespect me, mute? I'll make you my bitch. You fucking wait." With that, she walked away towards her cell on the upper levels of the prison wing. Annie watched as she left, knowing that soon, The Wretch would come for her with more than idle threats. She was no doubt an unstable woman, probably withdrawing from what little drugs she could get her hands on inside the jail. The fact that Annie hadn't bowed down to her when they had first met, she was channelling her anger on her. Annie looked and saw a guard above, looking down on her sternly. Annie felt like asking her for help, but she instead smiled and shook her head in a 'I'm fine, don't worry' gesture. The guard walked away and continued on her rounds. Annie walked back to her cell and continued reading her book. As she flicked through the pages, she knew she would be murdered by the Wretch.

#

A few hours later, Annie was lying on her bed staring at the ceiling as her mind fell to happier places, when a female guard walked into her cell.

"You have a visitor," she said to Annie, almost as surprised as she was. Nobody had so much as called the prison to check on her, but now she had a visitor, and Annie felt both happy and trepident, as who could this person be? She had no family, her work colleagues had long forgotten her, and any friends she had left on the outside had since abandoned her once they had read about the fire and the massacre. She got up and walked through the open hall to a large time locked door at the top of the wing, next to a woman who sat behind thick bulletproof glass. The guard spoke through an intercom and explained why Annie was to leave the wing. After a quick search of her person and clothing, the door clicked and was pushed open and closed with a heavy clack. Annie had forgotten what it was like to be outside of the wing, other than the 30 minutes of exercise she was allowed a day in the yard, where she mainly sat and read under a small tree away from the other prisoners. Annie walked through a light-coloured corridor which was lined with linoleum flooring and chipped wall paint. She continued through, looking at the windows that lined the corridor, which only gave the view of the wrong end of the prions enormous perimeter walls, laced with barbed wire which she saw a crow had made a small nest in. She thought this to be funny. Such a free animal had made its home on the walls of a place could leave. She walked through another room, a smaller one this time, with a few tables and chairs and a vending machine. She saw a woman sitting on a chair tucked into a shining brown table of polished wood which was chipped on the edges. She had dark hair that fell past her shoulders, a pale complexion and dark eyes like she hadn't slept in weeks. Next to her was a small boy who was drawing a picture on a piece of paper with some crayons. He was maybe six or seven years old, puffy blonde hair that looked like it had been cut around a dinner bowl and was equally as pale as the woman sitting next to him.

"You have an hour. I'll be waiting here," said the guard, as she stood against the wall and watched Annie sit opposite the woman and child. At first she didn't know what to say, and wondered if there and been a mistake. She had never seen these two before. A minute or so dragged by, before Annie broke the uncomfortable silence.

"Do I know you?" she said, sounding ruder than she intended, but the few weeks of being trapped with horrendous people had rubbed off on her. The woman rapped her fingers on the table, the boy still scribbling away on his drawing.

"You do not," she said. She spoke with a foreign accent, like eastern European.

"Then why are you here?"

"Because," she said. "I need answers. You were at the house, yes?" The house. Yes she was at the house. That god awful place. No matter how hard she tried she couldn't forget the place. She was reminded of it every damn second.

"That's right." Annie hissed. "Listen if you're another fucking reporter, I have nothing to say to you."

"I'm not a reporter," the woman said quickly. "My name is Ima, and this is my son Ivan. You murdered my husband Brian Callahan." Annie felt anger building inside of her. This woman had some nerve. Walking into a prison and speaking to her like this? So out of the blue? So boldly? How dare she.

"I didn't kill your husband," Annie barked. "The fact you walk in here and say something like that is..." she couldn't finish her sentence. Annie just stared out of one of the windows. It's going to be a long hours she thought, But she hadn't had a proper conversation in weeks. Maybe it would be good for her to speak a little?

"You admitted it. I have seen the transcript of your interview. You are in prison. So either you admitted it to the police and are lying to me now, or you lied to the police and went to prison for something you didn't do. Either way, I can't trust you." Annie looked back at her. Her face was hard. She had no doubt been through hell and back these past few weeks.

"Why do you care?" Ima reached into her bag. She dug around and pulled out a small plastic folder and placed it on the table.

"Because I wanted to thank you for showing me the truth about him." Ima unclipped the folder and spread out several photographs. All were of Brian and Claudia together. And they got more explicit the more you looked at them. Annie studied them with morbid fascination. So these were the photos John had spoken to Brian about. This poor woman, Annie thought. She must have seen them and then gone to the house to find it ablaze. Ima studied Annie as she looked at the photos. "He was not the man I thought he was. He was sleeping with that slut for such a long time. I pretended not to notice him coming home late, spending more time with Hugo playing golf and business trips." Ima's voice started to tremble. "I thought he was good. And then I got these through the letter box in a blank envelope the morning of the fire. I drove me and Ivan down to the estate immediately. But the traffic. The distance. It was too late. When I got there, the place was already ablaze. You were the only person I saw being taken out in the hospital. The rest..." Ima shook her head. Annie stopped looking at the photos. Understanding she couldn't go on. Ima wiped her eyes with tissue from her bag. "You are the only one that survived. I need to know what happened. I need to know what my husband was really like when I wasn't with him. I need to know how he died." Annie took a deep breath. She spoke freely. Explaining everything. She didn't hold back any detail. She told her about Claudia and Brian. Hugo and Annie. Edith. The fire. John. Ima struggled in parts to listen, but insisted that Annie go on. She purged everything. Attacking Claudia. Catherine

AKA Precious and John's love affair. Catherine sending Hugo crazy to the point of entombing himself in his own home. Annie told her about seeing hell and meeting her daughter in the in-between. Annie thought Ima would laugh at her. Tell her to shut up. Call her crazy. But she didn't. She sat there, stone faced and lapped it all up. Finally. Annie told her about the Shadow man. And Annie found this harder to talk about than Ima to listen. Annie felt that every syllable she spoke about him made him draw closer. She felt her skin prickle with the sound of his name. Like he was watching her. Annie finished talking, pushing through her fear. Ima sat there silently and a moment dragged by. Then another. Annie looked out of the window and saw a large crow on the window sill beginning to peck against the glass.

"So," Ima said. Annie turned back to her. She had out a piece of paper. "Brian, that lying cheating man, left me some money in his will. All of it actually. About the only decent thing he did. So that will get me and my son through." Annie had forgotten about the young boy sitting next to them. Lost in his drawings. Unaware of everything that was being discussed around him as he coloured in his green dragon breathing purple fire. Ima put her hand on his head. "I'm going to go back to the house." Annie flew to her and grabbed her hand. Her voice was trembling. Her body shaking. Like she was an infant being told that that ghouls and ghosts were real.

"Don't go back there." Annie urged. Ima pulled her hand away. She had to force it, Annie's grip like a vice.

"I'm going to go destroy the fire place. If it's still there." Annie felt something which she hadn't felt in a long time. She felt hope. Hope mixed with anxiety, fear and worry. But it was still hope, and it shone bright light through the other feelings of woe that convoluted her mind. If Ima succeeded, then the shadow might leave her. And then she could fulfil the promise to her daughter.

"Don't use fire." Annie whispered. She could feel a sort of bubbling inside her, like she was a drinks bottle that had been shook. Something rising. Something trying to get out. "It likes fire." Annie stood up quickly, feeling the anger in her build. She needed to get out of this room and fast. The shadow feeling threatened. Wanting to defend itself. Knowing it couldn't move on. Trapped in her as she was trapped with it. Its hunger wanting more. Ima reached out to grab Annie, to ask her more questions, to stop her from leaving. Annie turned and tried to grab for her hand but she resisted, pulling herself away, an internal battle wrapping around her body as she fell to the ground screaming and grunting. She saw her fingers grow black tendrils, as long snaking shadows licked at Ima's feet.

"Run! Go now!" Annie cried through gritted teeth. She felt like her chest was about to explode. Her muscles starting to spasm and her bones felt like they were going to break. She wanted to hold Ima, kiss her, love her. She wanted to be near her. Inside her. Devour her. Annie crawled to all fours. Her mouth foaming, eyes black. She saw Ima running for the exit. Annie shot up and sprinted to her, yelling her name over and over. "Come to me, Ima. Cometo meIma CometomeImacometomeIma!" Ima rattled furiously against the door, banging on it to get out. Annie was ten metres. Five. Two. She lept through the air to her, teeth bared and fingers aimed for her face. Annie felt a crashing pain in her jaw as she collapsed to the ground. She saw the door fly open and Ima and Ivan race through it with a guard. Annie let out a blood curling scream as she stretched her arm out to the closing exit. Laid on her front, eyes blood shot and burning. She felt the baton of the prison guard come at her again and then the swift kick of a boot in her ribs. She was restrained. Dragged back into her wing and dumped in the middle of the foyer ground. The guards moved back brandishing their batons as Annie thrashed at herself, tearing her clothing and her skin. Biting bloodied chunks out of her arms and howling like a mad animal. She rushed at a guard, speaking in a deep tone in a dead language. "Dona mihi animam meam!" Another strike of the baton caught Annie in the ribs and she struck out, sending a guard flying across the room into an audience of prisoners who tumbled like bowling pins. Annie raced to another guard and she dove on her, pulling clumps of hair and punching her wildly. She was mad with insanity. Destroyed with rage. Her humanity long gone. The shadow firmly taken hold of her. The beast looked up and saw a lining of guards in black helmets and shields. Weapons drawn, shouting commands to her that blurred in the beasts ears. It wanted blood. It wanted to feed. It wanted its pound of flesh and it was going to get it. The beast raced to the guards, toppling them. Gouging and cutting them. A gun shot went off and the beast felt hot in its vessels failing body. It continued its rampage. Gripping and biting. Another shot exploded in its vessels ears. It couldn't walk as well now. Its legs failing it as it limped then crawled to another bloodied guard who scrambled on the ground. Out the corner of its eye, it saw something else. A bony creature with black teeth running to it, as The Wretch buried a final bullet into the vessels head, before she was opened up too. The carnage subsided. The red alarm continued to blare for a moment. And all in the room fell silent, as they watched in horror as the mutilated body of Annie arched its back and spewed out a thick black gas which shot up to the ceiling and out the crack in the prison walls.

#

Ima raced to her car holding her sons hand tight. She hurried him in the back and she slammed the door and sired up the engine which roared as she slammed down the accelerator. Ima sped out of the car park quickly, crunching gravel and running red lights. She got far enough to stop hearing the gun shots and blaring alarm before she finally let herself breath again. Ima checked the rear view mirror. Her son blissfully colouring once again. Not a hair moved from his handsome face. She got further down the road, cruising at 85mph on the motorway. She punched in the address for the house and hit 'GO'. Ima's heart finally steadied and she allowed herself to turn on the radio. It was Beethoven's Moonlight Sonata. She allowed herself to feel safe for a few moments as the song drew her in. She glided down the fast lane with ease. The road was clear. Traffic was light. She had a plan to set things the way they needed to be. She had seen evil in Annie's eyes and she as absurd as it might be, she knew she needed to get rid of it. Ima heard the radio start to flicker, Beethoven's melody staggering like an old kick start engine. She tapped the radio until there was nothing but static. "Perfect," she said. She checked her rear view mirror. Ivan had stopped drawing and was looking towards her.

"Mum," he said, his voice quiet and meek.

"Yes Ivan?" she said. He didn't answer. She heard the sound of clicking coming from behind her. A swelling of fear crept up her legs and into her stomach. The hairs on her head standing up as she felt an icy chill run its nails down her neck. She looked in her mirror again and then turned to see her son staring back at her. "What's wrong?" He didn't move. His eyes fixated on her. She smiled at him. "You're so silly, Ivan. Go back to your drawing." Ima looked forward to the stretching road. She tapped the radio again and the sound of soft piano filled the car. Ima looked in the rear view mirror. Her eyes went black for a second, as she held on to the steering wheel tightly, with a silent smile on her face. "We'll be home soon."

If you enjoyed this title, please check out other works, blog posts and follow me on social media @jay_darkmoore_author for free titles, special offers and the occasional video of my dog.

Please leave a review of this title.

Keep a look out for the FREE upcoming title-

'The Space Between Heaven And Hell, Shadow Man.'

Exploring the insidious origins of the darkness within our hearts.

Normally authors have a website to send readers too. But I am not that organised. So keep your eyes peeled on my social media pages.

There might be some goodies for ya.

– J

Printed in Great Britain
by Amazon

35545954R00149